In the minotaur realm,
a new emperor sits on the throne,
beholden to his mother
the High Priestess of the death-cult
of the Forerunners.

The escaped slave Faros,
legitimate heir to the throne,
must overcome his personal demons
and lead an army of outcasts
into the heart of the empire.
The battle between rebels and dark forces
will determine the future of the throne,
the minotaur race, and all Krynn.

THE MINOTAUR WARS

RICHARD A. KNAAK

Volume
I
NIGHT OF BLOOD

Volume
II
TIDES OF BLOOD

Volume
III
EMPIRE OF BLOOD

THE MINOTAUR WARS
VOLUME THREE
EMPIRE OF BLOOD

RICHARD A. KNAAK

EMPIRE OF BLOOD
©2005 Wizards of the Coast, Inc.

Cover art by Matt Stawicki
Map by Dennis Kauth
Original Hardcover First Printing: May 2005
First Paperback Printing: March 2006
Library of Congress Catalog Card Number: 2005928120

9 8 7 6 5 4 3 2 1

ISBN-10: 0-7869-3978-8
ISBN-13: 978-0-7869-3978-7
620-95460740 -001-EN

U.S., CANADA,
ASIA, PACIFIC, & LATIN AMERICA
Wizards of the Coast, Inc.
P.O. Box 707
Renton, WA 98057-0707
+1-800-324-6496

EUROPEAN HEADQUARTERS
Hasbro UK Ltd
Caswell Way
Newport, Gwent NP9 0YH
GREAT BRITAIN
Save this address for your records.

Visit our web site at www.wizards.com

To my brother, Win,
Sister-in-law, Lisa, and their children—
Megan, Brandon, Austin, and Katie!

And not to forget Jason and little Riley, too!

Nethosak

Temple of the Forerunners

Headquarters of the Supreme Circle

Palace

Great Circus

N

THE STORY THUS FAR...

THE NIGHT OF BLOOD

The island empire of the minotaurs is changed forever by the "Night of Blood," a coup by the ambitious General Hotak that assassinates the rightful if despotic emperor and massacres the clans loyal to him. Assisting Hotak's rise to power is a new and powerful religious cult, the Forerunners. They are led by his mate, the enigmatic high priestess, Nephera, and Hotak's eldest son, Ardnor, who commands their fanatic warriors, the Protectors.

Some escape the Night of Blood. General Rahm of the Imperial Guard is one of the leaders who shapes a rebellion. Faros, the fallen emperor's nephew, is mistaken for a servant and sent to the brutal mining camp, Vyrox.

Rahm attempts to assassinate Hotak but fails. Nephera uses her dark gifts and her mastery of the dead to track the rebels. Faros is part of an ill-fated uprising, whose survivors are sold to the ogres of Kern to seal an alliance with the Grand Lord Golgren for a deal that will support the upcoming invasion of the elven realm, Silvanesti.

TIDES OF BLOOD

Hotak's son and heir, Bastion, hunts down Rahm. The rebels fall into chaos. Bastion's sister, Maritia, leads the assault on the elves, her legions crushing the defenders of the ancient realm. Faros escapes the ogres, then wreaks vengeance on them at the head of a growing band of slaves. Jubal, an old friend of Faros's father, tries to convince Faros to join the rebels but fails.

Just as all seems to go well for Hotak, treachery befalls his empire. Struggling with an assassin dispatched by his jealous brother, Ardnor, Bastion vanishes at sea. Hotak's growing rift with the Forerunners and Nephera leads to his "accidental" death. Ardnor assumes the throne, wielding his increasingly militaristic Protectors to crush any resistance.

Back in Kern, Faros faces imminent destruction by Golgren, only to be saved by Jubal's rebels. However, Jubal is slain by the Grand Lord. Faros severs Golgren's hand, but the ogre leader escapes. The action gives the minotaurs time to flee to their ships. They sail away, along the way picking up a half-drowned mariner who, unbeknownst to them, is the son of the emperor—Bastion.

As Maritia—seeking to realize her father's dreams of expansion and conquest—secures the empire's hold on Silvanesti, the power of the Forerunners grows ascendant, and a startling event turns the world on its head. Nephera, her powers without warning stripped from her, is among the first to understand its implications. The stars, especially those forming the constellations, are once more in the night sky after years of absence.

The War of Souls is over, and the gods have returned . . .

CHAPTER I

OBSESSION

As dawn broke, the two armies spread out, spilling over the jagged, parched landscape. The dry morning wind ruffled fur and added a mournful wail to accompany the constant clink of metal and the grunts of the warriors. The first rays of light reflected ominously on weapons poised for blood.

The differences between the amassed minotaurs and ogres were quite distinctive. The former formed well-trained, cohesive units that moved into position along the upwardly-sloping earth. Although they were huge, brown- and black-furred beasts with heads akin to those of bulls, they were among the finest, most disciplined fighters in all the world of Krynn. The legionaries' gleaming silver armor and rippling banners spoke of pride and experience. Their broad swords and twin-bladed, leather-gripped axes were honed sharp. Under wide, open helmets designed for use by a race that often boasted two-foot high horns, thick-browed eyes often tinged with crimson peered warily ahead. Plumed officers riding massive, muscular steeds, bred for generations to carry the bulk of an armed minotaur, bellowed commands.

1
▼

Determined and practiced minotaur crews snorted lustily as they maneuvered gargantuan wooden catapults and other siege devices over the chaotic ground of Kern. Mountainous dust clouds rose behind the horned army, as if their very movement stirred the world. A musky scent pervaded the air around so many heated bodies.

In contrast, the gray-furred ogres maintained the barest modicum of order. A head taller than the seven-foot minotaurs, the ogres shambled rather than marched, often dragged rather than carried their huge, well-worn, stained clubs, swords of varying length and condition—some rusting—and ten-foot long spears. The ogres stank and their fur was matted and infested with microscopic armies. Their faces had glimpses of human or elven background but were squashed flat, with heavy brows overhanging black, animalistic eyes. Ogres barely had noses, although, despite their own rank odor, their sense of smell was fairly keen. Their brutish demeanors were made more so by huge mouths filled with sharpened yellow teeth and their two tusks that thrust up at the sides. Like the minotaurs, many wore breastplates. However, where the legionaries' glittering armor advertised the black warhorse symbol of their late emperor, the ogres' were not only devoid of emblem but dented, dirty, and mostly ill-fitting.

What discipline there was among the ogres was maintained by leather whips applied to backs. Occasionally, the huge, sandy-green reptiles called meredrakes—the hounds of the ogres—had to be used to separate fighters concerned more with their private feuds than the upcoming attack. Monstrous creatures the size of a horse, guided by leashes, a meredrake could make one snap of its long, toothy jaws and sever the leg of even the hardiest ogre. Their curved, dagger-like claws could shred flesh and sinew with little effort. They competed with their handlers when it came to stench, and their breath especially smelled of rotting, half-digested meat. The constantly slavering beasts peered left and right, their noses aloft, tasting the air as they waddled along. They sensed the carnage to come and eagerly awaited the feast.

A full legion of minotaurs and twice that many ogres had journeyed to this dismal, mountainous region—the sun baking their backs every inch of the way—but at last their objective was in sight. The ruined structure perched on one side of a squat but pointed peak called *Mer'hrej Dur*—The Claw of the Meredrake—had once served as a temple, but had been forgotten long before the god to whom it had been raised had himself been forgotten. Carved from the very rock face, the jutting edifice spread across the peak. With high, toothy walls, a pointed crest, and only two visible, circuitous paths leading upward, the rust brown temple looked more suitable as a fortress.

That was exactly what those within were using it for now . . .

┼────────▼────────┼

Faros eyed the approaching forces from the cracked and crumbling battlements. Carved into the walls behind him, towering figures more beautiful than elves revealed the builders of the temple—the perfect, glorious High Ogres—offering wondrous gifts to the horned god Sargonnas. Such grand images were lost on the scarred, former slave. Where some among his followers, Grom especially, marveled at the artifacts of the past, the light-brown minotaur saw only the ruins' practical uses.

"The legion to the north, the ogres to the south," Faros muttered.

Deep brown eyes veiled, he turned to face the others. While some of his followers wore breastplates in addition to their knee-length, leather kilts, Faros typically left his upper torso unprotected. His thick mane hung loose, touching his shoulder blades. A myriad pattern of crisscrossing scars left by countless brutal whippings and vicious battle wounds bore witness to the ferocity of his life over the past few years. He had lived as slave, thief, and rebel. Gone were all traces of the privileged youth, the spoiled wastrel, who had once been nephew to Chot the Terrible, emperor of the minotaurs until the Night of Blood.

Faros had not boasted any connection other than lineage to his uncle, but he had paid a heavy price nonetheless. First he had been cast into the savage mines of Vyrox—located in the foreboding, ash-covered lands shadowed by Mithas's volcanoes—there condemned to toil for the glory of the usurper, Hotak. After an aborted revolt, he and the rest of the rebel slaves had been sent to a place that made Vyrox a paradise by comparison—the ogre mines in mainland Kern. There Faros had learned the true depths of cruelty. There he had forever changed.

Thus he had returned to Kern, not the empire, with a vengeance.

"Just as you said," remarked a darker brown fighter who quickly made the sign of Sargonnas. Grom's father had been one of the god's last priests, and Grom had always believed in the deity's guidance, despite the fact that the gods were known to have abandoned Krynn decades ago. His beliefs had only grown stronger after recent rumors that Sargonnas and the other gods had returned. "By the Horned One, this is certainly a sign—".

"A sign that Ardnor's generals have little more imagination than his father's," Faros retorted with a snort. His gaze shifted to a black-furred figure standing apart from the rest. "What say you to that?"

"Whether led by a hero or a fool, the legionaries will give their all," the slimmer minotaur responded.

"And if your brother himself is riding at their head?"

The other's coal-black eyes narrowed. "If Ardnor were among those below, I would be the first to seek his horns. You know that."

Faros nodded grimly. "That is why I let you live among us, Bastion." He suddenly stalked passed his most trusted followers, heading deep into the dusty labyrinth that led into the inner temple. "The others should be ready. Time to welcome our pilgrims . . . and guide them with our blades into the afterlife!"

The ogres and the legionaries believed they would be well-rewarded for this victory. Emperor Ardnor, who had ascended to the throne but months before, following the death of his father—an "accidental" death, it was always stressed—had placed at the head of many of the legions his own fanatic Protectors. Those generals served him and the Temple of the Forerunners first and foremost. They kept an iron grip on their subordinates, ruthlessly punishing any malcontents. The destruction of the rebels, especially the new leader, was their current priority and much wealth and status had been offered to those who brought Faros's horns—and the rest of his head—back to the imperial capital, Nethosak.

The ogres were also vying for that prize and other rewards. Their orders came not from the nominal leader of Kern, the Grand Khan, but from the true power of Kern and the other ogre kingdom of Blöde. The Grand Lord Golgren had decreed that the rebel commander should be brought first to him, preferably alive, but his head and hide if necessary. The Grand Lord had a personal score to settle. Faros had already cost him his right hand, slicing it off in battle. It itched horribly, that invisible hand.

The commanders of the two forces kept only the barest lines of communication open between them. They would not interfere with each other, but neither would they harmonize. Old racial hatreds still dominated, despite the pact made by Hotak with Golgren and the ogres.

Leather war drums beat among the ogres. The wind picked up. Meredrakes began to hiss eagerly, straining at their leashes. Warriors raised their weapons, barking at the distant enemy.

The ogre's war leader growled, thrusting a sword at the temple.

Roaring, the horde charged. To the north, however, the legion commander elected to keep his troops in check, waiting.

A wicked whoosh filled the air. Dozens of ogres tumbled back, bolts through their necks and chests. Blood splattered the dead and living as bodies twisted wildly before collapsing. Screams rose from every direction, but despite an initial heavy toll, the horde of ogres pressed on.

Rebel archers perched in and about the temple face fired again, sending scores more to grisly deaths. The archers launched a third barrage, but finally understanding the obstacles, the ogres made for cover and only a few arrows caused injury.

Barely a breath later, huge boulders savaged the ancient edifice, tearing apart with great accuracy those areas from which the defenders had fired. Taking advantage of the ogres' impetuousness, the legion general had let them draw out the rebels for the benefit of his catapult crews. Each strike sent thunder echoing through the region. The exploding rock face killed scores. Tons of rock collapsed upon the defenders. Archers plummeted to their deaths. With a low, long groan, one tower that had stood for centuries slumped earthward, landing not all that far from the legion, which had begun its advance.

A triumphant roar went up among the legionaries. Battle horns sounded. Both elements of the attack moved forward again.

The catapults began an incessant barrage. Under the protection of the siege machines, the soldiers closed ranks. Behind them, legion archers prepared to fire. To the south, ogres versed in the bow did the same.

Despite the carnage caused by the catapults, the rebels

continued to shoot their arrows and toss spears down. Wherever they materialized, they came under an onslaught.

A soldier bearing the legion banner—a sinister red scorpion on a field of brown—materialized near the base of *Mer'hrej Dur*, waving the flag for all to see. The foot soldiers had reached the tower. Immediately, trumpeters blared a new, high-pitched note. The catapults ceased their fire, the crews turning them toward fresh targets.

Archers from both forces pushed in, harrying any figures they spied among the rocks and ruins

Like the quickening of the warriors' hearts, the drums beat faster, insistently. The battle horns cried louder. The lusty roars of minotaurs and ogres alike filled the air.

Then, from the very bowels of the earth itself, shouting rebels rose up and fell upon the ogres' unprotected rear.

Bastion led. The black minotaur dove into the battle. He sliced through the chest of an ogre with his sword then buried the blade into the throat of another.

The shocking turnabout left the ogres completely dazed. Their broken-tusked war leader perished in the first seconds, a heavy axe buried in his chest. Bastion slew the next who sought to assume command. The ogres fell into disarray. Swiftly becoming a wild mob, they followed their most base instincts and charged their attackers with no thought of working in unison. They cracked skulls, leaving life fluids spilling on the hard earth.

The rebels eagerly met them in well-ordered battle lines. Under Bastion's command, the front line formed a deadly row of spears. Behind the spears stood more fighters with axes and swords who slipped between the protection of the longer-reaching weapons to cut down other tusked warriors. The rebels methodically advanced, forcing their opponents into a confused throng.

The legion commander noted the initial chaos but did not immediately act. A struggle between rebels and ogres could only mean certain victory for the minotaurs, but no sooner did the commander have this thought than his own rear flank was suddenly overrun in the same manner, rebels literally rising up from nowhere.

At the head of the second attack charged Faros, an axe in his right hand, a sword in his left. Unlike what was happening in the south, the legionaries quickly began organizing a coherent resistance to the abrupt assault. Dekarians kept their small units together, relaying the commands of their hekturions in swift fashion. Metal clattered and clanked as the empire regrouped. A line of lances quickly formed to meet the spears of the rebels, and as the legion turned to face the threat, Faros signaled one of his trumpeters. The human—one of many outsiders among his followers—blew a long, powerful note that resounded through the battlefield.

With a collective roar, those within the ancient temple poured out to cut off the invaders' only possible route of escape.

"Keep them divided!" Faros roared, as he plunged his sword through the throat of a legion officer. The distrust between the empire and its ogre allies would prove their downfall.

A legionary thrust a lance at him. Faros dodged the spear, then chopped it in half with his axe. The former slave lunged, catching his adversary between his breastplate and back. The heavy blade sank in; the soldier toppled. Faros grinned darkly as the fresh smell of death filled his nostrils. His eyes grew crimson . . .

"Faros!" Grom shouted, appearing from behind. "You must stay back! If anything should happen to you—"

With a venomous snarl, the rebel leader shook Grom off. Faces began to appear before Faros, visions of the dead who perpetually haunted him. He saw his family's hacked and soaked corpses, all stricken down by assassins on the Night of Blood. He relived the callous slaying of his loyal servant—Bek—who had pretended to be Faros so that royal blood might be saved. He remembered the brutish slaughter of the former brigand, Ulthar, who had befriended him in the mines of Vyrox.

Foremost among the images was piggish Paug, the overseer in the minotaur camps, who slew Ulthar. His leering visage mocked Faros. Behind Paug stood the helmeted assassin in his father's house, a fiery shadow, with Gradic's burning body lying at his feet. Behind them all was Sahd, sadistic lord of the ogre mine, who invited Faros to climb atop one of the huge, wooden structures shaped like skeletal flowers upon which he strung and tortured his workers.

Looming above all the rest was the Grand Lord Golgren—Golgren, whose pretense at civilized ways hid a viciousness none of the others could match. The well-groomed ogre stared at Faros with utter indifference, reducing Faros to the worthiness of a gnat. His contempt was as terrible a weapon as any blade or axe, and it burned deep into the rebel's soul.

With each nightmarish image, each memory, Faros grew more fanatical in his movements. He swept away two soldiers who rushed at him, severing the arm of one while at the same time cleaving the head of the other. A rider attempted to run him down, but Faros gutted the hapless mount, then, dropping his sword, he seized the legionary as he tumbled off. Throwing his armored foe to the already-bloody ground, the scarred warrior swung hard, chopping through metal, flesh, and bone, taking horrendous satisfaction in the groans accompanying each shattering blow.

Breathing rapidly, Faros rose and looked around. Ahead, a pocket of legionaries were busy establishing a defensive position. Behind them, their commander shouted to other soldiers nearby.

Retrieving his sword, Faros waved it high. A horn blew and the way parted for a band of figures barely controlling their slavering charges. The meredrakes they struggled to command padded along, tongues darting in ferocious anxiety.

Their eyes were narrowed. Taut muscles could be seen under rippling scales and their long, whipping tails nearly swept aside their handlers.

These meredrakes under the command of rebels had been gathered over the months. Faros kept them ever at the edge of hunger, which made even the slightest scent of blood enough to provoke a salivating frenzy. So many of his fellow slaves had perished because of the reptiles that Faros thought it the perfect irony to wield them against his former tormentors, ogres or legionaries.

Driven by bloodlust, the meredrakes moved quickly through the old tunnels once used for escape by the temple's founders. Against a fully prepared legion, the reptiles would have been slaughtered—their thick hides, sharp teeth, and ripping talons no use against a skilled fighting force—but the enemy was already in disarray.

Faros chopped the air, and the handlers released the meredrakes. The lizards thundered forward, leaving handlers behind. The thick scent of blood drove them wild.

To their credit, the minotaur soldiers tried to hold their positions. They might have succeeded if the meredrakes had been the only threat, but the legionaries were also harried by archers, spreading panic in the ranks as their numbers depleted.

Hissing hungrily, the reptiles tore into the minotaurs.

The first few beasts perished with lances stuck deep in their red gullets, but then teeth a foot long and claws as sharp as razors came ripping through breastplates. Lances—and then bones—snapped. Soldiers screamed as they were hauled down by the monsters. Muscular, seven-foot-tall minotaurs became rag dolls in the maws of the behemoths.

"Keep your positions!" shouted the minotaur general, a lean, fanatic-eyed figure, whose helm was not the silver one of the legion, but rather the ominous black of Emperor Ardnor's Protectors. "Keep your positions, damn you!" He swung his crowned mace at a recalcitrant legionary, battering the soldier so hard the latter went stumbling into the jaws of a meredrake.

Whatever their will, the legionaries could not obey. The line collapsed inward and the beasts swept over the soldiers. A force of rebels followed after. Grom tried to keep Faros from entering into the chaos, but Faros shook him off, as eager as the savage reptiles to claim another kill.

He passed one beast in the midst of devouring the leg it had ripped off a fallen legionary. The meredrake was crushing bone and sinew, swallowing both in large gulps.

A brawny dekarian tried to slice Faros in two with his axe. The pair battled for several seconds, weapons clanging again and again as they sought to reach under one another's guard.

Droplets of sweat blurred Faros's eyes, and he swung wildly. The dekarian snorted triumphantly.

Then Grom leapt from the side, barreling into the officer. The pair fell back into a mass of struggling bodies as Faros managed to wipe his vision clear. The rebel leader grunted but moved on, unconcerned about Grom. All Faros wanted was another opponent, another target upon which to focus his demons.

The legion general caught his hungry gaze. The mounted officer was in the act of striking down a rebel who tried to pull him from the saddle. The mace crushed its victim's skull, shattering one horn in the process.

Faros pushed his way toward the commander, swiping at anything in his path. A meredrake noticed his passing and turned toward him, but Faros batted it hard on the snout with the flat of his axe. The meredrake hissed viciously. Faros met its gaze, and after a moment of dueling wills, the monster turned back in search of easier prey.

The ground erupted.

Faros faltered as an avalanche of dirt and rock assailed everyone. Somewhere, a desperate catapult crew had made a strike, trying to drive back the rebels, but the hasty shot had done as much harm to the trapped legionaries as its targets. Blinded, stunned soldiers stumbled about, and when Faros sought the general, he only saw the Protector's wounded, riderless mount running off.

Then a crushing force struck Faros in the shoulder, nearly cracking the bone. Fetid breath filled his nostrils. Faros tumbled to the side, his weapons lost. Despite the pain, he rolled into a crouch and looked up at his attacker.

The ogre's expression was wild, harried. Blood dripped from a wound across his chest. The huge figure was covered in sweat. He stared around as if not quite certain what was happening. Another minotaur, a legionary, came within range of the gasping giant and the ogre instinctively swung at his ally. The heavy, well-worn club cracked the soldier's neck.

Faros looked past the ogre and saw other tusked warriors scurrying in chaotic fashion toward the north. Rebels closely pursued them.

As the first ogre turned toward him again, Faros hurled himself at the huge figure, eagerly wrapping his hands around the beast's thick throat. The ogre dropped his club and tried to pull the hands free, but Faros held on with a death grip. The former slave's eyes filled with blood. Again he saw Golgren.

The ogre's eyes swelled as his breath left him. Faros crushed his adversary's throat, the bones cracking. With a pathetic gurgle, the ogre toppled backward, taking his slayer down with him.

Pushing free of the gigantic corpse, Faros located his sword and eagerly looked about for someone else to confront. Instead, the black-furred Bastion met his gaze. The usually composed son of Hotak wore a startled look as he studied Faros's handiwork.

Grom appeared a moment later, fur slick from blood, eyes oddly sorrowful.

"The day is won," declared Bastion in a muted tone.

"Won . . . aye." Grom made the sign of Sargonnas.

A mournful horn blared. They looked to where the last vestiges of the battle raged. A desperate group of legionaries surrounded by a horde of vengeful ex-slaves waved the flag of truce.

Faros simply watched, not even blinking until Bastion whispered to him, "They're surrendering."

"Of course. What of it?"

Grom came up on his other side. "Faros, our people are caught up in a bloodlust almost as great as that of the meredrakes! The legionaries will be slaughtered wholesale—"

"As they intended for us," Faros retorted. He leaned down, wiping his blade on the body of the dead ogre, then slowly started toward the last battle.

"Faros—"

The glance Grom and Bastion received from their leader silenced them both. They followed as he wended his way toward the few remaining enemy. Faros picked up his pace, eager to claim one last foe, but as the trio neared the rebels began a systematic execution of the wounded—a standing command by Faros.

They passed the corpses of legionaries upon whom the meredrakes now fed in earnest. The beasts' heads were smothered in blood and gore, and their jaws made horrific sounds as they crunched flesh, bone, and even metal without discrimination. The huge reptiles paid no mind to the three. Their tails dragged slowly back and forth, a sign of their grim pleasure.

Bastion's ears went taut. Grom again made the sign of Sargonnas. Axe held steady, the latter moved to ward off one of the reptiles from its feasting.

Faros seized his arm. "No."

"Faros, this is monstrous! We should at least gather the bodies, build a proper pyre for the minotaurs—"

"Such minotaurs do not deserve pyres." Faros looked west to the heart of Kern, and beyond it, to Blöde. "They want to fight alongside ogres, they can rot with them. We will leave the dead for the carrion eaters . . . if they can stomach them."

Grom grew silent again, but now Bastion took up the argument.

"Faros, my mother is no doubt behind this and observing all. Her eyes are everywhere. It is one thing to send Hotak's loyal generals to oblivion, but the commander of the Scorpion Legion was one of her own. Do not provoke her. She will avenge her empire."

"*Her* empire?" Grom interjected.

"If Ardnor sits upon the throne, it is my mother's words he speaks." To Faros, he added, "She will unleash the full force of Nethosak—more importantly, the *temple*—upon us! I say again, we should abandon Kern and return to the others in the Courrain Ocean! It is vital we strike at the empire itself and quickly!"

Faros shook his head vehemently, his gaze fixed on the dark past. "No, I've not finished with Kern yet. That's why we came back. And Blöde . . . Blöde still beckons . . ."

"But the ogres are pawns—"

The blade poised below Bastion's jaw, touching enough to break the flesh but nothing more. "I have let you live, though by blood you should die . . . son of Hotak, my family's murderer."

"You are in your right to take that life now."

After a long hesitation, Faros lowered the blade and continued on alone, striding among the meredrakes and the newly-arrived crows feeding on the carnage. The stench rose from the dead.

Grom muttered under his breath as their leader dwindled from sight. Bastion's brow arched.

"Praying for the dead *again*?"

"Praying for the living. For him. We need Faros. Our people need him. He must see that!" The brown minotaur looked up at the heavens. "There are those who say that the gods have returned. If so, then surely the Horned One undestands our plight!"

Bastion grunted. "Rumors, nothing more. The only god is the evil thing my mother follows."

"I can't believe that! If so, then we're doomed!"

The black warrior nodded. "Aye, and maybe we are." He surveyed the horror surrounding them then added somberly, "We will follow Faros nonetheless, will we not?"

Grom exhaled. "Aye . . . we will. Sargonnas help us all, we will."

CHAPTER II

LORD OF VENGEANCE

As Faros wended his way through the ancient temple, he gave no thought to the dead bodies outside, not even those who had lost their lives serving him. All that mattered now was finding some new distraction from the thoughts and nightmares ever with him.

The nightmares had only grown worse since he and his followers had sailed off with the freedom fighters commanded by his father's former comrade, Jubal. Jubal, an ex-colonial governor, had sacrificed himself to save Gradic's son in hopes that Faros would help unseat House Droka from the throne. Instead, all Faros had done for days after was sit in Jubal's cabin, staring at nothing.

In the end, Faros felt himself drawn back to Kern, seeking revenge. His loyal followers had accompanied him, of course, augmented by a steady stream of fresh rebels drawn by his deeds.

The halls of the temple wound through much of the mountain, twisting and turning seemingly at whim. Only a handful of torches were needed to keep the temple illuminated, for the ingenious artisans had embedded in the walls pale yellow, diamond-shaped crystals that somehow magnified and reflected the flames. Those passing through would perfectly view the worn but still elegant images of the beautiful, robed figures that adorned the walls. The High Ogres were the ancestors, as legend put it, of not only the present-day ogres but the minotaurs, too. The carved figures were more than four times the height of even the tallest minotaur. They were depicted offering to their gods gifts of food and crafts, singing praises, and kneeling before altars. Such displays covered every wall in every passage. Surely hundreds of workers had toiled generations to complete such a massive mural . . . which, in Faros's eyes, only proved the depths of folly. The gods had abandoned the High Ogres too without the slightest remorse.

Pausing briefly at one of the reliefs, he eyed the horned figure that resembled one of his own kind. Seated upon a high-backed throne, this god looked almost like a benevolent father surrounded by his children.

"The great Sargonnas!" Faros mocked. "Savior of *no one*, father of *nothing . . .*" The rebel leader ran his blade across the image. As the finely-honed weapon scarred the god, the metal scraping against stone let loose an almost mournful wail that echoed through the passage.

Faros quickly pulled back the sword, glared at the desecrated image one last time, then the minotaur strode away.

Early on, the rebels had mapped out the entire complex, seeking all hidden passages and abrupt twists. Owing to that search they had uncovered the escape tunnels which had been used today to meet their foe with a surprise attack from behind. Faros had memorized each and every corridor, likely knew the temple as well as most of those who long ago had built it.

Yet . . . the passage he next entered was not one he expected.

The images were all wrong. Rather than suppliants honoring the Condor Lord with offerings of goat meat and wine, he came upon a long line of ragged-looking High Ogres, harried refugees fleeing toward the east. A huge, predatory bird with wings sweeping across the heavens led the way, the symbolism of the bird so transparent that the minotaur snorted.

Certain he was still on the right path, Faros followed the corridor for some time. However, when at last he turned down a new hall, it was to encounter more wall scenes that he didn't recall. Here, illustrated in stone, was the transformation—the "salvation," as the minotaur race put it—of those High Ogres whom Sargonnas had deemed worthy of rescuing from the decadence and downfall of their civilization. Faros could see the perfect High Ogre faces elongating, the ears twisting. Nubs bursting from the tops of heads. Robes falling away and bodies broadening, growing furred. By the time Faros reached the end of the corridor, all trace of his High Ogre ancestry had vanished. The last figure was pure minotaur . . . looking unsettlingly like him.

With a frustrated grunt, Faros headed back the way he had come. The dust of ages rising with each step, Faros marched past the mural of transformation, as if retreating back in time. He made a turn into the previous corridor just as the minotaur on the wall completed his reversion back to a stately High Ogre.

Around the corner was a wide, open chamber. Faros halted at the entrance, puzzled, his mind rapidly retracing his steps and finding no fault with his memory, yet here was proof that he had clearly wandered.

A mustiness permeated by myriad, ancient odors greeted him. There was no doubt as to the purpose of the vast room. There were rows of broad, crumbling stone benches, the wide, brown dais at the far end, and the huge, winged condor effigy—remnants of crimson paint still visible on the rust-brown stone. To each side of the square altar that stood under the stone avian was a towering figure of the god in his minotaur form, one hand holding high a sword, the other an axe.

Sargonnas.

Faros had stumbled upon one of the main worship chambers used by the long-lost priests. Even now Faros could detect residual traces of dried, centuries-old offerings on the altar—although whether flesh, flora, or some other gift, it was impossible to say. The last inhabitants had left hurriedly.

Then something occurred to him: the passage he had just departed, the images of the transformation. The High Ogres could not have carved that out. Someone else, even minotaurs perhaps, had created that mural. That was the only explanation.

His interest fading, Faros turned from the chamber. He had no use for a god as dead as the High Ogres.

However, the rebel leader froze in his tracks, for it was not the corridor he now faced—but rather again the priests' sanctum.

Looking over his shoulder, Faros saw the empty passage from which he had supposedly turned, yet when the minotaur tried to veer that way again, the chamber once more greeted his eyes.

"What trick is this?" Faros growled. He stood motionless for a moment, frowning . . . then charged ahead.

He did not know what he expected, but it was not the silence and emptiness that greeted him. Faros spun around, seeking the cause of this maze, finding only the silent images of the lost god.

A lost god whom Faros had the impulse to denounce.

"Is this your game?" he demanded of the nearest statue of Sargonnas.

The god figure, clad in armor reminiscent of the legions, did not answer. The carved eyes stared down imperiously, as if it was unthinkable for the god to answer to a mortal.

A rage filled the minotaur. This deity had not protected him, had not protected his family. Faros suddenly felt the urge to blame all his woes on Sargonnas. As he had done with the relief on the wall, the rebel leader took his sword to the statue, swinging with all his wrath and might at its mid-section.

The blade did more than simply score the marble figure. It sliced through the statue like water, cutting a massive ravine in the god's belly.

Out of the wound gushed a torrent of steaming red fluid that at first sight Faros believed was blood. He scrambled back.

As the horrific deluge poured down upon him, it also spread to each side. Twin red rivers spilled onto the stone floor, which hissed and sizzled from the strange heat. Despite his swiftness, these two rivers surrounded Faros, meeting together behind him and widening enough so he could not leap to safety.

With a roar, the fiery liquid continued to burst forth from the statue's wound but did not yet overflow the small area where the minotaur stood, crouched. The heat quickly covered his body in sweat.

Then, at last, the flow ceased. The roar became a hiss, then the chamber was again silent, save for the bubbling of the liquid. Not a single drop had stained the statue. The red lava continued to circulate, however, boiling furiously.

Faros's astonishment gave way to mounting annoyance. Some force was playing games with him and the first culprit that came to mind was Nephera, high priestess of the Forerunners.

"Come for me, witch!" he demanded. "My blade waits! By my father, I'll gut you or die trying!"

In response, a great bubble formed in the flow, swelling and rising. In moments, it had risen to loom over the wary fighter. Faros lunged at it, but the heat and molten flow kept him away.

Then, from each side, a limb suddenly burst out of the lava bubble. Before his eyes, the limbs solidified, becoming furred arms with huge hands ending in long, tapering fingers. Part of the top of the bubble slipped away, creating a head that further altered form. At the same time, the unearthly figure developed a thick, muscular torso, and more gradually, two legs. Garments formed about the body: armor plate over the chest and stomach, a kilt of fiery metal at and below the waist.

As the incredible figure defined itself, the molten earth retreated as if absorbed and sucked into the new entity. The floor retained no scars or burns from the flow. No lava blocked his escape. He could, if he desired, flee now.

The minotaur did not budge. Instead, under a furrowed brow, Faros studied the shape, recognizing and suspecting the truth at last.

As the final drops of fiery earth vanished within the towering form, two tremendous horns jutted up from its skull and the face solidified into one akin to Faros's, only sleeker, more perfect.

"Hail, Faros Es-Kalin!" thundered the crimson minotaur, his breath a hot steaming cloud. Everything about the giant minotaur was the color of blood—from his fur, his eyes and teeth, to even his mane, and the breastplate and kilt he wore.

The rebel leader tensed, ready to fight if need be. "I've no reason to greet you in turn . . . if the Condor Lord you truly are."

The fearsome figure's eyes narrowed dangerously as he nodded. "Yes, Faros Es-Kalin, I am indeed . . . Sargonnas."

Instead of fear or awe, anger was all Faros felt. "Is this where you've been hiding all these years, while your supposed children have been slaughtering one another? Is this where you came after you turned your back on us?"

An ominous expression crossed the deity's countenance. His body raged with fire and he seemed to swell further in size. "I do not have to answer to you, mortal, but know that I did what I had to do . . . and all the while I felt each of my children's suffering as if it were my own!"

"Small consolation to them!" Faros retorted with a snort, unmindful of the inherent danger. "And of no interest to me!" He lowered the sword contemptuously. "Just as you're of no interest to me."

He turned to depart, but his feet, instead of leading him out, spun him back toward Sargonnas.

"What I come to speak of has little do with either of us in the great scheme of things, Faros Es-Kalin, and much to do with all my children . . . and your people!"

"Stop calling me that!" Faros vehemently shook his head. "There is no Clan Kalin anymore!" His head throbbed. "There isn't—"

Sargonnas suddenly lifted his head to the ceiling and emitted a tremendous roar. The entire chamber shook, bits of rock pelting Faros, who struggled to maintain his footing. The statues of the god then took up his cry, shrieking. The flames that were the Horned One's mane flickered wildly, small droplets of fire scattering.

The crimson deity glared down again. "That the stars leave me but this one as my hope! I, who have guided Tremoc, Makel Ogrebane, Aryx Dragoneye, would be so reduced to this puny, ungrateful—to you!" He stalked forward, each step causing the stone to hiss. "You have been tempered in pain and battle! From the depths of slavery, you have risen to break your bonds and reclaim your pride! How I looked down at you in hope!

"But now you have sunk into this . . . this honorless, base shadow of a warrior! I have seen you ruthlessly behead captives bound before you! I have watched as scores who look to you for leadership perish bloodily in futile combat, so that you can add a few more skulls to your count! Ogre prisoners whose bones are broken have been left to be torn apart by meredrakes, while you watch with pleasure! You have taken the depravities of your slave master and added to the worst of his foul imagination!"

Sargonnas gestured, and before him appeared visions of the recent past. The flower-shaped towers of Sahd were recreated, but with ogres and legionaries hung from them. Other victims lay half-buried in the soil, their limbs stretched out with cuts strewn along their bodies. Drawn by the foul scent, scavengers and other creatures feasted on the tortured souls . . .

"There is what you have become, mortal . . ."

"What of it? I treat my enemies as they would me!"

This caused the god to bellow. A sulphuric blast assailed Faros. "You have become as low as your enemies! Even lower! Is this what Gradic of the House of Kalin taught his children?"

Faros brandished his blade angrily. "My father is dead! My clan is dead—no thanks to you!"

"Even a god cannot change what must be," Sargonnas replied stoically. After a pause the giant's face contorted and he grew angry, but this time his anger was not directed at the tiny figure standing before him. "There may soon be no clans at all, if the evil that commands the temple holds sway much longer! That is why I came to you, why I still hope to resurrect that which I early on sensed was deep inside you. I believe it still slumbers there! That is why you must behold the truth of what threatens us all!"

A firestorm surrounded Faros, a whirlwind of flame that spun around, obscuring all else. Clutching his sword tightly—though what aid it could give him now he did not know—Faros gritted his teeth as the fiery winds tore at him from all directions. He felt as if his body was dispersing into a million pieces. Sargonnas and the temple vanished.

Then the flames, too, disappeared and a darkness descended upon the minotaur.

In that darkness he was not alone. Immediately, Faros sensed a distant presence, a monstrous, malevolent presence that drew from his soul the basic fears of a child.

A shadowy form coalesced in the darkness. A horribly familiar form. Faros recognized the great temple in Nethosak. It lurked as if at the edge of a dream, but was just real enough to send angry chills through the minotaur.

The high priestess of the Forerunners.

Faros did not need to see the temple to know the menacing power of Nephera. Faros had lived through the Night of Blood and its aftermath, and was well aware of the part the empress and the Forerunners had played in that travesty of history. Sargonnas was revealing nothing new to him.

Then suddenly Faros sensed another shape superimposed upon the temple. It was vague, barely a shadow in the blackness, tall, narrow, yet more than that the minotaur could not tell.

A horrific sensation swept over him. He felt as if an utter evil lurking in that shadowy edifice had seen and noted his presence. Despite himself, Faros was filled with dread. A nightmarish sensation overwhelmed him, ate away at his soul—

As quickly as Sargonnas had cast him into the darkness, Faros blinked and discovered that he had returned to the god's chamber.

The fiery minotaur god was eyeing Faros intently. "Perhaps you see now . . ."

"I don't know what I've seen," muttered the former slave, trying to recover his bravado. "I don't care what I've seen. I want nothing to do with the machinations of gods, especially you!"

This brought a brief but incredulous look from Sargonnas. "Stubbornness is a trait not unknown among my children, but you are truly the most obstinate I have come across in many a century!" He shook his head, his burning mane sending off more flickers of fire. "So much you have betrayed . . . yet in you still lies my hope . . ."

Faros's ears went flat. His expression hardened. "Then you've no hope left! Begone, god!"

"Heed me well, Son of Gradic!" roared the deity, so loudly that Faros flinched at the noise. "I am the Lord of Vengeance and you, willingly or not, have followed my path well in that respect! I am many faces," and as he spoke, Sargonnas's countenance began to change. It became that of a somber, black-eyed elf, a pale, hawk-nosed human, and finally, a bearded, cunning dwarf, before shifting back to that of a minotaur. "And many facets!" This time the god swelled in size, growing nearly as huge as the condor symbol. The flames that were a part of him now lit up the chamber so brightly that Faros had to shield his eyes. "Above all, I am he who watches over his chosen, his children—"

"Watches and abandons!"

Abruptly, Sargonnas returned to his previous size. "I never wholly departed, Faros! I am—was—the consort of Takhisis, Queen of the Abyss! The others, even oh-so-noble Paladine, might have trusted her word, but I knew her like no other! When she took part in the oath to leave Krynn in the hands of the mortal races, I suspected her treachery, although never the astounding depths of it! Never did I believe she would steal the entire world!"

Faros did not understand the god's babble, nor did he care to understand. The squabbles of gods were not for him. "So you admit you are a fool . . ."

"No more so than my children, for they, like so many others, did not recognize either the One God or the power behind the Forerunners!"

All this strange talk made Faros's head spin. "Leave me alone, god," he said. "If you are truly a god, what need do you have of my help?"

"I am not the only god to return, mortal . . . and that is why I come to you now! I am much weakened and still not yet whole! One of the gods seeks an opportunity to expand his domain at the cost of mine! He will make of the minotaur an even more foul thing . . . unless one can be found who can lead the race back to the path of honor and tradition for which they were meant!"

Faros laughed loud, mocking the god. "Me? Your champion? I'm no emperor in the making, Horned One! I serve you in vengeance and nothing more! I will not be part of your intricate web!"

"Vengeance may whet the appetite, but it will not satisfy it, warrior. Only honor can give sustenance and strength to your race. Within you—despite what you've sunken to—remains the seed of greatness, of one such as Ambeoutin himself!" The fearsome deity pointed an accusing finger at him. "It is within your power to reunite the minotaurs and guide them at last to their destiny!"

"I am not your champion," Faros insisted, "and I will never be your emperor."

"Then you are destined to die for nothing, forgotten, and your bloodline will also die forgotten! Is this the bond you honor with your father?"

"Leave my father be!" Faros glared harshly at Sargonnas. "Say no more about my father! He's dead because of you!"

"The line of Kalin will end with your bones bleaching in the harsh sun of this benighted land," the Horned One retorted, "and those who sought to erase your House from history will have finally triumphed—"

With a wild cry, Faros charged at Sargonnas, swinging his sword.

The god stood motionless. The sharp blade easily sank into his chest. Having expected otherwise, Faros gaped. The fiery deity showed no sign of pain as the sword tore through his torso.

No blood or organs spilled, no bone slowed the sword. The gaping wound sealed itself almost immediately.

Withdrawing his blade, Faros quickly stepped back, fully expecting the wrath of the god to descend upon him. Instead, Sargonnas simply touched the wound, now healed, and nodded. "A bold thing, striking a god. Gradic would have been proud."

In reply, Faros threw down his sword. "I'll hear no more from you! I'm no emperor. I'm not what you want. Leave, or let me do so."

"I will let you be, Faros." Sargonnas gestured at the sword, which leapt up, hilt first, into the former slave's hand. The emerald gem in the hilt glittered as if with a fresh energy. "I see there is no dissuading you, but I will insist that, for the time being, you keep my sword."

"Your sword?"

"Mine. Fashioned when the world was in its infancy, for a champion serving my unlamented mate. You didn't find it by chance in that river, Faros. It has sought you for a long time. Have you not also wondered about that ring?"

The minotaur studied the black-gemmed ring he wore on his hand. He could not recall when he had found it, much less started to wear it. That it had magical properties he was well aware.

"Worn by the one most likely to protect my children. Given before you to General Rahm Es-Hestos, commander of the Imperial Guard . . . once believed by me to be a savior of the minotaurs."

Sargonnas had been wrong there, Faros noted, just as he had been wrong about so much else. There was not much about the deity to inspire faith and confidence. Faros briefly considered leaving the sword and tearing off his magic ring, but the former had saved him more than once and the latter had also served him since coming into his possession.

Yet to accept them was to accept the blessing of Sargonnas . . .

The god perceived his conflict. With a sweep of his head, he added, "There are no conditions laid upon these gifts, mortal. I will ask no more of you, save that you might consider beyond your own thirst for vengeance and look to the lives of others, as your father would have done."

Look to the lives of others. Faros almost chuckled. He cared nothing for the lives of others, nothing for his own life.

"I will trouble you no more," Sargonnas said. The fiery figure began to melt into the floor, the molten earth and flames simply vanishing into the cracks created by the ages.

As the god melted away, Faros took a step forward. His ears stayed flat and his nostrils flared. He felt the urge to say one last thing but kept silent.

The mound became a small, sizzling puddle. The chamber grew darker as the illumination created by Sargonnas's presence faded.

Suddenly, the Condor Lord's voice boomed throughout the chamber as if coming from everywhere. "Be wary, Faros, son of Gradic! Be wary of the master of the bronze tower. . . ."

With that, the last traces of the god disappeared into the stones.

The minotaur exhaled. He glanced up at the statue, now magically whole again. He shook his head, wondering if it had all been a dream.

"Faros?" came a tentative voice from behind him.

At first he thought Sargonnas had returned, then he recognized Bastion. The black-furred minotaur appeared at the entrance to the chamber, his expression as guarded as Faros's own.

"What is it, Bastion?" he snapped, eyes still searching around for signs of Sargonnas

The other's brow furrowed in concern. "The guard said I would find you here. Strange, I do not recall this chamber . . ."

"Guard?" Faros bit back a snarl. "Sargonnas!" he grumbled to himself.

"What was that?"

"Never mind! What is it that's so important?"

Bastion dipped his horns to the side in respect. "On that day when you revealed that you knew all along who I was, yet spared me, I gave you my life. Now I offer it in a special mission which, after the carnage of today, I believe may succeed."

"What is that?"

"There is an island in the north off of Kern, large enough to be settled." He hesitated then continued. "This is what I propose. There is only futile death awaiting countless numbers on both sides unless we offer a way of peace—"

Faros grew angry. "You want to surrender—!"

"Nay! Please listen! I offer no surrender but an end to the slaying of minotaur by minotaur! I would ask of the empire that we be allowed to colonize the island and be left alone with the assurance that we would never again become a threat! Our shores we would gird for defense, but never would we attack!"

"You're mad!" Faros almost struck him with the back of his hand, but then, oddly, his father's face appeared in his mind. Yes, Gradic would have sought such a peace, rather than continued slaughter.

Faros was silent for a long time.

Finally he asked, "How would you contact Nethosak?"

Bastion shook his head. "Not Nethosak. There is another who can speak in my brother's name. Maritia . . ."

Maritia had loved and admired Bastion almost as much as she had her father. If anyone would listen to such an audacious plan, the military commander of Ambeon might.

"Will she still listen to you, after she learns that you follow me?"

"I believe so. I hope so."

A grimmer image came to Faros. "What about the ogres? Why should they agree to this, after all we've done to spoil their land?"

"From what I have heard," Bastion muttered, his mood darkening, "the Grand Lord will listen to my sister. He will listen intently."

From what Faros had gleaned from Bastion, Golgren admired the Lady Maritia de-Droka, despite their great dissimilarities.

It was foolish and likely to fail, but perhaps urged on by Sargonnas's words and his own guilt toward his father, Faros grudgingly nodded. "If that's what you desire, go to it."

Much relieved, Bastion bowed. "I leave to make immediate preparations. I will not fail you. . . ."

As Hotak's son departed, Faros gazed up at the looming condor symbol. The bird's visage seemed to mock him. He turned his head from the icon, only to meet the eternal, knowing gazes of the twin statues.

With a furious snort, Faros sheathed his weapon and stalked out of the chamber.

CHAPTER III

AMBEON

Ambeon, as this eastern portion of the continent was now called, covered much of the former elven kingdom of Silvanesti.

There was no large area of Silvanesti that remained free. Minotaur legions had swept through every part of the conquered land—save the edge of the north, where their ogre allies still retained a modicum of control—securing vast portions through carefully-organized gridwork. At Lady Maritia de-Droka's command, teams of soldiers, with the forest-trained Wyverns at the forefront, divided the ageless, virgin woodlands into neat five acre-by-five acre squares. Legionaries swept over the squares with such thoroughness that no creature, however small, escaped.

Thousands of elves perished. Their nature craft could not save them from the methodical, overwhelming minotaurs. Lessons learned from centuries of war—including, perhaps especially, the failures—had enabled Maritia and her officers to draw up far-reaching plans that would, this time, guarantee victory.

As the legions cleared Ambeon, weekly shiploads brought new colonizers, who Maritia immediately assigned to various sectors. Hotak's daughter launched a systematic stripping of woods and structuring of new villages whose security would be linked to one another.

Roadways already extended from the harbors into the eastern third of the realm, making it easy for wagons to carry supplies and for reinforcements and colonizers to reach the next rendezvous before heading into the west. Sargonath, located on the shore of Kern, still acted as the main port before Ambeon, but work was already underway to build a greater, more expansive port that would allow heavier cargo vessels to sail directly to Mithas.

While so much had been accomplished in so little time, that very fact kept the minotaurs on high alert. Not content to leave the defense of Ambeon to settlers alone, Lady Maritia moved more and more of the legions to the very border. The minotaur military commander had a certain ambitious goal in mind . . .

Maritia rode along the area of construction, two legion generals and her personal guard accompanying her. Her helm hung secure on the side of her saddle, allowing her long, thick brown mane to flutter loosely. Her armor, ever polished and contoured for her lithe form, glittered in the sun, and the midnight purple cloak that marked her as military ruler of the colony draped her back. She wore a sword sheathed at her side. Her rich, brown eyes swept the near and the far, taking in everything.

As she passed, sweating legionaries clad only in kilts and sandals paused to salute her before continuing their heavy tasks. Admiration from the males among them had only partly to do with her beauty, for all knew well her reputation as a capable officer and leader in the mold of her father and her brother, Bastion.

Maritia turned her slim muzzle to admire the structure going up, a wide, high wooden fortress facing the setting sun.

The towering walls were huge trunks secured into deep holes by a concoction of stone, sand, water, and other ingredients. When allowed to dry, the substance became harder than rock, ensuring no enemy would be able to easily tear the wall asunder. Four minotaurs could have stood on top of one another and still not reached the sharpened tip of the fortress. When completed, the five-sided fort would have the potential to garrison an entire legion.

"How soon before the gates are finished?" she asked one of the generals.

"The whole of Basilisk Legion toils on this project, my lady," rumbled the barrel-chested male with a scar on his muzzle, "save a hundred pickets who are keeping watch. The gates should be up in a week at most. The surrounding wall completed in perhaps twice that time. Work should start on the main quarters immediately following."

Almost half a month ahead of schedule. Maritia gave the general a brief, curt smile. "That will make six. The northwest to the central west sector will then be secure."

Her plan was to arrange a series of forts covering the outer perimeter of Ambeon, each stationed with a full legion. They would surely defeat any attempt to retake the elven lands.

"We'll still need more soldiers," the second general declared, "if we're to cover the entire border."

Maritia did not bother to respond to the obvious statement. The speaker, Kilona, a fiery-eyed female with slight streaks of black decorating her brown hide, was a new addition to Ambeon's leadership. She commanded the Crystal Legion. Kilona's command had been ordained not only by Ardnor but directly by the temple. The general was a Protector like Bodar, leader of the Scorpions.

Like other Protectors, Kilona had shorn off her mane upon joining the ranks. The lack of hair, combined with her rabid eyes, gave her an otherworldly look, which suddenly reminded Maritia of her mother. Although ostensibly subordinate to Maritia, Kilona was not entirely trusted by Maritia's staff nor by the commander herself. Her obsessive devotion to the Forerunners made her judgment during moments of crisis suspect.

"Any signs of activity on the other side, Gorus?" Maritia asked Basilisk's first general.

"A few scouts noted. Some elves, a human. They all left thinking that they weren't seen."

"Excellent."

Every now and then, the elves made hapless forays trying to reclaim their homeland. They had a tendency to underestimate the minotaurs' own stealthiness, seeing the horned invaders as clumsy brutes little superior to ogres. Past lessons failed to have educated the haughty race, which was why Maritia expected the elves to return and fight again one of these days. Their persistence was almost comical . . . if it wasn't so tragic.

"What did the human look like?"

"He was dressed like a trapper, but he had the moves of either a Solamnic or Nerakian. The former, I suspect."

There had been no direct evidence so far of intrusions by the Knights of Solamnia, but the empire was anticipating them. Of all their potential opponents, the venerable knighthood excited Maritia the most. Their strict code of honor and extensive battle training made them the human equivalent to the minotaurs. A war against the Solamnics would be one for the bards and a sharp contrast to the easy victory achieved over the insipid elves.

"Inform me directly concerning any other humans spotted. I want the next one followed. Find out his ultimate destination."

"It'll be done, my lady!" Gorus said, saluting sharply.

Another subject long suppressed crept into her thoughts, darkening them. Clutching the reins tighter and trying to hide her growing anxiety, Maritia asked, "Any news from Galdar?"

The grand crusade supposedly led by the human waif named Mina—whom the empire believed was only a puppet of a minotaur renegade known as Galdar—had collapsed overnight with the return of the constellations to the heavens. What information Maritia's spies had gleaned indicated that both the girl and Galdar had fled after some catastrophic encounter in the west. There were even those who said that the pair had run afoul of the returning gods, but Maritia scoffed at such a tall tale.

Galdar had been a useful ally. Mina's crusade had kept the humans—especially the Knights of Neraka—distracted. More important, somehow Galdar had brought down the magical shield protecting Silvanesti, opening the way for invasion by the empire. In return for that favor, and the allegiance of the minotaurs, Galdar relayed Mina's wishes: that the minotaurs not advance into the capital, Silvanost. Silvanost and everything west belonged to her faithful, to which Hotak and his daughter had readily agreed.

Then came the unknown disaster that had befallen Galdar. Naturally, the moment word reached her—the crusade collapses! reported the scouts - Maritia had ordered the legions west. Even after securing Silvanost, she had been unable to locate the great, mysterious Galdar. Maritia feared the elves or Nerakians had claimed his life, and if so, it was the fault of that human brat, Mina. Galdar had been very, very clever, but entrusting his secrets to the waif had been perhaps his fatal mistake.

"No word, no sign of Galdar or that slip of a human, my lady," General Gorus replied.

"Her faith was misguided," interjected Kilona. "She served a false deity and paid the price!"

Maritia was fairly certain that Mina's supposed god—if genuine—was the Forerunners' own patron, one and the same, but she did not say as much. "Hmmm. A pity. Galdar's memory should be honored for his critical role in this conquest. I'll send word to the emperor." She slapped one fist against her breastplate in salute to the lost warrior, acting more chipper than she felt. "We will concern ourselves no more with Galdar nor his pet human then. All that matters now is strengthening Ambeon, eh?"

The others, Kilona included, readily agreed.

They watched as half a dozen minotaurs set into place another huge section of the wall. It would have taken more than a dozen elves to maneuver the huge, carved trunk into the hole. Three bare-chested soldiers used ropes to pull the piece up. Already set at the edge of the deep hole, the trunk slipped in easily. However, to avoid it sliding too fast, a second group of three pulled on taut ropes from behind. They eased off as a seventh warrior in breastplate brought forth a huge barrel of the stone and sand mix. With the utmost care, the female minotaur poured the contents into the hole, filling it to just overflowing.

The mix would need a few minutes to solidify before the different groups of soldiers could let loose the ropes. Maritia, satisfied at what she saw, urged her mount on, the others quickly following.

When completed, there would a main living quarters, stables, and a supply building. A walkway would run along the upper edge of the wall, with steps at each corner of the fortress.

"An excellent job, general," she told Gorus. "I'm quite pleased."

"More material will be arriving from Makeldorn tomorrow, along with additional laborers, my lady. It's possible we'll be even more ahead of schedule so."

Barely a half an hour's ride from the fortress, the newly-christened settlement of Makeldorn—"The Gauntlet of Makel" in the old tongue of the High Ogres—stood in place of a once-sculpted garden city whose name Maritia had already forgotten. The original city had been shorn of most of its trappings, only the bare bones left for reconstruction in the minotaur style. Instead of winding tree homes all but hidden by carefully-nurtured foliage and flowers, now there was a perfectly-measured, circular clearing filled with broad, rectangular common houses arranged in rows.

Two hundred colonists already dwelled here. A smithy that forged weapons as well as farm tools kept busy day and night. In addition to supplying its inhabitants, Makeldorn aided the construction along the border. The settlement also acted as a final waystation for food supplies for the legionaries. Maritia had mapped out a careful line of supply for each of her outposts guarding the west.

Yes, Ambeon thrived, even if to the north there still lay the stubborn problems in Kern. That was out of Maritia's hands, at least for the moment. The throne itself had taken command of that situation. All she had to concern herself with was the new realm.

"Your father would be proud," General Gorus called as they rode. "A pity he didn't live to see the day!"

Before Maritia could form an appropriate reply, Kilona spoke, "He serves a higher purpose now! He has ascended to the Forerunners, praise be!"

It was all Hotak's daughter could do to keep from swinging her fist at the idiot general for her remark. Her father a Forerunner ghost! Whatever ties others in her family had to the faith, Maritia knew Hotak would have found such a fate contemptible.

Yet . . . if her mother's teachings had merit, perhaps it was true, as people whispered. Maritia did prefer to think that Hotak stayed near her, guiding her efforts to make his dream a reality, but as a Forerunner ghost? Never!

Turning her mount toward Makeldorn, she shook the disturbing thoughts from her mind. All that mattered was Ambeon. As an officer of the empire, it was Maritia's duty to see that the new minotaur realm prospered to its full potential.

Spiritual matters were the province of her mother . . . and as far as Maritia was concerned, Nephera was more than welcome to spiritual matters.

"Someone comes from the direction of Makeldorn," a guard warned. Instantly, he and the rest of the retinue shifted position to shield Maritia.

As the rider neared, they saw it was an imperial messenger who anxiously pulled up before Hotak's daughter and thrust a sealed parchment in her hands.

"By order of his majesty, the Emperor Ardnor," the messenger informed Maritia apologetically. "I have sailed across the Blood Sea and ridden over half of Ambeon to find you. I was to see that you received this at first possible chance, no matter where you might be located." The musky sweat and heavy breathing of the minotaur bore witness to his arduous efforts.

Frowning, Maritia moved a short distance away from her companions, broke the red seal, and looked over the proclamation.

By the decree of his majesty, Emperor Ardnor I, lord of the realm, it is set forth this day that the capital of the new colony of Ambeon shall hereafter be called Ardnoranti. All previous designations, elven or historical, will be stricken from the records. Henceforth, the great capital of Ardnoranti will become the prime base of operations for all missions in Ansalon.

Furthermore, it is decreed that the artisans of Clans Tyklo and Lagrangli will begin work immediately on the commemorative icons of his majesty and the renovation of the temple of Branchala into a place of worship honoring the Forerunners. Second Master Pryas will arrive shortly after this message to oversee the latter mission—

Though she knew she was being observed by the others, Maritia couldn't help but scowl. Pryas was not only Ardnor's righthand servant, he had the favor of their mother. There were those who whispered he was being groomed to assume full control over the Protectors and eventually succeed Lothan on the Supreme Circle. Pryas's posting to Ambeon was not to Maritia's pleasure. There were already too many Protectors mingled among her officers.

The rest of the proclamation contained the usual blather concerning the beliefs of the Forerunners, nonsense added to each imperial message since Ardnor had ascended the throne. Maritia rolled it up and put it in a saddle pouch. Her brother need not have wasted messenger resources just to tell her his decision to name the city after himself, but Ardnor never failed to miss an opportunity to reassert his position, his importance as emperor.

For some reason, that made her think of Bastion, lost at sea many months before. He was intended to have been Hotak's successor. He would be signing the proclamations now, not Ardnor . . .

"Bastion . . ." she barely breathed his name, not wanting anyone to overhear. Strangely, Maritia often dreamed that her brother still lived, that he was trying to come back to her. There were rumors, rumors of a black-furred minotaur who fought alongside the rebel cur, Faros, and some warriors who had known Bastion swore that he was that unknown rebel. Maritia, however, refused to believe such monstrous rumors. Bastion would have never betrayed the minotaur nation in such fashion. If her brother had still lived, nothing could have prevented him from returning to the empire and his family—his destiny—and to her, especially.

Nothing at all . . .

Grom knelt before Faros, who had retreated to one of the antechambers likely used by the temple's high priest and—as he did for hours at a time—there dueled with invisible foes. Faros's practice sessions went on for hours, the manic energy built up during the day making it almost impossible for him to sleep at night. The rebel leader found rest only with short naps and those were so shallow that even the hint of a noise would cause him to leap to his feet expecting some confrontation.

Grom kept his head low and to the side. A cloud of dust churned up by the exercises caused him to cough, before he finally spoke. "Faros, forgive this intrusion."

With one last flourish of his sword, Faros beheaded the imaginary emperor he was fighting. The sword practically sang as it cut through the air. In the same motion, he sheathed the weapon.

"What is it now, Grom?" Faros asked impatiently, unmindful of the dust. Distant sounds drifted from the halls into the chamber—hammering, voices, the rebels keeping some semblance of life.

"In accordance with the rites, our own dead are finally all burned." The other minotaur coughed—harder—as he made the sign of Sargonnas. "I ask again to let me organize parties to begin doing the same for at least the legionaries we fought."

Faros responded to his request by drawing the sword again. This time, he began thrusting at the condor symbol carved into the nearest wall. He had not told anyone about Sargonnas's visitation, especially the pious Grom, who would have been unable to keep such a remarkable tale secret.

"Leave them where they lay! It'll be a reminder for anyone else who tries to storm our sanctum."

"Faros, the stench—"

"It will dissipate, is already dissipating!" Faros had smelled far worse during his years of slavery.

In truth, the odor aroused his obsession, reminding him there were more ogres to slay, more Sahds and Golgrens. When there were no ogres left to kill, maybe then he would start in on the empire that had betrayed him.

No, Faros reminded himself. He had agreed to Bastion's quest. Faros did not know whether he truly wanted that compromise to succeed or not, but he would allow the Lady Maritia's brother to try, which reminded him that Bastion had not yet departed.

Without a word, he stepped past the still-kneeling Grom. The latter quickly rose as Faros stormed by, but the rebel leader did not give him time to again plead his case. In the matter of the enemy dead, Faros would not be moved. The sun would dry their corpses and the scavengers pick them clean. The bones would serve to decorate this part of Kern in a manner most appropriate for both the hellish realm and Faros's own tortured dreams.

Grom, with a deep sigh, wisely did not follow. Faros marched through the halls, the echoes of his sandaled feet on the stone floor matching the pace of his ever-racing heart. The dead eyes of the ancient figures stared down from the walls, seeming to warily watch his progress. Torches flickered wildly in his wake.

He found Bastion in his quarters—a small, square domicile no doubt once used by novices. Bastion was the only one who, like Faros, saw little need for even the most meager ornamentation. Others sought to recall better times, better lives, with carvings they arranged or colored stones they had found, but nothing about the chamber gave any hint of the black minotaur dwelled within. Like Faros, when he departed Bastion would leave no memory of having been here.

"You are still here then," muttered the lighter-furred warrior. "Why the delay? The sooner this farce is over, the better!"

"The delay was necessary," Bastion responded in a clipped manner. He slung a small cloth bag over his shoulder, a week's worth of rations. Strapped to his back was a twin-edged axe. "Besides, I thought it would be wiser to start off closer to dusk, when we would be less visible." Bastion saw that Faros was not satisfied. "I was just about to alert you to my departure."

"You know where to find her?"

"I know those who do. They will contact her for me." Bastion shrugged. "As I said, I can promise nothing. When she realizes I have been fighting alongside the rebels, Maritia could throw me in chains or behead me on the spot. I trust she will listen first."

"Killing her own brother would be dishonorable," the former slave remarked sarcastically.

"True," Bastion said, chuckling, "but the definitions of honor has become quite fluid these days." Bastion dipped his horns in farewell. "I am in part responsible for that."

Ignoring the other's philosophical tone, Faros returned to the subject. "You're certain you want to risk your life on this mission?"

"Yes. "

Even if Bastion's sister agreed to all, it would still be up to Maritia and her brother to convince the Grand Lord Golgren. Though Blöde bordered the former Silvanesti, the emissary from Kern would have the final word. Blöde had become just a province of the northern ogre realm and Kern a land dominated by Golgren. The once powerful Donnag had been transformed into a grotesque mockery of himself, as if some disease he did not notice ran amok through him. Golgren . . . first Bastion had to convince Maritia, then Golgren.

Thinking of the ogres, Faros added, "The route through Kern and Blöde should steer you past the most populated areas, but you will encounter patrols. You still insist on only four companions?"

"They all served me at some point in the legions. They are skilled. Any larger a group would be more noticeable or slow me down." The black minotaur adjusted his pack then concluded, "Whatever happens, do not fear. I will betray nothing."

Faros brought the sword up, so that Bastion stared level at the sinister, unvarnished blade. "I do not fear anything, much less betrayal."

Bastion nodded, then, with a dipping of his horns, left the chamber.

Minutes later, Faros, sword sheathed, watched from an opening far overhead as the small party rode off to the southwest. Well, then. He had done his part; he had tried to live up to his father's memory. There was nothing else to be done for now.

Then a sudden sense of foreboding touched him. He quickly looked around but saw no one. Unconsciously, Faros rubbed the gem on the black ring. Sargonnas's ring.

A brief flash of something passed at the edge of his vision— a figure pale and deathly. Faros spun about, still touching the ring and concentrating.

Nothing appeared. With a silent curse, he glared at the artifact. "Some gift, Condor Lord! No wonder its last wearer is dead!"

He should take it off, hurl it away. No, not yet.

Faros clutched the hilt of his sword. That gift, at least, had served him well. It had bathed in the blood of many ogres and not a few legionaries, and still the blade was unblemished. Better that Sargonnas had given him a thousand such swords with which to arm his ragtag army, but gods never conducted affairs in a sensible manner.

At that moment, the briefest hint of a noxious odor that stirred foul memories assailed his nostrils. Faros glanced over the darkening terrain, finally noticing a slight, winding column of smoke to the north edge. If not for a sudden shift in the wind, the scent and smoke would have remained out of sight.

His eyes reddened as he realized what it meant. "Grom!"

Faros's fury rose as he rushed through the ancient temple, frightening many of his followers. Guards jerked to attention. Two humans playing a game of stones and sticks kicked away the pieces and scrambled away. Everyone had witnessed his explosive rages in the past, and no one wished to become the fresh object of his ire.

"A horse!" he roared to one of those tending to the rebels' small herd.

Most of the animals had been recovered from mining camps or slaughtered patrols. The outcasts took as good care of them as they could, although keeping the horses fed was a problem as persistent as feeding the army of former slaves themselves.

Someone quickly brought him a saddled mount. Faros leapt atop the huge ogre steed and urged it toward the northern gateway.

Those near the gate cheered him as he rode through. Faros ignored the cheers, focused only on the winding path leading down. The ogre horse was not the speediest of mounts, but it was sure-footed. Loose stone scattered as he swiftly made the descent, before long reaching the base of the mountain.

Faros veered the animal north. Once around the next bend, he would not be far from his goal.

Movement atop the ridge caught his eye. A figure slid out of sight behind the rocks. Faros had no fear of harm; the sentinel had been posted by Grom to call a warning, not attack. Grom had disobeyed a direct command, the worst offense in Faros's mind.

As he neared, the full extent of Grom's duplicity revealed itself. More than a dozen figures were working frantically to maintain a fair-sized pyre consisting of dried shrubs and other debris found amidst the harsh landscape. Another band of ex-slaves and former soldiers were tossing large burdens upon the fire. The odor of burnt flesh wafted toward Faros.

"Grom!" he shouted as he rode up. "Grom! Where are you?"

The rest halted their efforts, staring at their rebel leader in surprise and terror.

The focus of his anger finally materialized from behind the pyre. Stepping through the rising smoke, a sweat-drenched Grom strode defiantly toward Faros. The minotaur coughed as he approached.

"Blame—blame none of the others, Faros. This is my sin alone. They followed my orders and dared not disobey."

In response, Faros leapt off his horse, stepped right up to his second, and struck Grom heavily on the jaw. Grom tumbled to the ground. The others were frozen, not certain what they should do.

"I too gave an order. A specific order. You disobeyed me."

Grom embarked on a coughing fit, but finally managed to stand. Through tearing eyes, he faced Faros. "My conscience would not permit me to leave the dead, not even for you, Faros. At least the legionaries deserve a pyre! They only fight as they've been trained! They only follow orders, too."

"We've left their dead behind before. It never bothered you so much, then."

"Yes, it did. I never protested much. There didn't—there didn't seem much reason to, either, not with the gods gone."

There it was. Ears twitching, Faros snorted. "And now the gods have returned, is that it? Suddenly, you've got the fear of them again?"

"Not fear . . ." the dark-brown minotaur returned sharply, "Not fear."

Ignoring Grom, Faros looked to the rest of the guilty party. "Douse that fire! Leave those where they lay! The scavengers'll give them the last rites they deserve! Do it now!"

They raced to oblige. Whatever their convictions concerning the dead, first and foremost they had sworn themselves to follow Faros. Grom, Faros understood, had led them astray.

Grom and the intrusive Sargonnas.

Faros refused to let the god meddle with his life.

The others finished smothering the flames. Grom began coughing again, a series of harsh barks. Faros glanced distastefully at the minotaur who had once been among his most loyal stalwarts. Grom had inhaled too much smoke, the fool; likely he had been standing too near the pyre all the while.

"It would serve you right if—"

The other minotaur tumbled forward.

Instinct made Faros reach out and grab Grom before he struck the earth. With moist, red eyes, Grom tried to focus on his leader. Faros's own eyes widened as he noticed small, bloody pustules lining the other minotaur's lower lids.

"Faros . . ." Grom managed. "F-Faros . . . I—I'm sorry . . ."

He coughed again. His entire body shuddered—and grew still.

CHAPTER IV

THE DOWNTURNED AXE

The heart of the empire was beating soundly, and the high priestess took this as evidence of the absolute might of the power she served. Wherever her ghostly servants roamed, her own eyes seeing through theirs, Nephera saw proof of success and prosperity.

Mito and most of the other major shipbuilding colonies were at full capacity, shipwrights and dockworkers toiling day and night to strengthen the empire's expanding armada. Mito was constructing new shipbuilding facilities on the southern edge of the colony, and Mithas too was busy with plans for growth.

The additional ships would strengthen the new garrisons and outposts being established throughout the empire and police the outer colonies. They would help deal with rebel attacks. Not all the new vessels were warships, however. Huge squat cargo carriers filled with food supplies and raw materials—such as iron or oils—made regular runs to the main colonies, distributing to smaller vessels heading to lesser settlements.

All food distribution was overseen by the temple now. To Nephera, that made perfect sense and since the majority of the

Supreme Circle—the governing body under the emperor—were among her faithful, it had proven easy to obtain the required vote. Supervisors sent to the farming colonies made certain all growers brought their produce and meats directly to shipyard stations. Sow and yield was closely monitored, so that as the empire expanded, demand would not exceed availability.

Nethosak itself was the shining example of Nephera's achievement. What Hotak had envisioned, she had transformed into reality. The capital's full resources were focused on the needs of the empire. Every worker served the expansion. The Protectors commanded all levels, enforcing the priestess's decisions.

Her decrees . . .

The high priestess rose from the great marble bath that had once served the clerics of Sargonnas. Two acolytes clad in white, gold-trimmed garments quickly toweled her off while another brought Nephera her robes of office. As she donned the black and silver-lined outfit, leaving the voluminous hood pulled back, Lady Nephera allowed one of the servants to take a horsehair brush to her mane.

The scent of lavender drifted throughout the room. Steam rose from the waters of the huge, rounded bath. The temple kept a vat of water heated at all times for the high priestess, and the intricate plumbing system devised by some clever cleric long ago enabled Nephera to have the water temperature adjusted to her preference. Of late, she wished it hotter and hotter, almost to the point of scalding her flesh. The fur of her servants was matted by the constant humidity, not so Nephera. Those who came in physical touch with her often found her flesh strangely cold. Even now, fresh from the heated bath, she felt as though she stood upon a chill mountain top. Her fur hung smooth, crisp, and dry.

She little resembled the onetime young, glowing, beautiful (for one of her species) bride of Hotak, and had changed much even from the time of his ascension to the throne. The

Lady Nephera who now stood in the center of the chamber as her faithful toiled for her pleasure was a wild-eyed, cadaverous, vaguely repellant female. Little flesh filled her minotaur form and face, and her outstretched arms ended more in talons than fingers. Nonetheless, her servants attended her with rapt adoration, as if she were as she imagined herself to be, beauty and perfection incarnate.

"Send word to Lord Gunthin that his presence is requested in the temple tonight. I would speak with him concerning the disappointing news of shipping delays."

"It will be done, mistress," responded the one brushing out her mane.

"Is the chamber prepared for me?"

"All is in readiness, mistress," answered a second, adjusting the robes just so.

Nephera made a slight gesture with her left hand. Her acolytes immediately ceased their exertions, retreating several steps from her august personage.

"Clean this area. I want it perfectly clean and in order," she commanded, then murmuring to herself, "I want all in perfect order . . ."

As they scurried to obey, the high priestess strode from the bath toward the wall. Although she did not look behind her, she knew that the three did not dare watch as she touched one of the stones in the wall.

While part of the wall gave way to a black passage beyond, Nephera suddenly started. Her unblinking eyes blazed as she stared to her left, looking at a figure only she could see.

"Cease your reproachful manner!" Lady Nephera snapped at the figure, though others might have thought she was snapping at thin air. Her attendants shivered to overhear, but still none dared glance in her direction. Such things were not for them to question.

"Away with you!" she commanded, raising one clawed hand up to chest level. Her fingers flared a dark, sinister green and in their glow there appeared briefly the shade of a massive minotaur in armor, his head twisted, his limbs bent as if his death had been cruel. He showed no emotion, not even in the one good eye, now flat and dull, he once boasted.

Hotak's silent shade vanished at her command. That should have been the end of it, but Nephera had exorcised the spirit before . . . and each time her mate had returned. He was not like Kolot, a most obedient shadow, like all the rest. Hotak did nothing but stand and watch her, hovering close. No matter how harshly she sent him away, he always returned. When she commanded him to some hopefully lengthy task, he would obligingly disappear, only to materialize a short time later, the task forgotten, never started. He was alone among her ghosts in this stubborn, disobedient behavior.

Teeth bared in frustration, Nephera darted through the passage, the wall sealing behind her. For some distance she walked in total darkness. Then the high priestess paused at another wall. Her hand rose unerringly to touch the wall, which opened up into her sanctum, deep in the heart of the vast main temple of Nethosak.

The scent of lavender heavily pervaded her new surroundings, the scent designed to mask other, more foul odors that might arise. As she entered, three acolytes dipped their horns in acknowledgement. Unlike the ones who assisted her with her bath, these wore robes akin to hers, though with the barest hint of silver thread.

"It is fresh?" she asked, already knowing the answer.

"Drawn less than a quarter of the hour ago, as commanded, mistress," reverently answered the middle one of the trio. "As prescribed by ritual."

Nephera nodded, then with a frown, glanced about the chamber. Fortunately, there was no sign of the shade for whom she searched, and her confidence returned.

The three acolytes parted. Behind them stood a pedestal upon which sat a squat, brass bowl with the symbols of the Forerunners—the axe and avian—embossed five times around the upper edge. Next to it sat a small, less elaborate bowl and a cloth towel.

The lesser priestesses made way for Nephera as she walked up to the larger bowl. She gazed down into it then thrust her hands into its crimson contents.

An exclamation of manic pleasure escaped her. Although only her ears could hear them, voices whispered from the bowl. Nephera felt a tingle, a rejuvenation. Her body quivered in ecstasy.

From her mouth came words in a tongue foreign to all but a handful in all the world of Krynn. The dark red of the liquid within did not merely splash her wrists but flowed up her arms halfway to the elbow. Not one drop, however, so much as stained the sleeves of her garments, even as they dipped into the liquid itself.

Finally, with an exultant gasp, she pulled her hands free. Droplets fell back into the bowl, the surface finally settling.

"Not as strong as I hoped," Nephera whispered petulantly, causing her three attendants to glance fearfully at one another, "but it will do this time . . ."

Leaning over the bowl, she breathed in the warmth of the fluid. Then the high priestess stared hard. The contents of the brass bowl shimmered.

Nephera whispered, "Show me . . . show me what I desire . . . show me first . . . Ardnor . . ."

Without warning, most of the color faded from the rich fluid. It grew transparent, becoming a window, a direct vision of whatever person or place Nephera wished to observe. An image of a room filled the bowl, a room faintly tinged with red.

Despite the lateness of the day, her son, the emperor, lay in the vast round bed that was the centerpiece of his private chambers. A titan even for a minotaur, Ardnor de-Droka was a fearsome figure to behold . . . when he was erect and standing, that is. Brutish, broad-shouldered, and with eyes permanently tinged the same color as blood, the recently ascended ruler of the empire was Nephera's firstborn and most favored of her four offspring, although of late she had grown somewhat impatient with him.

Ardnor's chamber was filled with the trappings of the Protectors. The gold symbol of the order—the broken axe—hung on one wall. In a chair to the right of the bed lay his black, gold-trimmed breastplate and helm. Ardnor's favored mace and axe hung on the wall next to where he slept, easily within arm's reach. If her son had learned one thing from the Night of Blood, it was that an emperor was wise to keep weapons handy.

The muscular figure rolled onto his back. As with all Protectors, the symbol of his order was even branded on his chest. That had been Ardnor's own idea, a way of testing the fanatic loyalty of his followers.

On the far side of her son lay a light brown female, one of the young acolytes from the temple. Nephera's nostrils flared in disapproval, noting the empty goblets and wine flask on a bedside table.

The high priestess dismissed the sight with a curt wave of her hand. Her son had risen to power because of her, but he had a tendency toward certain disreputable activities. She must have another word with him, stir his better instincts. Nephera would see to it that he became the greatest emperor the minotaur race had ever dreamed.

So much of what Nephera had done had been, she admitted to herself, for Ardnor's sake. Not for Hotak, no, not even for herself. She reluctantly wore the mantle of power simply to aid Ardnor.

The high priestess put a hand to her breast, staring up at the dim symbols of the order hanging on the main wall. The ghostly avian and the broken axe handle seemed to tower over her. Nephera recalled the dream in which she had first been blessed by the force represented by those symbols

. . . and remembered bitterly the night that power had been stripped from her very soul without warning.

That had been the night when the stars returned, the constellations that many believed signaled the reappearance of the gods. For Nephera, there had been no rejoicing. The gods might or might not have returned, but the source of her magic had, at that same time, utterly vanished. The link had ceased, the ghosts—all ghosts—had faded away, then the high priestess had felt more bereft than at any other time in her entire existence.

That very eve, Nephera had locked herself away in her sanctum. She refused all visitations, even that of Ardnor, who constantly sought her advice even now that the throne was his. Even her beloved son had been barred from her sight.

Drinking little, eating less, Lady Nephera lay upon the dais below the Forerunner symbols for day upon day. Her gut twisted and her vision blurred. The slightest thought made her head pound, yet she could not keep from constantly praying that somehow her god would return to her. The high priestess did not even have a name by which to call the disappeared deity, but she did have her suspicions. Thus it was that, five days into her despair, Nephera finally called out to the one she believed her patron.

"Takhisis!" she shouted. "Queen of the Abyss, have you forsaken me?"

Yet even such a bold declaration had achieved Nephera nothing. The goddess did not descend, did not speak to her in her dreams. Takhisis, if she was the one, had forever abandoned the minotaur priestess.

Her lamps empty of oil, her candles melted, the emperor's mother had curled in total blackness, neither sleeping nor fully conscious. Cold chilled her bones, but she cared not. Death was suddenly attractive.

Then . . . then a presence pierced the shroud wrapped around her mind and soul. At first, Nephera refused to acknowledge the communication, fearful that it was but her own pain-wracked imagination playing cruel games. When instead of fading to nothing it grew to permeate every fiber of her being, the stricken priestess became ecstatic. Nephera fought her way from the abyss within her, embracing this new, wondrous force.

I have heard your yearning... came a voice in her head. Where the other had been suspiciously neutral in tone, this one hinted of a male personality. *I have come to offer you salvation*...

"Yes!" she shouted. "Please! I am yours!"

That Nephera so quickly and willingly offered herself to a new deity did not bother her in the least.

You have been abandoned, your soul left to rot despite your unceasing loyalty...

The minotaur felt a sudden rage directed at her previous patron. Yes, she had served unwaveringly, letting nothing and no one—no one—stand in the path dictated. Her every breath had been drawn in service to its desires, and she had been repaid so disdainfully.

Yes... feed on that... dwell on that... she left you empty...

She? The word verified at last her suspicions. She. Surely then, it must have been Takhisis. Nephera's swelling anger turned to impulses of vengeance. If she could only take the goddess by the throat and throttle her—

The Queen is dead... your vengeance is fulfilled...

"I am—grateful." Nephera could only assume that this new god had taken some part in Takhisis's destruction. It only made her desire to serve him greater than ever.

I can grant you all you had and more, my high priestess, power beyond what she could give you. All you must do is give yourself to me as you gave yourself to her...

Again, no hesitation. "Yes! Yes! I do!"

In that darkness within her mind, two cold orbs suddenly flared to life. They had no pupils and were tinged a green that reminded Nephera of a rotten grave, yet she suffered no apprehension despite that.

Come to me . . . the eyes commanded. *Come . . .*

Nephera felt her spirit separate from her mortal form. It soared toward those eyes, enraptured by the thought of what the god offered. The orbs filled her gaze.

You will know your master, minotaur, and thereby know my supremacy over all things living . . . and dead . . . Look . . . look close . . .

She would not have pulled her gaze from those eyes even if that were possible. At first, Nephera saw only herself reflected in the ominous green orbs, but suddenly her face vanished, to be replaced by the vision of a single, tall structure, a tower made of tarnished metal.

You know me now, Nephera of House Droka.

The high priestess did and still her hunger did not abate. Nephera had given herself to one who had proven to be the Queen of Darkness. How much different, then, was this decision?

Swear to be mine, body and soul . . . and you shall be my voice, my hand, on the mortal plane. Swear, minotaur..swear . . . .

"Yes! By my ancestors, yes! Grant me your gifts! Please!"

The eyes shut, leaving Nephera to the emptiness, but not for long. A sphere of dark emerald color exploded directly before her. The minotaur only had a moment to register its appearance, before something long and winding burst from its center.

The hand was even more skeletal than hers and covered in dried skin tinted the color of moss. It thrust at her chest with such velocity that when it scraped her Nephera was hurled backward. She spun over and over, crying out not from pain but rather fear that she would not after all be granted her desire.

The next thing the high priestess knew, she lay once more in her sanctum. Now, however, her lamps were lit despite no oil and flames flickered over the stubs of burnt wicks. Nephera surveyed the chamber and spotted the singular, familiar presence of a ghost, a ghost who smelled of something rotting in the sea, who wore a tattered mariner's cloak that did not obscure the bones of his burnt and torn flesh. His ravaged mouth did not move, but the specter's voice reached out and touched Nephera's thoughts in somewhat the same manner as the god's.

Mistress . . . the ghost Takyr said with a hint of a bow. *We stand ready for your command . . .*

As Takyr spoke, he was joined by an endless throng of other shades. Each and every spirit who had served the high priestess who had vanished when the stars had appeared, they were all returning. They were hers again.

She felt a powerful congestion in her chest exactly where the hand had touched her. Recalling another time, another god, Nephera leapt to her feet and flew past the waiting figures. She rushed to her private quarters, seeking a looking-glass. Then, with a dread fascination, the minotaur thought to open her robe wide enough to reveal where, to her eyes alone, the mark of the Forerunners had been seared into her by her former patron.

Nephera gasped, the glass slipping from her fingers. It shattered, the sound echoing loud in the stone chamber. The avian was no more. Instead, the high priestess reverently touched the axe symbol, which had been made whole again. And instead of being raised high, now it hung upside-down and looked rusted.

The vision of the tower arose once more in her mind, the tarnished tower that Nephera realized belatedly had been perched at the edge of a bottomless precipice. A tarnished, bronze tower—as much the symbol of her lord as the mark she now bore.

Morgion.

Her reverie ending, Lady Nephera touched once more the liquid contents in the bowl. The blood's strength was almost gone. She would need a fresh reserve soon, especially with what she was planning. Still, for one more glance, what was left would suffice.

"Attend me!" she called, not to her acolytes.

Immediately her sanctum filled with the numerous dead.

They were young, old, sick, strong, and from every facet of minotaur society. Some were whole of face and form, for their deaths had been relatively peaceful. So many more, however, had perished violently, and their macabre images portrayed that ending all too clearly. The dead came to Nephera in the forms they had worn at the exact moment of their ends. Warriors from the field bore gaping, red stripes across their throats or chests and not a few lacked limbs. Skulls were crushed, faces were mangled, sometimes beyond recognition as minotaur, yet those who had suffered outside of battle were no less horrific. Burned to the bone by fire, ravaged by the boils or pox of plague, they too were the things of nightmare.

To Nephera, they were nothing but tools of magic. She drew from them, drew from the magic that they collected from the world around them . . . and then she pointed at the bowl.

The blood boiled. In the center, an image struggled to form. It started to fade again, but the high priestess's fierce will fueled her spell, forcing the vision to materialize at last.

She drew in a harsh breath. She saw carnage, yes, as Nephera had expected, yet most of the dead who lay strewn across the landscape were not rebels, but rather the best fighters of the empire. The hacked and rotting bodies stretching as far as she could see spoke of a debacle as great as any in the history of the race. With a roar, the high priestess spun from the bowl, searching amongst the ghosts. No matter how horrific they appeared, these ghosts themselves were still capable of fear and shimmered under her baleful gaze.

Over row upon row, Nephera sought the victim of her wrath, until, almost bursting with impatience and venom, she cried, "Bodar! I know you must be here! Show yourself! I command you!"

From their ranks, a reluctant specter drifted forward, the Protector general who had led the Scorpions. As with all minotaur dead, his spirit was drawn like a moth to a flame to the commanding presence of Nephera. The dead had no choice, for it was the will of both the high priestess and the god she served.

General Bodar moved very slowly. He kept his head bowed, his horns to the side in deference. At first glance, he appeared whole, not even a wound scarring his chest or throat.

Hissing, Nephera commanded, "Look at me!"

Hesitantly, Bodar looked up . . . to reveal that the right side of his face, muzzle included, had been crushed in.

With a sneer, the high priestess declared, "You've failed me, Bodar! I promised you much and you failed me! In this one thing, I will brook no excuses."

The ghost rippled, a sign of trepidation.

"Takyr . . ."

From the host, the monstrous ghost that smelled of the rot of the sea fluttered forward, his tattered mariner's cloak a vast, writhing thing of shadows. Takyr's own ruined visage wore a dark look of eager anticipation.

Mistress . . .

"General Bodar is of no more use to me, alive or dead."

The sinuous folds of Takyr's cloak stretched out to engulf the other ghost. Bodar screamed, although no one living save Nephera could hear his terrible desperate cries.

Takyr spread his arms to embrace the lesser shade—and the cloak enveloped them both, Bodar's scream cutting off.

No longer concerned with the hapless general, the high priestess glared at the scene of carnage again, red eyes scanning the devastation wrought on one of her finest legions and a horde of ogres. Nephera scowled, outraged at this latest setback.

She studied the ancient temple, willing it closer, willing her gaze beyond its walls. As ever, the high priestess's attempt to probe deeper into the rebel stronghold failed. She was blocked at the arched entrance. Beyond the walls she could only sense a black nothingness that she felt mocked her.

"I will not be denied!" she roared, but despite her declaration and willpower, the vision did not change.

Her arm swept across, sending the bowl and its contents flying. The action sent her three acolytes scurrying and the ghostly horde edged back. Even Takyr, finishing with his monstrous task, flinched under the intensity of her fury.

Then the high priestess felt a light touch upon her soul. Immediately her anger faded, replaced by adoration. She looked to the empty darkness, envisioning a tower of bronze and, within it, a crowned and hooded figure seated upon a crumbling throne.

I have heard your anger, heard your pleas . . .

"I did as suggested, ordering my son to send forth a strong legion and a bloodthirsty contingent of ogres, too, to ferret out the rebels . . . especially the one *he* protects!"

And they now lie dead, your toy soldiers and the beastmen . . .

She bowed her head. Nephera knew that she followed an unforgiving god, one who, in some ways, punished for lesser offenses than her previous deity.

Do not bow your head, Morgion told her, *for you have done only what I commanded. The enemy is gauged; preparations are made. Your legionaries and their erstwhile allies have fulfilled their ordained roles. Unknowingly, they carried with them my kiss and now it is given to our enemies. Already it acts. What must be will quickly follow, you may be assured. Be prepared; when it is commanded that you must act, you must then act with all the power that I have granted you . . .*

With that, the god vanished from her mind.

Lady Nephera brightened as she mulled over his words. She had not failed. Her god had just not told her everything. He had not mentioned the gift he had secreted with the legionaries, a gift he now passed on to the unsuspecting enemy.

"*Morgion's Kiss*," Nephera murmured, smiling. "Yes, I will be ready, my lord. I will not fail. The rebels will fall . . . *he* will fall . . ."

Blinking, the high priestess finally registered the second bowl. She reached in, cleansing her hands of the rich crimson. Her imperious glare turned upon the acolytes.

"Attend to this!" As they bent to obey, Nephera considered her next step. There were lists awaiting her.

The lists never ended. The perfection of the realm could not be attained so long as there were those who did not give of themselves all they could. Even in Nethosak, the high priestess always discovered someone else wanting.

Tomorrow, the Protectors would sweep through the designated neighborhoods, collecting the layabouts and suspected enemies of the state whose names she had recorded on parchment. Already the latest lists spread three long sheets with more to follow. Nethosak, most of all, had to be prove itself to the utmost.

As she turned, Takyr unexpectedly drifted into her path. Nephera's ears twitched, knowing he must have a good reason for this affront. "You have news?"

Takyr kept his head low, a sign that, despite his special place, he knew he, too, could be punished if she so chose.

Mistress . . . mistress . . . eyes have seen him at last . . . he is discovered . . .

She knew immediately of whom he spoke. "Where? How? How did he evade me for this long? Bring his spirit to me!"

I cannot . . . the dread ghost dared look up. *He is alive.*

"Alive . . ." Her suspicions were verified. Of all shades, he should have been drawn to her if he was dead. "Where?"

Among the very rebels in Kern . . . with the hidden one, it seems . . .

The rebels! There had been rumors, but she couldn't bring herself to credit them . . . Her face, though, betrayed no emotion.

"And now?"

Takyr's voluminous cloak fluttered, reflecting his unease. *That is why I was able to detect him. Your son rides from their stronghold, mistress, heading with certainty to another of your blood.*

That could only be Maritia! Abruptly, Nephera lost all interest in lists. Bastion, thought drowned, now not only rode to his sister but had apparently departed from the side of the mysterious rebel leader, Faros.

Bastion . . . a rebel!

There had been no word of him since an assassin had tried to slay him aboard ship. Ardnor had sent one of his most trusted Protectors, and the fool had failed, so Bastion had escaped. Now, apparently, he had chosen the enemy over his own family. That could not be condoned.

She had to be certain. Her fists tightened until the knuckles turned as white as bone. Bastion, once a loyal officer of the legions, might simply be bringing information to Maritia. That information could concern the rabble in Kern, and the other rebels scattered throughout the Blood Sea and the Courrain.

Nephera had to know more. A thought came to her. There was one peculiarly well-suited to deal with Bastion, whatever the truth of it. After all, he already owed her very, very much. She would have him trace Bastion and discover what had to be done for the sake of the empire.

At this thought, the high priestess glanced around, but the shade of her husband was nowhere to be seen. Nephera took this as a sign that her impulse was the right one, the only one.

"Time to pay some of your debt, Grand Lord," she whispered, putting together her thoughts for the message she would shortly send. "More than time . . ."

CHAPTER V

BETRAYAL BY BLOOD

He should have been dead. Among ogres, the loss of a hand generally meant the loss of respect and status, and among the ruling caste, the loss of status generally meant a more powerful rival would soon crush in the scorned and maimed ogre's skull.

Although in the recent months two ambitious warlords had attempted such a traditional play for power—and perished quite horribly for their failure—Golgren had survived unscathed. More important, his grip—his single-handed grip on Kern and Blöde—had only tightened.

The clatter of hooves and the creak of wheels accented his caravan's journey over the rough terrain. The horses and covered wagons kicked up dust, which caked in grey the lines of warriors in his wake. The odor of heated horses suffused Golgren's nostrils, but it was a far more palatable scent than if he had ridden behind his unbathed, sweating followers. He reached with his lone hand to a pouch at his belt and removed from it a small, oval container of blue crystal, with a stopper attached by a thin gold chain. Manipulating the stopper free, he brought the bottle to his nose and inhaled. A hint of jasmine flower flowed into his nostrils. The perfume, taken from the wreckage of an elven lord's abode, momentarily eradicated the more strident aromas.

The Grand Lord rode through Blöde undaunted by how deep he intruded into the neighboring ogre domain. In the old days, his actions would have unleashed a monstrous war between the rival tribes. So much had changed during recent years, though. First the humans, the Knights of Neraka, had drawn the ogres together by invading both realms in their thirst for conquest. That invasion had precipitated Golgren's rise to power, for he had been of a sharper mind than the dull-witted chiefs serving the Grand Khan.

Then, along had come the Uruv Suurt—the minotaur—called Hotak. His ambitions had been the mirror of Golgren's own, and the ogre had used the minotaur's plans to draw others into his camp, those of his people who had become disenchanted with the Grand Khan's failings.

That they had come to him despite their differences spoke to Golgren's charisma and influence. Certainly it had little to do with his physical stature. He was not tall by his people's standards, and at his full height stood more than a head shorter than most. Moreover, Golgren was of a slim build and his countenance differed much from other ogres, being less flat and more narrow. The blunt nose was almost similar to a human's and instead of tusks, Golgren evinced only two nubs, the result of careful filing. His thick, black leonine mane was clean and brushed. The Grand Lord kept himself bathed—even forcing his followers to tote along a couple of wagons with water for that purpose—and wore a musky perfume to cover his personal scent.

His garments were of sturdy but fine make. This journey he wore a long, sand-brown cloak over an elegant tunic similar in color. His knee-length leather and cloth kilt was of minotaur design, and unlike most ogres, he wore sandals with leather straps winding up his calves.

There were those who claimed that Golgren carried some elven blood, but none ever said so within hearing of the Grand Lord. Certainly his eyes indicated some unique background, for under the heavy brow they were, in contrast to all other ogres, almond-shaped and emerald green. Those eyes missed few details, however, and when matched against the brutal, dark orbs of others of his kind in struggles of will or might, they never wavered.

Golgren seemingly had come out of nowhere, rising swiftly among the khan's followers and seizing control from the lord of Kern while the latter sat smoking the intoxicating essence of the Grmyn flower. His other rivals had fallen in short order. Despite Donnag and the treacherous Titans, the power of Blöde had come to him no less readily, although there he had needed a bit of outside help, help which he at times regretted.

Behind the Grand Lord marched line upon line of brutish warriors bearing clubs, axes, spears, and other, more creative weapons. The ranks alternated, with the taller, unarmored, grey-furred fighters of Kern marching in one row, then in the next the squatter, helmed, and breast-plated denizens of Blöde—their fur a more dusky brown at times—and so on. The alternating lines kept both groups from turning on one another, for if any got the urge to misbehave they only had to remember one of the victim's comrades marched directly behind. The ogres might be allied, but Golgren was no fool. He trusted his own kind less than he trusted the minotaurs.

To each side of the warrior horde, and adding immensely to the rank, pervasive stench, lumbered the mastarks, the huge, tusked beasts of war. Trained to be perpetually wary, several sniffed the air with their serpentine, prehensile noses. Atop each rode two handlers, one behind the other. The second also carried a bow and quiver, and from thick leather belts across the animal's back hung a set of spears. The mastarks wore iron helms with twin spikes, which they knew to use in conjunction with their tusks.

The behemoths also kept the warriors marching briskly, as the flat foot of a mastark was able to crush an ogre whole. Each step was accompanied by a low, thunderous sound, so heavy were the muscular beasts. If they were not enough to keep the warriors in check, on the outer flanks—always kept under leash—stalked several hungry, hissing meredrakes. Used to seeking out the smells of the enemy, the huge lizards were also quite adept at dealing with any unruly elements in their own ranks. Whenever even the slightest hint of disobedience arose, the handlers dove in with the long-toothed behemoths. Golgren's army might not have the training and discipline of the Uruv Suurt, but he knew well how to intimidate and maintain absolute authority over them.

The army had been marching over the winding terrain of southernmost Blöde, ostensibly hunting pockets of elven fighters who had taken to the inhospitable land in order to strike back at those who had conquered Silvanesti. These days it was Golgren who peered with eyes of avarice toward that lush, green realm, recalling the richer ground so briefly held by his kind during the initial days of the invasion. The Uruv Suurt had quickly sent more legionaries to secure most of the northern border of what was now Ambeon, leaving the ogres' holdings sparse and desolate by comparison.

Golgren quietly bared his teeth—the sharp, yellowed carnivorous teeth that, despite his outward attempts at cosmetic improvement, distinctly marked him as one of his brutish race—and suddenly barked out a command to the rider next to him.

The breast-plated ogre raised a curled goat horn to his mouth and blew two harsh notes. As he did so, Golgren and those near him reined their huge mounts to a halt, followed by the massive column.

The sun was already fading. Unlike the minotaurs—who would have organized an array of pickets, deployed scouts and no doubt ferreted under every rock for possible foes—the horde simply ground to a halt and slumped to the ground. Handlers led off mastarks and meredrakes for feeding. Both creatures were adept at foraging off the dry lands despite their large girths, and the cold-blooded lizards could especially go long periods without a significant catch. Warriors drifted together in small groups and began digging out the dried meat they bore on journeys. Several began to play games of chance, rolling polished bits of bone with markings on sides or betting on the outcome of wrestling matches. Others simply settled back and went directly to sleep.

"Harum i kyat!" snapped beady-eyed Belgroch, who was in charge of dealing with Golgren's needs, especially pitching and organizing his tent. The stout ogre was an uglier version of his toad-faced elder brother, Golgren's second in command, Nagroch. Both hailed from Blöde but had long ago cast their lot with the Grand Lord—which, naturally, did not preclude switching sides should the one-handed ogre face a sudden reversal of fortune.

Dismounting, Belgroch took a braided whip with nine sharp, metal hooks and snapped it in the direction of the second of two wagons directly behind them. From the rear of the tarp-covered vehicle, which still bore worn traces of a Solamnic emblem on the side, leapt two other Blödian ogres. Armed with swords, they shouted into the wagon.

The clanking of chains announced a dozen ragtag figures. One by one, the weary slaves—some human, others elven—dragged their gaunt, beaten bodies forth from the wagon. Many looked as filthy as the ogres, and their skin had blotches from disease and whippings. Their eyes were listless, for all hope, all life, had long ago been ripped from them.

"Harum i kyat!" Belgroch repeated, pointing to the other wagon. The slaves shambled forward, an occasional moan punctuating their movements. At the back end of the other wagon, they began unloading the wooden framework and the mottled, goatskin covering of Golgren's tent.

As the humans and elves erected the structure under the urging of stinging whips, Nagroch, who had ridden ahead with a small party, returned to his lord.

"No shelled ones," the repulsive, pockmarked ogre quietly reported in his best Common, referring to both Solamnics and the Knights of Neraka. Golgren demanded that those who served him closest learn the widespread tongue. Common was the language of civilization in this age, and Golgren considered himself as civilized as the great kings of the west or his own illustrious forebears.

"No pointy ears," Nagroch added, his own term for elves. "Scouts say no Uruv Suurt, either." Clad all day in the incessant, burning sun in an open helm and rusted breastplate, Nagroch stank even worse than usual. He leaned closer, crusted, brown teeth displayed in a wide, hungry grin. "No Uruv Suurt for days south. Could turn south, just accident, and—"

Golgren gave him a reproving look that stopped his lieutenant in mid-sentence. "You will not speak again of this, yes?" His eyes, narrow and unblinking, made the other, much brawnier figure, flinch. There was no doubt in either's mind that, even minus a hand, an annoyed Golgren would slay Nagroch with one mighty blow. "Not again . . . unless I say so . . ."

The Grand Lord adjusted a chain hanging around his neck. As he did, a large object near his chest shifted underneath his tunic. Nagroch grimaced, his blotchy skin growing a touch pale.

"Aye, friend Golgren, aye! Ignore this foolish one! A jest, nothing more!"

He was saved further disapproval by Belgroch's return. The younger brother bent as low as his massive girth would allow, announcing, "Grand Lord, tent is up!"

Golgren nodded, and without another glance at either of the two, headed for the rounded structure. The tent was half again as tall as an ogre and large enough to comfortably fit nearly a dozen muscular warriors. A thick, gray tarp cut from tanned mastark hide served as a tent flap. The slaves who had put the entire thing together now knelt near the entrance with their arms stretched forth and their faces pressed to the pounded dust. Two guards with whips stood wary watch over them, their own heads bowed slightly in fearful respect of Golgren.

The Grand Lord ducked slightly as he entered. His approving glance met the interior, which the slaves had already filled with his belongings. A lit oil lamp hung from the center of the ceiling. Thick furs covered the entire floor. Sacks of wine and water lay on a small, oval table whose wooden legs could be unbound and folded under for travel.

A young female elf clothed only in a scant goat fur slipped into the tent behind him. Unlike the other elves, her delicate, ivory skin was unblemished and her long tresses showed recent bathing and brushing. She even smelled of the same jasmine scent the Grand Lord carried—not all that surprising as she drew from the belongings of his household. Even with both her ankles and wrists chained, the silver-haired slave moved with grace. She was likely centuries old, but she had the appearance of a young woman edging into adulthood. Her wide, almost crystalline eyes were veiled by long lashes, and her features were gracefully angular.

As Golgren raised his arms, she silently bent down and removed his belt and sword sheath. To one side of the interior, Golgren's twin-edged axe already lay on a cushion of fur, as if it were a pampered infant. The female elf set Golgren's sword next to the rune-etched axe then scurried to another short table on the opposite side. There three small scrolls and the sharpened quill feather of a condor awaited. A tiny, square vial of ink with the Solamnic kingfisher emblazoned on it rested to the right of the feather.

The Grand Lord settled into the furs. He stretched out his maimed limb to the elf, who gently unwrapped the

silk-covered stump. Her perfect features finally shifted, gri-
macing unwillingly as she unveiled what lay beneath the
stained cloth.

Golgren chuckled at her obvious distaste, causing her to
gasp. With a grunt, he commanded her to continue.

As she drew away the last of the silks, the full extent of
the damage was revealed. The blade had made a very clean
cut, but to save himself from blood loss, the Grand Lord had
quickly located a torch, and there in the midst of battle cauterized the wound. Not once had he screamed as the flames
sealed what was left, but by the time he was finished, blood
from his lip and tongue had scored his garments. With the
burnt stump wrapped against his torso, Golgren had taken
from his pouch dried Grmyn flower petals, chewing on them
until their narcotic quality had eased—though not erased—
the agony. For an entire week, the ogre had secretly taken the
petals until he felt ready to accept the pain, then he immediately ceased using the addictive flora. To his followers, Golgren had performed something of a miracle, for from then on,
he had revealed no more struggle with his wound. In fact, he
had gone out of his way to display the maimed limb and show
that the loss was negligible, riding into battle and practicing
his combat skills against the very strongest opponents.

Now, after several months, the end of his arm was blunted
and black, but at least there had never been any infection.
Indeed, the scabs covering the stub had begun to heal as best
they probably could.

Reaching for a slim blue vial, the elf maiden poured jasmine oil over the wound and rubbed it in gently with her
smooth, tapering fingers. Golgren allowed himself a slight
exhalation of relief. There was still pain, but nothing he
could not contain. Golgren did not fear the elf revealing his
weakness, for she had seen what had happened to another
who had carelessly blabbed. The dried head of that one even
now hung to the Grand Lord's left.

"Wine," he growled, leaning toward her. The sharpness of his breath, the breath of a predator, caused her tiny nose to wrinkle.

She brought him a dark leather sack shaped like a thick grape from which he greedily drank. Once satiated, Golgren thrust the half-emptied container at her then pointed to the writing tools. The elf replaced the sack then immediately moved to the table, where she folded her legs and unrolled one parchment.

Peering over her, he eyed the flowing, elegant symbols of the High Ogres' ancient written language that covered the top half of the sheet. The Common tongue might be Golgren's favored manner of speech in public, but for this special project, only the perfect script of his mighty ancestors would suffice. Only the ancient script could adequately record his illustrious ascension for the future generations.

His slave, beaten into learning the style as quickly as she could, now acted as his stenographer. Mastark calls, the harsh laughter of gambling, the clatter of metal—all the raucous sounds of the horde faded into the background as Golgren started to dictate.

Before he could speak, a sudden chill rose up and down his spine. He jolted upright, his movements causing the elf to shake. Ink splattered the page, befouling the work done. She cried out, certain that in the next second he would slap her.

Her master no longer even noticed her quivering presence. The flame from the flat, elongated lamp had all but died. Out of the corner of his eye, the Grand Lord spied a shadow moving—a shadow without a form to cast it. Golgren swore under his breath.

Grand Lord Golgren . . .

The voice flowed like the perpetual tide. A hint of the sea touched his nostrils, but the sea when it was filled with death. The ogre watched as the shadow detached itself from the wall.

Only Golgren's furrowed brow gave any indication of his uneasiness. He stared hard at the shadow. Now and then he could make out a ghoulish soul, a burnt and rotting minotaur wrapped in a vast, shroudlike cloak.

The ghost had a name, he knew. Takyr. Golgren disliked that name. It reminded him too much of the dread Takhisis, although there appeared no connection.

He glanced at the elf, cringing, averting her eyes. The tent's interior was all but black, yet the shadow was distinct. The noises outside sounded muffled, almost nonexistent. Again the ogre heard the voice in his head. *Grand Lord Golgren...*

The elf was frightened, but because of his anger, not because of the ghost. Only he could see the intruder.

"Get out!" the Grand Lord snapped to the elf. "Go!"

With a whimper, the slave leapt up, and chains jangling fled the tent.

His unearthly visitor observed all in silence. Impatient and not a little unnerved, Golgren finally blurted, "What? You have something to say, say it!"

He felt Takyr's unearthly mirth. *My mistress would wish me to relay news of import to you...*

Lady Nephera wasted neither time nor Takyr on idle matters. Golgren's anxiety became wary interest. "I listen."

There are rebels riding through your domain...

"Always there are, ghost! What of it?"

They ride toward Ambeon. It is believed they seek a secret audience with the Lady Maritia and will meet with her near the crags that separate dry Blöde from the elves' lost paradise.

The ogre leaned forward, asking, "Why would the Lady Maritia allow this? She is loyal..."

Takyr's murky form rippled. He filled Golgren's tent, the tendrils created by the folds in his cloak moving as if of their own accord. *The one who leads the riders is her brother, black Bastion.*

"Oh, is that so?" The last the Grand Lord had heard of Maritia's brother, he had been lost at sea. In fact, fate had not been at all kind to Maritia's ruling family, two brothers and her father dead in so short a time. Golgren had even considered ways of consoling the female minotaur. While her face was not attractive by any stretch of the imagination—like all her kind she resembled a cow, of course—both her spirit and lithe form appealed to the Grand Lord as did none of his own race.

A wry chuckled echoed through his head. He snapped to attention, forgetting Takyr could sometimes sense his thoughts. The ogre's face darkened. "Huh? The son of Hotak is with the rebels? Why is this so?"

A matter of no significance, replied the specter almost curtly, which meant that it was a matter of great significance. *That betrayal is his, if it is such.*

"Your mistress wishes him captured? A small thing. I will send out Nagroch and—"

Takyr's cloak suddenly burst open as if seeking to swallow the ogre. Despite his best efforts to remain implacable, Golgren gasped and threw himself backwards. Takyr's cloak then withdrew, leaving the Grand Lord scowling.

None must seek to harm him during his journey to meet with his sister. My mistress is adamant in this. Bastion keeps his thoughts and actions well-guarded. Even she knows not all of them. It may be he comes to betray the rebels. She would like to know the truth.

"That is . . . understood, yes."

However, my mistress has much else with which to deal, lord ogre, and you owe her much for the favors done on your behalf. Donnag and the Titans would have been a great thorn in your side if it were not for their sudden . . . malady. The knowledge given to you also of their weaknesses, their need for the blood of elves ... Donnag is an excellent example to the others of what might happen without your leadership. Then there is all the weaponry, too, and the food supplied for hungry, willful warriors mercurial in their loyalty.

"Spare this one your mistress's lists," grunted Golgren, straightening. "The Lady Nephera wishes Bastion to reach his destination, wishes the black-furred one to meet with the Lady Maritia and reveal his secrets. So. Good. None will touch her son, this is promised." He looked away from Takyr. "Go. Tell her."

There is more, the ghastly shade persisted. *Lord Bastion is popular among the people.*

This was no surprise to Golgren. While he lusted after Maritia's warrior spirit, he himself respected Bastion's reputation— his self-denial and ability to take charge of a situation. Hotak had been correct to name his second son heir. Under similar circumstances, the ogre would have done the same.

"Aaah . . ." Understanding spread across the Grand Lord's face. His green eyes danced with dark thoughts. So that was Nephera's aim.

If a traitor, he may sway his sister, who was known to follow him in the past.

"This could be so," said Golgren, hesitantly.

If traitor he be, then it would be best if none of his party departed from the crags. None at all.

"This is wished of me?" Golgren growled, rising. He had not expected such an extreme measure. "All?"

A single baleful glance from Takyr made him back down. *The judgment is yours, lord ogre. So says my mistress. One, both, or none, it is you who chooses. Act as necessary.*

"It will be difficult for one to spy close on such a gathering— difficult to hear the truth and make such a judgment."

That has been taken into account. As he spoke, the dead figure's cloak opened further. From out of it suddenly emerged another specter who swelled to normal size the moment he was freed. Golgren's gaze widened briefly. The second ghost was slightly taller than normal for a minotaur, which still made him shorter than most ogres, but he was half again as wide as even the brawniest of the Grand Lord's warriors. He wore a dour expression, and if not for the gaping hole where his throat had once been, he would have looked almost alive, albeit translucent. From him, there was a hint of musk. *This one will assist you . . .*

Golgren bared his teeth, such audacity beyond even him. "The son of Hotak to watch over the son of Hotak?"

Kolot's ghost gave no hint of recognition. His eyes stared unblinking.

He will relay word for word what they say. You will know then what to do.

No sooner had Takyr finished than he began to evanesce. At that same moment, the din outside was heard anew. The macabre mariner became once more merely a shadow among shadows. It happened so swiftly that by the time the Grand Lord thought to speak, Nephera's servant was gone, and he was alone.

Except for the specter of Nephera's youngest son.

Golgren eyed the strange figure. Ghosts didn't bother him, as long as they didn't oppose him. This one remained as motionless as a statue. The ogre hissed then called outside, "Summon Nagroch!"

Moments later, the bulky warrior pushed his way into his lord's tent. He stood quietly, awaiting Golgren's command while the latter sought some sign that Nagroch noticed the third party with them. When it was clear that Kolot was invisible to all except the Grand Lord, Golgren smiled darkly in admiration of Nephera's magic and indicated that Nagroch should come closer.

"A task is to be performed, friend Nagroch, one that must be yours. It will involve a little bloodletting . . ."

The other ogre grinned wide in anticipation.

CHAPTER VI

MORGION'S KISS

The city that had once been called Silvanost stretched out before Maritia for as far as she could see, but it was no longer the forest-lined garden of halcyon days. As Maritia de-Droka and her bodyguard rode through the thick, new, wooden gates her soldiers had built, she surveyed a place that was much transformed.

Ancient towers that had gone unchanged for more than a thousand years were in the midst of being remade according to minotaur dictates. Delicate curves and gaudy ornamentation had been stripped to make way for smooth, efficient lines. Once-wooded pathways stood clear to the sun. Gentle and much-too-dim glow lights, the manner by which the elves had illuminated much of the city's walks, had been replaced by stronger, more durable brass oil lamps hanging from tall iron poles planted in the ground and lit each evening by patrols.

Despite so many alterations, Silvanost still was less changed than any other part of Ambeon. Here, in the former elven capital, Maritia had skirted Ardnor's order to eliminate all symbols of the past occupants by instead stripping down the wondrous towers and even the palace itself then reconstructing them more along imperial lines. *Waste not what should not be wasted,* her father had taught her, and she had followed that good advice. Why tear down what was functional? Ironically, it now seemed that Maritia had made the correct decision; had she followed Ardnor's original directive, the main temple would be in ruins and his new command to turn it into a Forerunner stronghold a futile one.

The first district through which they rode had once been the elven equivalent of a wooded market, but every structure there had been razed and the skeletons of rectangular common houses now arose. The constant need for housing made it a necessity to build wherever possible. Each house would be capable of temporarily sheltering up to two hundred new arrivals to the minotaur cause.

To the north of the new common houses, dust and the faint clatter of metal against rock signaled that the toil in the quarries going strong. There the bulk of elven prisoners slaved day and night to supply the city with enough stone to remake it in the empire's image. Maritia coughed as the evening wind whipped up the dust, but such minor inconvenience was the price of victory and progress.

Then a beautiful tower majestically rising ahead greeted her eyes. The Tower of the Stars glistened so much in the sunlight that even hardened minotaurs paused to gape at it in awe. Its design was simple, smooth, yet somehow so magnificent that Maritia, calling upon her brother's name to enforce her own edict, had so far forbidden absolutely any alteration of it. She had claimed it for Clan Droka, despite Clan Athak's early attempts to make it their own, and if not for her position as expedition commander, would have made her personal quarters there instead of in the sprawling yet effete palace visible some distance behind her.

The palace, over three hundred feet high and with three separate wings to it, would have impressed the minotaur conquerors more were it not for its rose-colored facade. The genteel hue was typical of the weak tastes of the elves, and when schedule permitted, Maritia planned to have it painted over in a good, honest grey. For the time, however, she tried to think of the color as being like dried, faded blood. Unfortunately, the soft woodland images decorating the entire structure inside and out in no manner aided her attempt to see the palace as other than it was.

Minotaurs everywhere ceased their tasks as she and her party passed through Ambeon's capital. Reluctant elven slaves—their once-shining finery now pathetic rags—were prodded or struck with the flat of a blade to remind them to acknowledge the emperor's sister. The eyes of most of the elves no longer held hope, although now and then one managed a brief if pathetic glare of defiance. The perfumes of the haughty race, which had assailed her senses when she first arrived in Silvanesti, were gone and replaced by the honest sweat of toil. The capital itself no longer smelled overwhelmingly of flowers; now the musk of minotaurs pervaded.

Guards in shining breastplates and helms saluted her sharply as she dismounted at the foot of the palace. Preferring some privacy, she dismissed her own retinue then strode inside.

Scarcely had Maritia entered when she was met by a treverian whom she knew was supposed to be stationed miles from the city. Helmet in the crook of one arm, the cloaked officer, his uniform dust-covered and his deep-brown fur dank, went down on one knee and in almost a whisper uttered, "My Lady Maritia."

"Novax? This is an unexpected visit. There's trouble in the north?"

"Nay—not exactly, my lady." Novax dipped his horns to the side. He did not look up directly at her.

Maritia's ears twitched. She noticed then that the sentries generally on duty in the hall were absent. "What does that mean? What brings a trusted subcommander, who once served alongside my own brother Bastion in my father's legion, so far from his own troops?"

Novax, a broad-muzzled male with horns scarred from axe cuts, cleared his throat. " 'Tis your brother that brings me here, my lady."

"My brother? What does Ardnor—"

"Nay! The very sibling of whom you just spoke! Good, honest Bastion . . ."

His hesitant manner disconcerted her. "Rise up and face me, Novax! Tell me in plain words what you're speaking about!"

The treverian obeyed. He stood more than a head higher than her, yet met her furious gaze. Novax's breath came in short, anxious bursts. "My lady . . . I bring a message from Bastion."

The blood rushed to her eyes and her nostrils flared wide. She clutched the hilt of her sword, barely containing herself. "Have you come from an audience with my mother? That would be the only way you might manage to speak with Bastion, Novax! I wonder what could possibly provoke your sick humor—"

He did not cower. Instead, the brown male handed her a small, crumpled parchment he had kept hidden in his other hand. "I ask only that you read this. If you find it lacking in truth, then punish me as you will."

Snatching the message away, Maritia unfolded it. She did not read the contents at first, seeking something else at the lower left corner of the page.

The mark was there. Two circles with a blade through them, so tiny most would not have noticed it.

Bastion's secret mark, known only to her and her father.

Her heart leapt, then sank. All the rumors she had heard. Was the unthinkable true?

Bastion among the rebels . . .

Then, her eyes narrowed as Maritia read what Bastion had written. Her nostrils flared, her breath quickened. Moments later, without divulging its contents, she crumpled up the note, sticking it in a belt pouch for later disposal in a fire.

"You know how to contact him?"

"Yes."

Trying to keep her expression neutral, Maritia said, "Tell him I'll meet him where he stipulates at the appointed time. There will be four with me, no more. All trusted."

"Aye, my lady." The treverian started to back away.

Maritia signaled him to wait. "Novax . . . how did he look?"

He grinned briefly. "As ever himself."

"That would be Bastion." She dismissed the officer.

Maritia went to one of the wide, open balconies thrusting out from the main palace. The rails were carved in the shapes of forest creatures, some fanciful, some real. The floor was a mosaic image of elven royalty communing with nature. Flowers and trees seemed to be sprouting to life at the elves' command.

The balcony gave her a view of much of the city. She could see five of the seven towers, each one once honoring a different god of light. Below, a lush, beautiful garden shaped like a four-pointed star filled the vast courtyard surrounded by the towers and the palace. Maritia had been so lost in thought on the way back from the frontier that she had not paid the garden any mind. Where most of the other plant life in Silvanost had suffered, the Garden of Astarin had remained untouched by the foul magic of the shield. Impressed by this, Maritia had renamed it the Garden of Triumph and allowed favored elves to continue to tend to it. She saw it as a symbol of her own race, determined to grow and thrive despite adversity. Bastion would have approved of her decision.

"Bastion . . ." Her eyes drifted over the capital, *Ardnoranti*. Ardnor's Glory. Maritia would have preferred to name the city after someone other than her brother, someone more deserving.

Maritia would have called the city *Hotakanti*.

Her hand slipped to where she kept the note. Bastion alive, but with the rebels. She could still scarcely believe it.

Yes, she would meet with him, if only to understand why.

"I'll do what must be done, brother," Maritia quietly declared. Her hand tightened into a fist. "Whatever must be done."

On the fourth day, Grom died.

He was only the first of many. The plague rapidly spread through the rebel stronghold. Not all who suffered from it died—but still scores upon scores of those who fell victim perished. There were few symptoms, few initial signs. The coughing became persistent, the ragged, barking cough that soon spewed blood. There appeared small pustules under the eyelids that soon swelled, pulsating and turning a fetid green. As the sickness progressed, the vomiting began. The bodies of the sick minotaurs radiated such heat that their fur was continually soaked in sweat.

The stricken lay in row upon row in the largest chambers of the temple. Unable to fend for themselves, unable even to maintain normal bodily functions, they were soon covered in filth. There seemed little anyone could do to help the ill or keep themselves from becoming afflicted. Each hour brought afflicted, until soon their numbers threatened to overtake those still fit.

Grom, who at his own request was brought to the worship chamber, woke but twice after his collapse. The first time he again asked Faros's forgiveness. Not knowing what else to say, Faros merely nodded. The second time, Grom rose up briefly and turned to his deity, praying to one of the towering statues that Sargas would see in him a worthy warrior and in addition watch over Faros and the rebellion. That was his last lucid moment.

After that, the unconscious Grom had twisted in agony, involuntarily clutching at his chest and throat. The pustules burst, spreading a thick, green fluid accompanied by the smell of rot. Like the others, he was bathed as best as possible, but it was a long time before his stomach had finally emptied itself.

When at last the news came that Grom had died, Faros nodded and said nothing. Faros had already reckoned him among the dead. Faros recalled Sargonnas's words and wondered if the temple was somehow to blame. The way the plague had arisen and spread was almost supernatural.

In two-wheeled wagons piled high, the rebels brought the dead out of the ancient structure and down to the battlefield where bodies were still rotting. Now Faros agreed to burn the dead, and parties scavenged the countryside for fuel. The harsh landscape provided little good wood or brush. The pyres that did get lit often burned out with their grisly work only partly done.

A pale human and a thin female minotaur came to Faros as night fell upon the temple. Seeing their hesitant expressions, he paused in his sword practice. Try as he may to drown out what was happening, Faros could not escape the sounds and smells that pervaded the temple. With a snarl, he asked, "What?"

"We—" the bearded human swallowed. "We wanted to know if it were all right to remove Grom for—for—"

"For the pyre," his companion managed to finish for him.

Faros snorted. "His body's still there? He's been dead a day! Go ahead and—" As he raised his hand to send them off, his mood shifted. "No. Wait. Be off with you! I'll let you know when."

As they rushed away, Faros sheathed his sword. He left his quarters, heading for the chamber where Grom lay.

Under the very statue that Faros had sliced open, the minotaur's corpse lay in repose. A single torch set in the wall enabled Faros to see how someone had carefully arranged Grom's axe in his arms. His garments had been straightened as best as possible, and if not for the marks of the plague—his gauntness was unsettling—he might have looked as though he died peacefully.

Faros suddenly found it hard to breathe. Visions swept past him. His father, his entire family. Ulthar the brigand. Bek the servant. Valun, who had escaped alongside Grom. Governor Jubal.

The procession of ghosts grew longer with each death.

Rage suddenly getting the better of him, Faros charged up to the statue. Drawing his sword, he threatened the figure.

"Where are you this time, Horned One? Here lies a fool . . . your fool! Here's one who imagined you would return one day and make all right! See the reward he got for his faith? To be burned with others in a mass pyre, then forgotten by all!"

He slashed at the statue, but this time all he did was leave a jagged line in the marble. No floodgates opened, no river of blood or molten earth poured forth.

With a frustrated grunt, Faros sought something stronger to wield against the statue. His eyes alighted on Grom's good, dependable axe.

As his fingers grazed the handle, revulsion filled him. Faros pulled back, staring into the face of the one who had followed him so loyally. Grom had courageously fought Sahd's minions, legionaries, and the horde of the Grand Lord Golgren. He could have remained with Jubal's comrades but had sworn to guard Faros's back.

Now, instead of battle, it was disease that had claimed the sturdy warrior. To minotaurs, such a death was a life wasted.

No glorious songs of final battle would be sung for him, no stories would be told to his children of the enemies he had taken with him.

Grom's head lay tipped slightly to the side, almost as if his lidded eyes watched Faros.

Going down on one knee, Faros readjusted his dead comrade's head so that Grom could stare up at the heavens.

"You should've chosen a different god," muttered the rebel leader, "and a different cause to follow."

He sheathed his sword again and hurried from the scene. The coolness of the temple would help preserve the dead. Grom's body could lie under the indifferent eye of his god overnight, then Faros would see to it that his second's body was burned. He owed Grom that much.

The sounds and sights of the plague continued to assail him all the way back to his quarters. He tried to return to his sword practice, but even slaying a hundred Golgrens did nothing to calm Faros. His heart beat faster and faster. Finally, Faros tossed his sword away in disgust.

As he did so, the rebel leader noticed the other gift of the god. Still caught up in his rage, Faros ripped the ring from his finger and threw it as hard as he could against the wall.

The ring did not break. However, it struck the stone with a loud clatter, making a brief, red spark, then clattered across the floor, leaving other sparks in its wake. Faros watched with some satisfaction as it rolled down into a crack in one corner.

"So much for your gifts," he murmured to the absent deity. "So much for your power . . ."

The sound of intense coughing made him spin about. An elder male with graying brown fur stood outside the entrance. Faros had seen him ministering to some of the other stricken minotaurs, but now he himself looked ill. Even as Faros opened his mouth to say something, the other minotaur abruptly fell to the left, striking the opposite wall in the corridor.

By the time Faros reached the entrance, the older rebel had slumped to the floor. Faros leaned over the quivering figure and turned his head so he could better see this one's face—especially his eyes.

The pustules were there. Faros cursed. Straightening, he shouted, "I need someone! Now!"

Perhaps it was the confusion of the echoing corridors or the simple fact that there were so many cries and coughs, but no one came. Finally growing impatient, Faros bent down. Straining with effort, he lifted the limp form enough to pull it down the corridor. The minotaur's feet dragged, slowing him.

By the time he made it to the chamber where the latest victims were being cared for, his fur was soaked with perspiration and his breathing had grown a bit ragged.

At last, someone noticed him. A sandy-haired human and a female minotaur with one eye covered by a cloth bound around her head raced up to take Faros's burden. As they did, he looked around in disgust. The number of victims grew by the hour.

"How many new ones?"

"Thirteen more," answered the pug-nosed human, who looked little healthier than the ones he supervised.

The minotaur shook her head. "Fourteen, Hanos. They brought in Guan when you stepped out for more water."

Hanos grew agitated at mention of Guan, though Faros didn't know why and could not concern himself with every individual who came down with the plague.

"Grom is dead," he said dully. "Grom was the first, wasn't he?"

"Grom was one of the first," the female said, "but there was also the human, Izak, and Sakron and Dor."

Faros did not know Sakron, but the names Izak and Dor were familiar to him. He tried to recall where he had seen them last—and realized that they had been part of the crew Grom had gathered to build the secret pyre.

The plague must have come with the attackers. They couldn't have known they were infected. The rapidity with which the plague spread made that very unlikely.

"Order those outside to stay outside as long as they feel healthy," he commanded. "If anyone comes down with the symptons, they're to be moved to the lower level of the temple. Maybe we can contain the situation." Faros doubted that, but he couldn't think of anything else to say. His head pounded. "That goes for you, too, if you are still healthy. Everyone out of the temple!"

Hanos and the female looked aghast. The latter blurted, "Who'll watch over the sick?"

"Can you really do anything for them?" he shot back.

Wearing defeated expressions, they hung their heads.

"Go tell the others!" Faros commanded again. "Now!"

As they reluctantly did so, he abandoned the sick room and started back to his chamber to get his sword and head outside himself. The corridor grew stifling as he walked. For some reason the halls also seemed to stretch on forever. Faros blinked constantly from the sweat that dripped into his eyes from his brow.

He spotted his quarters. Before he grabbed the sword, Faros would first drink some water from the leather sack near his bedding. That would finally cool him . . .

A voice suddenly whispered in his head. *Faster . . . swifter! So close! So far!*

The rebel leader shook his head, wondering if he had perhaps heard someone talking down a side corridor. He took another step, then paused at the entrance of his quarters, one hand against the doorway.

Do not stop, do not halt! The black kiss is upon you . . .

The words made no sense, whatever their source. Faros shook his head again, determined not to listen. All he desired was water, the sword, and maybe a few minutes rest. A short nap before he abandoned the temple. There could not be any danger in that—

His hand slipped at the very same moment that his legs buckled. Faros felt himself strike the floor with a jarring thud. The pain momentarily stirred him from his malaise and he realized with mounting horror the truth of his situation.

He too was a victim of the plague.

CHAPTER VII

F'HAN

Maritia eyed the unwelcoming landscape, so different from the fertile lands of Ambeon a few hours' ride south. The crags jutted up randomly like savage claws. The temperature was much hotter than when they had left the colony's capital. The musky scent of the minotaurs mingled with the sweat of the horses. What breeze there was served only to blow dust in their faces. The only life she had spotted for miles was a few scraggly shrubs and a brown viper scurrying off before it could be trampled by the huge warhorses. There was supposed to be a river around here somewhere, but they were surrounded by baked landscape.

"We should not be here," suggested an elder officer at her right.

"Be at ease," Maritia commanded. "We're in the land of our allies, after all."

One of the others snorted. Maritia gave him a reproving look. Despite her comment, she was well aware of the dangers. Golgren might have both ogre realms firmly under his governance, but there were always raiders or outlaws to be concerned about.

The sun had begun to descend. By Maritia's calculation, they did not have much longer to wait. Bastion had always been obsessively punctual and she had no doubt that he still was.

Shadows from the western crags lengthened. A bird's harsh cry echoed among the rocks. The party was flanked by the high formations. This area made an excellent spot for a trap, which bothered Maritia.

Maritia ordered everyone to dismount. She intended to meet Bastion honoring the minotaur traditions of truce, regardless of his possible affiliation with the rebels. Barely had her feet touched the baked earth when suddenly the slow, steady echo of hooves arose from ahead. Her escort immediately drew their weapons.

"Lower those!" Maritia snapped, despite her own gut impulse to reach for her sword. "We abide by the laws of truce!"

The clatter ceased.

A dark-furred figure, his axe slung behind him, materialized from the shadowed path ahead. Behind him walked four others. Each of the newcomers led a horse.

One of the soldiers couldn't help blurting, "Lord Bastion!"

Maritia had warned the four with her, four devoutly loyal to her, that her brother would be meeting them, but even she eyed the long-lost minotaur with some astonishment. To see Bastion living, breathing . . . and to have his betrayal verified in the flesh . . .

The black minotaur handed the reins of his mount to another rebel. The act was a signal, for all four of Bastion's companions stopped, leaving Hotak's son vulnerable as he approached his sibling. Maritia left her own horse and escort behind. She made certain to keep her hand away from her sheathed sword, no matter how much she was tempted to pull the weapon free. Bastion and she met midway, far enough from each party so that the two could speak without being overheard.

"Military commander of Ambeon," her brother announced respectfully. "An appointment richly deserved."

"As was heir to the throne," she countered coolly.

"I never desired that. That was Father's choice."

"I thought it a good idea at the time, Bastion."

His brow wrinkled. " 'At the time,' Mari?"

"What're you doing consorting with the rebels?" she asked bluntly. "If you survived your reported death, which is apparent, why didn't you return directly to the empire? How could you betray everything Father taught you to believe in, damn you?"

He started to say something then seemed to reconsider. After a moment, Bastion finally answered, "Because I had no choice. Because the path we chose for our people is tainted, and it grows more poisoned, leading to chaos and doom."

"Talk straight!" Maritia snapped.

"You want bluntness? Then consider this. I believe Ardnor is the one who tried to have me killed." He briefly recounted what happened: the assassin aboard the *Stormbringer*, how he had fought the attacker and tumbled into the sea, how he had been rescued by the rebels, and how the body of a Protector with the wounds Bastion had inflicted had been discovered by those same rebels.

Maritia listened to all open-mouthed.

"You—you can't be serious!" she uttered when he finished. "For all his faults, Ardnor would never stoop to that!"

Expression somber, Bastion nodded in disagreement, then slowly added, "There is more. Mari . . . I suspect that Father's death was no accident, either."

"What do you mean about Father? Of course, it was an accident! What else—?"

His countenance grew darker. "Mari . . . I think that Mother used her magic to lead Father to his death and bring Ardnor to power."

It was too much to bear, such heresy coming from her once beloved brother. "You're insane!" she said. "The sea must've poured through your ears and soaked your brain! I've my disagreements with Mother and Ardnor, but—but—"

she shook her head. "Maybe Ardnor is capable—maybe—but never Mother! She and Father were devoted to one another! They worked together all their lives to deliver our race from Chot's corruption! I don't believe it! They are rebel lies that you have foolishly accepted."

"No, Mari, I—"

The female minotaur thrust a demanding finger at his muzzle. "You've proof?"

"Proof is a difficult matter—but I know what I believe."

"How could you even know anything about what happened to Father? You were already gone, probably already turned traitor!"

Her outburst stirred the other rebels to movement. One drew his sword and advanced a few steps. The rest tugged at axes. Their response in turn caused the legionaries to wake up. Weapons raised, they moved toward the rebels.

Bastion whirled on his companions. "Get back! We will not dishonor the truce, no matter what!"

Maritia glared at her own soldiers. "You heard my brother! I'll not permit dishonor either!"

Maritia turned her baleful gaze on Bastion, who eyed her back with his usual calm. For the first time in her life, she found his placidity maddening.

"You called me here for a reason, Bastion! Spit it out and we'll take it from there. Are you ready to return to the empire now? Is that it? As long as your crimes are not heinous, perhaps—"

"No, Mari. I'm not going to return. Not so long as Ardnor and Mother control the throne."

Her blood raced. "Then what?"

"I have an offer to pass on that may put a peaceful end to this civil war—"

"Civil war? Insurrection!"

He snorted slightly. "Call it what you may. Faros has agreed to this plan, my suggestion. I propose that we—"

"Faros." The name she had read in reports, but very little was known about him for certain. The suspected leader of the rebellion, an escaped slave from the ogre camps. He had managed to defeat Golgren in personal combat, Maritia knew, not a trifling deed. She had never disgraced Golgren by asking him about it.

"So . . . " she said, her thoughts spinning. "You know this Faros?"

"You've met him yourself. Even before Vyrox. Faros, Mari. The son of Gradic, Chot's youngest brother."

She tried to match the name with a face and wasn't sure. "A wastrel? Perhaps I remember, but that one was everything that was wrong with the empire, a gambler and a drinker! A pathetic warrior, too! You can't be serious! That Faros?"

His expression changed, with an animation that Maritia had never seen before. Bastion quickly smothered his emotions, but his sister recognized the anger he had flashed in defense of the rebel leader.

" 'That Faros,' as you put it, survived the whippings and poison air of Vyrox, the slave rebellion to which you yourself were witness, then the indignities and horrors of minotaur servitude to the ogres. I need not remind you of the stories told of our ancestors' struggles as ogre chattel."

"This Faros is the blood of Chot! So what of his suffering? He should've been executed that night! Under what rock did he hide?"

"The Faros you knew is no more. This Faros realizes the truth of things, is growing as a leader. He has drawn to him not only slaves of many races—"

"The filth of Ansalon!"

"But legionaries as well."

"Traitors! Nothing more!" The nephew of Chot was the mysterious leader of the rebellion! Maritia would have found it laughable if not for the fact that her brother took it so seriously. "What is this grand offer?"

"There is an island off of Kern . . ." With his usual succinctness, Bastion explained the proposal. The end of fighting. The rebels living in an independent colony. The empire could expand onto mainland Ansalon without any distraction.

She could immediately see the advantages. The conflict here and out at sea badly drained the military. The ogres controlled part of Neraka, and even Ambeon extended beyond the recognized borders of old Silvanesti, but at the moment the empire was blocked from further expansion. To do so was to spread the legions and supply routes too thin. A capable enemy like the Solamnics exploited any weaknesses.

Yet it made no sense to authorize an island stronghold of malcontents. The nephew of Chot would, by his very existence, draw recruits from everywhere. Once it became known that Bastion was alive, loyal to Faros, the rebellion would blossom and not be contained.

"Out of the question," she said abruptly.

The black-furred minotaur did not intend to give up so easily. "Mari, if you would just—"

"I said out of the question!" Maritia flushed. She looked at Bastion as if having never seen him before. "How could you imagine I would even consider such a thing, much less speak on your behalf to Golgren or Ardnor? This betrayal of our father!"

"Father taught us that honor was first and foremost, Mari! Faros offers an honorable solution! Can you say that our brother and mother are acting honorably? I've seen the work of the Protectors firsthand! I know the tales of disappearances of any who speak out against the temple! Does such activity make you comfortable? Is this the imperium of which Father dreamed?"

"He certainly never dreamed that you would join a rebellion and accuse Mother of such horrors!" Before Maritia realized what she was doing, her sword was out and within an inch of her brother's throat.

Again the other rebels reacted, which in turn spurred the minotaur soldiers toward Maritia. Bastion didn't budge, though he waved one hand slightly to order the others to stay away.

"I will not dishonor the truce," he repeated, tersely.

"Nor will I," Maritia managed to say. Stepping back, she lowered her sword. "I've heard your words, Bastion, and in the memory of our father, I reject them! If not for the truce, I'd throw you in chains or even challenge you here and now to a duel!"

"Mari—"

"Go back to your rebel friends! My true brother drowned at sea! He would never have betrayed all his father had believed in, never followed one of Chot's lineage! Go! You'll all be dead soon enough!" Maritia forced the blade back into its sheath. "Go, before I fall as far as you and forget my own honor . . ."

He stood there for several seconds, studying her as if seeking something in her eyes. Whatever he was looking for, Bastion evidently did not find it, for he finally shook his head and turned away. Maritia watched him leave, a part of her ready to run him through, another simply wanting to run away from this.

As he rejoined his companions, the slim figure looked back at her. "Farewell, Mari," he said gently. "May Sargas watch over you."

She snorted at his use of the old god's name. Maritia had grown up worshiping only her father and the force of arms. Then, as he turned to go, suddenly she was gripped by doubt. She stepped toward her brother and shouted, "Wait!"

Bastion slowly turned. Rejoining her, he quietly asked, "What?"

"Why is Faros so eager to propose this pact?"

"I told you, it was my idea. He would fight forever, but for my sake, for the sake of his followers, and yes, the empire, he agreed to propose it," the black minotaur answered cautiously.

She nodded, thinking. No one but the two of them could hear what she said next. Nor could anyone but Bastion see when Maritia removed from one finger a signet ring with the warhorse crest as centerpiece.

"Father gave each of us one of these, all unique."

"Mine was lost at sea, unfortunately."

"You know I wouldn't part with this unless I was serious. Take it as a sign of my agreement, at least to meet with your Faros and discuss this plan of yours. Tell no one but him."

"Of course." A light seemed to come back into Bastion's eyes. "Mari, this is the best thing . . ."

She kept her emotions guarded. "You'd better leave now."

Nodding, Bastion slipped the ring into a belt pouch then started back to his comrades. Maritia returned to the soldiers, turning around to observe her brother as he mounted up and disappeared up the dark path.

"We're just letting them go?" an officer asked crossly, though he was acutely aware that Bastion was Maritia's brother.

"The traditions of truce!" Hotak's daughter snapped vehemently. Her mind was racing. She wasn't sure why she had just agreed to meet with Faros, wasn't sure whether she intended a treaty or not. "You have trouble with the concept of honor too?"

He bowed his horns. "Nay, my lady."

Immediately, she turned to her subordinates. "All right! Mount up! I want to be back in the capital before Pryas arrives! I don't trust that Protector. . . ."

Maritia leapt atop her horse and urged it around. She paid little heed to the legionaries as they scrambled to follow. All that mattered was returning to the colony as quickly as possible. Maritia had much to do and she would have to do it all quietly. The treverian, Novax, proved that Bastion still had admirers and friends among the legionaries. She did not want to alert her brother.

For all her talk of honor, Maritia knew now what she had to do. She planned a betrayal of her own brother. She had lied to him. She could not let this opportunity pass. She would agree to a meeting with Faros, then, unlike this time, she would arrange an ambush. She wanted the rebel leader taken

alive, but one way or another, Faros Es-Kalin would be elimi-
nated as a threat to the empire.

As for Bastion . . . he had made his foolish choice. Their
father had taught them to respect honor, but her brother had
forgotten that Hotak also believed first and foremost in victory. He had massacred Chot and his family during the Night
of Blood. She would finish the nephew during this false peace
parley. All for the good of the empire.

If, during the ambush, Bastion attempted to stop her . . .
she swore to herself she would do what she must, regardless
of how much it would pain her.

The hefty ogre Nagroch waited impatiently, watching
Maritia and Bastion finally separate. His party had been hidden in the high rocks overlooking the meeting for seeming
hours. His limbs were aching from not moving, his ears sore
from straining to hear.

"Bya syng . . . go now," muttered his brother, after the
rebels had gone, followed by the minotaurs.

Belgroch had not learned patience. He had not sat beside
Golgren long enough to understand. The older ogre knew
that command of this important task meant failure rested on
his head alone—a head that, in the case of failure, would be
forcibly detached from his neck.

Ten more warriors handpicked by Nagroch waited on
horseback some distance behind the pair. They had even less
patience, but they feared their leader and so satisfied themselves by rocking back and forth in the saddle. It was a primi-
tive form of relaxation, used by the shamans as they entered
their trances. Warriors made use of it when faced with inter-
minable waiting.

"Nya bya syng," Nagroch growled back. They would wait
for the sign that the Grand Lord had promised would come.
What form it would take he did not know, but his master

had promised that it would come and that it would be a clear sign.

Nagroch . . .

He jolted up. Had he just heard Golgren's voice in his head? Then the ogre suddenly noticed that someone stood before him. An Uruv Suurt! He pulled back and reached for his weapon, then gaped when he realized that the minotaur stood beyond his vantage point—and floated several hundred feet above the ground below.

"Zola un, i'Nagrochi?" asked Belgroch, gazing at his brother curiously.

Nagroch realized only he could see the ghostly figure hovering before him, a ghostly figure whose face he recognized from a meeting past. The Uruv Suurt called Kolot, son of Hotak.

Nagroch, came Golgren's voice again. Although the voice resounded in the warrior's head, somehow he knew the specter was the source. Nagroch's blood-shot eyes widened. Great was the power of the Grand Lord, who used the dead to speak his messages!

The ghost pointed toward the south, where the legionaries rode toward the minotaur lands. *The Lady Maritia goes untouched.*

He had suspected as much. Golgren had an unusual fondness for this particular Uruv Suurt.

Kolot, the gaping hole in his throat almost a second mouth, repulsive and frightening even to Nagroch, pointed then in the direction of the brother, Bastion. For just a brief moment, Nagroch imagined he saw a faint look of remorse struggle to the shade's countenance.

F'han, came Golgren's voice.

That said, the unearthly messenger faded away immediately. Nagroch needed no more. His froglike face relaxed, spreading into a grin again. He looked at his brother, who wore an expression of utter bewilderment.

"F'han!" Nagroch rumbled, indicating Bastion's group.

The two ogres eagerly rushed to their mounts.

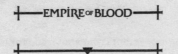

The journey through the badlands was a long one, made even longer for Bastion by second thoughts about having summoned Maritia to a meeting. He had expected little better, but the reality had been harsher than even he had calculated.

Scarcely noticing the steep, upward climb required of their horses to eventually reach the other side of the rocky hill and then to the rebels' stronghold, Bastion replayed everything in his mind. He could see no way by which the outcome would have differed. Maritia had always been the one most like their father, stubborn to a fault. There could be no reason in her eyes for joining those trying to bring an end to Hotak's dream, especially if the leader was kin to Chot. Perhaps if she had met Faros, things would be different, but she never would now. Bastion guessed his sister was trying to set up a betrayal, and he vowed to himself that there would be no second attempt at a treaty.

"Finally at the top," one of the others grunted.

In the distance, the silence of the region was broken by the sound of rushing water. At least there was one river in this godforsaken place. When they descended to the other side, they would refill their water sacks then finish their journey. A flat ridge ran off to their right, ending in a cliff overlooking the river. To their left and front, rock formations jutted up several yards high like the tusks of ogres.

"We should've taken 'em," another minotaur grunted. "We could've gotten the soldiers and captured her, Lord Bastion. Your sister would've made a good hostage in future, um, negotiations."

He stirred. "Out of the question. Whatever the outcome of the meeting, it was important to uphold the traditions of truce, otherwise we're no better than the brigands we're made out to be—"

A flicker of movement from above caught his eye. Bastion gazed in that direction but saw nothing. Nevertheless, he stretched in the saddle, his hand straying toward his axe.

"Never mind," the black-furred figure said at the same time. "We're in no worse position than Makel at the gates."

"Makel?" blurted one of his companions, fingers grazing the hilt of his sword. Every minotaur warrior knew the moment in history Bastion had mentioned. Makel Ogrebane had been ambushed by the enemy near the gates of an abandoned ogre settlement. Many of his followers had perished, but he had pushed the others to victory, leading the way and perishing himself.

Among legionaries, though, the reference had another meaning. "Makel at the gates" was code. Like the legendary hero, the one who uttered it warned his comrades they were about to be ambushed. A moment later, the ogres led by the two brutish brothers, Nagroch and Belgroch, fell upon them. Four ogre riders on huge steeds charged from the front. Four more came from behind.

"Forward!" Bastion shouted, making a decision as to the best possible escape.

Weapons out, the five met the first of the enemy. If they could carve a hole in the ogres' ranks, then they could escape. Minotaurs were always ready to die in battle, but they were outnumbered, and they had a duty to report to Faros. As soon as they collided with the ogres on horses, more dropped down from the rocks above. All were fully armored warriors of Blöde.

"*J'ara iy f'han i Uruv Suurt!*" thundered a particularly ugly one whom Bastion concluded must be the leader. He tried to force his way over to him, but another ogre jumped forward and blocked his way.

Out of the corner of his eye, he saw one of his companions drop as two ogres pummeled him with their clubs. Jaw broken, head askew, the minotaur fell limply from his mount.

Trapped in a compact area, he suddenly understood how stupid he had been; he and his small group were easy prey for the ambushers. He ran his blade through the ogre leering in front of him, but a second member of the rebel party slumped forward in the saddle then was dragged down by an ogre on foot.

"Stay together! Wedge!" With the two remaining rebels behind him, Bastion attempted to shove his way forward. An ogre on foot slashed at him with a chipped axe and was rewarded with the edge of the black minotaur's blade through his cheekbone.

Then Bastion's steed balked. He suddenly found himself tumbling forward. A spear had found the animal's neck. Throwing himself to the side, Bastion avoided grasping hands. He allowed himself to roll, breaking free of the tangle of bodies.

Unfortunately, Bastion rose to discover he was at the cliff's edge. One quick glance was enough to tell him that leaping into the river would prove his death as quickly as an ogre blade.

Heavy breathing behind him warned the minotaur of an lunging attacker. Bastion let the ogre's momentum work for him. Grabbing his adversary by the arm, he whirled the latter off the cliff. The river quickly drowned out the plummeting ogre's scream.

As Bastion turned back, the last of his companions died, the rebel's head detached by an axe. A little over half of the ogres remained, at least a dozen of the grotesque warriors, and they slowly began to collect around him.

One rushed to grapple with him. It was the ogre Bastion had initially mistaken for leader of the attackers. This ogre's breath stank so much that the minotaur almost vomited. He saw that his foe was too young, too careless, to be the leader.

He pushed the ogre back then thrust. The breastplate deflected his strike. Grinning wide, the ogre chopped at him. The wide arc of his swing forced Bastion to the precipice. The rebel tried to fend off the axe, only to have his sword batted free.

"F'han, Uruv Suurt!" his opponent barked triumphantly. Bastion knew the word well enough. *F'han.* Death.

Bastion understood how to wield an axe as well as any sword. He could throw a mace or fire a bow as well as any soldier. For a time, as a young officer, the son of Hotak had even served as a lancer. Now, though, he had none of those weapons at, so he used the one that legend said the god Sargonnas had granted his chosen so that they would never go unarmed.

With a war cry, Bastion bent and charged the ogre. The cry startled the ogre. He left himself open. One of Bastion's horns dented his breastplate, but did not pierce, but the other drove cleanly through the metal then sank deep into his foe's chest at the lung.

Blood splattered Bastion's eyes, burning them. He heard a gurgling noise from the ogre. The two spun about, the ogre dancing on the edge.

Bastion fought to pull free, but as his horn reluctantly sucked free of the dying ogre, a horrific pain shot through the minotaur's back. Every nerve, every muscle shook uncontrollably. He felt a gaping wound, moistness spreading down to his waist.

An experienced fighter, Bastion's last conscious thought was that he had probably been struck a terrible blow in the back by an axe. Vertigo overtook him. He felt desperation and regret. He had lost his place in the empire, lost his family, and had failed Faros. Now he had lost his life.

"I will not dishonor you . . ." Bastion was not certain who he meant—his father, Faros, himself—but with his last gasp he pushed forward, grabbing at the ogre he had gored, who had fallen and was trying to rise, and pushing both of them over the cliff.

He did not even feel the harsh, raging current as they hit the water.

Chapter VIII

Blood on the Jewel

The vast, oak dining table shuddered under the stress of two heavy minotaur bodies crashing against it. Roars of encouragement ensued from those seated around the table as the duo grappled. At the head of the table, the emperor sat shouting with the best of them. A jerk of his hand spilled wine and splattered his breastplate, but he paid the mess no mind. It was only the latest in a spreading series of stains from this evening's entertainment.

The high, intricate tapestries depicting some of the most renowned emperors also bore stains and several displayed cuts from wildly-brandished weapons. The marble walls on which the tapestries hung shared in the misfortune, as did the mosaic floor with its depiction of Ambeoutin leading his people to freedom. The image of the first ruler of the minotaurs was buried beneath strewn food. His followers peeked out from carelessly discarded garments.

Even the tiered, five-sided iron chandeliers had not escaped the drunken excess, and it was a wonder that a fire did not spread, what with so many candles askew. The chandeliers swung back and forth as revelers too drunk to stand leaned heavily on the chains in the walls that lowered and raised them.

Throughout it all, the guards at the door and against the wall behind the emperor maintained their erect postures. Despite bits of food and wine that disgraced their uniforms, the warriors showed no sign of reaction. Ardnor had punished for far less.

More than a score of participants—all members of the faithful—were celebrating. There was no reason for their celebration, but then, there didn't have to be. Such parties happened nearly every night and often during the day. Ardnor was emperor, after all, the undisputed lord of the realm. What he commanded was done immediately. He enjoyed commanding parties.

A young acolyte from the temple who looked very unlike an earnest priestess stumbled into Ardnor's lap. He clutched her tightly, forgetting the ongoing wrestling match until the two combatants spilled into the remains of the roasted goat, scattering plates laced with gold and silver. Crushed apples and mashed bits of wheat and rye bread covered the fighters now. Both laughed wildly as they fought, the more wiry minotaur with one slightly-bent horn finally gaining the advantage. They kicked over one of the high-backed chairs with the symbol of the warhorse carved in it as they twisted around in each other's clutches.

Onlookers bet on the outcome, tossing coins into the helms of the adversaries, which had been set upside down on one end of the table. The coins in the loser's helmet would be split among the smart bettors, with a share going to the winner himself.

One drunken wagerer, who leaned too close in order to encourage his chosen fighter, suffered for his foolishness as a stray fist caught him in the lower muzzle. The streak of blood running down his muzzle was more because the staggering figure accidentally bit his tongue than because of the force of the blow.

Still squeezing tight his giggling acolyte, Ardnor bellowed his approval. He glanced up—and his expression abruptly turned stormy. Without warning, he flung his companion to the side and leapt to his feet. Caught up in the game, the others did not notice until Ardnor slammed a fist on the rounded table, creating a foot-long crack.

"Get out! All of you! Go! Now!"

They froze, stunned and uncertain they had heard right, yet one look at the crimson eyes of the emperor and they quickly gathered their belongings and fled through the doors. The guards separated the two inebriated wrestlers and guided them out.

Even this did not satisfy Ardnor. He seized one of the guards stationed behind him, shoving the hapless soldier forward. "I said all of you! Everyone! Shut the door behind you!"

When at last he was alone, Ardnor turned to glare at the soiled and frayed tapestry with fresh spatters of blood. With an animalistic growl, Ardnor stared up at the image of his father. Hotak stood posed with his helm in one arm and one foot resting on the body of a fallen Nerakian. Gold and silver scrollwork surrounded the portrait. The artist had purposely designed it so Hotak's one good eye was dominant and appeared to meet the gaze of his son.

One of the blood drops trickled down from that eye, and in his imagination, Ardnor felt the condemnation of his father.

"I was your heir!" he snarled at the tapestry. "Groomed to take your place! I've only done what should've been done!"

The image, of course, said nothing in reply, but that only enraged the brutish Ardnor. Roaring, he swept his thick arm across the table, sending goblets, plates, food remnants, and more crashing to the floor.

He was emperor of all minotaurs. In his name, legions marched to war. Gladiators fought to the death in the Great Circus. His Protectors kept martial law throughout the realm. . . .

All this he had desired for as long as he could remember. From boyhood, Ardnor had been groomed to take his father's place and now, after many obstacles, Hotak's eldest had achieved that goal, yet the true power, he knew, resided not in the palace but rather emanated from the temple. It was from there that the dictates came, often bearing his name. He might be the emperor in name, but it was his mother who ruled the minotaur realm.

The figure in the tapestry appeared to be scrutinizing him. Ardnor finally seized the bottom of the tapestry with one huge hand, intending to rip the entire thing from the wall. Instead, after hesitating, with immense frustration he released the tapestry, grabbed his helmet, and stormed from the dining hall.

The guards stiffened to attention as he stalked through the corridor looking for something upon which to vent his foul mood. An unlucky legion courier was spotted coming from the opposite direction.

"You there! What're you doing here? You've some news of import?"

The courier quickly dipped his horns as he fell down on one knee. "Your majesty! I bring a private missive directed to you!"

Ardnor's ears twitched. "Well, give it over then, fool!"

Fumbling with his bound, leather pouch, the minotaur courier handed him a tiny, sealed note that had come by messenger bird. The emperor turned the note over, looking for a certain mark and finding the broken axe icon. It was discreetly placed.

"Dismissed!" he commanded the officer. Turning from the guards, Ardnor broke the seal.

Hail, First Master of the Protectors, Venerated Offspring of the High Priestess, Emperor of Emperors—

The list of titles went on for several lines. Although Ardnor snorted in derision, he found the faithful one's words quite flattering.

I, Genjin Es-Jamak, a mere acolyte not worthy to stand in your shadow, send this report at the utmost haste for your eyes alone. I felt it imperative to alert you to—

Ardnor's eyes widened. He read over the message three times, his ears flattening and the crimson in his eyes flaming.

When he had digested the contents sufficiently, the emperor crushed the note, almost pulverizing it in his powerful fist. Though his nostrils flared, he otherwise kept his emotions hidden from the sentries.

Whirling on one of the guards, he commanded, "Summon that courier back! Tell him to wait outside my quarters! He shall have a message in reply."

The soldier hurried off to retrieve the officer. Ardnor started toward his private chambers. As he stalked along, he bared his teeth in a grim, predatory smile. His mother had wanted him to be great emperor, and so he would be one. He was about to make a difficult but necessary decision, an imperial decision.

One even his father—the great Hotak—would have shrunk from making.

Faros drifted into and out of consciousness. How long he lay sprawled on the floor of the ancient chamber, he could not say. Hours, certainly. Days . . . at least one, possibly two or three. His body was wracked with pain, he felt horribly parched. He was both starved and nauseated, and his body felt as if it was burning up.

He dreamed . . . or rather, he had nightmares. The nightmares were more grotesque than ever. He was visited by the macabre faces of Sahd, of Paug, and the others, often by the Grand Lord Golgren. There were other vague, disquieting images, visions of a dank, foreboding realm over which shambling figures with disease-eaten bodies forever wandered in torment. At times, that realm would mingle with his memories of Nethosak, the imperial capital becoming a place of cadaverous ghouls and crumbling buildings.

Only one thing saved Faros from the madness brought on by the plague, a constantly-murmuring voice, that sought to draw him back to reality.

So close . . . so close . . . just a few feet more . . . it can be done, yes, it can be done . . .

The voice did not belong to any he recognized, not one of his followers. No help would come from them. The rebels had followed his orders and left the areas filled with the ill and dying.

Vaguely, Faros registered that he lay in the center of his quarters and that struck a chord. He had collapsed near the entrance. Somehow Faros had managed to drag himself inside, but to what purpose he could not remember. Ahead lay his sword. With a groan, Faros reached for it, but the weapon seemed an eternity away. Summoning what strength he could, the ravaged minotaur dragged himself a few inches closer.

The effort made him black out. The nightmares returned, as did the murmuring voice. At one point, Faros stirred again—and discovered the sword just barely out of reach. He could not recall pulling himself closer, but nothing surprised him.

The largest of the jewels in the sword's hilt—the great green stone in its center—provided the only illumination in the chamber. Faros did not question this odd fact, nor was he encouraged by it. Clearly the sword possessed magic.

His body wanted to sleep, but Faros dragged himself forward on his elbows. His fingertips grazed the handle of his sword, which unexpectedly shifted so as to fit firmly in his palm. Faros gasped. He felt the effects of the plague tremble and recede slightly. His body still burned, but at least he could think more clearly.

The ring . . .

The voice said nothing more. Faros peered through bloodshot eyes for the other artifact he had inherited from Sargonnas. A dry croak of a curse escaped his blistered mouth as he recalled where it was.

The ring . . . again he heard the voice's urging.

From somewhere deep inside, he summoned the ability to rise to his feet. His grip on the sword as tight as possible, he weaved recklessly across the chamber. At one point, he crashed into a wall and nearly fell, but somehow the sword caught on the stone floor enough to help him regain his precarious balance.

Finding the crack in which the ring had fallen, Faros dropped to his knees. He felt a resurgence of illness, so much so that he had to plant his snout against the opposing wall lest he slip to the floor. Faros tightened his grip on Sargonnas's sword, feeling a brief resurgence of strength. For some reason, it was paramount that he locate the ring.

Eyes blurred, he ran his fingers through the gap, at first grabbing nothing but grit. Then he felt metal, a round loop that surely had to be the lost ring. Faros tried to raise the object with his index finger, but it slipped out of his grasp. Cursing out loud, he tried his smallest finger. He managed to hook part of the loop and gingerly raised the ring into sight.

The ring dangled, almost ready to slip off. Faros's hand shook, as he pulled away from the crevice, the ring clattering to the floor with a spark, landing close by his knee. He snatched it up with his free hand, but as the minotaur prepared to put the ring on, the voice sounded again.

Blood there must be, for it and me . . .

Despite his struggles, Faros frowned. Blood?

A drop to each, centered on the eye . . . or the plague take you . . .

Whoever was murmuring, even if it was Sargonnas, he felt sick and weary, tired of riddles. "A-all right, damn you . . ." He readied the sword, eyeing his shaking hand, then brought the weapon's sharp edge to his palm. It took the barest touch of the blade to cut open the skin. Blood spilled out—and at the same time Faros could have sworn he heard a wail coming from the sword.

Once again, he felt the renewal of the plague. Blinking away tears, Faros turned his palm, allowing the first drop of blood to fall. It landed square on the black gem . . . sinking in without a trace. Faros almost reached for his sword then recalled the rest of the command. He turned the sword to view the emerald in the hilt.

He saw an eye staring back, but then he blinked, and Faros saw nothing. Taking a deep breath, he twisted his palm around again. The droplet touched the emerald, and as the first had, this too vanished into the jewel. The sword suddenly flared a brilliant green. The light completely filled the chamber.

The ring . . .

Shaking more than ever, Faros let go of the sword just long enough to put the ring back on his finger. The moment he was done, a jolt went through him. Faros screamed and would have dropped the weapon, but his fingers kept their tense grip. His entire body felt as if a wave of fire was coursing through him.

Then the agony of the plague abruptly diminished. The pressure in the minotaur's head eased, and suddenly he could breathe properly again. His strength began to return. All of a sudden the pain ceased. Now it was possible to stand, even move.

Your blood is bound, your blood is cleansed . . .

The sword barely glowed, but the ring had a warmth to it. Faros looked around and found his water sack and some dried food. He ate and drank greedily, water spilling across his fur.

Afterward, Faros stumbled into the halls beyond. He heard no sound other than his own footsteps. The temple was dark save for the faint radiance of Sargonnas's blade. Holding the weapon ahead of him, the rebel leader wended his way. Only the faint wind met his ears.

As he finally neared a window—and saw by the darkness outside that it was surely night—he heard a horrific sound. He froze, listening and trying to decipher the noise, a great cry. Beyond the temple, grotesquely illuminated by torches and fires dotting the landscape, Faros saw his followers. They had not escaped the insidious plague. The cry he heard—and heard again and again—was the combined voices of the hundreds suffering from it. Everywhere he looked, he saw the sick and dying. Few stood or moved about. The stricken lay all around, spread out over the ground, their bodies mingling with the enemy dead.

Nephera had at last succeeded. Where force of arms had failed, foul magic was destroying the rebellion. Peering up, he saw the stars glittering. The peace of the heavens contrasted sharply with the scene below. The smell of decay and disease overwhelmed even his jaded senses.

One set of stars caught his eye. It took a moment for Faros to identify the constellation representing his would-be patron. A sense of responsibility he had never experienced before touched his heart. With a shudder, Faros recalled his father.

"All right!" the rebel suddenly roared at the stars. "All right, damn you, Lord of Vengeance! I need you! Not your toys, but you! You want to hear me plead? Well, I do! Help us! Help us now or you won't have a single worshiper left! You hear me? Help—"

A fierce rumble of thunder shook the temple. The minotaur grabbed hold. He heard startled voices cry out. Silence followed the thunder . . . and after the silence came the caw of a single bird.

A moment later, a second avian responded to it. Then another, and within the blink of an eye, it seemed that every bird in the world was answering, though as yet none could be seen. The raucous sounds drowned out all else. Suddenly, there came the flapping of wings. Hundreds, thousands of wings. The racket grew so loud that Faros's head pounded.

A fat, ugly crow darted in through the window. It flew past Faros, entering the chamber where the dead lay. The crow landed on one of the corpses and pecked out a bit of flesh, then, swallowing that, eagerly took a second morsel.

Another crow flew past Faros's shoulder. It alighted on another corpse and proceeded to imitate its counterpart. Without warning, birds by the scores suddenly filled the temple. They ranged from the tiny to the huge, but each was a carrion eater. They fell upon the corpses with eager abandon. Some of the plague-ridden bodies were so blanketed by feathered forms they could no longer be seen.

Aware that this was something he himself had somehow unleashed, the rebel leader raced through the temple and to the outside, hoping to reach his surviving followers and aid them. More and more avians poured into the stone structure as he ran, darting around the various corridors. Faros stumbled across corpses reduced to little more than heaps of bones, but in many cases the birds devoured everything—flesh, sinew, even bone.

With the cries of the voracious feeders resounding in his ears, Faros finally staggered outside. There he was struck dumb by the sheer magnitude of what was happening. Visible under stars that now shone nearly as bright as the sun, the carnage before him was worse than any battle he had ever experienced. Both the heavens and the ground were black with carrion eaters. Out here were not only the dark crows and their cousins, but the giant vultures, buzzards, raptors, and condors. They had all come and were attacking the field of dead. They tore off huge ribbons of flesh and made a horrific sound as they feasted.

Everywhere, survivors huddled together, watching the grisly business. All they could do was stand and stare with wide eyes. After what felt like forever but what was in actuality mere minutes, the work was all done. Of the sea of dead, there was little left except for empty armor, lost weapons, and some overlooked straps of leather.

The source of the plague had been entirely eradicated. Or at least, the dead would spread the disease no longer. Next an incredible deluge struck. Rain poured down, drenching all, including the birds. There were no clouds, no warning. The storm began from nowhere in the clear night sky.

From the rain emerged a mist, a pale, white, yet somehow comforting mist. It covered all but seemed thickest around the temple.

Indeed, it felt to Faros as though the rain and mist had washed away some foulness deep within him. He glanced down and snorted in surprise to see a foul, greenish puddle forming at his feet then dissipating into the earth. Looking around, he saw the same insidious substance pooling around most of the others—especially those lying desperately ill. It was as if each surviving rebel was being purged of all remnants of his illness. Those caught up in the worst throes of the plague had the largest, most vile puddles, and as the puddles washed away, the sick began to stir as if healed.

No one else but Faros saw and understood all, though. Gradic's son understood that Sargonnas's gifts had rescued them. The last of the foulness sank out of sight. As it did, the rain and misting ceased. Normal darkness returned, with normal stars.

As if on cue, many of the birds took to the air, flying off to wherever they had come from. However, hundreds more remained where they were perched, watching, waiting, as if expecting something else to occur, but it was over. No one who was there could doubt that it was a miracle. Several who had lain at death's door were already sitting up, looking little the worse. No one cheered, though, for all were worn out and dazed by the sudden turn of events. As for Faros, he stood silent among them, reflecting . . .

Everything that he had tried to bury inside of himself finally exploded to the surface. Arms raised to the sky, Faros roared both his pain and his awakening to the knowledge of the path he must take. He screamed over and over, with those who had followed him so loyally watching dumbfounded, uncertain.

When he could scream no more, Faros turned in the direction of faraway Mithas. He stood there, peering into the distance, envisioning Nethosak—and the grandiose palace of the emperor and the sprawling temple of the Forerunners.

Envisioning them awash in fire and blood.

CHAPTER IX

THE HANDS OF GODS

The summons came as Ardnor rode beyond the city. Too bad, for it was a pastime he relished; the speed with which he drove his black charger allowed him to forget everything and revel in a basic pleasure. Minotaurs had long bred their mounts for swiftness as well as strength. Their massive steeds had to carry heavy weight; but in battle quick maneuvers often decided the day.

Across the wooded hills—the same wooded hills where General Rahm Es-Hestos had slain Kolot—the emperor raced. Two Protectors atop their own black steeds did their best to keep pace, but of all the horses in the capital, perhaps even the empire, Ardnor's was the fastest. He took great care in training and raising his animals, and this particular one was his pride and joy. Even his father had admired Ardnor's expertise with horses.

He sighted the lone figure just as he was he returning to the gates of Nethosak. A blunt-nosed male, with the shorn head of a Protector, but wearing the gold-trimmed, white robes of the temple. The messenger bowed his horns as the emperor approached, then reverently uttered, "She would see you, First Master . . ."

There were only a few things that Ardnor allowed to disturb his entertainment. A summons from the temple was first and foremost among them.

Quickly returning to the palace, he took special care to wash away the sweat of the ride before donning his armor. Then, flanked by his Protectors and surrounded by a contingent of the Imperial Guard, he rode to see what his mother desired.

He traveled with the pomp and circumstance of an emperor. Horns blared as he and his retinue exited the gates, led by a single rider bearing the banner of the Forerunners. In contrast to his father, Ardnor flaunted his relationship with the temple.

The citizenry dutifully gathered on the walkways on each side of the streets. They cheered, many calling out his name. They threw sheaves of horsetail grass in honor of their emperor or waved their fists in salute. Such was expected of the citizens whenever he bestowed his presence upon them.

Behind the crowds, Protectors kept a vigilant watch, making sure that the organized enthusiasm stayed orderly.

Midway to the temple, Ardnor slowed as he spotted a squadron of Protectors—their commander mounted—crossing a street ahead. The helmed warriors trotted along at a brisk pace, their maces held ready as if expecting trouble. As the emperor passed the street, he glanced and saw the unit stop before the business of a prominent miller. Ardnor realized their dire task, all of a sudden, for he himself had signed the warrant at his mother's behest. Despite the absolute authority he had given the temple to supervise food distribution, there were still those who thought they could secretly flout the rules. The miller had attempted to increase his profits despite his duty to the imperium and its expansion. The Protectors were already smashing the doors in and breaking through the windows. By tomorrow morning, every mill owned by the miscreant would be operating under imperial management.

By tomorrow night, the former owner and his workers would be serving Ardnor in one of the mining colonies.

He sighed with exasperation as the gates to the temple grounds opened. Leaving the crowds behind, Ardnor entered to a single, deep-bellowed bark emitted from a waiting line of stolid warriors. As a second salute to him, they raised their weapons as the First Master rode up to the steps. Ardnor leapt easily from his black beast and climbed the steps two at a time. Once atop, he turned and beat his fist against his breastplate, striking the area of his chest upon which the symbol of the order was branded.

Acolytes in white robes with red trim bowed low as he bulled his way into the main hall. A thin, fanatic-eyed male in the hooded robe of a mid-level priest hurried to greet him.

"The high priestess is not in her quarters any more, your majesty. She expects you to meet her in the meditation chamber."

Ardnor grunted, his expression hiding any unease he felt about joining his mother in that dread place.

The halls grew deathly quiet as he left the public area of the temple. The subtle scent of lavender drifted through the air. Gargantuan statues of shrouded, ethereal figures gazed down upon the emperor. These were the high priestess's interpretation of the Forerunners, those who supposedly had gone on to the next plane and now guided the progress of the living. Some had faces, others were obscured. No two were alike. They lined the path on both sides and although they were made of marble, Ardnor sensed their energy, powers only he and his mother could note.

Chanting broke the silence as he neared his destination. Two Protectors stood guard at the bronze doors, their tense stance owed not only to his arrival, but also to the ominous aura even Ardnor felt emanating from behind the doors. Ardnor girded himself as he neared, telling himself that the power he served would sustain him.

But as he reached the doors, the sentinels crossed axes, barring his path.

"She ordered that you not enter until word's given," the senior of the two warriors informed him anxiously.

The emperor considered ignoring the command, but thought better of it. It was his own tardiness that had put him into this position. Besides, he was in no hurry to go inside.

The chanting abruptly ceased. All three instinctively tensed.

Without warning, what felt like a monstrous wave of cold coursed through the hall. Ardnor, his senses extremely acute due to his training, saw first the doors, the guards, then the hall ripple with the cold. The chill touched not only the flesh, but the soul. The torches all but died . . . then burst to life again.

Silence hung over the area like a shroud.

The bronze doors swung open. The deep darkness prevailing within seemed to seep out. Without realizing that they did so, the two menacing Protectors edged away from the lengthening shadows.

Needing no other sign, Ardnor strode past the pair and into the high priestess's sanctum.

"So," a voice echoed within. "My prodigal son comes at last . . ."

He did not see her at first. The chamber was so dark his eyes needed time to adjust. At the same time, though, the emperor felt the presence of the others, the many unseen forms flitting back and forth, awaiting Lady Nephera's commands.

"I was . . . detained," he answered.

Something came into vague focus ahead of him. A wide stone slab was set at an angle. The scent of lavender was stronger there, as if masking an odor more baleful. Something lay upon altar, a loose form. Even as he squinted, trying to see it in detail, two shadowed forms—priestesses, he belatedly realized—took the form up and carried it into the deeper dark.

From somewhere, Lady Nephera returned, "I was not referring to you."

A trickling sound, as if someone was washing their hands in a bowl, turned his attention to his right. He waited, but nothing became visible.

Then from beyond the altar, his mother's voice added, "The fates conspire. He lives . . . he still lives . . ."

Without warning, torches in the walls erupted. Their flame was not blazing red or sun-searing gold, but rather a sickly, infectious green.

And at last Ardnor faced his mother . . . or saw her. She now sat upon a high-backed chair—almost a throne—atop the dais behind the altar. Her silver and black robes draped her as if she had no flesh, only bone.

Above her, tainted by the flames, hung the massive, silver symbols of the Forerunners. Yet, for all their size, they did not seize his attention as did the glittering icon burned into his mother's upper chest. He couldn't help but stare at the icon etched into her skin as he approached, knowing only he and she were aware of its existence. All others saw nothing unless the high priestess ordained it.

A war axe, turned upside down. The true mark of the god behind the sect, the god who had come to his mother when all others had abandoned her.

He shrugged. Morgion or Takhisis, one deity or another did not matter to Ardnor, so long as he was emperor.

His mother did not look up as Ardnor went down on one knee at the base of the dais. Her tone, when the high priestess finally spoke, made the hairs on his neck bristle. Her hands lay curled upward.

"He lives . . ." Nephera repeated, her words filled with venom. "Even after all this, he still lives."

"The slave in Kern, mother?"

"The slave in Kern, yes, my son . . ." The high priestess raised her head slowly. Ardnor swallowed. In the flickering light of the torches, she looked more than ever like a corpse torn from the grave. Her eyes burned into his, but he couldn't turn away. "The slave who is Faros Es-Kalin."

The emperor blinked. After some thought, he said, "Kalin. Chot's clan was Kalin . . . ?"

"A brilliant, astute deduction!" the robed figure spat, rising. "Yes, he is Chot's nephew! A weak, whimpering gambler is the cause of so much trouble!"

"Faros . . ." The brutish warrior rubbed his chin. "I think I remember the little snot . . . it can't be him, though. He could've never—"

"Cease overtaxing your mind, my son! It is indeed him!"

Thrusting his helmet on, Ardnor rose decisively. "Then, I'll go hunt him down like a rabbit! His hide'll become my cloak and his horns will make a good hook to hang the cloak on!"

"No!"

"Let me take him, Mother! I am emperor! The last of Kalin should rightly be mine! I'll hang his head on the gates of the palace for all to see! It'll prove to all who it is that rules here!"

Darkness enveloped the high priestess so suddenly that Ardnor stepped back in surprise. In the dark, half-seen figures collected, dire warriors with monstrous, dead faces and twisted bodies.

But Nephera waved away her horrific servants with the least of gestures. "No, my son, that task you must give to others. It is Maritia and Golgren who shall finish this rabble off for us. If I have to send all the might of Ambeon and the combined ogre realms, Faros will be crushed! His ghost will then bow at my feet!"

"Golgren and Maritia?" The huge minotaur snorted. "A one-handed, foppish ogre and my sister? What makes you think they can take care of this problem, when they have failed for so long?"

"The Grand Lord will because I wish it. Your sister . . . have you any cause to distrust her, any suspicion you would like to discuss with me?"

Immediately, he shook his head. "No. None."

"Then, we are agreed." She raised her hand to her left, and a priestess came from out of the shadows to hand her a goblet. Nephera paused to sip its contents, letting Ardnor wait until she was satisfied. "So that all is done officially, I have written up orders for you to send to both." She gestured, and suddenly there appeared two rolled parchments, hovering before her son. "They will need your imperial mark before they are sent."

With a grunt of annoyance, Ardnor dipped his horns to the side. He took the parchments, replying, "I'll see to it."

"Do not feel so slighted, my son." Nephera reached the goblet back to her attendant, who, as before, vanished with it into the shadows. "You have not been called here simply for this purpose. You see, I have a very special mission in mind for you. You may consider it a brief taste of what is to come." One hand lovingly outlined the symbol scarred into her flesh. Lady Nephera's gaze was like that of one deeply enamored. "It is close coming to the time when you should knew your god better . . ."

Ardnor had the sudden urge to tear his gaze from the downturned axe, but could not. He could not even blink, much less close his eyes. As he stared, the axe first pulsated, then swelled. It became the only thing that he could see, a living, fearsome thing.

And then the axe became a tower in the distance, a tarnished bronze tower from which there came the rasping voice.

My champion . . . the voice grated. *My champion . . .*

As quickly as that, the voice and glow vanished.

Ardnor felt an immense, inexplicable loss.

"Very soon, my dear son . . ." Nephera said, rising, and, as she did, two priestesses flanked her. "I am weary. I wish to bathe and then retire for a time. You may go."

The brevity of their encounter did not surprise him. This was his mother's strange way, especially of late. He started to leave—when a gasp from his mother made him spin back.

He opened his mouth to say something, but froze. Nephera stood in the shadows, her expression mixing anger and concern. She gestured at the darkness, as if trying to repel something.

"Go! I will not have you here!" she suddenly blurted. "Away!"

Ardnor squinted, and just for the briefest moment imagined he saw a familiar form fade away. He involuntarily bared his teeth in consternation. Had he seen—?

Her countenance once more neutral, Nephera turned and nodded to her son. "There is something you wish?"

Ardnor shook his head. "Nothing. I'm going."

She nodded again, continuing on. Clutching the parchments tightly, the emperor headed for the bronze doors. Ardnor could not help but glance over his shoulder as he left. Not in search of his mother, who had vanished through a passage, but rather for proof of something.

Proof that the condemning shade of his father did not now follow behind him.

While they waited for Bastion's return, Faros led the exercise of the meredrakes. Left penned up, they would soon turn on one another, creating an orgy of blood and gore.

With the handlers, Faros used whip and torch to urge the beasts in the direction desired. Others among the group used long lances. Everyone kept a sword or axe handy, just in case of sudden disorder. Being bitten by a meredrake generally caused death, for their saliva was poisoned by the foul things they ate.

While the other handlers kept as safe a distance as possible, Faros always waded in close. To the surprise of many, the reptiles treated him with the obeisance and caution, perhaps recognizing, in some manner, a more fearsome predator.

Faros roared at one hesitant beast, the crack of the whip accenting his guttural command. The stench of the monstrous creatures' breath and body odor forced many of the minotaurs to wrap cloths over their nostrils, but Faros went unmasked.

The scouts rode up as Faros urged the matriarch toward the pens. The matriarch hissed, forked tongue darting, displaying her savage, stained teeth, but she obeyed his signal.

But the nearby arrival of horses stirred the reptiles up again. One young, eager male tried to break from the herd. His tail flickered, bowling over an unprepared handler.

Faros signaled two others to grab the male. He, in turn, leapt toward the fallen figure, driving back a mature female with an open maw. The lash struck her squarely in the snout. Shaking her head and hissing vehemently, she turned from her intended prey.

When the matriarch entered the pen, Faros deemed it safe enough to leave matters in other hands. Passing the whip and torch to one of his subordinates, he approached the newcomers.

"Well? What did you find?"

Their grim expressions told all. The lead one spoke. "He is dead, my lord. They are all dead. We didn't find his body, but we found fragments of his belongings and the evidence of a scuffle leading to the cliff overlooking the river."

Despite himself, Faros felt dismayed. "Which way were they heading?"

The lead scout, a worn veteran with a thinning, grey mane, sounded bitter. "Back to us, my lord."

Faros snorted. The meeting had taken place. Bastion had been betrayed . . . and by his own sister. Faros, who had lost his entire family to the Droka ambition, still could not believe the depths of their evil. Bastion had spoken of his sister as someone with a mind like his, but he had also called her the most like their father. Maritia had proven that, indeed.

So there it was. So much for any pact. If the unnatural plague had not been enough to convince Faros of the throne's determination to exterminate him and his followers, the diabolical assassination of Bastion by his own sister left no doubt. There would be no peace. No hope of ending this before more minotaurs perished. If Maritia had betrayed her own brother, then she certainly would not bargain fairly with Faros. With peace out of the question, the bitter feud between him and House Droka could only end in war.

As he turned from the scouts, a black bird the size of his head dodged his foot, then landed nearby. Faros stalked past that avian and dozens more before even making halfway to the winding path leading up to the temple.

Suddenly, the birds were everywhere. They filled the field, perched on the mountainside, and even infested the ancient edifice itself. They didn't utter a sound. Even when frustrated warriors tried to sweep them away, all the birds did were silently flap out of reach, then settle down again. They looked as if they anticipated something, but what it was, no one could say.

Regardless of their overwhelming numbers, the creatures were mostly an annoyance, nothing more, and so Faros attempted to ignore them. Of far greater concern was how to contact Captain Botanos and the rest. It could take weeks, even months, for any message to be delivered.

But there was no choice, not any more. Faros knew he had to try.

From the wreckage of the legion, he had procured a supply of ink and parchment. In his quarters, spreading the latter across the crude, stone table he had constructed out of natural slabs from the mountainside, Faros tried to compose the necessary message.

But the words did not come easily to him, and he struggled. As if to mock his efforts, one large black bird alighted onto the table. Faros made a half-hearted attempt to grab the avian, but it leapt a couple of feet in the air, then landed only when he withdrew his hand. With a snort, Faros returned to his work.

Unfortunately, hours later and he was no closer to success. Nothing he wrote could articulate what he desired to express.

With a roar of mounting frustration, Faros shoved everything aside. His winged companion fluttered up but did not fly off. Ignoring the bird, Faros looked to the ceiling, silently cursing the deity. Before the Night of Blood, the only writing Faros had done had been notes of debt for his gambling losses. His father had been the one who wrote speeches, not him.

"Would that they could hear the words from my own mouth," he muttered to himself. "Then I might at least have a chance . . ."

"From my own mouth . . ." his voice repeated from nearby.

Faros shoved back from the table, looking for the speaker. The black bird glanced in the same direction as him.

"Who said that?" he demanded.

The bird gazed up at him. "Who said that?"

Ears flat and eyes narrowed, Faros said, "So, now you speak?"

"You speak?" it imitated.

The rebel leader growled. Had Sargonnas provided him the means to send his message? Leaning toward the creature, he tested his theory. "Hear my words . . ."

"Hear my words . . ." The bird answered back, every syllable, every inflection, that of the minotaur's.

It was all the proof Faros needed. The message came spilling out of his mouth. He began to dictate, telling the other rebels of the plague, of the deaths, and of Sargonnas's rescue. He spoke of his realization that the nightmare could only end with the destruction of House Droka. He pledged his life to that goal, swearing on the names of his father and mother . . .

Throughout his speech, the avian watched him intently. It did not interrupt his chain of thought with any more repetitions.

Even after Faros finished, the bird only cocked its head to the side, waiting for instructions.

Without hesitation, the minotaur commanded, "Speak the message."

Word for word, the black bird—in Faros's voice—told of the new crusade. The minotaur listened carefully, but the avian did not make one mistake. Even the deep emotions of the words it somehow conveyed perfectly, astonishing the hardened former slave.

When it reached the end of its spiel, the bird simply clamped its beak shut and preened its feathers.

Before he could consider the matter further, the raven abruptly ceased its preening and leapt off the table, flying from the chamber before Faros could stop it.

And even as it vanished, he heard the bird begin proclaiming his message. Faros pursued the bird, wondering if he had made a mistake in entrusting his voice to the Condor Lord's minion.

He had gone only a few yards down the corridor when he heard himself speaking from a side hall where the bird had not gone. A moment later, a third echo came from another direction. As Faros passed a window, he heard himself from the outside.

Pausing, Faros peered through the window—and saw that every bird had suddenly taken to the air. The sky was filled with black birds. Yet, even more astounding than that sight was the clamor. Not the caws of crows and ravens—but rather it was the voice of Faros Es-Kalin speaking over and over and over, echoing proud and strong.

When it seemed that they all had spoke his message, the huge flock dispersed, heading off to every point of the compass

The die was cast. As Faros watched the feathered messengers wend their way over the world, he willed them on as fast as they could fly. The sooner they reached their goals, the better.

When the last had vanished over the horizon, Faros spun from the window, calling out to the nearest of his followers. "Spread the word! From tomorrow on, I want everyone to gather everything of value from the region—food, especially! I want all weapons sharpened and the animals prepared for a long, hard journey!"

He made a calculation of how long it would take for everything to be prepared, then added, "I want us ready to march in three days!" He smiled grimly. "It's time we headed home . . ."

CHAPTER X

FATEFUL MESSAGES

Second Master Pryas was an aloof figure who clearly reveled in the glory of his swift ascension in power. With ranks such as Legion Commander and Procurator General to his credit—the second giving him free rein in almost any critical situation—he was now one of the most powerful minotaurs in the empire.

To Maritia's dismay but not her surprise, General Kolina and the other Protector officers fell all over themselves to please Pryas. In the short time since he had arrived, more than half of the legionaries and colonizers who were supposed to be helping renovate the capital had switched to appeasing the temple first and foremost. Even as Maritia angrily rode toward the sprawling edifice, she estimated a good hundred or so soldiers from the Crystal Legion were busy at work on it. Several were in the midst of building a massive framework that would eventually hold gigantic versions of the axe and bird aloft over the entrance.

That Kolina's warriors, Forerunner faithful all, had come here did not astonish her, but there were also dozens of soldiers from various other legions, including the Snowhawks and even one or two stalwarts from her own.

She met the steely-eyed Protector at the base of the temple steps. Pryas wore the black and gold of his calling, his helmet tucked in the crook of his right arm. At his side hung a powerful mace whose thorny head looked capable of cracking either rock or bone with equal ease. Four of his towering guards stood near.

"My Lady Maritia!" he called as she approached. "Your presence is a blessing!" The Second Master swept forward in a bow, his dark cloak fluttering. "Had I known you were coming, I'd have had a more formal welcome prepared!"

"You've pulled enough of my soldiers from their appointed tasks, Pryas. There's no need to borrow any more."

He did not look at all chastened. "The people are the soul of the imperium and the temple is the soul of the people, my lady. It should've been open for worship long before this."

"There were a few other priorities. Supplies, housing, the enemy . . ."

He turned from her, seizing an unhelmed dekarian from the Gryphons and commanding, "Go tell those laggards to put hammers to those blasphemous icons now!"

As the officer hurried away, Maritia glanced to where several minotaurs were piling elven statuary that represented Branchala to one side of the entrance. Most of the figures were already cracked or broken.

"Why not just cart them off to a refuse pit like the rest of the trash? It would save time."

"In the presence of that which we serve, there must be no false deities or even their graven images," Pryas said, frowning. "As her holiness's daughter and his majesty's sister, you should understand this better than I, blessed one!"

"I'm a soldier, Pryas, a legionary like my father. I understand war, like most of our people."

"With our ancestors to guide us, we all take our appointed places, perform our appointed deeds, for the good of our race and the glory of that which we serve."

Trying to keep a straight face, Maritia said, "I understand also that your subordinates have moved into the distribution centers. When one of my treverians attempted to procure our allotment of food supplies, he was turned away by swords and axes!"

"A misunderstanding, of course! Your treverian should've known better. Ambeon's foodstuffs and other essentials are under the auspices of the Protectors! It's the same in Nethosak; it surely follows that the colonies would do likewise."

It was all she could do to keep from using her fist to wipe the sanctimonious expression off his face. "I am military commander of Ambeon—"

"I simply follow the dictates of the emperor, as do you."

She could little argue with that logic. Still, Maritia stared hard at the Protector. "I trust you've collected enough laborers here, though. I can't have lapses in other crucial areas of colonization or security. Those Snowhawks, for example. Their duty is supposed to be securing and guarding the northwest. If you need more help, there's always the slaves—"

Drawing himself up, Pryas, nostrils flaring, growled. "No elf scum will touch anything regarding that which involves the Forerunners! I'll not trust their soft, treacherous hands! Better an ogre or a gully dwarf than one of them! The elves should all be executed! There will be no place for them in the pure realm!"

As much as Maritia despised elves, she found the Procurator General's attitude extreme, but she forced a smile. "As you like . . . just talk to me before any other 'requisitions' of personnel, yes?"

His expression altered immediately. Pryas acted as if she had granted him a great gift. "I look forward to your company at the next best moment, my lady."

Maritia recognized the look in his eyes. She had had her share of lovers but never a Protector. She had already shunned advances by the Supreme Councilor, Lothan. If the Second

Master thought to rise higher in status by binding himself to her, he was deluded.

"A simple written request will suffice," she managed.

He revealed no disappointment. Instead, Pryas gazed past her. Ears straightening, the Protector remarked, "It would seem that one of your adjutants is looking for you."

While Maritia had an official headquarters, she could rarely be found there. However, she always left word with her subordinates where she could be found, in case of important messages.

"My lady!" gasped the rider. "There are ogres at the northern gate!"

"Ogres?" blurted Pryas, eyes narrowing suspiciously. He started to signal the working soldiers, but Maritia forced his hand down.

"Hold!" To the newcomer, she asked, "How many? Are they attacking?"

"Four, my lady. Two fat ones from Blode and a pair of thinner ones from Kern. One of the former said this was for you."

She took the small, sealed parchment. A fierce mastark image marked the wax. The fact that it came from the ogres meant only one person could have written it.

Golgren.

It would have been best to return to her quarters before reading it, but Maritia's curiosity got the best of her. Ignoring Pryas, she turned to the side and cracked the seal.

I await you.

That was all it said . . . and for Maritia, that was more than enough.

Rolling up the missive and secreting it in a pouch, she told Pryas, "If you'll excuse me, I need to attend to this matter."

"I can have every soldier toiling here armed and ready—"

"These are our allies, if you recall, and I doubt four ogres could conquer this place."

"There may be more in hiding," he suggested. "In my capacity, I should at least come with you and ascertain the exact danger."

"That won't be necessary." Before the Protector could say anything further, she left. Pryas's spies would find out soon enough what was happening, but for now, Maritia had to meet with Golgren.

Why had he journeyed so far?

The four ogres were seated, waiting, when she arrived at the gate. The Grand Lord was not among them.

"Wait here," Maritia commanded her guards.

"My lady—"

"I'll be safe." To the ogres, she asked, "Where are we headed? Only a short distance?"

One of the Blodians grunted, the closest thing to an affirmation.

Leaving her reluctant underlings behind, Maritia plunged into the woods. Despite her seeming comfort in their company, she had already calculated her course of action should the ogres prove treacherous. The one to her left Maritia could gut, then, as he fell, she would drive her horse past his. She was very familiar with these woods, having journeyed through them time and again. There were dips and gullies that would help her leave her pursuers behind.

All thought of flight vanished a moment later as a lone, hooded figure astride a brown devil of a steed met her, bowing his head. That he was roughly her height—and, therefore, at least a foot shorter than her guides—was enough to identify him, even before he pulled back the thick, brown hood back.

The Grand Lord Golgren flashed her a smile . . . which might have been charming if not for his ugly sharp teeth and Maritia's knowledge that the ogre smiled even, perhaps especially, when cutting throats.

"Offspring of Hotak, Commander of All Ambeon, good ally to the Free Ogres of Kern and Blode . . . I give greetings!"

Maritia didn't feel like smiling. She had the impulse to frown. Golgren's cheerfulness had a strange artificiality about it. That and his very presence in Ambeon was worrying.

"I greet you in turn, Grand Lord." She skipped his list of titles, which would have required several minutes of oration. He had come this distance to alert her to something, and Maritia was impatient to hear the news. "I am surprised by this visit. The border station's proven reliable enough for passing on messages."

There were actually two border stations, one located on the ogre side, the other in Ambeon. A small group of couriers attended each. When messages came from Golgren, an ogre would bring them to the neutral zone in between, where a minotaur would take custody of the missives. From there, one of the legionaries would bring the message to the colonial capital. The system worked equally well in reverse.

Early on, the two sides had tried messenger birds, but the avians did not fare well in the clumsy care of the Grand Lord's followers.

"This was . . . a delicate matter," he replied, much of the false cheer vanishing. He waved his sole hand at his compatriots, sending them off. His maimed arm the ogre kept obscured under his travel cloak.

Most of the riders headed off to the east, but Maritia noticed one ride in the opposite direction. Storing that information, she eyed her ally. "Are you in need of supplies? Has there been a setback along the Nerakian border?"

"No, all is good," the Grand Lord said with justifiable pride. What had once looked like the subjugation of his kind by the black knights had become a debacle for the humans. True, he had employed minotaur assistance, but the actual fighting had been done mostly by ogres under his leadership. "As, I know, all is good in Silv—Ambeon. Excuse, please."

"Then if things are going so well for both of us, what, by my father's axe, causes you to risk coming here?"

He looked in the direction the single rider had gone. Maritia saw that the lone ogre had now returned with another horse laden with packs. Her brow arched.

"What goes on here?" she uttered, suddenly wary.

Golgren indicated the animal, then, his voice flat, he told her, "I bring back that which was the Lord Bastion's, who is dead."

She stiffened in the saddle, unable to speak.

"I do not lie," Golgren insisted, perhaps believing she thought him telling tales. "I—"

Maritia found her tongue. "Tell me everything—everything!"

"Little to say. Much guessing. The body, viciously cut, was found by Nagroch's people. Your brother was alone, but the tracks of horses led to the northeast. One there was who knew of your Bastion and brought the body to this humble one." He slapped his fist against his other shoulder, an ogre salute to the dead. "I had believed the son of Hotak was already lost, yet when I saw the body I knew it was he."

"Where's the body? I see only a horse . . ."

He grimaced. "Our lands are no more kind to the dead than the living. The body was no longer good, so it was given to the flames—as Uruv Suurt prefer—and much singing was done to honor the warrior. I saw to this myself."

Golgren then explained where Bastion had been found. Maritia gritted her teeth as she heard the details. He had been slain while still in the same region where he had met her. It was likely Maritia had been mere hours away. He must have been betrayed somehow, she thought furiously.

"*Nya orn i'fhani ge!*" Golgren snapped at the other ogre.

The other sullenly brought the packed horse to Maritia. Taking the reins, she glanced at the pouches, some of which were of minotaur make. One had her brother's mark etched in it.

"What was recovered," was all the Grand Lord said.

Dismounting, Maritia searched through the items, which proved a paltry collection. A dagger, a bedroll, the saddle from his mount—with blood splattered on it—and so on. Little that spoke of the owner, which, somewhat ironically, made her all the more certain they were indeed Bastion's effects.

As she rummaged through the pouches, her blood raced faster. A tension such as she had not felt since first hearing of her father's fall took hold of Maritia. Even before, when she had thought Bastion lost at sea, she had not reacted so strongly to his death. Without a body, it had been simple to pretend that he might still return some day. Of course, when he did return, it was as a rebel.

Now there was no pretending.

"The wounds!" she snapped, still staring at his skimpy belongings. "Describe them for me!"

The Grand Lord did not reply at first, which caused Bastion's sister to pause and look at him. The ogre appeared much distressed.

"The wounds," Golgren finally said. "Deep in the back and neck. All from behind. Many . . . many wounds . . ." His brow furrowed. "A base death. His weapon, it was not drawn."

Maritia's ears flattened. All in the back. His weapon unused. A base death, indeed! "Were there any other bodies? Ogres? Minotaurs?"

"Only tracks to the northeast . . . One there was who later claimed to see minotaurs riding that way, but too far and too fast to catch.."

Only tracks . . . to the northeast . . . other minotaurs riding away . . .

The other rebels . . . ?

Faros Es-Kalin. Yes, that made sense. He must be responsible! Why the rebel leader would kill Bastion, she didn't understand. Her brother had proposed peace, and she had countered with her own offer of another meeting. Maybe that was enough of a failure in the eyes of one who was reputed to be crazy with bloodlust. Her brother's escort had been his own assassins!

Such a dishonorable death. Stabbed in the back by his supposed comrades! Maritia felt the blood fill her eyes. All the animosity she had felt toward Bastion vanished, to be replaced by a burning hatred for the nephew of Chot.

"Faros . . ." she muttered to herself.

Golgren heard and understood. He nodded and brought his other arm out to view. The stump was expertly bound with silk and cloth, obscuring what was left. "Faros it may be, yes. That would be my guess, too."

"Who else?" Maritia closed the pack again. Still holding the reins, she leapt back up onto her mount, her fury rapidly building. "Who else would deal so treacherously? Who else but some misbegotten refuse of Kalin?"

"My lady," the Grand Lord Golgren murmured soothingly in his best Common. "This is news not good, of course. I will ride with you to the city—"

"I thank you, but that won't be necessary," the female minotaur replied, steeling herself. "I mourned my brother once already. That he is now truly dead, I accept. That his murderer is Faros, I readily believe." Maritia lined up the second horse with her own. "That I'll see Faros's head and horns on the end of a pike, I swear!"

This caused Golgren to grin, a cruel, savage grin. "A delicious image, yes . . ."

The urge to return to the capital swelled within her, then Maritia remembered Golgren. She turned to him. "You have my gratitude, my lord, and more. If you'll wait, I'll provide you with safe escort back north."

His grin grew devilish. "There was no need in, will be no need out."

She nodded, knowing that if he said as much, it was the truth.

"Then I bid you a swift journey, my lord," Maritia said. "My thanks for all you did for my brother."

"What was done was done necessarily," he said.

Without warning, he veered his mount away from hers. At the same time, Golgren called out to his other companions and they rode off.

Maritia had already lost all interest in the ogres. Pulling the reins of the second horse, she led it back toward Ardnoranti. As she rode, her mind continued to replay what she believed to be the circumstances of Bastion's death. By the minute, her fury grew. Maritia smelled blood—Faros's blood.

"I'll hunt you down, wastrel!" She spat. "I'll hunt you down like the jackal you are!"

The other horse snorted, reminding her of Golgren. He had risked his life to bring her this news and these mementos of her brother. The minotaur and the ogre had their mutual mistrust, true, but he had proven himself by this deed and she was grateful.

It was telling, Maritia thought, that even an ogre had more honor than Faros Es-Kalin.

CHAPTER XI

DEMONS IN THE NIGHT

Faros drove his followers to complete their preparations for the journey in as short a time as possible. He barely slept, constantly overseeing the pace of activity. If their leader had seemed a creature possessed before, now Faros's urgency gave him a manic appearance that caused unnerved whispers and fearful glances.

Huge plumes of dust marked their departure. Dry winds combined with the dust. Faros rode at the head of the rebel force, his eyes surveying the landscape as if daring some interference, but the column traveled untouched. The journey northeast was arduous, but most of the rebels had long since been hardened by adversity. They traversed the unstable, winding paths through the foreboding land. A few were lost and left behind along the way.

Finally, the badlands gave way to the wooded regions of northeastern Kern. Despite the more tranquil atmosphere of their surroundings, the rebels grew more wary. The salty sea called to them, but they also knew that, this close to the Blood Sea, an imperial vessel might be nearby. Ogre ships, too, were a viable threat. Faros almost would have gladly welcomed one last strike at his former tormentors, no matter how weary his followers might be.

As they neared the coastline, Faros sent out more scouting patrols. Despite protests, he himself led one party consisting of twenty riders. Somewhere ahead was the site where he remembered Jubal's crew had made camp once. Captain Botanos—assuming he still lived—might have left some sign or message.

With the coast near and night falling, Faros sent two riders back to the main party to let them know the way was clear. The small scouting party made camp within sight of the shoreline. Eagerness ran high among the minotaurs and even the pair of humans who accompanied them were beguiled by the lapping waves. The Blood Sea sang its siren song even to Faros, who thought he had long steeled himself against such nostalgia.

A thin, swirling mist drifted over from the waters as night lengthened. The party kept close together; sentries were posted on the edge of the encampment. As the rebels settled down, the sound of the sea proved so soothing that most fell asleep quickly.

Faros was not among those. He lay with eyes closed, trying to focus his thoughts on the dangers ahead. His thoughts roiled. There were so many risks involved in his plans. In an attempt to calm himself, Faros tried—as he had sometimes done before—to recall peaceful moments from his youth, yet those moments always twisted into vile reminders of what he had lost, even bucolic scenes transformed into ravaged, gore-drenched nightmares.

The scent of the sea overcame him. He heard snores, the shifting of bodies, and the occasional call of woodland creatures. Then suddenly he heard furtive whispering. The words were hard to understand, but the urgency of the tone was unmistakable.

Sitting up, Faros glanced around. No one around him seemed awake. In the distance he made out the shadowy form of a lone guard watching the dark woods. All looked as it should. He pricked his ears, but he no longer heard the whispering. Deciding he had imagined things, Faros lay back down. This time, though, the stars caught his attention. Through the sea mist, they had taken on an ethereal quality. They were forming images, such as a snapping turtle and a rose. One even seemed to him to resemble a face. No, not exactly a face, for he noted a hooded crown and what appeared to be eyes, but nothing more.

The eyes stared at him. Faros could not look away. He felt as if he floated toward the star eyes, as if they meant to engulf him . . .

A frenzied shout jolted him free. He rolled to the side, grabbing his sheathed sword.

All around the encampment, the soft earth erupted. Huge mounds rose then crumbled open. From them emerged massive, shelled forms armed with odd, curved blades almost like scythes, but with harsh, angled and edged teeth. Other shadows held wicked, three-pronged spears with barbed heads.

The mist-enshrouded crustaceans swelled in size, growing broader and taller than the minotaurs. Their heads were buried so deep in their shells that they were barely visible. The monsters' eyes were grotesque, knoblike protrusions and their snouts long and flexible. The shells were tinted crimson. They made a bubbling hiss, then, trundling forward on four lobster-like limbs, the demonic host closed on the startled rebels.

One minotaur dropped his weapon, he was so astonished. Another shook his head and began muttering prayers. More than one set of ears stood taut as the nightmares of childhood were resurrected before their very eyes.

Magori . . .

Faros's father had fought in the war against the aquatic horrors, as had the parents of most of the minotaurs in the party. The monsters had arisen from the depths during the time that other races called the Summer of Chaos or the Chaos War. As a child, Faros had heard the tales of the gruesome slaughters, of the relentless hordes of crustaceans pouring onto ships, onto the islands of his people, and the bloodbaths that ensued. Where the monsters struck, they left little recognizable of their victims. They offered no chance for surrender; butchery was their one desire.

The Magori served an entity called the Coil—itself in the thrall of some dark god—and desired nothing less than the total annihilation of the minotaur race. Gradic had murmured of finding entire settlements razed—heads, arms, and other body parts scattered wide. Not even the ogres rent such horror.

The fiendish creatures had overcome much of Mithas and ravaged part of Nethosak, yet in part because of Sargonnas himself, the Coil had perished and the leaderless Magori had retreated. At the very edge of annihilation, the minotaurs had fought back and sent the Magori slipping back into the deep. No one living had seen a Magori in a generation, but they remained the demons of memory, the fears of troubled sleeps . . .

"Form a square!" Faros shouted, but only a few could obey before the hissing Magori plowed into them. The crustaceans slashed and jabbed with surprising swiftness, forcing the rebels to defend rather than attack. Half-hidden by the mist, their hisses echoing chillingly, and the Magori were terrible to behold.

They were still mortal, Faros knew. He jabbed twice against the one facing him, seeking a vital spot. However, his blade only encountered a shell more protective than a steel shield. Worse, his sword felt uncommonly heavy, almost as if it were resisting his will. When he tried to thrust at the pale, fleshy part beneath the snout, he felt his arm jerk to the side, nearly leaving him open to the Magori's vicious counter-attack.

The nightmare swung, its wicked scythe cutting a jagged trail across Faros's forearm. The minotaur cried out as the weapon bit into his flesh. The Magori leaned close, so that its bulbous orbs nearly grazed the minotaur's own. There was nothing in the creature's gaze, though, except blankness.

This was a thing of carnage, of savageness beyond any race born of Krynn.

Another scream ripped the air. Faros caught a glimpse of a minotaur victim—the head flying from the torso. Something struck the ground with a dull thud near the rebel leader's feet. Faros tried again for the fleshy area of his opponent and again the sword felt heavy, awkward in his hands.

"Damn you!" he snapped at the blade. Whatever the cause for his trouble, Faros would force the weapon to obey. With a grunt, he deflected the scythe then thrust ahead with all his might.

The sword sank deep. A hideous squeal, the Magori's death cry pierced his eardrums. A putrid, yellowish fluid spilled from the crustacean's quivering body. The stench, akin to rotting fish, forced Faros to cover his nostrils. Droplets struck his wrist, burning him. With a final hiss, the Magori slumped over.

Shaking from pain and effort, Faros looked around. His dwindling party was hard-pressed. One human had fallen under the savage attack of two Magori, his body severed into three pieces that briefly flopped about on the ground as the vestiges of life drained away. The shelled horrors surrounded the scouting party like a wall.

Faros tried to dredge up childhood memories of the beasts. The Magori had other weaknesses, he thought, besides their narrow patch of soft flesh. If he could only remember . . .

The other human screamed, his chest ripped open by a barbed spear. As the nightmarish warrior stood over his victim, the heads of his lance still bearing gobbets of bloody flesh, a female minotaur leapt forward, burying her axe in one of the creature's bulbous eyes. The Magori squealed and fell.

Such heroics were dwindling. More common were simple, desperate acts of survival, as each of Faros's rebels struggled against the inevitable. Forced back, Faros stumbled over something. He slipped, tumbling. A searing pain swept over his left shoulder. The minotaur frantically rolled away, his fur singed by the campfire.

Then something Gradic once told his son came back to Faros. Ignoring the heat, he seized a long piece of driftwood from the flames and thrust it toward his adversary. The Magori ducked but showed little fear of the flames. The rebel leader's brow wrinkled; that wasn't what he expected.

Before he could ponder the matter, his foe charged again. Faros dropped the wood, throwing himself back. He deflected another strike then cut the creature on one limb. The three-digited claw twitched, and the weapon slipped.

Then he noticed something: The holes from which the Magori had burst were no longer there. Even in the dark Faros could see the tall, shattered mounds were gone, and the ground was smooth and quite solid.

That was impossible . . . unless the tunnels had magically sealed themselves. Unless there were no tunnels and mounds to see, because they had never really existed in the first place.

If that was so, what did it say about the monstrous crustaceans?

On a hunch, he rubbed the black ring. The Magori did not vanish, but almost as one they certainly rippled—and briefly Faros saw another, more familiar form in the place of each. What he did next, Faros knew, might cause his death, but if his eyes had seen true, it was his only option.

Planting the tip of his sword in the earth, the minotaur bent down on one knee. At the same time, he shouted to the rest of his band, "Stop! Do as I do! Now!"

It spoke to the trust they placed in Faros that the other rebels immediately obeyed. The Magori encircled them. Their bulbous, unyielding orbs twitched atop their stalks. Several hissed and the foul odor of death washed over the rebels.

The Magori raised their monstrous weapons. Then the one looming over Faros hesitated. It signaled the others to lower their blades, then leaned forward, as if studying its adversary.

Faros clutched Sargonnas's ring and struggled with every

iota of his willpower to understand what he had really been fighting.

The lead Magori shimmered. Its shelled body transformed, one pair of the horrific appendages vanishing and the others becoming furred arms and legs. Its snout stretched out, expanded, and transformed into a broad muzzle. The bulbous eyes became ears and—as Faros had guessed—a pair of long, sharp horns.

Horns belonging to one of his own kind.

With a startled expression, the other minotaur demanded, "Faros? Faros Es-Kalin?"

He was looking up into the stout face of Captain Botanos. The mariner's horrified astonishment gave way to dismay. Botanos looked at his bloodied axe, which had nearly cleaved Faros in two. With sudden repugnance, he dropped the weapon and bowed his head.

"Faros! I swear I didn't know it was you!"

With that, every Magori became a minotaur. The two parties look at one another, the terrible truth now revealed. Allies had met one another as deadly foes. More than half a dozen lay dead and several more were wounded, some badly.

"I saw—" Botanos swallowed. "The *Crest* dropped anchor about an hour north. We set out to scout the area. I—I heard noise and we snuck up—but it was ogres we saw! An ogre band with minotaur pelts set in a pile!"

Several of his crew quickly grunted or nodded assent.

Faros slowly rose. Unlike the captain, however, he did not toss away his sword. There was still a chance that this manifestation, too, was nothing more than vile illusion.

"We saw Magori," he tersely told Botanos. "They burst from the earth, each armed with a scythe sword or barbed lance . . ."

"Magori? By the Sea Queen, small wonder that you fought back so fanatically! I'm old enough to recall those horrors, lad! 'Tis a wonder that you didn't kill us all, regardless of surprise and numbers!"

Faros nodded bitterly. "That's what some enemy had in mind. That's what was supposed to happen. We were supposed to destroy each other." He recalled gazing at the face formed by stars in the sky, just before the attack. "A crowned head," the rebel leader muttered loud enough for Botanos to hear. "Eyes without a face . . ."

Botanos made the sign of Sargonnas. "Eyes without a face? A crown? It sounds like the lord of the bronze tower—dread Morgion!" The heavyset captain snorted. "Faros . . . are you saying that this deadly trap, this double illusion, is his foul work?"

"This and the plague that struck us earlier, the plague that was supposed to have annihilated all of my followers . . ."

Several of those nearby began muttering to one another. Botanos evidently did not like their tone, for he quickly said, "Aye, the temple might have Morgion to play dishonorable and scurvy tricks, but there before you is one who stood up to Sargas himself! You all heard that in the message spoken by the birds, remember? By the Maelstrom, I'll take the battle might of Faros over a deity who dwells in filth and rot any day, eh?"

His words heartened the dispirited minotaurs. They cheered, despite the carnage. It was not truly their hands that had slain their comrades, but the foul, cowardly spell of their enemies.

"See to the wounded," the captain commanded. Then, somewhat sheepishly, he looked at Faros and added, "With your permission, my lord."

Faros nodded, exhaling with a sigh. While some tended to the wounded, others went about the task of dealing with the dead. Both sides had suffered, but at least the worst had been avoided.

Alone now with Faros, Botanos dipped his horns to the side, saying, "This error still rests on my head, lad. You've a right to take my head, it would seem, or my horns, whatever you see fit."

"Which would only add to the tragedy," growled Faros. "Keep both, Captain. I'll demand more of you than that! Your precious *Dragon's Crest* will be my flagship when I sail into Nethosak!"

If he thought that would shake the veteran sailor's morale any, Faros was mistaken. He received a grateful grin. Botanos almost gave him a slap on the shoulder, then he saw the rebel leader's wound.

"Gods above, Faros! You need to see to that!"

Only then did the younger fighter feel intense agony where he had been burned. So used to burying his pain deep, Faros had not even notice that his fur was in places completely charred. In one or two spots, his flesh had already begun to blister.

"There's no time for it now," he said, forcing the pain away.

"Oh, I think there is! This is one time I'll be giving the commands, lad!" Looking over his own shoulder, the captain roared, "Joak! You've some mender training! Get over here and look at this!"

A shorter, narrow-eyed mariner joined them. Seeing Botanos would not be satisfied until something was done, Faros resigned himself to treatment. He sat while the other minotaur fussed over his burn.

"Can make a poultice out of some herbs I've got and a plant I saw, but it'd be better if I had 'im aboard the *Crest*."

Mention of the ship sparked Faros's interest. "How far is it off shore? An hour, you said?"

"Aye. A safe harbor, at least for now. We skirted half a dozen imperials only a couple of days ago, though! There's lots of activity goin' on."

Most of it aimed at Faros, no doubt. It would only increase now that Bastion de-Droka was counted among the dead.

Botanos misread his expression. "Oh, we'll get you aboard quick enough, lad, no doubt about it! I'll not lose you now that you've taken up the cause! Soon as you're secure, we'll set sail for the Courrain!"

"We'll be going nowhere, Captain, at least, no farther than your ship. The rest are a day or more behind us. I swore I'd leave no one in Kern." In his mind's eye Faros saw his father's face. When Gradic had given an oath, he had kept it. Faros could do no less.

"But—"

At that moment, Joak, the mender, made the mistake of probing a particularly sore area. With a growl, Faros shoved him and leapt up. Blood briefly filled his vision.

"No one gets left behind for the ogres, do you understand?"

"Aye . . . aye, lad—Lord Faros."

The rebel leader picked up his sword, which once again felt like a natural extension of his arm. "Take us to your ship."

They left after the dead and wounded were dealt with. One of the rebels who had fallen under Grom's influence said a prayer to Sargonnas. Faros glanced up at the constellation representing the god, but as usual, the deity did not appear. When the short ceremony was done, those wounded who could not walk were carried on makeshift stretchers built from cut wood and blankets. The trek was not an arduous one, but after the sinister illusion, each step was made warily. It no longer appeared that Sargonnas's power obscured Faros from the sight of his enemies.

"I wish you'd be reconsidering," Botanos muttered as they neared their goal. "The *Crest* could reach a safer location in a handful of days, and with luck, enough ships for most of your people could be arranged shortly after. A week, maybe three at the outset—"

"Everyone left behind would already be dead or worse."

" 'Tis you that matters! You're the only one who can lead us to victory!"

The rebel leader met the mariner's gaze. "Would you follow someone who abandoned so many for his own hide?"

Botanos could say nothing to that. He finally nodded. "As you say, then. At least get aboard and stay there. If we are discovered by Imperials, you can't argue if we take you away!"

"No, I'll stay ashore. If any ship comes, I'll melt back into the woods then return to the column."

They broke through the last line of trees. At any moment, at least according to what Captain Botanos had told him earlier, they would spot the legendary rebel vessel.

"Now see here, my lord!" Botanos was saying. "If you'd only—"

The mariner broke off, his mouth agape. Faros quickly followed his eyes to where the *Dragon's Crest* lay anchored—and surrounded by more than half a dozen other large vessels.

"Into the trees!" he snapped, pulling away from Botanos. "Captain! Get—"

Yet Botanos laughed. Faros looked at him as if he were mad.

"Rest easy, my lord! There's nothing to fear!"

"Those are warships!"

"Aye! Ships of the Eastern Fleet, most of them! Led by Captain Tinza, if you'll recall . . ."

The veteran naval officer's face briefly came to Faros's mind. She had been one of those who had first sworn to follow him, if only he would make his focus Nethosak, not Kern.

"Truly the Horned One watches over you, my lord!" Botanos gestured at the fleet. "There lies the end to both our concerns! You wanted ships to carry the others? I'll wager these'll do! The birds spread your message quicker than even I thought, and it seems your heartfelt words did the rest!"

Faros surveyed the ships, every one of them having come this far because of his entreaties. Every one, because they would follow him, even if their seemingly futile quest ended in death.

Against the unearthly power of the malevolent Morgion that was the likely outcome.

Chapter XII

Blöten

Blöten, capital of Blöde, once one of the primary cities of the venerated High Ogres, was nestled high in the mountains of the north. Thousands of years earlier, its tall towers—some, according to legend, made completely of white crystal—and vast, extravagant manors were known the world over. Everyone came to Blöten; the riches of Ansalon flowed to it as if compelled. The marketplaces held exotic items from across the oceans—including rare essences taking years to distill and animals found in captivity nowhere else. It was said that if one could not find something in Blöten, it was because it did not exist. The capital of Blöde compared favorably with greatest High Ogre cities in Kern.

Like Kern, the ogres of the second kingdom fell into decadence then savageness. Abandoned by all but a few of the barbaric descendants of its original inhabitants, Blöten became a mockery of its once-mighty self. As the ages progressed and violence and natural disaster took its toll, the outer walls crumbled and many of the unique, wondrous towers collapsed. The glistening, polished cobblestone streets sank as tremors cracked open the earth, swallowing entire sections of the city. The sprawling dwellings left behind became broken shells, stripped of value and used by the ferocious heirs of the godlike race as homes for entire clans of bloodthirsty warriors. Blöten became a shadow, a ghost of glory lost because of the arrogance of its founders.

Of all the cities of the ogres, even Kernen to the northeast, Blöten had done its best to resurrect that magnificent past. What few towers remained had been repaired as best as possible or were in the midst of reconstruction. There were traces of the supposed crystal structures, and whenever bits of such marvels were found, they were skillfully incorporated into the new buildings, causing the towers of the revived Blöten to glitter in the sunlight.

Once the cherished symbol of the capital had been the brown mountain hawk, a fierce, red-crested raptor with a wingspan more than twelve feet. Most of the images of the avian had been lost to time, but now a giant marble behemoth stood watch over each of the four towering wooden entrance gates, wings outstretched as if Blöten's fabled protectors were about to launch against its enemies. The four were but a recent addition, commissioned not by the great Donnag but by the true master of the kingdom.

In and around the towers, the remaining quarters of the capital had also been cleaned, polished, and touched up. The curved walls rose high again, the replaced stone covered in brown plaster. Here and there, slaves with a talent for carving restored or chiseled fresh images of tall, beautiful figures who seemed to descend from the very heavens. They were, in their way, as beautiful as the High Ogres, but taller, more imposing, and with a powerful cast to their expressions, they seemed almost threatening.

Golgren, who entered the city at the head of his army, only sniffed in disdain as his eyes swept past these images. Those who had ordered them to be made lived in a delusion they were allowed to keep only at his sufferance. The great column of warriors and beasts that passed through the arched gateway were but a fraction of those at his command, yet they made for a spectacle. The armored warriors, the helmeted mastarks, and the ever-hissing meredrakes impressed the many onlookers. Never in the history of the ogres had such power been accumulated by one figure, not even by the khans or chieftains.

The guards on the walls hailed him. The people flocked to demonstrate their approval. Clubs beat the battered street in unison, creating a thundering effect. Other onlookers barked, the harsh sounds honoring the Grand Lord's might. A few southern amolaks—the shorter necks and yellow brown bodies of the lupine horses marking them as distinct from their taller, longer cousins in Kern—joined in the cries. Many of the well wishers were clad only in kilts, but some wore garments akin to Golgren's. These bowed and acted in a more civilized manner. Several had filed their tusks in the fashion of the Grand Lord. His chosen were among this group, those who watched over his domain in his absence. In Blöten, there was much reason for vigilance.

The crystalline fragments in the high towers glittered brilliantly, Golgren noticed with satisfaction. He had timed his coming for this hour, aware that the sunlight would be at its brightest. To the crowds, the Grand Lord took on an almost celestial appearance, the glow surrounding him enhancing his prestige.

The wind picked up. The smell of so many filthy bodies would have caused anyone other than an ogre—or gully dwarf—to pinch his nostrils tight. Golgren strapped the reins to his saddle, then reached into a saddle bag and took out a small vial, which he held to his nose. The heady scent momentarily drowned out the stench of his people. With the bottle once more secreted, he seized his mount and steered it toward his destination.

Another smaller procession shifted to one side, as the Grand Lord passed on his way through the city. Clad in grey cloth robes, four massive ogres were carrying a wood and goatskin litter, upon which lay the body of a prize amalok. The beast's throat had been cut and around its bound corpse lay small, round clay jars filled with its drained blood. The lids of the dusky brown containers had been sealed with wax to keep the contents from escaping. Behind the litter, five other ogres, also in grey, stood with their heads bowed. The lead figure, his hair tied in a tail, was a local authority favored by Golgren. Those behind him were members of his clan and also ogres of some high caste. The leader and one other had filed their tusks down. Each of the five carried a small, leather sack in which something squirmed.

Golgren glanced beyond the procession, beyond the walls of Blöten itself, where the high, jagged mountains stood as sentinels around the capital. Their snow-covered caps and the harsh outcroppings on many peaks made them resemble giant, helmed warriors, to superstitious ogres.

The other procession was heading into the ominous terrain to honor those warriors and ask their blessings. The amalok was a prize animal that had been sacrificed. Part of the ritual was making the journey barefoot while carrying such a precious sacrifice. The smaller sacks contained adolescent baraki, the fighting lizards so prized by the upper castes. Another sacrifice, and this one would be made fresh on the spot, so that the spirits would be most pleased. The baraki would die by knife as the amalok corpse burned on one of the rock cairns dotting the mountainsides.

It was not poor timing that caused the procession to cross Golgren's path. By embarking on this arduous trek at this time, the other ogre did his duty in honor of the Grand Lord. The sacrifices would be offered for the continuing glory of Golgren.

As the master of Kern and Blöde passed, the Grand Lord reached into a pouch. From it, he drew a piece of broken tusk, which Golgren tossed to the feet of his follower. The other ogre dipped down and seized the offering. His head remained bowed at all times, but he clutched the bit of tusk with clear avarice.

The piece of tusk had been taken from a rival of Golgren's long dead. The power of that dead rival was now the Grand Lord's, and by giving a portion of the dead one to his follower, Golgren had granted the other a small fraction of a glorious death.

The other procession already forgotten, Golgren looked ahead once more. A structure more imposing than the great towers loomed in front of him. It was said that the palace of Donnag marked the birthplace of the High Ogres. It was twenty times the size of other palaces. The massive square structure appeared part fortress, part temple, with battlements and wide bronze gates. The main tower rose above all other rooftops. The palace looked almost new, but that was because it had recently been repainted and touched up, and now its color was a pristine ivory white. From the high windows hung lavish tapestries depicting tall, blue-skinned figures.

Donnag had begun working on his palace almost immediately after seizing the city some years past. The palace, indeed all of Blöten, was intended as a monument to Donnag's greatness. Now, even though Donnag still nominally ruled, the palace and other official buildings would serve Golgren. Already he had ordered replacement tapestries—large, intricately-sewn pieces glorifying him, not the remote past.

"*Ky i grul*," he commanded.

One of his subordinates raised a goat horn and blew a series of notes. The crowds grew silent. The vast army ground to a halt. Only the Grand Lord and Nagroch, who looked unusually dour, continued riding on.

Tall, massive warriors with breastplates and spiked helms stood guard at the palace. The guards were slimmer, more wary of eye, than most of their ilk. Their armor was polished, their weapons new and sharp. They came to attention with a crispness worthy of Solamnics. As Golgren dismounted, the ranks raised their weapons in salute.

"*Juy i foroon i'Donnagi kyrst, ke?*" muttered Nagroch.

"*Fyan,*" his leader returned indifferently.

At the palace doors—new, high, bronze doors that featured identical tall figures in mirrored poses of godliness—a pair of guards holding the chains of two slavering meredrakes watched respectfully as the newcomers approached. Nagroch, in turn, watched everyone distrustfully, his hand never straying from his weapon. In contrast, Golgren walked blithely along with the confidence of one certain of his safety even in the house of an enemy.

They were met by an ogre who, like Golgren, had filed down his tusks to mere nubs. Although he stood as tall as most others of their race, his figure was far slimmer. His mane was nearly as groomed as the Grand Lord's, and he looked more like an inhabitant of Kern than Blöde.

"*Herak i Jeroch uth Kyr i'Golgreni,*" the servant uttered, bowing his head as he spoke. He launched into a litany of the Grand Lord's titles, but Golgren dismissed the formality with an indifferent wave of his hand. The servant nodded, then gestured straight ahead, to the audience chamber used by Chieftain Donnag. "*Koloth i Donnarin ut.*"

Foregoing a reply, the Grand Lord gazed at the walls of the palace. Unlike so much else, they were conspicuously devoid of ornamentation, although there were marks that hinted of removed decoration. The floor and ceiling both had lines of silver trim.

"*Kojya,*" Golgren finally rsaid. He pointed at a narrow corridor leading to the right past the audience chamber. "*Mera i Daurorin ut.*"

The servant frowned, saying nothing.

Golgren stared hard at the servant, who was much bigger and stronger-looking than the Grand Lord.

The servant looked away first. Bowing his head again, he muttered, "*Mera i Daurorin ut . . . ke.*"

With clear reluctance, the servant guided them down the side corridor. In contrast to the rest of the palace, the path was not well lit and grew darker with each step. The torches appeared to have trouble sustaining any worthwhile flame, almost as though they struggled for air. Nagroch's hand rested on his weapon, but Golgren continued to stroll without the slightest apparent concern. The servant, meanwhile, grew more and more agitated and kept glancing over his shoulder at the Grand Lord.

At last, in the gloom, they came upon a small, bronze door. Before this door stood a brutish guard whose helm covered all but his eyes and mouth. He was twice as wide as most ogres and almost a head taller. Even in the dim light, the protruding veins in his arms and throat were impressive, and his eyes held a malevolent light.

"*Haja,*" began the servant. "*Haja i'Golgreni ot mera i Daurorin ut.*"

The monstrous sentinel remained impassive, save for a slight narrowing of his unsettling orbs.

"*Haja!*" repeated the servant, with more insistence. "*Haja i'Golgreni ot mera i Daurorin ut! Haja!*"

Nagroch let out a low growl and started to draw his weapon. However, just then, Golgren stepped past their guide, gazing solemnly up at the guard. The bestial figure's breathing grew rapid, and at last he shifted aside. Recovering quickly, the servant stepped beyond the Grand Lord and touched a finger to the center of the door.

Of its own accord, the door swung open. Their anxious guide moved to one side, indicating the two should enter without him. Nagroch snorted at the other's faint heart as he followed his master. They had no sooner stepped inside when a voice from the darkness murmured something in a language like pure music. Behind the pair, the door shut. A shadow glided ahead of them, vaguely hinting of tremendous height and perfect grace.

Something near Nagroch's leg hissed. A reptilian form poised on its thin hind legs then snapped at the ogre. Nagroch snarled and kicked at the baraki. The fighting lizard jabbed at him once with its claws then receded into the dark, still spitting.

Again the shadow figure spoke, this time directly to Golgren.

"Jya uf heref," returned the Grand Lord.

In reply, his unseen host answered with more in the same, lyrical tongue, yet despite its beauty, somehow the words and tone also conveyed menace.

"You speak the tongue of the ancients no more than I." Golgren snorted. "If you wish this game to play, we will speak in Common then. Choose."

The other spoke a single word. The chamber grew just bright enough to reveal another ogre, but one not at all like Golgren or Nagroch . . . or most others of their kind, for that matter. This ogre rose high over them, nearly fifteen feet in height. His skin was a brilliant blue, like an azure gem. If Golgren's features hinted at possible elven blood, one could easily have mistaken the other figure for a giant of that race, so handsome was his face. Yet no elf was so perfectly and broadly muscled, none had eyes of pure gold that seemed to glitter from some tremendous force lurking within. Even more telling, there was no delicacy in this face, but rather a smouldering darkness. The smile that greeted the newcomers was tight-lipped, secretive. His garments were richer than any they had seen thus far in Blöde—long, flowing, silken—and enhanced the idea of a being more akin to the gods than ogres.

There was no mistaking that this ogre was one of those depicted on the tapestries outside. The tall blue figure radiated a powerful presence that would have overwhelmed most ogres . . . but not the Grand Lord Golgren or his most trusted officer.

"If that is your desire," the giant acquiesced, even his Common sounding elegant. With long, tapering fingers that ended jarringly in black talons at the tips, the blue one gestured to the door behind the Grand Lord. "We can speak more comfortably in the audience chamber—"

He received a knowing smile from Golgren. "With Donnag, I have no need for speaking. Donnag understands. Donnag knows his place and hopes. It is the other Titans I question. Do they know the lesson of Donnag, who smiles with me, slaps the back, and drinks as blood brother—who in silence curses this one, but still obeys?"

In a telling moment, the Titan's lips parted. Instead of the perfection the rest of his face displayed, he showed two savage rows of teeth better suited for a shark.

"We . . . understand things very well, Grand Lord. The hand of the witch and your own maneuvering force us to understand. There will be no betrayal."

"Even this from Dauroth?"

The Titan looked uneasy. "He is not here now. I would prefer not to answer for him, even in this—"

As he spoke, a mournful groan escaped from the shadows behind him. The blue figure gestured. His hand briefly flared orange. The groan immediately subsided.

"Many elves there are in Ambeon," Golgren remarked, purposely using the minotaur name to add to the value of his point. "Few and fewer in Blöde, yes? Dauroth searches even now, but fruitlessly." He studied the subtle shifts in the Titan's expression. "Oh, yes . . . all is known. Dauroth comes empty-handed. Where once could be found many healthy, hardy elves, even one is harder and harder to find now."

The Titan said nothing, though he bared his teeth. His hands trembled slightly, a sign of his pent-up rage.

"Not only elves, but certain plants, herbs . . . items. Very hard to gather all that is needed . . . especially in time . . ."

Clearly straining to keep control over himself, the giant

reluctantly went down on one knee. "He only sought our survival! We will not strive against you, Guyvir."

He had said the wrong thing. Golgren's eyes almost burned. He eyed the kneeling figure with such vehemence that even the Titan edged back in fear. "There is no Guyvir!"

The Grand Lord snapped his fingers and pointed in the direction of the moan. With sudden animation, Nagroch eagerly seized a dagger from his belt. He vanished into the dark, and a voice clearly elven began babbling fearfully. The Titan immediately started to rise, but Golgren's furious gaze lowered him back to his knees.

"This was Dauroth's doing, not mine! I have been obedient!"

"This is not for Dauroth's folly," the Grand Lord stated blandly. "This is to remind. I am Golgren . . . Golgren . . ."

In the shadows, there was a brief gasp and the mournful elven voice was cut off. Seconds later, the brutish Nagroch reappeared. He wiped blood off his blade with a piece of soiled, green cloth of elven make. With an evil grin at the Grand Lord, he thrust the dagger back into his belt.

"The elixir was not finished!" the kneeling figure whined, almost rising.

Golgren's gaze, however, kept him at bay.

"Something to remember."

"Where will I find another?"

Golgren smiled, showing his own predatory teeth. "Ask Dauroth."

"But—"

"No more warning. All will obey or all will suffer."

The Titan's head slumped forward in defeat. He said nothing.

His smile still in place, the Grand Lord walked serenely out of the chamber. The massive guard crouched low against the corridor wall as Golgren passed. Beyond the brutish sentinel, the servant waited expectantly.

"*Kyi ut i'Donnagi?*"

Golgren ignored him. There would be no need to see Donnag. To ensure his own survival, the Lord Chieftain would see to it that none of the Titans attempted any trickery while Golgren was away. As for Dauroth, the lesson the Grand Lord had taught his underling would remind the Titans' leader sufficiently of his proper place. There could be only one power among the ogres, and that was Golgren.

"*Nya i f'han i'Titani,*" muttered Nagroch with narrowed eyes as they descended the palace steps outside. He patted the dagger at his waist.

Golgren replied with a small shake of his head. There was a time when enemies had to be removed and times when they simply had to be kept on reins. The Grand Lord had many plans for the future, and even the Titans might play a role. They would serve him well if they wished to keep their pretty faces and magic powers.

If they did not . . . he would deprive them of their precious elixir—and watch them wither away, until they begged him to slay them.

Chapter XIII

SPECTER OF THE STORM

It took some maneuvering of cargo and space, but they managed to get everyone aboard. Quarters were cramped, though, and after waiting another day to see if any other ships were coming, it was decided they had to leave or risk discovery.

"We head northeast," grunted Captain Tinza. "If any of the others plan to join us, they'll have gone to the safe point beyond Karthay, to prepare for the journey across the Courrain."

Setting such a course meant many days sailing in the opposite direction from the capital, though Mithos and Kothas lay so tantalizingly close.

Captain Botanos read Faros's flashing eyes. "If we sail into enemy waters in such a cramped fashion, we'll be more danger to ourselves than any Imperial force. We need more ships."

Faros reluctantly nodded. "Get us there as soon as possible," he commanded Botanos.

"Consider us already underway, my lord."

The rebel ships left Kern's shore under cover of night. Imperial warships still patrolled the waters, and the rebels could not afford to spend much time fleeing from or engaging the enemy. Thundering clouds accented their departure, and the weather only grew worse as they headed toward Karthay. Barely two days into the voyage, the heavens unleashed their fury. Lightning raked the sea and waves grew as tall as the masts. Winds roared, seeming to blow unwary mariners overboard and fill the sails so they tore, yet the rebels pushed on, for they had no choice.

The weather made it impossible for Faros to sleep, for each heavy rumble or unusual bolt of lightning made him wonder if they were once again being stalked by the temple's dark magic. He tossed and turned in the cot attached to one wall of his cabin, then, when sleep failed, made futile attempts at whittling—a traditional pastime for minotaurs at sea. However, it was not long before he threw the dagger and stick of driftwood to the side, and securing his sheathed sword, he burst from his cabin onto the main deck to see firsthand what was happening.

The crew was working hard to keep the *Dragon's Crest* on course. Shouts from the first mate to a pair of hands trying to control the mainsail greeted the rebel leader. Faros, however, barely glanced at their hard toil, his mind on his own matters.

He found a place of seclusion near the portside. Standing at the rail, the spray soaking his fur, Faros eyed the storm. There was nothing to mark the shifting clouds as anything but normal. If the high priestess was behind this weather, he could not tell.

On impulse, Faros drew his sword, studying the jewel in the hilt. The enchanted sword was, in its own way, more mysterious than his magic ring. It seemed to pulse with a life of its own. However, he admitted, with the exception of the Magori attack—which was illusion after all—the sword had served him well.

An immense exhaustion filled him. He had not asked for the destiny that was being thrust upon him. If it could have been avoided, he would have done so. Faros was aware of the looks and whispers of those around him. These rebels followed him, yes, but some likely questioned his sanity, his often cruel decisions.

He glared at the enchanted sword. Over the crashing waves and howling winds, Faros shouted, "Are you listening, Sargonnas? I'd gladly give this sword and all else up to another if I could . . . I'd gladly be rid of it all for some peace of mind . . ."

Peace . . . The word resounded within him. *Escape and peace.*

There is always the sea, a voice in his head murmured. *The sea of the ancestors of all minotaurs. How many of your brethren have found peace in the sea? How many have nestled in its soft depths? How many have escaped to its eternal peace?*

Watching the evening waves lapping against the *Crest's* hull, Faros saw them as soft, inviting blankets. The soothing darkness of the waters called to him. His slumber was always haunted by nightmares; how good it would be to finally sleep soundly. Almost as though hypnotized, he clamped his free hand on the rail then put one foot up on the lower edge. The ship rocked, tossing him forward. He would have slipped over the rail, but the sword twisted, catching its point in the wood and propping him up.

There are no enemies in the ocean, only the sweet bliss of oblivion . . .

Faros peered into the water, seeing the faces of family and friends lost to him, beckoning.

Toss the sword over, then follow . . .

Just then, lightning flashed. The gem in the hilt reflected that light into his eyes, making him blink.

Faros's brow furrowed. He thought he felt something nudge him from behind, something evil.

The minotaur summoned all his will, and steeled himself. The urge to leap into the sea faded, replaced by fresh determination. With a savage growl, Faros spun about, slashing with his blade. Then he heard an inhuman cry that pierced his very soul.

A macabre figure flashed across his vision. Under a thick hood draped over thrusting horns, a decaying muzzle and blazing orbs met Faros's gaze. Tatters of clothing hung over a body ripped open so completely that the innards looked as though ready to pour free. A stench emanated from the monstrous specter.

His blade had not cut the ghost, but it had sliced at the voluminous cloak that surrounded him like a protective kraken. The folds and corners of the cloak fluttered like tentacles, as though eager to seize and choke the mortal. One ghastly fragment lay limp, though, the end of it sheared off where Faros had struck.

Rising up as if borne on the wind, the sinister phantasm loomed grandly over the rebel. The fold of cloak that Faros had severed repaired itself then joined in reaching for him.

"Keep back!" Faros roared, "or see if the dead can die again!"

One fold of the cloak darted to the side. It touched a set of barrels secured by strong rope against the whims of the sea. Like a serpent uncoiling, the knot undid itself. The barrels bounced toward Faros.

He leapt out of the way of the first one, but the second caught him in the leg, knocking him over. A third and fourth barrel rammed into him, momentarily pinning the rebel leader. Faros almost lost his sword. Gasping, he shoved away the heavy containers and rose just in time to avoid the last one hurtling at him.

Toward the stern, shouts arose. The ghost glanced at the ruined rope. Suddenly the rope whirled itself at the minotaur, snaking around his legs and sword arm and quickly constricting his movements. Faros chopped away at the animated rope. His blade cut through it easily, leaving small pieces that wriggled around the deck.

A crackle of thunder so close that it shook the *Dragon's Crest* jolted the minotaur. He looked up just in time to see a bolt of green lightning strike the rigging above. Flames spread over the sail and much of the rigging rained down upon him. Faros tried to dodge, but the rigging dropped on the minotaur. His sword tumbled away. As Faros reached for the weapon, the cloak of his horrific foe stretched to enshroud him.

The *Dragon's Crest*, the sea—everything—disappeared.

Faros floated in a smothering blackness. He waved his limbs but found no hold nor footing. The trapped rebel strained to breathe. Although his lungs filled with air, not water, he still felt as though he were suffocating. Voices assailed him. They pleaded for mercy, pleaded for rescue. Faros felt desperate fingers grab at him, but he saw no one, nothing. Something seized his arms and legs, pulling his limbs tight, tighter. He felt his muscles and tendons stretch to their limits.

You are mine now, the ghost's voice mocked. *First you shall die and then afterwards you shall truly be punished . . .*

Blood-chilling laughter overwhelmed the pleading voices. Fighting whatever bound him, Faros clutched at his own throat. He couldn't breathe!

Where was Sargonnas now? Certainly he wasn't waiting for Faros to call out! Only a god could aid him in this infernal netherworld. Then, in the midst of the darkness, a brief glimmer of red, like a tiny spark of flame, caught his attention. It took him a moment to realize that it emanated from his hand.

The ring.

Sure enough, a deep, red fire emanated from within the black gem. Faros focused on the stone, trying to summon its power. He concentrated his willpower on it, each breath feeling like his last.

The spark grew stronger. Then a crimson flame erupted from the ring. The flame ate away at the emptiness. Its terrible light drove back the suffocating blackness. The tentacles of darkness retreated from Faros, who could suddenly breathe.

Vertigo shook him. His feet landed on a hard surface. Once more, he found himself standing aboard the deck of the *Dragon's Crest*. Around him, sailors were frantically trying to put out the fire and restore the ship to order.

One crew member nearly collided with him, then stared in shock. "My lord! Where did—"

Something rolled across the deck, rattling to a halt near the rebel leader's feet. Faros's sword. As he bent to retrieve it, he heard Captain Botanos's baritone voice nearby giving orders. Faros looked up just as Botanos turned his way. Like the sailor, the captain looked at Faros as though he saw a ghost.

"Where by the Sea Queen did you come from all of a sudden? Faros, you shouldn't be out here in this!"

Storms and fires did not concern the younger minotaur at the moment. Nostrils flaring, he glanced anxiously among the figures racing around. "Where is it? Where did it go?"

"Where did what go?"

"The ghost! That thing with the cloak that moved like it was alive! Where'd that demon go?"

Botanos spun around as if expecting to confront the nightmarish monster. "But . . . I see nothing!"

Neither did Faros. He cursed.

Botanos came over to him. Lowering his voice, the mariner asked, "What happened?"

Faros told him, leaving nothing out. When he had finished, it was the captain's turn to swear. He quickly surveyed the area again, but the menace was clearly gone . . . at least for now.

"We must get you below!" Botanos insisted. "Put a guard around you day and night! I'll have the hold searched! He could be down there even now—"

"It—Never mind, Captain. He comes and goes at will and is already far from here. I can't say how I know—" The ring felt cool on his finger now. "—but he is gone." Faros grunted. "Time is running out for us. They're getting bolder."

"What do you mean?"

The rebel leader thrust the ring up for the heavyset minotaur to inspect. "This was once worn by General Rahm Es-Hestos."

"Aye, I wondered. It looked just like it—but no! That ring burned with his body—"

"Afterward it came straight to me." Faros sheathed his sword, then lowered the ring. "From what I've heard, it seemed that the general was brilliant at eluding the temple."

"He was that."

"For awhile, even I couldn't be noticed by them—or else, I think, they would've hunted me down before this."

Captain Botanos's frown indicated that he understood. "The Lady of the Lists," Botanos began, referring to Nephera by one of the lesser epithets the rebels had given her. "Perhaps she just got lucky a couple of times."

"Or her powers are growing . . ." Faros hesitated, then finished, "and even Sargonnas is intimidated."

"That's not possible!" the mariner nearly bellowed. "There's no force stronger than the Horned One! He—"

"Quiet!" The former slave looked past his companion. None of the sailors, it appeared, had heard Botanos's outburst. "Keep your voice down! I don't want to spread panic!"

Much more subdued, the captain murmured, "How can we hope to defeat such evil as the empire and the power of the temple?"

"How, I don't just know," Faros finally answered, after a long pause. He glanced out to sea. "We'll fight our best . . . because even if Sargonnas fails us, we really don't have any other choice."

As her servants removed the body, the high priestess bathed her hands in the bronze bowl next to the larger brass one. It took more scrubbing than the previous ritual, which had taken more than the time prior to that one. The crimson stains refused to completely wash out of her fur, regardless of what soap or other cleaning substance Nephera utilized. She could have worn gloves, but that she considered an affront to her god.

Nephera had dismissed all, even the ghosts, desiring the utmost privacy, but suddenly she could not help the feeling she was being watched. The high priestess glanced over her shoulder, but no one-eyed specter drifted there, his lone orb condemning. She returned to the frustrating task of cleansing her hands. The stains had to come out! Nephera scrubbed hard, scraping away fur and flesh, but the stains themselves never seemed to diminish.

Again, the sense that she was being watched burned into the high priestess's consciousness. Nephera spun about, water splashing all around. The armored figure stood nearly muzzle-to-muzzle with her.

"Away, damn you!" she blurted, not caring how high and shrill her voice had grown. "Away!"

She thrust a hand through the silent shade, which vanished the instant her fingers reached him. The robed minotaur swore then turned in a circle to make certain the figure had not materialized elsewhere.

"I did what had to be done . . ." Nephera muttered to the emptiness. "No matter what the cost."

There was no reply. She expected none. Her husband's shadow never spoke; Hotak never did anything but stare. Nephera spun back to the bowl, back to washing her hands of the blood. Attempting to put her mind at ease, the high priestess reviewed the tasks ahead. She had prepared a proclamation for Ardnor to announce: a new holiday to be celebrated throughout the empire. Galh'Hawan—The Day of the Risen—would be explained as a way of honoring the spirits who guided the living. Not coincidentally, the night following the proclamation would be when the constellation of Morgion fell into perfect alignment.

A pain-wracked voice filled her head. Nephera put a bitter end to her cleansing and seized the sheepskin cloth next to the bowl.

Mistress . . . came the voice. *Mistress—I return.*

She looked to her right, where what materialized at first seemed a mound of rotting rags. Nephera raised an eyebrow; she had recognized the voice of Takyr, but never had she seen him so weakened. Whatever the shade's state, she had to know immediately.

"Is he dead or alive?"

The ghost kept his head bowed. *Alive . . . alive . . .*

"And yet . . . you still exist."

Forgive me . . . mistress . . .

Though she was stunned by this failure, she kept her face impassive. The high priestess dried her hands with the cloth, rubbing the stains vigorously but still to no avail. "It is of no consequence." Her unblinking eyes looked momentarily to where the silver Forerunner symbols hung high. "Tell me this: Does he, as I suspected, bear gifts of the Condor Lord?"

Two . . . mistress. A sword . . . and a . . . and a ring with a stone of black that spits fire . . . This last was said with some venom, a clear sign the ring had caused ghost's disheveled state.

"A sword," she whispered. "Could it be—?" Nephera eyed the fallen ghost. "A ring, you say? With a black gem?"

Aye . . .

She had heard vague descriptions of just such an odd piece of jewelry worn by General Rahm. Ardnor insisted Rahm had used a magic ring to cause Kolot's death. A light had shone from the ring, blinding her youngest son long enough for Rahm to slay him.

Now Faros Es-Kalin wore the very same artifact.

Nephera brooded. Such weaponry, such magic, could spell disaster for her . . . for her lord's goals, yet even with these magical aids, Takyr had found him once and he could find him again. Perhaps Sargas had given him these trinkets then chose to leave him to his own devices. She chuckled, a sound that made Takyr prostate himself lower yet.

"Excellent!" Nephera abruptly shouted to the ceiling. "You hear, my beloved lord? You see the weakness?"

The high priestess laughed merrier yet. Her earlier distresses faded away. She gazed down upon her servant, who, seeing her fierce expression, recoiled in expectation of punishment.

"Rise up and have no fear, Takyr! You bring me good tidings after all! Do you not see? The gifts of his god do the son of Kalin little good any more! Sargas clearly lacks the strength to protect his chosen! Soon, very soon, Faros will fall—either to my spells or to the combined military efforts of my daughter and Golgren! One way or another, he must, he will fall!" Lady Nephera gazed up at the ceiling again. "And soon after, my dear lord . . . soon after, so too will his god!"

CHAPTER XIV

DEATH AT SEA

The inhabitants of Ardnoranti—the name still stuck in Maritia's craw for some reason—watched solemnly as the selected legions marched out through the eastern gates. General Kalel of the Direhounds, a tall, slim minotaur with a down-turned muzzle, saluted Maritia sharply as he passed with his crack troops. She returned his salute, hiding her frustration that it was the Direhounds, not Kolina's Crystal Legion, that departed the capital. Pryas had invoked Ardnor's name to keep Kolina near. He seemed to think he was the temporary commander of all Ambeon.

She could not permit Pryas to supersede her authority. The Protector's demands put a strain on everyone. Many projects had ground to a halt so he could focus time and resources on his infernal temple. The master plan Maritia was following had to be postponed, thanks to Pryas's obsessive allegiance to his faith.

Maritia herself could have stayed behind, could have chosen Kalel to command the pursuit of Faros, but her own urge to lead the hunt was strong. She was impatient to catch the rebel leader, the one she now knew was responsible for Bastion's murder. She could scarcely wait to present his horns to Ardnor.

"My Lady Maritia," said a somewhat nasal voice behind her.

She glanced over her shoulder to see the burly General Bakkor, commander of the Wyverns, who had ridden up to join her. He studied the Direhounds as they passed, before continuing.

"Your note—brought so interestingly to me—said you wished a few last words."

A treverian from the Direhounds shouted out to his troops. Immediately the legionaries turned their heads and saluted Maritia as they marched along. Her legions would journey to the small ports on the eastern shores of Ambeon, where warships from Sargonath waited for them. At her request, Maritia's flagship would be the *Stormbringer*, once Bastion's own vessel.

"I hope you're still not upset at being left here to monitor things, general," Maritia murmured as she nodded to the ranks.

"I question not the orders of my superiors."

Despite everything, she almost smiled. "You should. My father did."

"Aye, my lady."

"I want you to know that I've sent a message by bird to my brother, to encourage him to increase your authority over the Protector while I'm gone." Pryas thought he would be sharing command with Bakkor. However, the emperor's sister did not trust the Protector while she was gone. Pryas was too ambitious.

"May the emperor see your wisdom," the officer murmured.

Glancing around, Maritia said, "General Bakkor, you will be in charge while I'm away, and I trust you completely. However, I have one request for you, one that should remain between us, if I may."

"You are my commander, Lady Maritia. Your will is mine."

"I appreciate that, Bakkor, but hear me out first. Pryas is very eager to impress his master." From the officer she received only a noncommittal grunt. "I ask you to do nothing beyond your normal duties, general . . . but at the same time keep an eye on him if you would. See he doesn't overstep the bounds we have agreed to."

Bakkor, his eyes following the departing legionaries, responded, "He always tests the bounds, Lady."

Maritia nodded grimly. The last of the Direhounds passed by. She scanned the crowd, eyeing Pryas atop his mount, watching the departure. His black helm obscured his gaze from Maritia's eyes. General Kolina sat next to him, with a more telling look. She seemed to mentally urge the legionaries out the gates.

A regiment of Protectors stood around the pair, as still as statues, their maces held before their chests, their eyes staring straight ahead, never blinking. They even appeared to breathe in unison.

Maritia suppressed a shudder. "I'll be back as soon as I can, Bakkor."

He bowed his head. "May you have good hunting, my lady."

All worry about Pryas and Protectors vanished as Maritia grimly turned her thoughts to the quest. Eyes narrowed in prospect, she answered, "Oh, I will, general . . . you may count on that."

With her bodyguards surrounding her, she rode off to join her own legion, which marched far ahead of the column. She had already forgotten Pryas. Nothing would distract her from Faros Es-Kalin.

She hoped Golgren would be ready. They had traded messages concerning their preparations, and he had promised to meet her at the appointed rendezvous. Maritia would need the help of the ogres to make certain the rebels did not escape this time. Trapped between her forces and one commanded by the Grand Lord, they would be cut down one, until she faced Faros himself.

There were risks, of course. Golgren might consider going after Faros himself, for his own glory. For the honor of the empire and her brother, though, Maritia would make sure that didn't happen. Surely, in the end, the ogre would see reason.

Faros was her enemy above all. He had slain her brother.

The vast smithy radiated a heat akin to standing atop one of the great volcanic craters of Argon's chain. More than two hundred skilled crafters toiled day and night for the glory of the emperor. Sweat matting their fur, their breathing labored, the minotaurs hammered, pumped bellows at gargantuan forges, and expertly manipulated molten metal into molds.

Ardnor watched as one apprentice held a hot, metal plate with long tongs out toward a vat of water. A searing hiss and spouts of steam marked the plate's descent into the vat.

Shadows created by the many furnaces danced on the walls of the huge, stone building. There were windows up by the base of the ceiling, but merely for ventilation; they allowed in no light. The fiery glow from the furnaces provided the only illumination of the blood-red tableau.

Sulfur from the coal tainted the air, but at least it smothered the odor of sweat. Ardnor found the acrid scent as pleasantly aromatic as his father had the lavender perfume of his mother.

Over to the side, one of the smiths raised high a finished product. The black breastplate bore the broken axe symbol. The smith turned the breastplate over to an apprentice, who respectfully hung it next to another plate, which hung next to another. Ardnor chuckled as he inspected the endless rows of breastplates, helmets, maces, and more. Each already had a wearer waiting, one of the many ready to do the emperor's bidding, but even working in continuous shifts day and night, the smiths could not keep up with the demands of the empire. The master smith, who had accompanied him for this inspection, waited for Ardnor's comments.

Nephera's son hid his approval, instead saying, "The pace must be increased."

Dipping his horns, the smith said reluctantly, "I'll have to borrow workers from those who regularly supply the legions."

"Then do it."

A figure already clad in armor materialized in the midst of the smoke-filled chamber, helmed eyes searching. He spotted the emperor and hurried over. Another messenger. It must be important for the officer to search for Ardnor here.

"From Ambeon, my lord," coughed the warrior. The smoke had thickened.

Stepping to the side, Ardnor studied the missive. When he saw his sister's mark, he grunted with disapproval. Unscrolling the parchment, the emperor quickly skipped over the imperial salutations and read:

My brother, by now I know the news has reached you of the true death of Bastion, whom we thought lost at sea. Slain most cowardly by the rebel Faros near the border of Kern and Ambeon. I have chosen to lead the legions in pursuit of him, coordinating with the Grand Lord Golgren . . .

She then went into some details of her plan, which Ardnor skipped.

In my place, I've appointed General Bakkor to govern alongside your Pryas. However, I respectfully ask, for the sake of stability, that the general be granted full command. He is more familiar with the activities and layout of the colony and was instrumental in setting up the vital supply distribution network. I request you send word as soon as possible making this so—

The emperor read no further. He crushed the note, stuffing in in a belt pouch.

"You!" he demanded of the courier. "I sent off a message directed to Protector General Pryas some days ago! It went on its way?"

"Aye, my lord! It should've been in his hands long ago!"

"I thought so . . ." Ardnor rubbed the underside of his muzzle, trying to hide his frustration. "Come with me! "I've two messages to send!"

"To the Protector General?" the officer asked, trying to keep up with the emperor's long strides.

"To him," muttered Ardnor, trying to think, "and to another . . ."

The tiny island north of Karthay was a miserable, wind-blown place covered in twisted trees with needles instead of leaves, and bushes that cringed close to the ground. There was fresh water from two springs and a creek, but the only food and supplies were those abandoned by prior ships. Stored in cold, underground caves, the dried, salted fruit and jerky were edible but unappetizing.

Eight ships awaited them. Four more arrived the next day. At Faros's behest, the leaders of the various rebel factions met in the largest of the caves. The low ceiling forced the tall minotaurs to duck and stoop, but once seated, they were relatively comfortable.

Squatting on a rock, Faros surveyed the group. Botanos represented those already loyal to him and sat to the left of Chot's nephew. On Faros's right sat Captain Tinza, with the marine officer Napol next to her. They could likely be counted on, although the former Imperials eyed him a bit warily.

Some of the other two dozen or so figures he knew only by sight or reputation, and not a few he was meeting for the first time. They could be lumped into three parties. One consisted of those from the outer colonies whose freedom had been squashed under the iron hand of the throne. Several had their fur trimmed short and sported tattoos. The second category were former members of once-prominent clans whose holdings had been expropriated. They still dressed like the wealthy merchants they had been, and despite the loss of their clans, they still boasted prestige and power. They were among the most reluctant of the factions who had come, at Faros's summons, to Karthay.

The third group was the most unpredictable. These minotaurs were more on the fringes of the empire than even the escaped slaves. 'Brigands' and 'pirates' were the terms most aptly applied to this bunch and not simply because they attacked ships of other races. They freely committed all kinds of crimes, yet they could contribute to the rebellion too. Surveying the assembly, Faros saw that everyone there wore the same hardened face. They had all come too far to turn back; it was either attack and defeat the throne or go on the way they had been going on – eventually to die at the hands of the empire. None trusted the other, however. No one could unite and lead them.

"You all know who I am," he began.

"We wouldn't be here if we didn't," one of the tattooed figures declared.

Faros nodded. "First, I'll tell you that if you're looking for another Chot, you should leave. I'm not my uncle."

"A good thing," interjected a female privateer wearing an eye patch and with one ear missing. "We'd all be sailing with Nolhan if you were."

That surprised him. The former adjutant to the late Councilor Turibus, once head of the Supreme Circle, Nolhan had grandiose ambitions. There were rumors Nolhan was Turibus's bastard son. He was Faros's only real rival among the rebels and was absent from this parley. Nolhan had sent with one of the ships a note saying he refused to recognize Chot's nephew. According to Captain Tinza, Nolhan was leading a number of rebel ships into the empire along its southeastern edge. That meant passing near Thuum, where the Eastern Fleet often anchored for restocking.

It was evident what the former adjutant intended. Nolhan planned to surprise the Eastern Fleet. Attacking the Eastern

Fleet would spread his name throughout the realm. Warriors would flock to his banner. Even some of Faros's own followers might be tempted to defect to such a daring leader.

Tinza explained, "With your pardon, my lord, Chot was no treasure, though he had our sworn loyalty."

"Speak for yourself!" growled the female privateer.

Tinza ignored her. "Hotak could've had a number of us on his side, if he'd done matters differently. In his own way, though, he was as arrogant as your uncle. The Night of Blood and what followed proved that. Now, though, 'tis even worse than when Chot ruled. Ardnor de-Droka and the Lady Nephera have assumed the power of Hotak but surely not his sense of honor. The Protectors and the temple will ruin the empire in the end, mark me."

"Jubal was right when he thought you being Chot's nephew could draw us together," added Botanos. "That is because we understand vengeance, but that's where any tie to Chot leaves off being any use. It's not who your uncle was; it's what we've heard from those who follow you—the things you've survived, the deeds you've done. You're Tremoc crossing Ansalon four times to avenge his mate. You're Makel, cutting a bloody swathe through the ogre realms. You're Mitos, outwitting a far superior foe."

"You've got an aptitude for . . . well, survival," grudgingly added the lead merchant, a grizzled but well-muscled figure in flowing sea-green robes.

The other privateers said nothing, their leader folding her arms and watching Faros intently.

"Hotak claimed he could restore the empire to its glory of old," the captain of the *Dragon's Crest* went on. "He turned out a fool, but we think you can actually do it, my lord."

"Not all of us think that," another merchant interjected. Next to him some of the pirates nodded.

"Droka's hereditary throne. We don't want that, Kalin," a tall, tattooed outlander growled. In addition to small, gold rings in his right ear, he wore one huge ring through his nostrils. "Not if it means the likes of Ardnor ruling."

Faros eyed the parties most resistant to his authority. "If I win this for us, should I expect a challenge the next day?"

Botanos stared at the rebel leaders, daring anyone to speak. When none did, he shook his head and answered for them. "Nay, not you, Faros . . . but if your sons and daughters wish the throne, they'll have to contest for it like any other good minotaur."

Again the others agreed. Faros grunted. He had no children and did not believe he ever would. He would die first, so the point was moot. "Then it's time we spoke of what we need to do."

"Is it safe?" asked Tinza. "Is it safe to conspire here, with the Lady of the Lists no doubt listening to us even now?"

"Kern's parched ground is covered with the bones of ogres and Protectors who knew exactly where I was and what I was trying to do." His bold words met with approval from most of the rebel representations, but the merchants looked uncertain.

"Not so fast, we've not agreed that we'll follow you," one of the merchants pointed out. His gaze swept over the others. "What stands before us is an ex-slave without a bloodline that matters any more, a minotaur without land, status, or reputation—"

"Oh, I think he's got reputation," put in Napol, "and the ability that goes with his reputation. You all know that."

"We are aware where you stand, Napol. What is unclear is whether the rest of us share your view."

"Then let me hear bluntly," Faros demanded, eyeing the leaders. He stared at the privateers. "What say you?"

The one-eyed female grunted, then glanced back at her companions. "Dagger up or down?"

"Up," rumbled one.

"Down," another.

Two more declared "up," another called "down." Another "down" followed.

Botanos leaned close to Faros, whispering, "A dagger up means you'll fight for someone. Turning it down means you stand against them. An old voting ritual of mariners. I'd forgotten it."

One brigand muttered, "Mine stays sheathed."

To Faros's curious glance, the captain added, "Means he's abstaining."

One more brigand chose "down," but then the next five declared up.

"There 'tis," the female declared. She slapped her fist against her chest. "Majority rules. We always act together, as one. We're yours, Lord Faros!"

The merchant leader sniffed.

"What of you?" asked Tinza of the sniffing merchant.

"We wait and see."

That left the outer islanders. Unlike the privateers, they did not hesitate. "You are marked. The condor guards your back. We have not forgotten our place with him, so we will follow you."

At this, the leader of the clan merchants abruptly added, "As do we, of course!"

The female pirate sniggered, but Faros pretended to pay no attention to the sudden change of mind. He glanced around at the few independent captains and saw they were leaning with the majority.

"It's decided, you're our leader," Captain Botanos declared with satisfaction, "not that any sane warrior could've argued otherwise!"

A few of the brigands and islanders scoffed at the merchants, who feigned ignorance.

Captain Botanos looked up at Faros. "Command us now! What would you have us do?"

"First, is this all there will be? Are the ships that surround this miserable place all we can trust to?"

"There's some others," rumbled a broad-shouldered figure among the independents. He had a gleaming, almost mirror-like axe slung on his back. "They're still hesitating. They think Nolhan might still manage a miracle."

Faros looked to Botanos and Tinza. "Can he?"

"He has the heart," answered the former Fleet officer, "but I don't think so." She shook her head. "No, I don't think he can."

"Then we make do with what we have," Faros decided, "because we set sail tomorrow."

"Tomorrow?" blurted Napol, with others muttering their surprise at Faros's urgency.

"Most of the imperium's forces are either in the Courrain or on Ambeon. If we sail as swiftly as possible, we can catch them before they're fully organized." He unfurled a massive map showing the Blood Sea and the edges of the Courrain. In the center were the twin islands, Mithas and Kothas and to their east, Mito and other islands.

Faros used his finger to circle the main pair, then Mito. "We need to attack all three, almost simultaneously. Toroth once said it," he added, referring to the emperor who had initiated the greatest expansion of the realm. " 'Who holds the heart of the empire holds its soul.' Take these three swiftly and any who wish Droka gone will seize their chance. You all know our people. It will happen."

Eyes were wide among the rebel leaders, astonished at Faros's boldness.

"The majority of the empire's soldiers might be spread east and west of the heart of the main islands," argued the minotaur with the axe, "but Protectors are settled in on every island."

"Enough to keep all the inhabitants in check, if they are heartened by a rebellion against the evil throne, that might succeed?"

Several looked around, slowly nodding. There were many Protectors, many Forerunner faithful . . . but most minotaurs belonged to neither group. Everyone knew that discontent was rife in the realm. The strategy would be bloody, but it was possible.

"What of the temple?" asked Napol. "What about what your message said, the powers of Morgion, the dread one?"

"That stinking cadaver will learn he can't pirate in the Condor Lord's waters!" the one-eyed female declared passionately. "Sargas will use him for bait for hunting krakens—if even they are attracted by such putrid fare."

This brought confident laughter all around. Faros himself said nothing about Sargonnas. He didn't think Sargonnas watched over him or them, and it was up to the rebels to make their own destiny.

Seeing they were with him, Faros outlined his plan. He spoke in great detail, even though he was acutely aware a ghostly spy might be peering over his shoulders, recording all for the sake of Lady Nephera. Faros, though, no longer cared. Let her report to Ardnor. Let him send every warrior at his disposal, let the high priestess exhaust her dark spells. If the rebellion was meant to fail, better it lose a great battle than fade away shamefully.

Hours passed before they were finished with the plans. Faros listened to suggestions from each captain and incoporated those that seemed sound. He had seen too many deaths of comrades not to heed valuable advice, though he always reserved the final decision.

At last, the gathering broke up. The factions returned to spread word to their comrades. Faros sat staring at the map by the light of the fire. Soon, only Botanos was there to keep him company.

"Should we head back to the ship?" asked the captain.

"Finish what you need to do, then come for me. I want to be alone and think."

"As you say." Grunting, the heavyset minotaur wended his way out of the cave.

Staring at the map, Faros's eyes wandered toward Ansalon, and he thought of the Grand Lord Golgren and Lady Maritia. One day he would reckon with them both. His eyes strayed far to the east. Faros almost imagined the ships there, where the rebels of Nolhan and the might of the Eastern Fleet were locked in mortal combat. A victory by Nolhan, however much it might complicate the leadership of the rebellion, would invaluably boost Faros's cause. If he only knew what was happening—

The truth can be known.

Faros looked around, certain one of Nephera's ghosts had caught up to him again. However, no shadowy specter was visible.

You have but to wield me . . .

He looked down at the sword.

Draw me, use me . . . I can show you the truth . . .

With some misgiving, the former slave drew his dark blade. The weapon slipped from its sheath with a mournful scraping.

The battle, you would see . . . the fate of your rival, you would see . . .

He stared at the sword, Sargonnas's sword. "Nolhan? You can show me what's happening to Nolhan?"

What is happening has happened. What happened cannot be changed.

Faros frowned.

"Show me, then."

His arm lifted—the sword rose—and cut a huge circle before him. The very air seemed to quiver. Through a shimmer, Faros suddenly heard thunder, shouting, and the clash of arms. He leaned forward . . . and without warning the hole enveloped him.

Storm clouds rumbled overhead and lightning flashed. Faros's footing shifted. He found himself standing on the deck of a ship in flame. Minotaurs were running around everywhere, some trying to douse the flames, others grabbing weapons. There were ships all around the one he was on. Some floated singly, others were packed together. Many were either on fire or in the midst of sinking.

"They're coming alongside!" roared someone. "Prepare to repel!"

Wooden hulls groaned as they collided. An imperial warship was alongside. Marine fighters waved swords and axes. Grapplers swung hooks onto Faros's ship, sealing the two vessels together. A flight of arrows hissed through the air, striking more than a dozen attackers. The rebel arrows were answered by twice that number from the Imperial. Screams erupted from all over the deck. A sailor, his left eye pierced by bolts, crumpled at Faros's feet.

"Look out!" someone called.

The warning was punctuated by a massive crash near the bow. Huge javelins from the Imperial's ballistae had crushed in the hull, shattering part of the deck.

"To the rail!" Faros suddenly felt compelled to cry. "Meet them at the rail! Don't let them get a foothold!"

As every available hand ran to obey, Faros started after them. He realized that he was acting through the body and seeing through the eyes of another person, most likely the captain. More than two dozen hooks now secured the ships together. A few fell prey to quick axe chops by the defenders, but archers and marine fighters with long pikes forced the rebels back.

Aboard the warship, a horn blew. With a collective roar, the marine fighters leapt over. The first several died quickly. Two fell between the vessels and were crushed as the pitching of the sea pushed the hulls together.

"Hold them!" Faros shouted.

A half dozen archers fired. Three bolts caught marine fighters on the rail, but the long pikes kept the defenders at bay, enabling a small group of the enemy to gain a hold near the center. The marine fighters pushed forward. Many were killed, but the rebels also paid. Axes clashed against axes. Swords bit through flesh and bone. One rebel was lifted high by a pike buried in his rib cage.

"The mast is falling!" a voice to Faros's right called.

Burning rigging collapsed onto the deck. The foremost mast came crashing down, breaking through the wooden deck. Faros stumbled back, sliding against the half-buried mast. A sharp pain went through his left shoulder. A huge, jagged splinter from the broken mast stuck out of his flesh. Blood stained his fur, which he saw for the first time was gray brown, or silver and—

Silver brown.

Nolhan. Faros was experiencing the disaster through Nolhan.

A stocky figure bent down before him. "There's a long boat prepared for ye! We need to get ye aboard!"

"Where's the captain?" Faros heard himself gasp.

"Dead when the ballista opened fire—my lord, your wound! By Zeboim's Cradle!"

Faros heard himself shouting in what he now recognized was Nolhan's voice: "Help me bind it, then take anyone you can and get away! I'll have the line hold as long as it can to give you time!"

"Ye can't stay!"

The Faros who was also Nolhan seized the stocky minotaur by the fur below his throat. "Do as I say! Get to—"

He suddenly shoved the other minotaur aside as a snarling marine fighter descended upon them. Faros twisted, avoiding the axe, but winced from the pain. With a shout, the figure who had come to Nolhan's assistance barreled into the marine fighter. They struggled over control of the weapon. Faros/Nolhan rose, thrusting with his sword, but the two fighters spun about, and instead of the marine fighter, the sword sank deep into the back of Nolhan's savior. With a startled grunt, the other minotaur dropped to the deck.

Faros/Nolhan was aghast at his understandable mistake. He tried to raise the sword again, but he was too slow. The marine fighter's axe struck between his eyes.

The world became a mix of burning blood and chaotic agony. Muffled shouts came from everywhere. Faros/Nolhan grasped at empty air. A second later his feet crumpled and his head struck hard on something. Numbness took over. A darkness settled over him—and Faros once more found himself back in the cave, his sword quivering before him. Frightened, he dropped the blade. There was no doubt in his mind that he had experienced Nolhan's death.

After a long while, he slowly bent down and seized the dropped sword. "How long?" Faros snarled. "When did this happen?"

Now Sargonnas's gift was mercilessly silent. In truth, it did not matter much. Nolhan had battled . . . and lost.

A scuffling sound alerted him to someone entering the cave. Back bowed low, Captain Botanos rejoined him. "All set. Finished here?"

Faros blinked then looked at the fire. It was nearly burned to embers, even though Botanos had rebuilt it just before his departure. How long had the sword's vision gripped him?

"Yes, I'm finished here," he answered, quickly rising. Faros said nothing of what he had witnessed, knowing it would only cast doubt on his own cause for him to tell the others about Nolhan's failure.

Botanos scooped up the map as Faros hurried past. "Is there something wrong?"

The rebel leader paused to look back, then shook his head. "No. This changes nothing. Everything goes on as planned."

Faros moved on before the confused captain could say anything.

Botanos shrugged. He finished rolling up the map then followed the last great hope of the rebellion outside.

Chapter XV

Dark Designs

Haab, governor of Mito, considered himself a pragmatic creature. He had followed Hotak loyally during the Night of Blood and for his loyalty had gained control of the third largest region—until Ambeon, that is—in all the imperium. Haab had strictly performed his duties as he felt Hotak would have preferred, maintaining an iron grip on the large colony.

When Hotak fell victim to an accident, the slim-snouted Haab had quickly lined up behind Ardnor. He had even joined the Forerunner faith to which the new emperor belonged. Of course, his conversion had been more expedient than religious. As a member of the faithful, the colonial governor could better handle the Protectors sent to strengthen Ardnor's rule. Haab found the officers of the order obnoxious and overzealous, but they did keep order—at least until now.

The ebony-armored figure stalked into his official chambers. "I've come, Brother Haab."

As was his habit when he was either in thought or irritated, the governor tapped his fingers over and over on the desktop. This particular Protector insisted on calling him by his religious title instead of his proper governmental one. "I am greatly disappointed in your brethren, Brother Malkovius. There was another disturbance in the central square today."

Malkovius removed his helmet, revealing the shorn mane of his order. His eyes displayed the red tinge around the edges that was an increasingly familiar sign of the real fanatics among the Protectors.

Malkovius shrugged. "There were some who thought their apportioned supplies were wanting. They believed they were due more, despite the gift that is taxed each citizen for their expected pledge to the temple. We were forced to arrest five radicals."

"Two of whom are now dead."

"They resisted arrest."

Haab snorted. The deaths of enemies of the throne never bothered him, but other behavior of the Protectors did. His fingers went tap-tap on the desk. "I have reports that indicate the situation almost spilled over into a riot."

The Protector's eyes blazed. "We maintained order. Punishments will be meted out to the sector involved."

"This is becoming too frequent. Worse, productivity is slowing. We're going to be hard-pressed to meet the throne's goals, Brother Malkovius. Goals I've not had difficulty meeting in the past, I might add."

For the first time, the armored figure betrayed emotion: anxiety. Failing the throne meant not only failing Ardnor—which would be terrible enough—but also the temple. Clearly, Malkovius did not wish to fail the Lady Nephera.

"Order must be restored," the Protector insisted. "Disciplinary action is vital when people fail their duty to the imperium."

The governor tapped his fingers, considering "You may need further assistance. I'll withdraw half the legionaries from the outposts and place them under your command. They've been idling for months, waiting on the movements of the rebels, but according to all reports there is no longer any imminent threat."

"I am grateful, Brother Haab! Those who guide us have spoken wisdom in your ears—"

"Yes, yes! I'll see to it. If—" Haab paused to recall the legion commander's name. She had been a thorn in his side since Hotak's death and was clearly not enamored with the Protectors. Haab considered this officer short-sighted and had transferred her legion to shore protection in part to get rid of her. "—General Voluna—protests, have her come see me."

"As you say." Brother Malkovius beat his fist against his breastplate then eagerly departed.

Haab ceased tapping his fingers. Every report reaching his desk said the nearest rebel fighting was either in Kern or far beyond the eastern edge of the realm. The rebellion was clearly in tatters, but he knew Voluna; she would protest being reassigned to the Protectors. He smiled to himself. If she protested too hotly and slandered the throne, then he would have her removed from command. Otherwise, let her deal with Malkovius.

"Where are they?" muttered Maritia, peering out at the Blood Sea. "They wouldn't dare be using galleys on this mission."

"Surely the Grand Lord is not such a fool," the barrel-chested mariner next to her said in a startlingly soft tone. Captain Xyr's voice belied his huge form. The streak of gray running down the front of his fur was the only evidence of his many years on the sea. Otherwise Xyr looked young for his years.

As captain of the *Stormbringer*, Xyr had been the one who had first reported Bastion lost at sea. Xyr had taken it upon himself to search long after everyone else had lost all hope. That dedication, in Maritia's mind, was exactly what she expected from an officer of the empire, and so she had made Xyr senior captain of her fleet.

"No, he's not," she reluctantly agreed. "He's far from that."

The lookout suddenly shouted, his exact words drowned by the strong sea wind, but his meaning quite clear. Maritia shifted her gaze to the west. Golgren coming from that direction puzzled her. Imperial intelligence reported the majority of the ogres' warships were much further north. Either Golgren had taken a wide swing, or the empire was wrong about the location of his sea might. Maritia made a mental note to have her officers look into the matter. It was unsettling to think so many ogres could go undetected so near to Ambeon.

Most of the ships in Golgren's fleet had once either belonged to other races—including minotaurs—or had been crafted to imitate those of the empire. They were generally more bulky vessels, and as the ogre ships neared, Maritia saw a banner she did not recognize—a severed hand grasping a bloody dagger set in a field of brown that matched too closely the color of her own fur.

Assuming the lead vessel was the Grand Lord's flagship, she had Captain Xyr give the signal of recognition. A sailor blew five short notes followed by a longer, higher one. Seconds later, the long note was returned, with the five quick ones coming after.

"Prepare my boat, Captain," she commanded.

"With all due respect, my lady, it is better protocol that he should come over here."

Maritia's ears twitched. "The *Stormbringer* is the latest design in the imperium. I'm sure that Golgren would like to have its hull and sails studied by what passes for shipwrights among the ogres. Let them make their crude copies from a distance; I don't want them aboard to study the smaller details." She snorted. "They are allies, not equals . . . and certainly not to be trusted."

Xyr turned to give the order. "You'll get no argument from me on that."

In a few minutes the long boat was readied. Maritia took only two guards with her. The more minotaurs aboard the ogre ship, the more likely some trouble might stir up. She knew her soldiers would not start any tiff, but they would spill blood if provoked.

Four rowers brought them across the dark waters of the Blood Sea. As she waited, Maritia studied the Grand Lord's ship. It was the newest and sleekest ogre vessel yet. It was definitely in the minotaur style, probably captured at some point in the past. At the bow Maritia could make out the old imperial designation. The letters had been crudely removed and replaced with the funny symbols that ogres preferred to represent their names.

Maritia puzzled out the symbols, finally arriving at the ship's name: *Hand that Devours All*. What did that mean exactly? She had a suspicion it had to do with Golgren. Since the loss of his appendage, he flaunted his missing hand in various ways.

The *Hand* rocked slowly in the water. The deck was all but devoid of ogre sailors. Only a mere handful could be seen.

Just as she was about to call up, a shaggy beast in a simple gray kilt came to the rail and tossed over a rope ladder. One of the rowers took hold of the ladder, tested its strength, then held it against the side while the first of the guards ascended. Maritia followed, her other escort taking up the rear.

"Most welcome, most welcome, offspring of Hotak, blood of the emperor and khan of Ambeon! Most welcome!"

The Grand Lord Golgren was costumed in all his finery, looking more like an elven elder than an ogre overlord. His green and brown robes swooped nearly to the deck. His mane was far more well-kept than Maritia's herself. She had been forced to bind her own mane behind her in a tail, due to the constant dampness.

Accompanying Golgren was his omnipresent shadow, the hulking Nagroch. For some reason, Nagroch did not look directly at her. The frog-faced ogre eyed her guards, peered at his master, and even feigned to gaze at the sky—but never met her eyes. Maritia marked that oddity for later consideration.

One of her companions leaned over the rail and tapped the flat of his axe against the hull. Maritia heard the rowers begin to return to the *Stormbringer*. It attested to her trust in her host—and her trust in her own power—that they did not linger.

She greeted Golgren. "Hail, Grand Lord of Kern, Liberator of Blöde, and Protector of his people! I thank you for your good hospitality!"

He grinned. "It is pleasure. Come! My cabin has a welcome more proper!"

Maritia walked beside Golgren, as both their bodyguards walked close behind. Nagroch stalked ahead. Again, Maritia thought Golgren's lieutenant was behaving strangely. Two armored giants of Blödian origins stood sentry at the Grand Lord's cabin door. Nagroch barked an order. They immediately stepped to the sides, raising their axes to form an archway.

As Nagroch opened the door, the Grand Lord gestured for her to enter ahead of him. "Please! It is the guest who first is in."

As Maritia stepped inside, her eyes could not help but widen. In contrast to her own cabin, her host's was an explosion of grandeur. Silks of many colors draped the huge room, all but obscuring the excellent wood. A gossamer veil hanging from the ceiling further gave a dreamlike quality to their surroundings.

There were no chairs or tables, only countless plush pillows and elaborate rugs that were spoils of the former elven kingdom. To the sides were some tools for writing and a small platform upon which lay charts, but otherwise the room was like the personal chamber of a Grand Khan. The more she thought about it, the more the minotaur felt certain the room intentionally resembled one she had seen on her single visit to Kernen. Glittering plates and goblets had been set on the floor for two. A high, curved glass flask of wine stood near.

Sudden movement in the far corner of the cabin startled Maritia. An elven slave, her hair bound like the minotaur's, knelt with her head low. The creature was so ephemeral and blended so much into the background that Maritia couldn't see her clearly.

"Please to sit," Golgren offered.

The female minotaur found a place among the cushions near the setting. Maritia removed her sword, laying it within reach. As an afterthought, the minotaur also removed her dagger.

Golgren's eyes admired the latter. "A most exquisite blade. Ivory hilt, fine steel. Legion, yes?"

"A gift from my father when I joined. I treasure it."

"Of course."

Nagroch tried to assist his master, but the Grand Lord shook him off and deftly seated himself. He didn't seem discomfited in the slightest to maneuver with one hand. The bodyguards and Nagroch took positions close to their respective leaders. Maritia caught Golgren's second scowling at her companions, but when he noticed her watching, his expression quickly became neutral.

"Please to have some wine." The ogre leader snapped his fingers, and the elf scurried forward, gracefully reaching for her master's goblet.

Golgren's seeming good humor vanished in an instant. The Grand Lord slapped at the elf with the back of his hand and snarled a reprimand. Maritia understood enough of his language to know that if the slave made another mistake, it would be her last.

He pointed angrily at Hotak's daughter. "Guest first!"

The elf slipped over to Maritia and poured her some wine. However, as the minotaur reached for it, the slave raised the goblet to her lips and carefully sipped, testing the liquid.

Once the elf had swallowed, it was another few seconds before she handed the drink to Maritia. As the latter took the wine, the slave went back to Golgren and repeated the action.

He accepted the goblet but held it away from him, swirling it thoughtfully. With a smile, he said, "Care must be taken, yes?"

Poison was not unfamiliar in minotaur circles, and Golgren certainly had many enemies who would like to see him dead. Waiting, Maritia didn't drink until the Grand Lord himself finally did so.

"Most excellent, is it not?"

Indeed, she thought to herself, it was delicious. "Elven?"

"Yes. Will be a rare pleasure as years pass."

She was never certain exactly how good Golgren's grasp of Common was. At times he could wax most eloquently, but at other times his speech was very murky.

Lowering her wine, Maritia began, "My lord—"

"Please! Call me Golgren . . . this is insisted."

"Very well. Golgren, I want to make matters clear about our mission. I know that this is not one we both—"

Handing his goblet to the elf slave, he waved for her to be silent. "Let us eat first, enjoy, then speak of this difficult matter."

He snapped his fingers. When nothing happened, he bared his teeth in annoyance and looked up at Nagroch. A quick word sent the heavy ogre marching out of the cabin.

Maritia's eyes must have lingered too long on the other ogre, for when she glanced back at her host, the Grand Lord immediately said, "Must forgive poor Nagroch! Brother Belgroch killed not long ago."

"Belgroch dead?" She recalled the other ogre, a younger version of Golgren's underling. Belgroch had briefly commanded the ogre contingent during the last days of Ambeon's liberation.

"Yes. Neraka we entered, you know. Some of the dark ones, they still fight now and then. Not bad fighters, at times."

He said it in an off-handed manner, as if speaking of the clouds. Small wonder, though, that Nagroch was so distracted. The two brothers had been close, Maritia knew from her spies.

"So you have been exploring Neraka?" the legion commander suddenly asked. "I was not aware of this. Nor did I

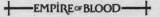
know the knights were active in the east. I've been told they were busy regrouping further west."

"A mere scouting party. Probing weaknesses."

Maritia frowned. More intelligence her people had missed.

They were interrupted by Nagroch's return. Behind him came four more elven slaves, each bearing a tray with food.

Maritia's nostrils welcomed a heavenly aroma. The goat meat on two trays carried an unusual scent. The meat had been broiled well. The two slaves carrying the meat passed both by Golgren, who sniffed each and nodded. He pointed at the tray with the slightly larger portion, and one elf brought that over to Maritia.

The remaining trays each held fruit and a red soup with a heady texture. Both again passed under the Grand Lord's attentive gaze, then one was handed to him and the other given to her.

She had hardly expected such a feast aboard an ogre ship. Golgren chuckled at her clear surprise. "Elves. They are masters of food."

"I wouldn't have thought they'd know how to prepare goat so well. They were never known for eating meat much."

He gestured at the slaves. "With everything, it is the teaching. They learn."

Before Maritia could sample her meal, Golgren had two of the slaves repeat the ritual of tasting. He then bade them sit in the corner, where one of his bodyguards kept wary watch over them. When at last it was apparently safe to eat, Golgren signaled her to choose first. Without preamble, Maritia ate some of the goat, discovering it to be even more delicious than it smelled, yet as she dined, she found herself stealing glances at Nagroch. He seemed to be brooding, eyeing the minotaurs.

She had dealt with Nagroch many times before and while both had a healthy distrust for one another, he had never shown such animosity in the past. She kept on guard through the dinner.

His personal slave aided the Grand Lord as he dined, handing him food and even feeding him like a babe at times. Golgren spoke grandly of their alliance and its successes thus far.

"Great is the word I hear in Ambeon! Fortresses beyond old Silvanesti! Many Uruv Suurt building new realm, yes?"

"We've made many advances. I've been told that the ogres thrive, too. Is that not so?"

"All very good!" he responded much too cheerfully, hoisting his wine glass. "To the glory of our ancestors we will someday make!"

Golgren paused to adjust the chain hanging from his neck. Maritia had seen him shift it more than once. Each time, a large object lying across his chest shifted along with it.

Trying to puzzle out what it was, Maritia asked, "Is there anything you need in terms of supplies?"

"So gracious! This will be considered, but likely nothing. My gratitude."

The meal was excellent. The minotaur had to admit that she had not eaten such splendid fare in many years, which made Golgren beam. He leaned toward her in a manner she found slightly discomforting and poured her some wine with his lone hand.

The trays were cleared away. With another snap, Golgren dismissed all the slaves, including his personal one, the beleaguered female elf. He then startled Maritia by whispering, "It would be best, yes, if we talked without any others around."

"Are you suggesting that our bodyguards leave, too?"

His smile had vanished. "Would be wise."

Maritia considered this and finally nodded. She turned to her top-ranking soldier. "Wait outside the cabin."

"My lady, this is not proper—"

"You heard me. Both of you. Outside."

Golgren interrupted. "With permission. They will trust more if mine leave first." He pointed to the door. "All! Go!"

Nagroch seemed as reluctant as her guards, but he obeyed. The other ogres filed out. The two legionaries reluctantly followed suit.

After they had all departed, Maritia looked at the Grand Lord and commented, "Don't worry, I can kill you without their help."

Her host chuckled mirthlessly. "Would be a very good fight, though. An interesting fight, Maritia. Most interesting."

It was the first time he had used her name and the intimacy did not appeal to her. "Let's get on with this then. We have to coordinate our plans perfectly. This rebel has caused the deaths of too many of our people – ogres and minotaurs. I want his head."

"This I understand well."

"I don't think you do. I mean I, personally, want him, Golgren. I want to see his body stretched out, his gut opened, and his horns cut off. Is that clear?"

He grinned wide. It was not a pleasant sight. "So very ogre, Maritia! So very ogre . . ."

"He killed my brother, Bastion! I demand my vengeance! In that respect, our people are alike!"

"Agreed. I, too, would this Faros want." The Grand Lord held up his stump, flourishing his deformity.

"Yes, you lost your hand," conceded Maritia, "but I lost—"

Golgren cut her off. "To Uruv Suurt, a hand is important, yes?"

Visions of the colonizers filled her mind. Most were minotaurs who had been maimed and deemed incomplete as warriors. Losing a hand was terrible enough to lower a minotaur's status, too.

"It is, yes."

"To ogres, this is death." He unwrapped the limb, revealing to her the cauterized wound. "Ever death."

"But you survived—"

Again the mirthless grin. "I am *Golgren*."

Leaving the maimed arm uncovered, the Grand Lord reached up and tugged on the chain around his neck. The object on his chest rose with it.

"I survive, Maritia. I survive, but also I remember. Have this ever at my heart to remind."

Out from his the neck of his robe came a chain bearing a grisly sight that almost made the minotaur drop her wine—a hand. A mummified hand.

Golgren's hand.

Someone had painstakingly dried and embalmed the hand. The nails were even perfectly filed and cleaned with no sign of blood.

"Remember it every sleep, every hour. I survive, yes, Maritia, but always this is at my heart. Keep it there to remind all others, too, that Golgren is more than a hand." He let the chain drop, allowing the lost appendage to bounce against his garments. His good hand thumped his chest. "Golgren is power. Golgren is might. Golgren is Kern and Blöde . . ."

His eyes glittered fanatically. Maritia wisely remained silent until the Grand Lord had calmed down. His tone abruptly shifted to one of conspiracy and camaraderie. Gaze upon Maritia, he gently—almost reverently—replaced his lost hand inside his robe.

"Come! This is not a necessary argument! This Faros is still far from us! We decide who gets kill when it is more needed!" He leaned to one side, reached among some pillows. The Grand Lord pulled free a rolled-up chart. "Please! I would hear your glorious plan!"

Taking a deep breath, Maritia outlined her strategy. The knowledge that Faros was no longer in Kern had reached Maritia just before her departure, but she was surprised when Golgren added that it was believed that the rebel's followers were gathering north of Karthay. When she probed for the source of the Grand Lord's intelligence, the ogre simply smiled and urged her to continue.

Their talk went on for a long time, slipping into evening. When all had been agreed upon, Maritia gave a sigh and stretched her legs. She then rose and reached for her sword and dagger.

"There is no need to depart so quickly," Golgren urged politely.

"I have much to communicate with my staff and officers. I know you need to do the same."

"Please . . . would wish to speak with you about your brother, Bastion."

Maritia hesitated. "Bastion? Why?"

"Know that you were close. Closer than others in your family—other than your father, the great Hotak, of course. Understand your thirst for vengeance."

She sat back, listening.

"Must admit," the Grand Lord went on, pouring himself more wine. "Heard rumors . . . rumors of Bastion fighting alongside the rebel, Faros."

"I heard them, too. Just scurrilous rumors."

He downed the wine. "But he was alive . . . and he was living in Kern."

Her hand tightened on her sheathed weapon. "He did what any good legionary would. He survived."

"A pity, though. So close, yet you could not see him one more time living."

Maritia fought to keep her expression blank. "A pity, yes."

Golgren leaned forward. For the first time, she noticed he now gripped something in his good hand. Something small, unimportant. She was no longer interested in the conversation. All Maritia cared about was returning to the comfort of her own ship.

"Loyal you were to your brother. Would have done anything for him, yes?"

She stared at him. "Is there a point to all this?"

His reply was a shrug. "Answers, nothing more."

Again she rose to leave.

"It is sorrowful you did not speak with him one more time," the Grand Lord declared, pushing himself to his feet.

Her blood was racing now. Maritia turned for the door. "I already told you, yes. Now, excuse me, my lord—"

"Would not want to leave without this," came the ogre's insistent voice.

As she glanced back, Golgren tossed the object he had been holding toward her. He threw it slightly past her, but instinct made Maritia reach out and catch it before it could hit the floor. It was rounded and made mostly of metal. She opened her palm.

A signet ring.

Her ring. The ring she had given to Bastion to show Faros her "good" intentions.

Proving her a liar.

All the questions the Grand Lord had been asking suddenly took on ominous meaning. Maritia instinctively reached for her sword—but it was no longer there. She spun about and found it, held by Golgren. Her hand went to her dagger. The sword knocked her hand away.

"Please to not do that," murmured Golgren. He held her blade with such obvious skill that she had no doubt he could cut her a second mouth before she could move fast enough to draw her dagger. "As demanded by your brother—the emperor—I must regretfully make you prisoner, Maritia de-Droka."

"Are you mad? Prisoner?"

The blade briefly came down to tap the ring before coming close to her throat. Golgren's eyes drew so narrow they were slits. "For conspiring with your brother and the rebels, offspring of Hotak . . . for betrayal of the empire, of course . . ."

CHAPTER XVI

ZEBOIM'S CRADLE

Lady Nephera had created a new list, one differing from past efforts. This list did not tally up her enemies—suspected or otherwise—but rather was aimed at only one enemy.

The greatest enemy of the imperium: Sargonnas.

The Horned One, the Condor Lord, the Lord of Vengeance— by whatever title or name he went by, the former principal deity of her people was, she had decided, the reason for the growing disorder in her domain. First he abandoned the horned race, then he returned unwanted to bestow his blessings on Faros, of all people. Sargonnas was a meddler. Nephera was convinced she needed to eliminate his interference, indeed eliminate Sargonnas from the minds and souls of the minotaurs who once revered the god.

Her own power was growing, thanks to Morgion. With her present patron's help, Nephera thought, almost chuckling with glee, she should be able to hand Sargonnas a stinging defeat. Nephera looked over the first few pages of the list. The priestess had itemized strategic locations throughout the empire, prime centers of population, areas she had filled with her devout Protectors, areas where new temples honoring the

Forerunner faith—and her patron—were already being built and attended.

"There can be only one god," she whispered reverently to the symbol on her chest. "You, my lord."

"Holy one?" asked a grey-robed figure just beyond her. The Supreme Councilor Lothan looked up from another document he was working on. "You said something?"

"Merely asking for the blessing of the Forerunners, my dear friend." She rose from her desk, the parchments quivering in her hand. "Well? Do you foresee any trouble with passage?"

The gaunt minotaur thrust his wrinkled snout into the page he had been studying, then looked up. "Nothing I foresee. Iolin will vote against it. Negarius will abstain, and the rest will vote with me. The people will be satisfied that the Circle has performed its proper, independent function. The funding then will be distributed in short order, praise the Forerunners!"

Nephera nodded approval then stretched forth her free hand. Lothan went down on one knee. The high priestess gave him her blessing.

"You are dismissed with my gratitude."

She watched with barely concealed impatience as he departed. Lothan would act as she commanded, dealing with imperial officials. Now, though, she must send word to the faithful beyond Mithas. Mortal messengers, however, would not be fast enough. Let her followers marvel at the powers Morgion had granted her; their admiration would stimulate their fervor for the cause.

"Takyr!"

The phantom was at her side in an instant. His cloak billowed around him. He had fully recovered from his earlier setback.

Mistress . . .

She held before him the message she had composed, along with the extensive list of locations. Takyr eyed both silently.

Nephera commanded, "Let it be done! Let them all be told!"

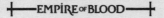

The dread ghost shimmered, a sickly green aura blossoming around him. His rotting and ravaged muzzle opened wide—and out of it Takyr spewed forth another ghost. The faint form, little more than what seemed a shroud and hungry eyes, howled as it flew upward and tore through the ceiling.

No sooner was this done then a second spirit was spewed forth from the maw of Nephera's servant. This ghost seemed a little more substantial, having the semblance of arms and a general countenance, but it, too, howled, and raced off to pass through another part of the thick stone ceiling.

One by one but in a swift blur, they burst forth to do the high priestess's bidding. These were the spirits who had been 'punished' by Takyr on behalf of his mistress, and their souls were ever tormented in the monstrous abyss within him. Their escape now was but a momentary freedom, for when their task was done, they had no choice but to return to his horrific care.

Nephera observed their departure with wide, bloodshot eyes. All was at last falling into place. Mortal weapons would end the life of the Horned One's chosen champion, but for a god, a different battle was envisioned. The high priestess's decree would demand that all work be shifted to the building and perfection of the new temples. Not only that, but the faithful—and that meant *every* minotaur—would be required to attend services three times a day, extolling the Forerunners and their patron. All memory of the other gods would be discouraged and punished. The only god for the minotaurs was Morgion, who would be revealed by name only when the faithful had been properly and firmly indoctrinated. Without the minotaurs, his once favored race, Sargonnas would be bereft. He would retreat and shrivel to a minor deity known only to a few. Gradually he would fade into obscurity.

Smiling faintly, Nephera touched the axe symbol on her chest, murmuring lovingly, "First, I will slay his mortal hound, my lord. Then, for your glory, I will slay the god himself."

The ghostly messengers soared through the heavens, shrieking and screaming as they darted over all parts of the empire. They descended swiftly over the colonies to which they had been sent, honing in on individuals targeted by their mistress.

On Mito, on Amur, even on Ambeon, the ghosts hovered before these individuals then materialized for their eyes only. The Protector General of Dus nearly toppled from his saddle when the pale, mournful young child appeared, hovering in the air before him. His counterpart on Thuum, in the midst of pronouncing sentence on a legionary who had been heard uttering unkind words about the emperor, instead blurted out a shocking epithet when he was startled by a ragged, thin male, who formed before his eyes.

For Second Master Pryas, the visitation of a ghost dispatched by his priestess brought exaltation. He considered it the greatest honor of his life thus far. The pale yet still beautiful female stared with hungry, pained eyes at the Procurator General. Pryas ignored her agony, eager to know her message.

"Hear my message, faithful one," the drifting, translucent figure began in the high priestess's voice. "I have been given a vision from beyond, a vision of a task of such magnitude that when it is accomplished it will forever change our world . . ."

Pryas listened as Nephera's messengers outlined her intentions. For the Procurator General of Ambeon, the job was an especially challenging one and proof he had been blessed with favor. Truly, the Forerunners had guided his destiny. Only an hour later all the riders had been dispatched to give the good word to the rest of Ambeon, and a short time after that Pryas was disturbed by the furious entrance of General Bakkor.

"What in the name of sanity is this?" asked the Wyverns' commander, waving in front of the Protector's muzzle one of the documents hastily scribed by Pryas's assistants.

Pryas perused the document, whose contents he well knew, then responded, "This defines your duty, General . . . and you're hereby warned against speaking such blasphemy again. Be grateful for my good mood, or else you'd be facing punishment right now."

"First of all, we share authority equally here!" Bakkor said, pulling himself together and staring angrily at the Protector. "Second, with all due respect, if we follow this decree to the letter, Ambeon will collapse. You've got the western fortresses all but stripped of power, our ogre allies are nibbling at the north, and there'll be hardly anyone tending the fields—"

"We have elves for that chore."

"They need to be watched by more than a few overseers! They'll slip away! The same goes for the workers at the quarry."

Judging by his equally angry expression, the Procurator General was unmoved by this argument. "We embark on a more important, more ambitious project than Ambeon! This will set the course for the future of our people . . ."

"There won't *be* a future if we don't keep a constant eye on the day-to-day aspects of empire-building. I'll not permit this—"

Pryas beat his fist on the table. Immediately, four massive warriors in black helms entered, surrounding General Bakkor on all sides. "You'll perform your duty as dictated." To the guards, the Protector said, "Escort the commander to his mount."

"Never mind! I'll happily see myself out!" Nodding curtly, Bakkor turned and stomped out the door.

The Second Master signaled an underling. "Tulak. Earlier, I sent a dictate from the throne, which ordered the arrest of Lady Maritia. I've heard nothing back. What happened to that message?"

The brawny aide's thick brow furrowed. "I took it only as far as the eastern gate. A legionary took it from there."

"From Wyvern, no doubt. That settles it. Interference with the throne. A sign of treason. I'll bet the legionary took it to General Bakkor . . ." He frowned. "Begin gathering a force from Crystal Legion. I'll have an important task for you soon."

An evil grin spread across Tulak's muzzle. "Aye . . ."

Pryas, too, allowed himself a smile as the officer left to obey. The high priestess would be very proud of him. Nothing would stand in the way of the temple's work in Ambeon. The minotaur race would be exalted, the people saved—even if a few, like General Bakkor, found themselves ascending to the next plane a little sooner than they had expected.

✦ ▼ ✦

The storm erupted just before dawn and grew more intense as the day progressed. Although the ships had anchored in safe waters, the harsh currents and high winds scattered them. Many drifted near to the island, threatening to run aground.

The ship closest to Faros's was the first to suffer. A sudden cracking sound was followed by a low groan. As rebels on the other vessels watched helplessly, the ship's main mast collapsed. It dropped into the savage waters, taking with it the rigging, part of the rail, and two slow-moving sailors. The hapless figures were immediately swept out of sight.

"She's not goin' to last!" cried Botanos. "They'd better get everyone off before it's too late!"

"The *Champion of Duma* and the *Karak's Avenger* are veering into one another!" warned someone from the aft.

Sure enough, the bow of the *Champion* was only yards from the portside of the smaller *Avenger*. The crews tried frantically to avoid a collision, but the same anchors that had failed to root the two in deeper waters now tangled their efforts.

The *Champion of Duma*'s stronger hull crushed into its sister ship. *Karak's Avenger* listed, tossing several hands overboard.

"The rebellion will end here unless we do something!" Faros called. "Give the signal to set sail! My father once said it's better to ride out a storm than let it strike you in the muzzle!"

"We might capsize in deeper water!" Botanos warned him.

"Would you rather wait and pray?"

Nodding, the captain went to the rail, sending the word by lantern to the rest of the fleet. The *Dragon Crest's* crew worked to ready the sails. Grunting with effort, minotaurs fought the whipping lines. Crew members scurried up the rigging to make sure the sails filled properly.

Aboard the damaged ships, the survivors began filling the long boats and heading to other vessels. The crossings were hazardous. More than a few minotaurs were washed overboard into what many dubbed Zeboim's Cradle. At last, the ruined ships lay empty. The sea had already engulfed the *Karak's Avenger*. One by one, the rebel fleet abandoned the island.

As they headed away into the storm, Captain Botanos pointed. "It's rough ahead! There's no chance of heading on a proper course for the Blood Sea! We'll have to steer for the Courrain!"

"How long?"

"Storm like this? Couldn't say! Hours certainly, days maybe!"

With a curse, Faros nodded. Even he could see that heading southwest of Karthay would be courting death The *Dragon's Crest* took the lead. Thunder boomed as the sky darkened.

"Get those lanterns lit!" shouted Botanos. "I want that stern blazing like the Great Circus at festival time!"

The show of lights would help the others keep the flagship in sight. The fear of the ships getting separated was far greater than the remote possibility the Imperials might be near enough to spot the lights.

Slowly, *Dragon's Crest* wended its way deeper into the northern Courrain. Against their hopes, the storm worsened. The waves rose higher than the masts. The lookout had to abandon the crow's nest for fear of being washed away.

"Hard to port!" Botanos called, looking to Faros. "We've got to slow down a little. We're starting to leave some behind! If we lose 'em here, we may never find 'em again!"

Then, without warning, a massive wave washed over the deck. The rebel leader was knocked over and sent flying. He collided with another body, struck a wooden framework and flipped over the rail. Just as quickly, something thrust him back up and over, onto the ship. As the wave died, Faros, half the ocean rising up from his gut, found himself lying face down on the deck. Pushing himself up, he gazed through waterlogged eyes at another form tumbling through the tempest. Captain Botanos was trying to swim back to the boat, but his efforts were pathetic in the storm.

Looking around, Faros found a long coil of rope. He yelled at the nearest sailors. "Over here! Your captain's overboard!"

They came to his assistance as he bound one end of the rope around his waist.

"You shouldn't try this, my lord," a sailor shouted. "Let me—"

"No time! Secure the other end!"

Faros looked to Botanos. Although the larger minotaur still remained afloat, his strength clearly was flagging. Each stroke seemed an effort. His drenched fur pulled him down. Faros dove in. Striking the water was like hitting a stone wall. Shaking his head to clear his dizziness, the rebel leader started for Botanos.

At first the waves aided him, tossing Faros toward the captain, but when he tried to grasp the other's hand, he was thrown back. Worse, the rope drew so tangled it threatened to strangle him.

Faros struggled with the rope—which suddenly slipped free, vanishing in the water. The younger minotaur grabbed for Botanos. The captain remained afloat but was barely moving.

"Botanos!"

The other did not respond. The ocean abruptly tilted. Faros looked behind him and saw only a wall of water. The high wave came crashing down. It pushed Faros deep beneath the surface. Water filled his lungs.

Abruptly, he was surrounded by a strange calm. The storm, the crash of the waves . . . all turbulence vanished. A startling green glow filled the water.

A short distance ahead, he could see Botanos drifting limply underwater. Faros tried to reach the captain, but his limbs felt like stone. Then a giant hand with slender fingers materialized under the captain. At the same time, another cradled Faros. He tried to swim away, but to no avail.

The fingers parted slightly as Faros came to rest upon the palm. He saw webbing among the fingers. The skin was ivory with just a hint of sea green, although that might have been an effect of the light. The two hands drew together, cupping both minotaurs. It occurred to Faros that by all rights he and Botanos should be dead—perhaps they were dead. They had been underwater for far longer than any surface creature could hold its breath.

A feminine chuckle, soft and reminiscent of a tidal breeze, startled him. He looked around but did not at first see anything clearly. Then Faros noticed a pair of creatures swimming toward him. At first they appeared to be Magori, but then he saw that they were huge sea turtles of an unsettling grey color, yet as they drew near, their forms grew murkier. Rather than turtles, they looked like eyes—grey eyes, the color of storms. Feminine eyes, too. The more Faros stared, the more he was sure they were giant orbs, beautiful, hypnotic, but ominous.

When they blinked, revealing themselves to be heavily-lidded eyes, the rebel leader finally understood. Around the eyes, a pale, surreal countenance formed. The female figure seemed neither elven nor human. Indeed, the beauty of the Irda did not compare to her beauty, yet as the perfect, full lips parted in a smile, the slim, elegant nose twitched, and the long hair of white sea foam floated around him, Faros felt unsettled more than entranced. In this being, the minotaur sensed death.

With what awkward effort he could muster, Faros bowed his horns to Zeboim, feared mistress of the darkest seas. Again, he heard the female god giggle. Legend had it that Zeboim was a capricious spirit, as inclined to seize a mariner off his ship and sleep with him as she was to feed the unfortunate to the sharp-toothed denizens of her realm. The Sea Queen, as she was often called, constantly battled Habbakuk— the Fisher King—for sovereignty of Krynn's waters. Zeboim was mistress of all those who had died in the seas and the races who lived underwater.

When she did not immediately drag him deeper down into the darkness, Faros dared to meet her eyes. Under a graceful brow, the grey orbs studied him. Her expression mingled curiosity, disdain, and amusement. He felt strangely drawn to her as to no other female. She was the promised shore that all sailors yearned for, yet also the turbulent deep to which some were doomed.

One hand gently tipped Botanos toward Faros. Zeboim drew the pair near her chest as if they were babes. The sea queen wore a gossamer green and blue gown that looked spun from the very sea. The pale goddess swam through the ocean. As she did, she waved her hand toward the darkness below, as if beckoning.

From the black depths emerged a presence so huge that it even dwarfed Zeboim. It was some kind of fish, for it had fins and gills, but it was round with a mouth filled with needle-like teeth. So huge was the behemoth it could have swallowed the entire rebel fleet whole.

Thinking that this was perhaps Zeboim's intention, Faros tried to wriggle from her hand. The moment he did, however, his lungs filled with water and he started to drown.

Naughty, naughty! came a female voice both melodious and hideous in the minotaur's thoughts. The Sea Queen—her expression vexed and eyes suddenly a violent green—held him up and shook him as one might a disobedient puppy. Gasping, Faros could only watch as the goddess—a hint of dark mirth now spread across her face—and the beast rose close to the surface.

Zeboim pointed up at the ships. Through white, horrific orbs without any pupil, the monstrosity seemed to understand. It started for the unsuspecting rebels, its canyon-wide maw opening. Raising her hand to her face again, the deity looked deep into Faros's eyes. Hers were now the color of the deep azure of the sea.

For my daddy . . . came her susurrating voice again. *And because your little people understand proper respect for a queen* . . .

With that, Zeboim laughed and tossed the two mortals to her gigantic pet. Faros tried to hold his breath as he started to sink. His vision blurred. Faros saw Botanos tumble past him, a single twitch of the captain's arm the only sign his comrade lived.

Swimming up from beneath them, the abomination opened its mouth to swallow the duo. A huge, serpentine appendage, the sea beast's tongue, thrust out at them. The blood-red appendage snared both bodies and sucked the minotaurs inside.

CHAPTER XVII

DUEL

The two fleets lay locked in position despite the foul weather. The minotaurs had the strength of numbers and better equipment, while the ogres held the advantage of ferocity. They also held the key to the minotaurs' continued cooperation.

Maritia had not suffered in the days since her capture, at least not physically. In fact, Golgren had gone out of his way to make her comfortable. Even her two guards had been treated moderately well, although their quarters were down below and far more cramped. The guards were fed decently and left alone by their captors. True, they did not receive the fine food and drink, nor plush pillows upon which to sleep, like Maritia, but all things considered, Golgren had been very gracious indeed.

The Grand Lord had turned over his own cabin to her as her cell. Maritia had searched the place as thoroughly as possible but could find no way out other than the barred, guarded entrance.

The stalemate could not last forever. Golgren had to decide what to do about her. The minotaur fleet had only held back so far because of her safety. His best bet was to sail back to his own realm, but that would not be a permanent solution, and surely the minotaur ships would maneuver to block him if he tried.

Why did he "arrest" her anyway? Could she really be condemned by Ardnor and her mother? Maritia doubted it. They would want to avenge Bastion's death as much as she did.

She couldn't figure out Golgren's motives.

Golgren did not like feeling off balance. Everything had been going perfectly. He had his people under his thumb, the Titans in check, the beginnings of a solid expansion into Neraka, and strong ties to his minotaur allies, to the Lady Nephera—the true emperor. Now because of Nephera, all of it threatened to unravel.

"*Jahara i du f'han i'Maritia'n,*" muttered the seated Nagroch, from behind his pacing master.

"*F'han i'Maritia'n?*" the Grand Lord snapped, turning to glare at his huge second. "*Kyal nur f'han i'Nagrochi, ke?*"

The ogre from Blöde pulled his head back, his eyes round with uncertainty.

"*Ngi,*" added Golgren dismissively.

The Grand Lord had taken over Nagroch's cabin. The Uruv Suurt was kept prisoner in his quarters. Unlike Golgren's perfect paradise, however, Nagroch lived in the squalor to which most ogres were accustomed. The huge warrior slept on soiled skins on the floor. Bits of old food lay scattered about; the floor had stains of spilled wine. Only one weak oil lamp lit the cabin, a preferable thing to Golgren, who did not wish to see every foul detail.

A rank odor filled the room. While bathing was all but impossible on such journeys, Golgren at least attempted to counter his own sweat with scented oils. It was doubtful that a barrel of such oil would have done anything to douse the smell prevalent here. The cabin also appeared to be infested with bugs.

Nagroch stood and leaned in a bored fashion against the wall. Golgren paid him no mind, more interested in the absence of the one he had been expecting for days and nights.

Kolot's ghost should have returned by now. The specter had the ability to travel great distances in but the blink of an eye, Golgren knew. There had been more than ample time for him to deliver the Grand Lord's message to his mistress and bring the reply.

Did the high priestess have no concern for her own daughter?

Nagroch grunted something under his breath. Although he did not understand the other's words, the meaning was clear. Nagroch wanted the Lady Maritia's horns, blaming her for the death of his brother at the hands of Bastion. This stupidity—considering Maritia was totally in the dark—was not lost on Golgren.

"*G'hai!*" the Grand Lord snapped, finally irritated with his second. "*Roch g'hai!*"

With a sullen expression, Nagroch bowed his head and left the cabin.

Golgren scowled after him, but his annoyance was not entirely directed at the other ogre. His good hand pressed against the one hanging from his chest as he considered the benefits and dangers of his alliance.

Grand Lord . . .

His only hint of surprise was the suddenly tightened clutching of his severed hand. Golgren gazed over his shoulder, but it was not the now-familiar youngest son of the high priestess he saw.

Steeling himself, the Grand Lord eyed the foreboding, cloaked specter. He knew that Takyr sensed his unease despite his apparent composure. "So, the mistress's hound! I have been waiting . . ."

She has far more important tasks than guiding you by one hand . . .

Ignoring the jab at his maimed condition, Golgren responded, "But her own daughter? Have done all you requested, all the son of Nephera demanded . . ."

And now you shall let her go. The emperor has reviewed the situation and found error. Maritia is loyal. The priestess has been informed of that.

The ogre's eyes narrowed. "Just so? All a jest? Proclaimed her a traitor in her brother's name. Waited days for word." Despite his distaste for the ghost, Golgren approached the malevolent shade. "I am the Grand Lord. To let her go now, in such a manner . . . this is a loss of face to my own, even I cannot explain."

Takyr suddenly seemed to fill his view. The folds of his cloak spread toward Golgren, who refused to move. *The mistress has commanded. All . . . all will obey . . .*

"I—" Before he could say more, the damnable spirit vanished. Golgren spat where moments before Takyr had floated.

The high priestess's decision had done nothing but worsen his mood. Golgren did not like being played like a puppet and then having his strings jangled. It was simple for the Uruv Suurt to tell him to let Maritia de-Droka go, yet to do so now, without the explanation he dare not give, would make his followers believe he had weakened. Then there was Maritia herself; how to tell her?

Teeth bared, Golgren hissed. It would do not good to reveal the emperor's part in Bastion's death to his sister Maritia. She would not believe him over her mother and brother. Indeed, she was clever enough to wonder about the ring, perhaps even follow clues to the truth regarding his own dire connection to the death.

Too bad, because actually he preferred the daughter to the mother.

"This alliance," the Grand Lord muttered to himself, "not

so worth the trouble, any more . . ." He stroked his chest where the mummified hand dangled. "Not worth it at all . . ."

He nodded to himself, making his decision. The Lady Nephera had left him with the proverbial baraki in the bag, but the Grand Lord would do what was best for him, not any Uruv Suurt. If Nephera did not concern herself with Golgren, then he would not concern himself with the high priestess.

Then the solution dawned, a solution so obvious it amazed him that he hadn't immediately thought of it.

Nagroch would be very eager for it too. "Nagroch!"

Maritia sat casually plumped against some pillows, eyeing Golgren. He had come to see her with Nagroch and a couple of guards. What was he up to now? Her captor was quite cunning.

"It is to your comfort?" the Grand Lord asked, indicating the surroundings.

"A little genteel for my tastes. I prefer my own cabin."

Golgren glanced around, saw there was no ready flask. "You have no drink?"

"They took it away when I tried to beat in the skull of one of them with it."

He chuckled, his eyes admiring her. There were times, Maritia suspected, when Golgren wished she were one of his kind. She did not know whether to be flattered or disgusted.

"You've come to tell me when I'm to be executed, I suppose," she declared, her expression unchanging.

"Ah, not so! I come for a different, happy reason. You are to be released! All a misunderstanding!"

"A misunderstanding?" She rose abruptly, trying to hold her temper. "Like my ring?"

"A crossing of communication, as you say. All is well now."

"If what you say is true, then I'll be leaving immediately. My guards?" She moved about, as though to gather

her things. To her surprise, Golgren did not balk or try to stop her.

"Will join you on deck."

"What about my weapons?" To be among so many ogres without even a dagger . . .

"Nagroch?"

At the Grand Lord's command, the hulking ogre, standing there and glaring at her, all but shoved her sheathed sword, breastplate, and dagger to her. Maritia glared back at him then slipped on the breastplate. She belted her sword and was about to slip the dagger in place when she saw it was not her dagger.

"This isn't my father's blade!" Glancing up, Maritia saw Nagroch's hand curl over a dagger at his side. "Give that back!"

"Not have your knife!" Nagroch snarled.

She started toward him, only to be restrained by two guards. Frowning, Golgren called, "Kul itak! Itak!"

The guards pulled back. Maritia shoved toward Nagroch, but now the Grand Lord stood in front of her, blocking her way.

"You claim him a thief?" he asked casually.

Hotak's daughter threw the dagger she had been handed onto the floor. "This is not mine. I demand the return of my father's dagger!"

Pointing at Nagroch's belt, she no longer saw the dagger. Maritia stared at the leering ogre, but her father's gift was gone.

"No thief!" Nagroch rumbled. "Lies!"

"You have it somewhere!"

The ogre spat at her feet. The blood surged to Maritia's head. She tried to maintain calm, but the days of captivity, the loss of a precious memento that belonged to her father, all this took a toll. Nagroch had stolen from her and now impugned her honor.

"*G'lahdi i suug . . .*" Nagroch continued to speak with much venom. "*Nera i suug . . .*"

She knew enough of the ogre tongue to realize that, roughly translated, Nagroch had called her a female unable to bear children. On the surface, a weak, almost laughable insult, but she was fed up, and she struck Nagroch across the jaw.

He flinched from the blow but held his ground. Nagroch leered evilly. "*Ih hita f'hon!* Duel! Honor demands!"

"Draw your weapon!" Maritia countered.

"No!" The Grand Lord rushed between them. His expression was very aggrieved. He looked from Nagroch to Maritia. "Enough bad has happened. Must not endanger yourself, offspring of Hotak!"

Her temples pounded. His words only made her more determined. "I'll endanger *him* now!"

Golgren shook his head. "The emperor would never understand!"

"Summon my guards! I'll have them as my witnesses!"

"What if you die, who is to blame?"

Maritia straightened proudly. "None!"

He sighed. "Maritia, Nagroch was struck. Declared duel. Ogre law says, ogre rules."

Meaning the arrangements would tend to favor Nagroch. Maritia, however, did not care. "Do it!" To her adversary, she added, "And when it's done, I'll have my dagger back!"

Nagroch only grinned. He seemed quite happy with the outcome.

The Grand Lord barked orders to his followers, including his second. The other ogres departed, leaving Golgren with her.

"Certain of this?" he asked.

Maritia already regretted her rash outburst, but her honor would not permit her to retreat. "Deadly certain."

"Then prepare." The ogre leader gave her a look of sympathy. "And beware. For Nagroch does not lose."

They came for her as the sun set. The beating of the leather drums preceded Golgren's grand entrance. The Grand Lord wore a solemn expression, though inwardly he felt like grinning. The daughter of Hotak had forgotten her mistaken imprisonment, and everyone else had forgotten Golgren's "mistake," so focused was the minotaur upon revenge. Nagroch had accepted Golgren's plan unquestioningly as a way of avenging his brother by slaying Maritia.

Revenge begets revenge, the Grand Lord thought with a rueful sigh.

"All is made ready." Golgren wore not his usual fine garb, but rather a simple kilt. In contrast, his breastplate—of minotaur manufacture—had been polished as bright as that of any legionary. "Such a tragedy it is, coming to this."

Maritia displayed no emotion. *Never show an enemy or an ally weakness,* her father had more than once instructed her. The Grand Lord was enemy and ally both, she thought to herself.

As she stepped out of the cabin, guards flanked her. Golgren led the small procession toward the open deck. There, Maritia saw the rails had been lined with torches. She wondered if those aboard her own flagship knew what was happening. Would they attack, if they did? She hoped not. Now was not the time to smash the uneasy alliance. Especially with the rebels threatening, the ogres were still important to the long-range plans of the imperium.

The drums continued to beat. There was no sign of her bodyguards. She had talked with them earlier, made them understand she had chosen this duel. They had protested, in the end acquiescing. Now Golgren likely kept them out of sight to avoid flare-ups between them and the crew.

A hexagonal pattern had been drawn with chalk on the deck. Each point was inscribed in the bastardized High Ogre script utilized by Golgren's caste. The only symbol the minotaur recognized was that of a snake. The snake seemed to be eating a tiny skull.

The drums ceased. The ogres began what sounded like a chorus of barking. Several batted the tops of their clubs or the tips of their axes on the wood, at times audibly cracking the rails.

"*Kya du ahn di i'gorunaki!*" the Grand Lord called, raising his hands to the sky. "*i'Nagrochi ut i'Maritia'n!*"

The ogres repeated his shout, obviously thirsty for blood, preferably Maritia's. The female minotaur strode to meet her opponent. Nagroch grinned eerily at her and then waved to the crowd.

The Grand Lord pointed to the center of the design. As the two positioned themselves where he indicated, Golgren waved another ogre over with two much-abused hand axes. Nagroch took one, tested its balance, then proceeded to discard his breastplate.

As she took the other chipped and rusting axe, Maritia felt a sudden flash of panic and considered rushing to the rail and leaping over. No, it was too late for that dishonorable move, and besides, her guards below would suffer the most for her cowardice.

Ogres surrounded the pattern, holding their clubs steady. They were not simply there to watch. If she or Nagroch tumbled outside any part of the fighting area, the ogres there were to beat the unfortunate until he or she returned to the duel. Once the duel begun, it wouldn't end until one combatant lay lifeless.

They studied each other for weaknesses. However, Golgren had chosen his second wisely. Even though Nagroch had shed his armor, her adversary appeared to be a veritable small mountain of muscle.

"Be ready," the Grand Lord cautioned.

Maritia crouched, her axe gripped tight. Nagroch's froglike

features spread wide in grinning anticipation. From somewhere behind her she heard a single drum beat.

Axe high, Nagroch leapt at her. The deck erupted in roars.

She barely deflected the first strike. Every bone vibrated as the monstrous warrior's blow landed. The minotaur fell to one knee, struggling to push her opponent's axe away from her skull.

"*F'han, Uruv Suurt,*" Nagroch breathed at her. "*F'han . . .*"

Her snort was partly an attempt to clear her nose of his stench. Straining to push herself up, Maritia suddenly kicked at the ogre. Her foot harmlessly bounced off Nagroch's thick leg, but the maneuver startled the pockmarked warrior and he backed up a step.

Leaping to her feet, the minotaur swung low, seeking Nagroch's belly. His own weapon came down, pushing her axe away, though she managed to crease his side. The meager cut likely did not even sting, but it was symbolic. First blood was hers. Last blood was what mattered most, however.

Cheers rose, for the ogres relished the violence, the spectacle, and the promise of more blood. Maritia looked around for Golgren but couldn't see him, and Nagroch gave her no time. The frog-faced ogre swung again. When the legion commander shifted to defend herself, Nagroch's beefy hand thrust at her. The feint had caught her by complete surprise.

He seized her throat and began throttling her. Choking, Maritia grabbed his wrist. However, she might as well have been trying to tear the Great Circus down, so solid was the warrior's arm.

Nagroch chuckled. "Skin you, Uruv Suurt! Wear you close!"

He intended to do just that. Ogres sometimes used the skulls, horns, and fur of their dead enemies for home and body decoration. Minotaurs, on the other hand, saw little value in collecting such grisly trophies. Perhaps a tusked skull here and there lay in some legionary's home, but that was uncommon.

Nagroch's fingers closed tighter. Maritia felt her neck twisting, but using his bare hands made Nagroch negligent. He momentarily lowered his axe, and Maritia jabbed upward with her own weapon. Nagroch fell back rather than risk a deep wound on his arm.

Maritia slipped to one knee. She inhaled deeply, trying to overcome the dizziness she felt. A harsh pain ripped across her weapon arm. Her axe skittered across the deck. She rolled away from the ogre, clutching her shoulder. Stomping feet warned her that Nagroch was close behind. Instinctively backing away, Maritia collided with a pair of hairy legs.

"No!" she gasped.

The female minotaur leapt back into the fight just as the guard on the line swung his club at her, grazing her thigh. Barreling forward, Maritia collided with Nagroch. Her left horn struck him hard. He gave a yelp, as Hotak's daughter looked out of dazed eyes and saw his blood dripping down on her muzzle.

"*Nya i koja eza f'hani, Uruv Suurt!*" roared Golgren's second.

His axe struck her hard on the side of the head, but fortunately he made contact with the flat of his blade. Still, her ears rang, her jaw felt numbed. The minotaur stumbled back.

Nagroch limped to one side. His right leg had a deep, round wound. The limb shook. The ogre now had to favor his good leg.

Clutching her axe, Maritia rose to face the giant. Nagroch grinned anew, and if anything seemed more eager for the fight. The crowd jeered their momentary hesitation. Shouting his own taunts back at his fellows, Nagroch stomped toward Maritia, swinging his axe back and forth in a series of savage arcs.

Maritia swung her weapon. The clanging of the two axes resounded beyond the ship. The minotaur and her foe whirled around and around as each sought advantage. Among the sea of roaring ogre faces, Maritia spotted Golgren's. As ever, the Grand Lord seemed unreadable, watching the duel with almost clinical detachment.

"You fall!" grunted Nagroch. "Fall and save your hurt! Will make your death swift, I promise . . ."

"I feel no pain, no weakness," the minotaur commander lied. "Can you say the same?"

"I am Nagroch! Nagroch, He Who is the Mastark Bull! Named so by Donnag at birth!"

Maritia could well believe the Lord Chieftain of Blöde had given this brute such a name. Despite his quivering leg, Nagroch seemed very much like a mastark bull, ready to fight all night if necessary.

Maritia knew that she could never last the night. The minotaur focused on Nagroch's lower right side. Every opportunity, her axe attacked his vulnerability. Again and again, she forced the heavy ogre to lean on his weakened leg. Soon her efforts began to tell. Nagroch's bleeding didn't stop, and his leg grew more and more unsteady. Maritia, risking herself at times, continued to drive him to the right.

Still he hammered hard at her. Twice he slipped past her guard, the first time grazing her side, the second time piercing her thigh. Maritia bit back the pain and again pushed to the right.

Then . . . Nagroch stumbled and fell to one knee.

The audience roared loudly at this surprise. Whether they cheered for Maritia or to encourage Nagroch, it was impossible to say.

The ogre pushed up, but his limb buckled. He swung wildly. Sensing her opportunity, Maritia lunged for his open chest.

Nagroch's weapon shifted to block her, but the minotaur abruptly feinted and drew her adversary off-balance. As Nagroch tried to compensate, Maritia adjusted for her true target. The blade sank deep into Nagroch's thick throat, a spray of blood soaking the weapon to the handle.

He let out a piteous, garbled sound. To Maritia's horror, though, Nagroch did not fall or die. Rather, moving with a swiftness that should have been impossible, he tore her axe away from her hand, tossing it beyond the gathering.

His chest bathed in his own life fluids, Nagroch then rose slowly. Like a clumsy puppet, he took one awkward step, then another, toward his opponent. Each step was accompanied by a wide, jagged swing of his own blade. Forced to retreat, Maritia found herself dangerously close to the line of waiting ogres. One took a swing at her but stopped his club at the line.

Nagroch tried to speak, but his words emerged as guttural gasps. If anything, his grin was wider, wilder, crazier. He left a trail of red drops on the deck, but still he advanced.

Now he was so close she could smell his horrible breath. Feeling all but spent, Maritia twisted to one side and at the same time kicked out at him desperately with both feet. This time, she caught Nagroch's legs, striking them with her last might.

The massive ogre twisted backward. The planks beneath him cracked as he hit with a thud. Maritia rolled over and tried to rise. The crowd grunted loudly. Nagroch, too, struggled for his footing.

Swearing, the minotaur sought her weapon. Finding it, she crawled over to the ogre.

Eyes still filled with venom, the dying ogre reached for her and managed to seize her by the ankle. His fingers tightened, almost crushing the bone.

"*Nya—nya i f'han—i'Bastioni—*" he growled, baring ugly teeth.

"What?" About to land a death blow, Maritia faltered. "What did you say?"

She struggled to remember her ogre tongue. What was this brute trying to say about Bastion?

Suddenly, Golgren stood beside them. Maritia glanced up, saw his darkening face.

"Duel is yours, Maritia. Death must be demanded."

"Not until—"

"You will shame Nagroch's clan by letting him die slow, like a sheep blooded. Slay now!" Around them, the ogres barked 'f'han' over and over.

Maritia did want to finish the duel as decreed, but she also wanted to know what Nagroch had said about Bastion.

Nagroch's grip on her faltered. He opened his mouth, eyes narrowed.

"*i'Bast—*"

He got no further. A curved blade suddenly glided across his throat, opening a ravine through which the last of Nagroch's life poured.

A hush overtook the assembled warriors. With a sigh, Nagroch finally fell still. Maritia tugged her leg free of his death grip.

"You shouldn't have done that!" she said angrily, looking up at Golgren.

The Grand Lord stared back indulgently, almost fondly. "It is the way of our kind. Your life I might have saved from them." He indicated the other warriors, who had now resumed their cheering and shouting.

"But he—"

Golgren would hear no more. He handed his own dagger to a subordinate, who, in turn, gave the Grand Lord a small water pouch.

"Drink! You need."

She could not argue. As she sipped, Maritia's thoughts whirled. Nagroch had been trying to trick her, babbling. That had to be it. He could know nothing of Bastion.

Why had the Grand Lord interfered?

"Will have Nagroch's things searched, Maritia. Will find your father's dagger."

"Good . . ." Maritia swayed. The fight had depleted her. Her eyes swam. She could barely think.

"Fought well, Uruv Suurt," Golgren remarked, with only the barest smile. He peered at her. "Fought well, Maritia."

"I-I won, Golgren. Now, I demand m-my freedom as—as is my right!"

The Grand Lord said nothing, his eyes narrowing. The smile took on a predatory appearance, all sharp teeth clamped tight.

He said nothing else, nor did she. Exhaustion and nausea overwhelmed Maritia. The water sack slipped from the female minotaur's hand, the contents spilling. The deck spun about.

Maritia collapsed.

Chapter XVIII

Gaerth

Faros was drowning. The intense pressure squeezed his lungs. The darkness of the deep embraced him. He knew he was dying.

Still, he clawed futilely. A thick forest of seaweed wrapped itself around him. The long, sinewy plants clutched his arms and legs. He felt as if bound by ropes. Faros desperately tore at the seaweed, yet it only appeared to grow thicker, stronger . . .

He woke up gasping.

For what seemed an eternity, Faros couldn't fill his lungs. No matter how many desperate breaths he took, it didn't seem enough.

Something grabbed his arms. Faros struggled.

"Easy now, lad! Easy!"

The familiar voice soothed him. Shaking, Faros slowly came to grips with his surroundings. He could smell the sea, but was no longer in the water. His breathing began to return to normal and, as it did, the memories returned.

Memories of the behemoth from the deep . . . and the mercurial goddess who was its mistress.

"My Lord Faros!" the voice growled. "Do you hear me? Snap out of it, lad!"

"Botanos?" the rebel leader managed to gasp. He gazed through blurry eyes at a male minotaur, yet neither the voice nor the shape was that of the *Dragon Crest's* captain.

"Here." A cup was thrust in Faros's left hand. "Drink this, slowly."

If there was one thing he wasn't, it was thirsty, but his murky companion pushed the cup toward the younger minotaur's muzzle. With great reluctance, Faros swallowed the contents.

Fire erupted in his head, his belly, and his limbs.

"By Vyrox! What—?"

"Aye, they said it was potent." The other minotaur coalesced into Napol, the marine commander.

Napol sailed with Tinza aboard the *Sea Reaver.* How had Faros ended up on the other ship? Had they plucked him from the waters? Had the entire vision of Zeboim and her creature been nothing more than his waterlogged imagination?

Slowly, things around him registered. He was in a high but narrow hut. His bed, a brown, cotton mattress atop a six-legged wooden cot, was stuffed thick with down. A blanket of similar make covered him. The floor was soft, white sand. A tall candle in a boxy, silver holder sat upon a table whose top was made of planks that had once been part of a ship. The door was the treated hide of some animal. It flapped lightly from the ocean breeze outside. Faros could tell it was day, but nothing more. There were no personal items in the hut other than the candle holder, nothing that told him where he was.

"Where—?"

Napol stopped him. "They won't tell us the name of the place, even though it's only a way station. That was a promise made."

"Who're they?"

"You'll meet them soon enough. They want us out of here. They weren't too happy when we appeared like that."

Trying to hide his confusion, Faros asked, "Captain Botanos. Is he dead?"

Napol's eyes widened. "Dead? He's been awake for a day already. You're the one who's been worrying us, my lord! If I hadn't seen it with my own eyes! If I hadn't lived through it and I'll tell you I was sure none of us would—I'd have never believed it!"

He raised a large leather sack and offered Faros some more of the drink. Quickly refusing it, the rebel leader said, "Tell me."

"Better you rest. I'll tell you when we take the long boat back to our ships—"

Faros's expression hardened. "Tell me . . ."

Under that gaze, the veteran soldier swallowed anxiously. "Aye, my lord! Aye . . ."

Napol kept the story simple. Aboard the *Sea Reaver*, they had known nothing of the two lost at sea. Tinza had had her own problems to worry about, chiefly a mast that was cracking and ships behind her that were starting to scatter recklessly.

"We feared that once those behind us lost direction, we'd have rebels sailing off in every direction. We'd be lucky if some of them we'd ever find again!"

Faros nodded.

"Then . . . you'll swear I've been drinking sea water instead of good rum . . . but it's true what happened next: the water became deathly calm! We stood on the deck, wondering at it. The sails hung as limp as a hanged corpse, and there wasn't a sound!" He grimaced. "Was a mighty stench, though! Smelled like every fish in the sea had gone and died, and we'd found the place they'd chosen to rot!"

So caught up in his own story, Napol unthinkingly nearly took another drink from the sack. Only at the last did the minotaur pull it away, his lips curling in distaste. "Pfah! Forgive me, lad! 'Tis what happened next that makes me forget myself . . ."

"What was it?"

"You'll think me daft, but everyone else save Botanos will swear to it, too! We were all looking around, trying to decide what happened—when the tentacle of the largest kraken I ever saw rose from the water!"

A sailor at the stern saw it first. Giving a cry, she pointed up. As Napol, Tinza, and the rest stared, the huge appendage rose out of the sea. Its diameter was greater than the height of the tallest ship. It stretched into the dark heaven, thrusting forward far beyond the sight of the *Sea Reaver*.

"Your ship saw it, too, after you'd gone missing," the marine commander added. "The most curious thing about the tentacle, however, was that it hung in the sky for the longest time. Not only that, but no one among any of the rebel vessels reported seeing the rest of the giant. Still can't fathom how it could be swimming like that—one limb up in the air.

Faros said nothing. Napol's words were too frighteningly close to describing the tongue of the Sea Queen's creature. There was no longer any doubt in his mind: his encounter with Zeboim had been real. Faros attempted to rise. Napol reached to help, but the rebel leader shook him off.

"How did we end up here—and where is here anyway?"

"The first I can't say much of, lad. Suddenly the tentacle dropped back beneath the waters, and the sky returned. The stench faded and we found ourselves in the calm of this island. They came out to meet us at first light . . . and told us they had you and the captain."

" 'They' again. Just who are they, Napol?"

"He means us."

Faros spun toward the voice. A minotaur stood at the entrance to the cabin. Tall and lean, he moved like a predatory cat. He wore a simple green kilt that reminded Faros of Napol's, though clearly they were not related. The newcomer looked down his tapering muzzle at the younger minotaur.

"My name is Gaerth. My people . . . are no longer yours."

With a snarl, Faros tried to leap at Gaerth. However, his brain was swimming dizzily, and it was only Napol's aid that kept him from toppling over.

Gaerth watched all with complete indifference. "After taking the durag brew, you should make no sudden actions for the first hour. Did you not tell him?"

Napol's ears flattened. "I didn't have a chance to warn him, my lord."

"What do you mean, your people aren't mine?" asked Faros, fighting the dizziness. He straightened.

"We long ago parted ways with the empire. Our home is ours, our destiny is ours, we belong neither to the throne nor the Horned One. You are here because of a request of another, one to whom we owe respect and homage. The Lord of Just Cause has asked that we do what we can for you, but we shall do no more than that."

" 'Lord of Just Cause'?" repeated Faros. "Who—?

Gaerth had already turned back to the door. "Your ships make ready. You'll be leaving soon . . . and you will not be returning."

Vertigo or no vertigo, Faros struggled free of Napol's grasp and seized Gaerth's shoulder. The taller minotaur attempted to shrug him off, but Faros grabbed his arm and twisted it back. Gaerth grunted in surprise.

Immediately, two others burst into the cabin. They reached for Faros, but Gaerth waved them back. Napol, despite having no weapon, tried to defend Faros, snarling at the pair.

"Listen to me," Faros muttered between clenched teeth, his head feeling on fire. "I never asked for your help, nor that of your 'Lord of Just Cause!' I was brought here without my knowledge by the whims of a goddess—"

"Zeboim," Gaerth declared, rubbing his freed arm. " 'Tis a strange time when such gods ally themselves thusly . . ."

"She's Sargonnas's daughter, nothing strange in that."

"She brought you to those who follow the ways of Kiri-Jolith, Faros Es-Kalin. She brings her father's champion to his arch-rival for our race. Truly they are strange shieldmates . . ."

First I am bothered by one god, then two, and now three. Faros snorted. "As far as I'm concerned, that's three too many gods. What do they want of me? Can't three gods defeat Morgion?"

Gaerth shrugged. "This is not the only battle going on. Zeboim and the bison god have their own struggles to overcome. The pantheons as we know them are a thing of the past. Already no Takhisis, no Paladine. Who can say what will happen next?"

"I can . . . and will!" Faros searched around. "My sword!" His expression tightened. "Where is it?"

"The weapon . . . all your weapons . . . are being held in safety until you leave these shores. We will not take any chances—"

"You'll return my sword to me now!"

The guards moved close to Gaerth, blocking the rebel leader from reaching him. Gaerth's eyes became slits. "No outsider bears arms in our domain. You will cease your demands and—"

Faros's fingers folded and folded again, as if he already tensely gripped the weapon. "I demand my sword!"

The two guards moved toward him—then froze. A flash of black light burst from Faros's empty grip. It stretched long, shaped itself to a sharp point—and became the blade created by Sargonnas.

One of the sentries gave a cry and lunged. Faros sliced his axe in two, then took a swing at the minotaur, nearly slicing him in two.

"Get back!" snapped Gaerth. He gestured at the sword. "Stay away from that ... thing!"

They retreated, leaving the way open for the rebel. Without waiting for Napol, Faros pushed past Gaerth, through the doorway and a moment later stumbled to a halt in absolute shock.

A city of high, silver spires and curved structures, reminiscent of the shell of a nautilus, met his disbelieving gaze. The city was surrounded by water dappled with foam green and glistening blue colors. A blue banner with the silver outline of a twin-edged axe fluttered atop many of the city's structures. A thick, serrated wall of iridescent pearl protected the city from the waters to the east, where the rebel ships lay anchored.

Circling the rebel ships were several low-slung, green-tinted vessels with shorter, slimmer masts. Their bows ended in elongated, narrow points looking to Faros like ideal spears to puncture the hulls of an enemy. The bows of each ship also sported a ballista aimed at the outsiders.

"Lord Faros!" Napol shouted. "Remember, the durag brew—"

The moment the other rebel spoke, Faros's world spun about. The fantastic city vanished, leaving only a rocky, foreboding set of hills with no sign of life in his vision. He looked out at the water, this time seeing only three ships near the rebel vessels. Faros blinked and looked again at the hills, then back at the ships, but nothing had changed. He eyed his sword and ring, but even then the silver city did not reappear.

"Are you all right, my lord?"

"Where is it? How is it hidden?"

Napol looked perplexed. "Where's what?"

"The city! What magical veil covers it?" He turned to Gaerth, who had calmly followed them out. "What is this place?"

"A way station for our people. A half dozen man it at any time. The rest of us sailed here at the behest of the Lord of Just Cause."

"A way station." With a snort, the rebel leader pointed at the hills. "What if I climb up for a better look at your mighty fleet?"

Gaerth shrugged. "If you wish to do so, I will not prevent you from climbing."

"Which means that I shouldn't bother . . ." The illusion had to to be a potent one, Faros thought.

"The brew is very heady, outsider. It can cause one to imagine things . . . at least temporarily."

The two guards approached. Faros readied his blade, but Gaerth sent the pair back inside. To Faros, he said, "Your Captain Botanos is back aboard the *Dragon's Crest*. He has been directing the taking aboard of supplies and weaponry. I would venture that he is just about done. You look fit for travel now, so it is time you left."

As Faros had no desire to keep Gaerth's company any longer, he nodded. "What did you mean about supplies and weaponry?"

"A promise kept to our patron. You have all we can give. The empire is yours to win . . . or lose. We do not care. Our ships will guide you to a familiar point, then our part in this is ended. Be warned, though. Do not sail from your escort until signaled."

"Why?"

"Because if you do not follow the escort, you may be forever lost. Even we will not be able to save you and none of us will risk ourselves to try."

"All this protection for a mere way station?"

Gaerth did not answer, instead gesturing at Napol, who anxiously sought to guide his leader away before another argument ensued.

"I've no war with you," Faros declared to the stranger. "I'll not come hunting you if I win the empire."

"You could never find us again."

The younger warrior bared his teeth at the slim minotaur. "I would . . . if I needed to."

Gaerth's nostrils flared but he said nothing.

Faros turned and followed Napol away. At the edge of the white, sandy beach upon which the cabin sat, a long boat awaited them. Four sailors from the *Dragon's Crest* saluted as he neared.

As the boat launched, Faros glanced back. Gaerth stood near the tiny, unprepossessing cabin. The structure looked well-worn, ready to collapse. The island seemed as stark and uninviting a piece of ground as the rocks north of Karthay.

They passed one of three green ships. The crew, all built like Gaerth and with similar, less pronounced features, watched them in silence.

"An arrogant bunch for so few in number," Commander Napol commented.

"They supplied us with what we needed?"

"Aye! Every vessel!"

Faros looked over the closest green ship from stern to bow. As swift and as deadly as it appeared, it clearly could hold no more than a third the number of crew and fighters of his flagship.

"Every vessel," he repeated back to Napol.

The veteran warrior did not see what Faros did. Three ships could not restock his fleet. They could not possibly have held enough supplies, much less weaponry.

It would take more than a dozen . . .

The *Sea Reaver* sat anchored to the port side of the *Crest*. Faros climbed aboard the latter. Napol took another long boat and headed back to the *Sea Reaver*.

A boisterous Captain Botanos greeted Faros. "My lord! Praise be, you're finally up and well!" The hulking minotaur went down on one knee, his horns lowered to the side. "You saved me from the depths! My life is yours, once again!"

Faros frowned. "Tell me what you remember."

"Little enough! Tossed into the water, the ocean in my lungs, and you jumping in after me! I know you reached me, but after that . . . nothing until I woke up on that forsaken rock *they* use."

"You sound like you know them."

As Botanos rose, his cheerful mood faded. "I recall them from a brief encounter once. They aided my captain, Azak, and General Rahm Es-Hestos, in fleeing Hotak's sharks, then, just like now, cut off all further contact." Ears twitching, the master of the *Dragon's Crest* snorted. "Captain Gaerth was there, too. Azak nearly came to blows with him. Gaerth and his fellows then sailed off. Never figured to run into him again. An odd one."

Faros grunted. Again, he squinted at the island, but no new vision was granted to him. Shrugging, the rebel leader turned to more pragmatic matters. "We're ready to go?"

"Aye! We were just waiting for you."

"Then let's be gone from this place." He glanced at the green ships. "Those three are to be our escort, eh?"

Botanos nodded dourly. "I'm to signal them when we've set our proper course. Don't know why I need the likes of those to lead me out to sea! I was born and raised in my craft and taught by the best, good Captain Azak!"

"Follow them. Follow them exactly. Don't try to deviate."

The mariner studied Faros's face. "As you command."

As Botanos turned to issue orders, the former slave went to the rail to watch. Using triangular flags, the *Dragon's Crest* signaled to the other rebels. When Captain Botanos was satisfied, he himself signaled the nearest of the green ships.

Almost immediately, the three strange vessels moved out. Their curved sails caught the slightest wind with ease. Faros studied their unusual design.

"Look at them cut through the water!" one of the crew blurted.

The trio were indeed swift and very agile. Faros recalled the brief vision he had experienced. If there was any truth to what he had seen, there were more than three ships surrounding them, enough to bring his fleet to ruin if he broke his word.

The *Dragon's Crest* got underway. The rebel ships clustered together. As the entire armada left the island behind, Faros looked back. Gaerth's isolated domain took on an indistinct appearance, as if it had lost some cohesion. The way station now seemed little more than a shadow. Faros felt disoriented. Even gazing up at the sky did not help, for the clouds—and the sun—appeared to shift randomly, making it impossible to say which way was which.

Thinking of the other ships, Faros snapped, "Botanos! Signal the other ships to stay close!"

The captain obeyed. As the signal passed from one ship to another, some of Faros's unease faded.

But a moment later, Botanos suddenly shouted, "Answer, damn you! Answer!"

The rebel leader turned again. "What's wrong?"

"No one is answering from the *Fury of Harnac*! Worse, I think she's drifting south and taking one of the others with her!"

As they helplessly watched, the *Fury* veered completely away from its sisters. It sailed south, with another ship blindly trailing it.

"Start a signal fire!" urged Botanos to a sailor.

"That'll take too long!" Faros looked about, saw the ballista. "Fire at them!"

"You'll not reach 'em at this distance!"

"That's not what I want! Let's get their attention!"

As quickly as possible, the trained crew had the weapon manned and ready. However, the two confused ships had sailed far away from the others.

Faros gave the order. The steel-tipped lances flew as high as the weapon could send them. The missiles darted over the water, then dipped. They hit the water with a high splash.

Those aboard the *Crest* waited. Botanos let out a gruff exhalation of relief as the last ship began to turn back toward the fleet, but the *Fury* failed to respond. It moved in a strangely haphazard, chaotic fashion, as if its crew had lost control.

"Get back here, damn you!" the captain called in frustration. Gold rings jingling, he shouted to his own crew, "Prepare to come around!"

Faros seized his arm. "No! Let them go!"

"There's still a chance we can catch them—"

In response, the rebel leader shoved Botanos's muzzle heavenward. "Look!"

The larger minotaur gasped. Shaking off his leader, he tried to focus on the swirling and shifting clouds. The effort was too much and Botanos fell against the rail, eyes blinking. "What's happening to the sky?" he gasped.

"The same magic that protects this place! You follow the other ship and you risk losing complete control of your direction! Gaerth said to follow the escort! Do it, no matter how many sail wrong!"

Botanos swallowed. Clutching his head, he shouted to the crew, "Belay that last order! Stay with the green ones! Make sure the other ships know that!"

He and Faros took one last look at the *Fury of Harnac*. A splash occurred some distance behind it, the second vessel's own desperate attempt to signal their comrade. However, the *Fury* paid them no heed. Like the island, it began to lose definition.

"What do you think is happening to them?" Botanos murmured.

If Faros understood Gaerth, they would sail until they died. Faros thought bitterly of Sargonnas, of Morgion, of all the deities. "One god or another will claim them. Aren't we all pawns of the gods?"

The huge mariner had no reply.

Faros watched the *Fury* vanish toward its fate, then started toward the bow. He had no idea where Gaerth's escort would take them, but the sooner the island was just another buried memory, the better. For the price of one ship, he had the supplies and arms for the rest. The rebellion could go on as planned.

And more minotaurs could die as the gods stood by and observed.

Chapter XIX

Broken Alliances

Maritia dreamed she was still a prisoner in Golgren's cabin. However, this was not her current nightmare. It was worse than that. She awoke to find the Grand Lord himself lying at her side.

She rolled away from him, one hand reaching for a dagger that she couldn't find. To her horror, Maritia discovered she was clad only in a blanket.

"I'll flay you alive!" she growled at Golgren. Her eyes darted around the cabin. There had to be something she could use as a weapon.

The Grand Lord calmly rose. He had been sitting right beside Maritia's head. To her relief, she saw he was dressed in dark brown and green pants, tunic, and cloak, along with high, leather boots.

"No harm is meant," he said, smiling.

Well aware of the duplicity always lurking in that smile, Maritia was not at all assuaged. She gestured at her bare garment. "No harm? What of this?"

"There were wounds to tend to. The armor, it had to be removed for your sake."

"By you, of course!"

He chuckled, an obscene sound to her ears. "No, no. My servant." Golgren gestured. "Please, look."

Among the pillows, Maritia saw her clothing neatly arrayed. The armor had been arranged meticulously. Her sword lay nearby . . . and her father's dagger next to the sword. All had been freshly polished.

"Nagroch gave false words. The dagger he had."

"As I said." Pushing back her loose mane, Maritia bared her teeth. "I'd like to get dressed."

Golgren simply turned his back, a gesture meant to prove both his trust and his power.

Still a little unsteady on her feet, Maritia reached for her clothing. The Grand Lord politely admired the cabin wall. When she had her breastplate and kilt on, she muttered irritably, "If you wish to turn and face me, you can do so now."

As he turned, Golgren bowed like a human courtier. He dressed like an elf sometimes; now he was bowing like a human. Maritia wondered what race he would next emulate. The Grand Lord was a rare ogre, a contradiction at times.

"The warrior queen!" the ogre declared grandly. "The victor!"

"The prisoner," she countered tersely. "The betrayed."

"No betrayal, Maritia. This humble one but made certain you would not yet follow your father and brothers to the Field of Crows."

She understood the reference. The Field of Crows was an afterworld where the ogres believed champions of their race fought epic and eternal battles. Huge carrion eaters feasted on the losers, whose bones then regenerated with the coming of each new day. They would then rejoin the combat, this time seeking to make meals of the others for the scavengers. To the ogres, it was a warrior's paradise.

To Maritia, however, it was a hell only for Golgren's race. She hoped whatever afterlife her sire and siblings had passed on to would be better than such fruitless, chaotic struggle. Maritia bent toward her weapons, watching her companion. Golgren spread his arms wide, showing he was not even armed with a dagger. Not at all comforted, she secured her belt. Maritia checked her sword for any damage or interference, but found none.

"By your own guards the polishing done," the ogre lord informed her.

"Obviously so." She stared Golgren in the eye. He had piercing orbs that tempted her to flinch. "What isn't obvious is what you intend to do with me now."

"Now? You shall depart . . . as promised."

"That's all? I just walk out of this cabin and take a boat back to my fleet?"

His smile grew toothy. "Not to your fleet, uh, no."

Her hand went to the sword's hilt. "What?"

Golgren indicated the door. "Please! All is answered outside."

"You lead, then."

With a dire chuckle, the Grand Lord strode toward the door. It swung open, revealing a shaggy sentry. The ogre sentry hunched down to keep his head below that of Golgren's.

Her fingers hovering near her sword, the legion commander followed Golgren outside. The first thing she saw was dozens of ogres. It almost seemed as if every creature aboard the ship awaited her entrance. Her own bodyguard knelt near the bow. Looking ashamed for their failure to protect her, they bent their heads low to the deck, the tips of their horns almost touching the wood.

"Rise up," she hissed. "You are minotaurs."

They immediately obeyed. Maritia didn't think there was anything they could have done to prevent her situation, and sacrificing their lives in the effort would have been a waste.

Golgren indicated the starboard side. "This way, offspring of Hotak."

Flanked by her two warriors, Maritia walked over, the ogres parting way for her. She stopped dead in her tracks, gaping. A small boat rocked in the water. Beyond the rail, there were no other ships. A small speck not at all worthy of being called an island was the only break in the otherwise endless waters.

She spun on Golgren, causing many of the ogres to growl and her own guards to brace for a fight. "Where have you taken us?"

Unperturbed, he answered, "Not far, not far. The last ride will be short." Golgren used his stump to point at the forlorn rock. "Only there."

"Then what?"

"Then we go. Uruv Suurt come."

"You 'go'?" her brow wrinkled.

"Return to Kern. The hunt . . . the hunt is yours, Maritia. The rebel Faros is yours . . . if catch him, you can."

"Why are you forfeiting your revenge? Why—"

"Please, the boat," Golgren said, gesturing.

Maritia stared at him, not understanding. He stared back, smiling grimly.

"Come," she finally commanded of her soldiers. Whatever the ogre chose, her own mission was clear. Faros had to be hunted down.

As she peered over the rail, she noticed the six burly ogres at the oars. One of her guards descended first, followed closely by Maritia. As she stepped into the long boat, her other guard climbed down the rope ladder—after which, to her surprise, Golgren also started down the ladder.

Maritia sat and watched the maimed figure lower himself. Golgren moved deftly despite his incapacity, she had to admit. He was strong as well as sly. Had it been the Grand Lord who faced her in the combat, she wondered whether the outcome would have been different.

"You needn't have joined us," Hotak's daughter mocked as the ogre leader sat near to her.

"No?" he replied, his visage grim. To a whip-wielding ogre at the boat's bow, Golgren roared, *"Tyraq i gero! Kya ne! Kya ne!"*

The other snapped his whip. With a collective grunt, the rowers went to work. Their muscles strained as they fought against the current. Wondering where they were headed, Maritia admired the rowers' strength. The current was powerful and even minotaurs would have found it tough going.

The small island proved no less bleak as it drew closer. Nothing in the landscape identified the place to Maritia.

One of her guards leaned close, whispering, "This is some trick, my lady! They mean to kill us!"

"Quiet, Rog!"

Golgren pretended not to have heard the conversation, but Maritia knew better. He trusted her to keep her warriors under control, just as she trusted him to do the same.

The boat jostled. There was a thump and the ogres started leaping out of the vessel.

Rising grandly, Golgren commanded, "Please. Ashore."

Her other guard stepped from the boat then offered Maritia his assistance. Most of the ogres were already ashore. Two stayed behind to mind the boat. Rog suddenly roared. His axe came out in a blur, slicing into one of the two ogres still with the boat. The second rower reached for his own weapon.

Immediately, the rest of Golgren's followers swarmed Maritia and her other bodyguard. She drew her sword and managed a cut to one attacker's side, but then she was hemmed in by the press of bodies. Hotak's daughter saw the Grand Lord take a hand axe from one of his own protectors. With careful deliberation and clear skill, he threw the axe at Rog's back.

The spinning blade struck the neck and skull of its target with perfect accuracy. There was an audible crack of bone. The legionary toppled into the water.

Golgren barked at his followers. Those hounding Maritia pulled back. Her remaining bodyguard moved to her side, his arm bloody from a savage cut near the shoulder. At the legion commander's sign, both put away their weapons and waited.

With a snap of his fingers, the Grand Lord had the remaining ogres form two lines flanking the minotaurs. As he stalked to the head of the party, he looked ruefully at Maritia.

"Regrettable," was his only comment.

It took a short while for them to march to the center of the islet. There, Golgren indicated that the two prisoners—for prisoners they were again, Maritia believed—should stand.

"Here," he told her. "Stay until the boat is far."

She did not reply, but the ogre was obviously satisfied. He looked to one of his underlings, who brought forth a small leather sack Maritia had not noticed on the boat.

As the bestial warrior dropped it unceremoniously at her feet, Golgren added, "For thirst and hunger."

Maritia did not bother to pick up the sack. The Grand Lord sent the other ogres back to the boat, keeping with him only two giant warriors.

"Most regrettable," he said again, this time more broadly.

"No, not regrettable. This is a terrible mistake on your part," she told him. "I will not forget it, Golgren."

He looked pained. "No, do not forget me. Farewell, Maritia. I wish you the good battle against the blood of Chot. May many enemy die screaming at your feet."

"They will . . . and some of them may yet be ogres."

He chuckled, then with a solemn bow, he left her. The legion commander watched bitterly as her sworn ally abandoned her on the wind-whipped rock. Her stare burned into his back.

"Do we go after them, my lady?" asked her companion.

"Why? To fight gloriously but fail my father's empire by dying here? There'll be time for the ogre, mark me. Now we've

other matters to attend to. We've got a rebellion that must be crushed . . . and the last of a cursed bloodline to sever."

Golgren studied the banner fluttering atop his flagship, admiring the design for which he was responsible. The wind made it look as if the severed hand moved, slashing again and again with the dagger. Each cut was a mortal blow against some rival, some foe . . .

The die was cast. The pact with the Uruv Suurt was finally broken. The day had been inevitable, if not the manner of its occurrence. Lady Nephera and her dark powers had become more of a burden than they were worth and this debacle had cost Golgren more than he had desired. Nagroch had proven a disappointment, and perhaps Hotak's daughter had actually done Golgren a favor by defeating him. It was not the outcome the Grand Lord had expected, but he found it pleased him more, for Lady Maritia's sake.

His enemies would think him weakened now, but Golgren had planned for this opportunity. Even the hellish powers of Hotak's mate would not deter him from his ultimate goals. He had other methods, other sources of strength, from which to draw. His rivals might think him easy prey now, but he would be like the jakary—the spindly, wide-mouthed lizard that lulled its victims with an appearance of illness, then clamped its highly-poisonous fangs on the unsuspecting. The jakary's potent venom killed in seconds. Golgren would try to be just as swift.

As ever, the Grand Lord had more than one reason for his actions. Maritia still served a purpose, an important one. Let her hunt the cursed Faros and let much Uruv Suurt blood be spilled. Golgren wanted many, many minotaurs drawn into the conflict before it ended. Already, essential legions had left Ambeon . . . beautiful Ambeon, or as the Grand Lord saw it, *Dyr ut iGolgrenarok*—the Realm

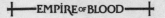

of Golgren's Supremacy—a much more fitting title than the one that honored some worthless, long-decayed king of the Uruv Suurt.

The long boat bumped up against his flagship. As Golgren ascended—accepting no aid—he paused to look at the island he had left behind. The pact he had made with the lead captain of the imperial fleet would give him the time he needed to depart. His other vessels had already long before left the area. The Uruv Suurt would pick up their commander then sail off to fight their own kind.

Whoever won did not, in the long run, matter to the ogre. Golgren allowed himself a genuine smile as he imagined the fate of imperial colony on Ansalon. His hordes would surprise them. The Uruv Suurt there would replace the slaves Faros had freed.

There was much to plan, much to do. The Uruv Suurt—the minotaurs—believed themselves the children of destiny, but they were wrong. There was only one child of destiny, one being fit to rule all.

And Golgren would humbly accept that mantle . . .

✠————▼————✠

The *Stormbringer* arrived several hours later, much too late to catch Golgren's *Hand*. The sun was nearly at the horizon. An apologetic Captain Xyr met Maritia as she climbed aboard her flagship.

"Should've stormed his vessel, my lady." He presented his axe and the back of his neck. "I've failed your brother and failed you. 'Tis yours to take." The mariner crouched low.

Maritia refused the weapon and spared his life. "I'll not waste your blood, Captain. Rise up. You did what you thought right." She snorted. "I'd likely have done the same."

"Thank you, my lady."

"What about the rest of the ogre fleet?" she finally asked. "Have they all fled?"

"Every single ship. I'd say that the Grand Lord is meeting up with them even now."

"That's the end of it, then . . . for now. Get us underway, Captain," Maritia declared bitterly. "We need to get back to the others. We've got rebels to catch."

"Aye."

Maritia calculated the time. "How many days lost, Captain?"

"Five."

She was stunned. "Too damn long, then! Wherever the rebels were before, they won't be there now. By my father's axe, they could already be slipping into the heart of the realm!"

The captain looked even more downcast. "A thought that occurs to me, also, my lady."

"Has there been any word—or sign of word—from Nethosak?"

"None, my lady. Were we to expect a messenger bird?"

"No," Maritia replied at last. "No messenger bird."

"With your permission, then, I'll get us going."

"Do so."

As Captain Xyr shouted orders, Maritia marched to her cabin. Her charts and notes lay within. Two sentries saluted her, one opening the door. However, as the door closed, the darkness within suddenly made her halt. Maritia felt a chill along her spine that made her shiver. She imagined Golgren's grinning face in the shadows. Swearing with the skill of a veteran legionary, Hotak's daughter hurriedly lit the round oil lamp hanging near the bolted oak table. The illumination pushed away her fears.

"That's better," she muttered to herself.

Like her father and Bastion before her, her cabin held few personal items. She had a place on the wall near her cot for both an axe and her sword. A niche in the wall held some bottles of wine and heavily-salted strips of dried goat in a clay jar. The table where she worked out her strategies dominated the room, the squat, square piece of furniture sealed by pegs to the floor. The charts and notes, all held in place by lead weights, lay open for her perusal. Despite the weights, the parchments had shifted some and Maritia spent a few moments organizing her papers. By the time she was done, she already had decided. The rebels were somewhere in the empire. If she tried to follow their trail, she could end up on the opposite side of the realm.

"He won't like this," she muttered, "and neither will she."

Whether Ardnor or their mother would have agreed with her, Maritia did not know. She felt she had no other recourse. She had to follow her gut, and her gut steered her in one direction.

A shout brought one of the guards. "My lady?"

"Summon the captain! Immediately!"

Moments later, Xyr hustled into the room. Slightly out of breath, he had clearly been in the midst of some hard labor.

"Aye, Lady Maritia?"

"As soon as we rendezvous with the others, I want a new course." She thrust a finger at the map. "Get us there as quickly as possible! Everything may hinge on seconds!"

He eyed her destination. "Sargonath? You think to go back to Ambeon?"

"No, but we'll need reinforcement for what I've planned. I can't take them from Ambeon . . ." Maritia did not dare borrow from Ambeon, not with Pryas eager to usurp her and Golgren acting unpredictably. "There's two legions stationed there just sitting around. Let's pick them up and then head on to Nethosak!"

"Nethosak?" Xyr's confusion mounted. "We're going to the capital? What about the rebels?"

She nodded grimly. "Faros Es-Kalin wants nothing more than to go home. Let him. When he arrives, the least we can do is be waiting with a proper welcome . . . an axe in his chest."

CHAPTER XX

MORGION'S GIFT

Scores of ghosts swarmed around Nephera, each seeking to relay some important piece of information, but she had no time for them now. With her Protectors in charge in most of the colonies, certainly any situation short of a crisis could be handled.

The ogre had betrayed her. The betrayal that Nephera had expected had come too soon, but she refused to be daunted. "You are a nothing more than a gnat to me," she whispered to the distant, departing figure of the Grand Lord Golgren, "and when I feel in the mood, I will crush you as easily as I would any insect."

She would have done so today, if Faros was not more of an immediate concern. He came from the bloodline of the old emperor, and was the champion, however inept, of a rival god.

Nephera eyed the vision rippling in the bowl. Through the crimson liquid, she watched the *Stormbringer* wend its way back to the rest of the fleet. "First Kolot, then Bastion, and now you, my Maritia. My children are becoming such disappointments." The cadaverous figure touched the surface of the fluid, causing it to ripple more. "But punishment and redemption can wait."

Maritia had made an important decision on her own: She had decided that rather than pursue the rebels, she would let them come to her. Yet perhaps Nephera's daughter had inadvertently chosen the perfect course. Here in Nethosak, everything was to Nephera's advantage. Faros would be sailing into the heart of the empire to confront a force more terrible than the Maelstrom.

But where was the rebel fleet? She had to keep close track of it, and for some reason, it had vanished from her sight again.

"Takyr!"

Mistress...

As was his wont, the monstrous ghost materialized right next to her. The high priestess looked at him with eyes as ghastly as any specter's. They had sunken into her sockets, as Nephera had delved deeper and deeper into what Morgion taught her; they danced nervously after the incessant visitations by the condemning spirit of her mate.

Even now, even as she spoke, Nephera's eyes darted around for signs of the cursed shade, "Spread word to all others. Let them understand there must be no exception. They're to seek out the rebels of Sargonnas, target the one called Faros, and alert me as to their whereabouts. All other commands are to be superceded by this! Is that understood?"

The hooded shade slowly nodded then spoke sonorously, *There is unrest in the Imperium... the building of the temples drains resources—*

"All prior commands superceded!" Her skeletal hand thrust out at Takyr's throat and although he was already dead, the fearsome specter cringed from her wrath. "All else is of negligible concern! The Protectors know their orders! They will raise the temples to the Great One and will continue to convert the rabble! All memory of gods past—The

Condor Lord in particular—must be eradicated from the minds of our kind . . ."

In due time Morgion would become the dominant god, first of the minotaurs, then of all creatures. Nephera did not wonder whether her notions were possibility or madness. She had long since ceased to think of anything but her deity.

Soon, in fact, another sacrifice would be underway. Even now, the chosen approached the temple. They came in secret, entering the vast complex through a series of hidden passages built by the high priestess's predecessors. The irony that the priests of Sargonnas had supplied her with means to aid in the defeat of their own patron amused Nephera.

Takyr vanished without another word. Nephera gazed lovingly at the huge symbols of the Forerunner faith that decorated this room, only her eyes seeing the downturned axe imposed over them. A scraping of stone alerted her. Attempting to look as kindly as possible, Nephera pushed her hood completely back and loosened her mane. The high priestess covered the bowl with a black silk cloth, then with a smile made to welcome her guests.

The wall to the right shifted open, the rectangular gap barely wide and high enough to admit a minotaur. The lanky figure who first entered immediately fell to one knee when he saw Nephera.

"My beloved mistress," rumbled Lothan. Underneath the voluminous, brown travel cloak he wore, his grey robes could just be seen. "You honor us this evening. Such an occasion I thought never possible for myself, despite my loyalty, which you know."

Nephera touched not his forehead—as she did when blessing the faithful—but instead briefly rubbed the side of his muzzle. Lothan tried to contain his ecstasy, but his entire body quivered with pleasure.

"Dear, darling, loyal Lothan . . . tonight I promise that you will reap my eternal gratitude. Tonight you will be rewarded for all your years of service."

"I am grateful."

He rose as a second figure entered. The immaculate older female wore a cloak identical to Lothan's, but under hers was a clean and polished breastplate and kilt marking her as belonging to the fleet.

"Admiral Sorsi," Nephera greeted, extending her hand.

Going down on one knee, Sorsi took the high priestess's hand. In a scratchy voice, she said, "I live to serve the faith, my lady."

"You shall, you shall."

Three others appeared in short order, all from the highest ranks in the imperium. Tonight they would learn the truth about Morgion.

"Faraug . . . Lesta . . . Timonius . . ." The trio dipped their horns as she uttered their names; merchant, another councilor, and the patriarch of one of the most loyal Houses.

"This is truly an honor," gasped Lesta, a young but steely-eyed female. She had been a late convert to the faith, but her diligence and devotion put even Lothan to shame.

"It is I who am honored with your presence, all of you. You have served well, served loyally, even in dark days. Now we are in ascension. Now it is time to secure the world for our god."

"We will know the god, then?" murmured hefty Faraug. "We will know the truth?"

"You will know the face and the love of the god, my children!" the high priestess declared, gazing at all of them, one by one in turn. "You will know the perfection, and you will understand the need for your ultimate devotion to that perfection."

Some of them looked slightly perplexed. They would realize everything soon enough, though. When Morgion blessed them, they would understand all.

"The time draws nigh," Nephera told them. She indicated the center of the chamber, where the symbols of the Forerunners had been meticulously etched in the stone. "Please. Your places."

They went to the five points designated on the symbols. Three stood at the head, end, and point of the breaking of the axe. The other two took the upper wing and head of the ghostly avian.

Nephera positioned herself directly between the axe and the bird. The moment she did so, her smile, persistent until now, vanished. The torches that lit the chamber dimmed, yet the room did not darken. Now an unsettling silver glow radiated from the huge symbols hung over the high priestess's empty chair atop the dais. Aging Timonius let out a small, surprised snort, but no one else broke the silence. The five stood entranced by this clear sign of the god's presence.

Raising her hands, Nephera opened herself to the dread lord she served. She felt his nearness. Compared to him, the entire minotaur race were worthless cockroaches. That her god granted her some tiny bit of his glory was so overwhelmingly generous that, not for the first time, tears were brought to her eyes.

Nephera drew with her finger the symbol of the downturned axe. Her nail left a streak of dark green flame in its wake. She completed the axe then drew around it a five-pointed star. The moment Nephera completed the star, the axe flared. From each tip of the star, a tendril of light darted out, seeking one of the supplicants.

"What—" Lothan began. He got no further, for the moment that the tendrils touched the chosen, they froze.

Turning in a circle to view her companions, Lady Nephera read their uncertainty, even fear in their faces. She smiled to reassure them and said, "He is with us, all around us! Let yourselves see and feel now the Great One . . ."

Within the minds of each of the five, a voice spoke, *Know me ... know me ...*

And to each, the Lord of the Bronze Tower revealed himself.

"The gods preserve us!" Faraug blurted.

Lothan shook his head once. Lesta evinced a look of rapt devotion. Admiral Sorsi gritted her teeth and Timonius only stared.

I am Morgion ... the voice continued. *I am the end of all things ...*

Faraug tried to struggle free, annoying Nephera. The five had been chosen at Morgion's command. They had been given an honor. If they were short-sighted, that was unfortunate for them.

She reached up to the blazing images and, muttering under her breath, caused them to invert. Sorsi howled. Timonius shook as if some giant, invisible hand throttled him. Lesta was the only one who did not move, perhaps because her devotion was so strong that it had not been unaltered by the revelation of her deity's identity.

You will serve me, said the dread lord's voice, *and your sacrifice will serve your high priestess.*

"Sacrifice?" Lothan asked. "My—My Lady Nephera! What—?"

"It is all right, dear, darling Lothan," she replied, cupping both hands under the burning symbols. "I will love you all the more for this. I will love all of you for this."

"Not the Lord of D-Decay!" the admiral murmured. "Not for—"

Her words ended in a hellish keening. Timonius joined her, then Faraug added his voice to the shrill choir. Lothan struggled, but even he was overwhelmed by the god's work. Only Lesta remained silent, though tears poured down her cheeks.

"Know that through your actions, the temple will be stronger," the high priestess informed them. "The empire will be stronger." That most of them did not even hear her any more through their screams did not interest Nephera in the least. They were in communion with their god, as they had long begged of her. "You will have served the Great One as few others."

With that, she seized the tiny axe by its handle.

Above her, the huge symbols flared so bright that even Nephera had to shield her eyes. The fiery axe burned her flesh, but if she suffered, it was little in comparison to the ravages that overwhelmed the five. Pustules swelled over the bodies of the chosen, covering their flesh rapidly and then bursting. A green and yellow pus spilled forth, eating away at what remained beneath. In mere seconds, the five could no more be identified as minotaurs, save that they had horns. The pus had rotted away their muzzles. Their decaying flesh sloughed off in great gobbets. Throughout it all, they continued to howl. Now even Lesta joined in.

The green fire surrounding the tiny axe grew more intense. It burned away the skin on Nephera's fingers. Nephera felt none of the pain, though, as she was enraptured. Then, from each of the chosen, a thick, ghastly haze arose. The tendrils drew the haze forth, and as they did, the spell entered its final phase. With one last howl, Admiral Sorsi twisted as if she was a rag wrung out from the wash. Her flesh, her sinew, and her bones melted. Her shining breastplate reddened with rust, her cloak rotted.

The bodies of the chosen crumbled. As the tendrils tore free their prizes—the souls—what little remained of the five's shells collapsed in horrid heaps. Sorsi's armor clattered as it struck stone, the rusted breastplate cracking in two.

The tendrils retreated into the star and the star into the axe. Breathing heavy, eyes moist with tears, Nephera continued to clutch her creation, though her hand was now a charred, twisted ruin. Without warning, the fire ceased. The Forerunner symbols still glowed silver but with their intensity diminished.

Nephera's breathing was the only sound. Heedless of her ruined hand, she stared with awe at what Morgion had wrought through her. The dread god's symbol fit in her palm, its edges still glowing. It was no larger than the one emblazoned on her breast, but she could sense its tremendous power.

"It is done . . ." she whispered, her voice cracking. "It is good."

It is good . . . agreed the voice within her mind.

Facing the Forerunner symbols, she fell to her knees in gratitude. "I thank you, my lord . . ."

Five nights . . . the moons will be in conjunction in five nights . . . the hour of that night's zenith . . .

"I understand."

With that, Morgion's presence receded. She felt the same great disappointment every time communion with her deity ended, yet this time, he had left something of himself behind. Out of the corner of her eye, Nephera noticed the remains of one of the chosen. Morgion had demanded that for what he would bestow on her, she would have to sacrifice followers of value.

The disappearances of the five, especially Lothan and Admiral Sorsi, would not go unnoticed, but there were always rebel elements to blame. That, in turn, would allow her, through Ardnor, to have the Protectors and State Guard clamp down harder on those she found wanting.

A slight clink came from the direction where the admiral had stood, the rusted pieces of armor still settling. Folding her monstrous fingers around the tiny axe in order to keep it secure, the high priestess summoned her power.

A high wind swirled through the chamber. It ruffled Nephera's robes but otherwise touched nothing else except the grisly remnants of the faithful. Like a hound fed by its mistress, the wind scooped up first one, then another pile. In swift fashion, all trace of what had happened spun high in the air.

Nephera drew a circle with her finger and the wind spun faster. Dust, fragments of bone, and bits of brown metal spun around and around. The faster the wind raced, the more it condensed into a shrinking mass. It became a funnel cloud, a tiny tornado.

As quickly as it had arisen, the wind ceased. With it went all trace of the awful event. Nephera bared her teeth in pleasure, a genuine grin.

With minor matters out of the way, the high priestess again stared lovingly at Morgion's gift. Only five nights to wait.

When his head finally felt clear again, Faros knew that the rebels had left the spell surrounding Gaerth's island. This was verified minutes later when the three escort ships suddenly veered away. There was no signal, no warning. The strangers wanted nothing of the empire or its rebels and Faros desired nothing of them.

"I can't see any hint of land behind us," Captain Botanos remarked. "I know we should be able to see at least a speck from here, but even the glass doesn't help."

"Leave it. Forget it." Faros eyed the descending sun. Night was almost upon them, not that it mattered. Minotaurs were skilled sailors. The stars made for excellent points of reference. "What we need to find out now is where we are."

"We're probably east of the empire," Botanos suggested. He grunted. "Or northeast . . . or southeast."

The rebel leader thought of drawing his sword and seeing if it could provide some guidance, but then his eyes fell upon the ring. General Rahm's ring. Sargonnas's ring. A faint glow radiated from within.

He raised it to chest level. "Show me the way, I command you."

Thinking of Mithas, thinking of a home no longer standing and a family no longer living, Faros turned toward the east. The glow did not intensify. Undaunted, he turned some more. Still nothing.

Botanos watched, clearly puzzled. Faros's nostril's flared as he thought of how foolish he looked. Despite that, he turned some more.

The black gem flared, its brilliance startling him.

There was an intake of breath from his companion. Faros smiled victoriously. This time he had not begged for aid; he had demanded obedience. "There lies our path, captain! Mark it!"

"Already done," returned the mariner, recovering. "I suspect us to be east by northeast from that." Some of his enthusiasm waned. "What distance we are is clear, much farther than we'd like."

"Set sail, anyway." Faros looked from the ring to the deep waters. "She brought us here. She can help us get back."

" 'She'—" The massive minotaur shook his head, his eyes wide. "Lord Faros . . . you'd not be thinking of talking to the Sea Queen again!"

"Keep the ship on the course I showed you," Faros said, heading further up the bow. "Make sure to pass it on to the others." He looked back one last time at the *Crest's* master. "And see to it that I'm not disturbed."

"Oh, aye! I'll see to that, all right!"

As he neared the forward rail, Faros contemplated drawing Sargonnas's sword, all the better to show himself to the Horned One's tempestuous daughter, yet it might also diminish him in her eyes. Foregoing the blade, he leaned over the rail. The waters rocked against the hull, the darkness below absolute. Faros was not a seasoned sailor, but he had a healthy respect for the power of the ocean . . . and its mistress.

He rubbed the ring, thinking that it would somehow connect him to her. "I know you're down there . . ."

The *Dragon's Crest* rose as a strong wave lifted the ship

like a toy. With his ring hand, Faros clutched the rail tighter. He would not be so easily repulsed.

"I know you're down there, Sea Queen," the minotaur repeated steadily, his gaze never leaving the water. "I know you hear me . . ."

The last traces of the sun sank beneath the surface, turning the ocean blacker yet. The wind shifted, picking up. The salty spray burned Faros's eyes, but he continued to lean precipitously over the rail toward Zeboim's domain.

"You know what your father wants," he muttered. "You know what I want."

A brief sound made his ears go taut. For just a moment, Faros thought that he had heard feminine laughter.

Gripping the rail with both hands, he cried, "Laugh if you like, Sea Queen! Keep laughing when Morgion's greedy grasp comes for your domain as well! Don't you think that the Lord of Decay covets those lost in your seas? Don't you understand that if he takes what is your father's, he can certainly take what's yours?"

Faros waited, but only the waves and the wind answered him. Snarling, he turned from the bow. Even if it took the ships a year to sail back to the empire, they would accomplish the task. He would not fail. He had chosen his course, and whether his destiny was the throne or death, he would not be dependent on the whims of a capricious goddess.

The minotaur had gone only a few steps from the rail when again he thought he heard the laughter. At the same time, there was a peculiar shift in the wind and the ocean began to rock oddly.

Shouts rose from the crew. Captain Botanos met him, the generally-stalwart mariner shaking. "By the Sea—By her! What did you say? What did you do?"

"Get a hold of yourself!" Faros demanded.

The *Crest's* hull creaked ominously. A thump shook everyone, causing one crew member to nearly slip from the rigging.

"The stern!" someone called.

Faros and Botanos ran. The rebel leader shoved aside a stunned sailor in order to see what was happening. Behind the flagship, a great wave arose. It was not as high as the masts but massive enough to do quite a bit of damage if it hit.

"Never demand of the Sea Queen," uttered Captain Botanos. "She'll brook that from no one!"

The wave crashed toward the ship. Most of those standing at the stern fled, but something inside Faros made him stand and face the disaster.

Just as it reached the *Dragon's Crest*, the wave split. Brow wrinkled, Faros thought he saw the upper part form fingers of water. The dusk made him uncertain of what he saw but not of what the wave did next. Instead of smashing part of the ship to flotsam . . . it pushed almost gently against the stern. The vessel lurched, then glided forward. Simultaneously, the wind filled the sails to their fullest. The *Dragon's Crest* coursed through the waters at a clip no sailing ship had ever managed before.

"Hold tight!" Faros shouted to the others. "Get everyone off the nest and rigging!"

Wiping his eyes clear, he looked for the other ships. Knowing Zeboim's wicked humor, he expected them to be far, far behind, but they, too, were racing along the turbulent ocean at the same remarkable clip. Behind each pushed a massive wave.

"Gods above!" Botanos had wrapped rope around his waist, securing himself to an inner rail. "What'd you ask of her?"

"To get us to where we're going, and quickly enough!"

"Did you ask her to do it in one piece?!"

Faros did not bother to answer, for he had asked no such thing. Still, while the others hung on for dear life and no doubt prayed for the goddess to spare them, he stared eagerly ahead.

The empire awaited him.

Chapter XXI

Return to the Empire

As General Bakkor returned from his evening ride, he noticed a contingent of soldiers approaching from the opposite direction. Aware that most of his own troops would not be out this way, his grip on the reins tightened. Around him, the nighttime forest seemed more dark and threatening of a sudden.

"We've company," the muscular figure informed his three guards.

"Aye, General," responded his senior guard.

The legion commander did not have to see the emblem on the first rider's breastplate to know that they hailed from Kolina's Crystal Legion. The arrogance with which they rode was characteristic of the Protectors and their ilk.

The captain leading the newcomers—his helmet poorly concealing the fact his mane was shorn off—saluted Bakkor as they rode up. A quick estimate by the general put the Protectors's numbers at roughly twenty. Twenty against his four.

"General Bakkor, legion commander of the Wyverns?"

"You know I am, Captain Tulak," Bakkor responded in his clipped, nasal voice.

Tulak's legionaries immediately started to fan out around the smaller party. As they did, Tulak announced, "General Bakkor, by the authority of the Procurator General, Pryas, you are hereby under arrest for insurrectionist thoughts and actions—"

Bakkor scoffed. "Me? Insurrectionist thoughts and actions? I'm a good, loyal soldier, as your precious Procurator General well knows!"

"Any sign of resistance," the captain went on, eyes wide and fanatical, "will be dealt with harshly!"

"You mean, such as this?" Drawing his sword, Bakkor gave a yell.

From the branches above rained down countless armored figures with short swords, hand axes, and taloned gloves. The Protector captain spun around in the saddle as several of his fighters were knocked off their horses by the minotaurs raining from above.

"Never ambush a Wyvern in the forest!" the general barked, closing on Tulak, but the captain swiftly raised his mace, swinging it heavily, and Bakkor had to adopt defensive measures.

All along the path, legionary fought legionary. A Wyvern's clawed climbing gloves ripped open the side of a Protector's muzzle. One of Bakkor's troops fell to a blow from an axe.

"Heretic!" cried Tulak as he battered at the general.

While the Protector was a good fighter, General Bakkor had experience as well as talent with the blade. He finally managed to deflect the mace, driving his sword under the captain's arm.

Pierced through the lower shoulder, the other legionary fumbled his weapon. Still his hands reached for Bakkor. Seeing that his foe would never yield, the veteran mionotaur general thrust for the unprotected underside of his adversary's muzzle. Clutching at the red river gushing down his chest, the captain beholden to Nephera and the Protectors slumped in the saddle.

The other Protectors fought on, showing no willingness to surrender, but the Wyverns finally bested them. When the last of Kolina's soldiers had fallen, Bakkor called a weary halt. One of those who had dropped from the trees marched up and saluted him. The minotaur was tall and lean and moved almost elegantly.

"All elements of resistance crushed, General!"

"Well done, Vacek. You're commended for keeping pace with us. They were supposed to come for me half a mile back."

The first hekturion snorted. "Kept half my number there and half ahead here. Thought I'd catch them between, but this worked as well."

"Yes . . ." Bakkor eyed the strewn bodies. "Losses?"

"Seven to their twenty-one. We have four more with wounds, two serious. They fought well for being entirely surprised."

The general grunted. "Minotaurs against minotaurs . . . of course they fought well. Where will it all end . . . where's the honor that Hotak claimed to be returning to the empire?"

Vacek shrugged. "In the trust of his son."

"Where it'll die malnourished." Bakkor stared grimly in the direction of the city whose name was now Ardnoranti. "The Procurator General has forced our hand. Let the others know. That damned Protector's not going to get away with this."

The first hekturion nodded. "Aye, General. Right away."

"Hold there a moment, Vacek." The Wyvern commander's ears flattened. "Talk to the others. Make sure they understand what we're doing here. Talk to all the sub-officers and legionaries."

"Aye, General. We're protecting the true empire."

" 'Protecting the true empire.' Yes. An apt way of putting it. Be on your way."

As the officer hurried off, General Bakkor wiped his blade clean. " 'Protecting the true empire,' " he repeated to one of his personal guard. "I wonder if that's how the damned rebels see it."

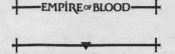

Through the night, the ships sailed mercilessly fast, cutting across the ocean as if across a slick, endless patch of ice. Faros felt certain they would encounter some catastrophe or one or more of the ships would founder. How could every mast and hull survive such a fantastic journey? Yet all appeared intact.

"By the Abyss!" roared Captain Botanos. "How much longer can we endure? 'Tis just coming on dawn!"

Barely had he asked . . . then the ocean stilled. The huge waves tapered off, spilling harmlessly. The terrible wind expended itself abruptly. The sails fell as limp as rags. The only sound was a gentle lapping of water against the hull.

Twisting himself free of the rail, Faros surveyed the rest of his fleet. Despite the speed and distance they had sailed, each vessel appeared to be in position - in almost exactly the same position with regard to its sisters as before the amazing journey.

"See if they're all in one piece down below!" Botanos called. "Signal those nearest and find out how they fare!"

Faros wasn't surprised when none of the other vessels reported distress. There were a few broken limbs, but no loss of crew overboard or any deaths. Not one captain reported cracks in the hulls or the masts, and even the sails needed scant repairs.

"Unbelievable," the captain muttered to Faros. "Only you could've persuaded Herself to do all this without extracting a fearsome price!"

"She's sending us into war. She'll collect her due then," the rebel leader replied grimly. "Where do you figure we are, exactly?"

Botanos tried to convince Faros to get some rest. However, despite having spent the entire night holding on for his life, the younger minotaur felt not the slightest exhaustion.

Faros ordered the captain himself to get some sleep for a few hours, while he stayed near the bow, watching for a hint of land.

At midday he saw something else—not land—and quickly shouted to a sailor to wake up Botanos and summon him on deck.

The captain, rubbing his eyes, emerged moments later. "What is it?" The other minotaur followed his gaze. "A ship!"

Far behind them but coming from another direction, a lone vessel plied the same waters as the *Dragon's Crest*.

"Can we intercept them, Botanos?"

The other minotaur did a quick calculation. "Aye, easily too, I think!"

The *Crest* veered toward the newcomer. Four other ships followed, swinging wide to cut off the vessel, should it try to run. Either the other ship did not spot them at first or it assumed them to be friendly, for the strange vessel continued on at its same stolid pace.

As they drew close, the lone ship suddenly turned from the other five, trying to angle away. The maneuver cost time, however, and the *Dragon's Crest* came within hailing distance. By this time it was obvious the lone ship was also manned by minotaurs. Botanos called for the lone vessel to slow and in reply received a catapult shot that flew far past his bow.

"She ain't friendly, and she flies the emperor's flag," he growled.

"Take them. Try not to sink the ship, though."

"We'll do what we can."

Bringing its ballista about, the rebel vessel fired. The lances tore into the port side of the stern. Wood from the upper deck flew everywhere, and a chorus of cries arose. Minotaurs raced along the ruined deck, seizing axes and other weapons.

"I want this done quickly!" urged Faros, drawing his weapon.

Another rebel ship, captained by one of Tinza's former comrades from the imperial fleet, came along the lone ship on the opposite side.

"Lower your flag!" Botanos demanded of their adversary.

An arrow struck the rail before him.

"That was their last chance!" he snarled. "Grapplers to the ready! You up there! Bring us even with 'em!"

Aboard the enemy ship, the catapult crew readied their weapon, but Faros's forces were already too near for the missile to be any threat. Meanwhile, the other rebel ship fired its own ballista, raking the trapped ship's opposite side.

"Make sure the crew knows I want to keep the enemy afloat, Botanos!"

"Aye, they know!"

The *Crest* drew neatly alongside. As a barrage of arrows peppered the rebels, grapplers began tossing the hooks over the enemy rail. Two of Botanos's crew fell dead and another pulled back with a wound to the arm, but most of the grapplers held their positions. More than a dozen hooks were strongly fastened.

"Heave, blast you!" Captain Botanos shouted.

Faros signaled their archers. "Fire!"

The second barrage was larger and decimated the front ranks of the foe. A few bolts answered back, but little damage was done. Grunting hard from exertion, the grapplers brought the hulls together. A roar of anticipation burst from the throats of the rebels.

Caught between two larger opponents, the crew of the imperial ship could not battle equally on both fronts. With the second rebel ship harassing them on one side, Faros led the boarding party on the other. Sword high over his head, he let out a shout and leapt over the rail. Faros eagerly slashed at the first soldier to face him. His blade cut through the enemy's throat. He stabbed a second foe deep in the forearm then traded blows with a third.

The rebels were swarming over the opposite deck. Quickly beaten back from the rail, the imperial crew tried to regroup. A narrow-muzzled, graying female who was likely the captain managed to create a line, but before Faros could reach her, an arrow from the second rebel vessel caught her between the shoulder blades.

The surviving defenders swiftly changed into a confused rabble. They fell easy prey to the superior attackers. Before long, all resistance had crumbled. Faros contemplated executing those who surrendered, but decided prisoners might prove of value.

"The ship's a good one," Captain Botanos told Faros as he came aboard. "The damage at the stern and the other rail can be dealt with in short order. She's fit enough to go into battle."

"Appoint someone to take command. Have a complement made up."

"Aye."

The eye-patched second mate of the *Crest* dragged up a disheveled figure that turned out to be his counterpart aboard the imperial. "This is what's left o' the enemy command, my lord!"

"I be Orym," the prisoner muttered abjectly. "My horns are yours! Take 'em and be done with me!"

Faros brought his sword up to one of the horns and ran the edge against the latter. The well-honed blade cut into the bony growth. As Faros expected, Orym shivered with humiliation and pain. A minotaur's horns meant more to him than an arm, or even a leg.

"You can keep your horns and your life for the answer to one or two simple questions."

The captive tried not to look hopeful, but there was a slight glint in his eyes. "What sort of questions?"

"What island lies closest ahead?"

Orym blinked, almost choking. He seemed to find something funny, a humor that quickly vanished as Faros again tapped his horn with his sword.

"You sailing these parts and not know? Fine fighters you be, but as mariners you're not so educated as a gully dwarf!"

"The name." This time Faros cut deeper.

"Okay! 'Tis Mito, of course! What other place would it be?"

Mito. Gradic's son could almost hear the Sea Queen's laughter. He had wanted Zeboim to return them to the empire and she had. They were now surrounded by imperial ports, and one of the largest outside Nethosak lay but a short distance ahead.

"Mito," Faros repeated, savoring the name. He lowered his weapon. "Take him and the others away. Spread them among the other ships so that they can't organize themselves."

As the second mate dragged the prisoner away, Botanos eyed his leader. "Mito! Is that good or bad news?"

"Well, we can't sail the waters of Mito for very long without being noticed, unless we head so far out we waste precious time."

The captain shook his head. "I say, waste the time. If we attack Mito, even assuming we have unlikely success, someone's bound to rush the word to Nethosak! Mito's close enough that they can send the fleet before we've barely left the docks."

Faros nodded, thinking. "Yes, they'll do that, won't they?"

Governor Haab tapped impatiently on his desk. Special missives from Amur and other key colonies were to have reached him two days earlier, but the ship carrying the messages had still not materialized. One day late, he could understand, but the courier vessel should have easily made it to Strasgard by now.

An aide entered. Daring the governor's wrath, she announced, "Brother Malkovius is here."

Haab's ears flattened. With a snort of resignation, he said, "Send him in."

The Protector officer removed his helmet as he stepped into the room. "Brother Haab."

"May the Forerunners guide your path."

"And yours." Malkovius was clearly impatient about something. "Governor, has there been word of the courier ship?"

"I was just looking into that myself. None. A little later than usual—"

"I am expecting important instructions from my counterparts. Progress on the temple-building in each colony must be synchronized according to the high priestess's command. I—"

The governor cut him off. "I'm aware of your needs, Brother. I've already decided to dispatch a scout along the route the courier should have taken. If they have encountered any delay, I'll soon know about it and you'll be informed."

That satisfied the Protector. "There is another matter. General Voluna's legionaries are not cooperating with my orders. Most recently, she refused to crack down on protesters at the allocation centers."

"A niggling matter. Voluna has overstepped herself for the last time. I've already written up orders for her removal—"

Noise from without made both minotaurs straighten. As Haab came around his desk, Malkovius went to the window overlooking the port.

"What is it?" asked the governor.

"A ship coming in!"

"The courier at last!"

"No, another ship—and three more!"

Sure enough, Haab could see four huge warships sailing into Strasgard, their line virtually sealing off the harbor from the outside.

At that moment, a horn blared. Haab listened. "The northern outposts! That's the signal they give in case of attack!"

Another sound filled the air, growing stronger by the second. The governor's ears pricked. He knew that sound—

The wall across the room exploded. Both were sent tumbling to the floor. The roof near the governor's desk collapsed. Beams of wood and blocks of stone flew at Haab and the Protector.

When the dust finally settled, the governor had to fight his way out of the debris. His left leg felt numb and blood poured down his cheek. He noted the remnants of a huge rock, a catapult missile. Someone had aimed a very good shot.

"Guards!" Haab cried. "Malkovius—?"

The Protector's armor had failed. A huge chunk of stone had crushed Malkovius's unprotected head. Dismissing him from his thoughts, Haab lifted himself up and reached for his axe, which he kept near his desk. Using it partly as a crutch, he hurried into the next chamber, as one of his guards rushed over to him.

"Governor! Rebels on land! They're pouring into the city!"

"I know, you fool! Get me to the messenger birds! Quickly!"

With the aid of the guard, the governor reached the small room where they kept the birds. Shelves lined the walls and on each shelf were cages. Generations of training had schooled the small, predatory avians. Each clutch instinctively knew its birthplace, and no matter how far away, they would always return.

Each cage held a single bird, with its birthplace designated in markings above the door. There was no sign of the handlers. Haab searched for the avians he needed, then quickly seized several of the small parchments used for messages. Quill in hand, he quickly wrote an urgent message. The governor took the missive, rolled it tight, then, keeping the avian within the cage, popped the note in the tiny leather pouch strapped to one of the bird's legs.

"Send it off!"

Taking the cage to the window, the guard opened the door toward the sky. The messenger bird immediately fluttered off.

Haab copied the information several times over. Twice his work was punctuated by loud crashes. Some distance away, he heard shouts.

"The last!"

When the last bird flew off, the governor felt relieved. He had sent messages to fleet elements in the capital and the emperor himself, among other places. Within hours they would learn what was happening. The fleet, poised to sail at a moment's notice, would head to Mito. The legionaries and Protectors must hold out until then.

He heard horns signalling the arrival of the legion.

"Find Malkovius's second," he ordered the guard. "Inform him that I will be taking command of both the Protectors and the soldier in the name of the emperor. Tell him that the spirit of Malkovius has guided me to this decision."

"Aye, Governor."

Haab tested his leg, finding it sturdy enough. He snorted at the rebels' audacity. "We'll turn their tactics into a trap and finish the revolt here!" The governor hefted his axe with a smile. "Perhaps I'll even have the opportunity to take the leader's head myself!" He suddenly blinked at the guard. "Well? Get going!"

"Aye, governor!"

As the soldier left, Haab peered out of the window, where he could see another of the rebel ships. He stared incredulously.

"Fools!" mocked the former provost captain. "Fools! What did they possibly think that they would accomplish?"

Chapter XXII

The Blessing of Morgion

The ogre ships slipped into the southern harbor, which was strategically close to Ambeon. The harbor was well-hidden by the high, barren rocks all but encircling it.

Golgren's flagship was the first to dock. Ogres onshore and those crewing the other nearby ships paused to bark their allegiance. The Grand Lord—his hulking bodyguards surrounding him—strode imperiously down the gangplank and waited.

From the flagship, an underling led down the Grand Lord's favored steed. The massive steed moved unsteadily at first, but quickly regained its footing. Golgren patted the animal on the side, inspecting it with care before mounting up. However, as the Grand Lord did so, another ogre trotted anxiously over to him. In one hand, the newcomer carried a goatskin parchment, in the other a wooden cage holding a squawking messenger bird. The ogre set the cage down then bowed low.

The avian was one of the few that had survived the attempt to create a communication system between the ogres and the minotaurs. Golgren recognized from the plumage a bird he himself had trained, likely the reason it had prospered when others had died.

"Halag i kira tuk?" snapped Golgren, eyeing the bird.

"Wosagi mun dreka . . ." replied the bowing subordinate, indicating the sun and holding up three fingers.

"Hmm . . ."

Snapping his fingers, Golgren had the cage raised higher. The bird's demeanor grew more antagonistic when the other ogre lifted the cage but changed as the Grand Lord leaned close. Murmuring to the creature, Golgren removed the messenger from its prison, setting it on his maimed limb. He removed the missive from the tiny container and let the bird calmly preen itself as he read.

More demands from the emperor. More drivel. Without finishing, the ogre leader crushed the note, dropping the fragments. The avian sensed his darkening mood and squawked, but Golgren soothed the bird with a few strokes of its plumage, then reached for the goatskin parchment.

"Ambeon . . ." he murmured.

The script of the message was crude but legible, and it was written in Common. Nephera had her eyes, but Golgren had his, and not all of them were among his own kind. What he read in the goatskin parchment made his own eyes widen and his mouth open hungrily.

. . . armed conflict between legions . . . between temple and army . . .

The rest of the message provided details, which Golgren readily absorbed with an almost careless glance. What mattered was the crux of the situation. The legions loyal to Maritia had risen against those controlled by the Forerunners. The reasons were not clear, but that hardly mattered.

Golgren chuckled. If the gods were indeed back, they were certainly smiling upon him. It appeared he would not have to wait so very long, after all. His destiny was quickly approaching.

Stuffing the parchment in his belt, he reached down to return the messenger bird to its cage. Already the Grand Lord's mind was awhirl. There would need to be a rearrangement of his forces, a shift of more strength to the southern regions. It looked as though it would be his duty to restore order to a troubled land.

The avian shrieked and hopped about on Golgren's arm as the other ogre sought to grab it. The bird snapped at the handler and spread its wings wide in order to make itself too large to shove through the opening. A scowl erased Golgren's smile. Swiftly he took the raptor by the neck. The messenger bird managed one final squawk before a deft movement by the Grand Lord crushed its windpipe.

Tossing the mangled corpse to the ground, the Grand Lord wiped blood and bits of feather off onto the parchment. He eyed the dead avian for a moment. There had been no reason to save the bird for future work anyway. With the news brought to him, the last tie to the Uruv Suurt had been severed as decisively as his hand.

"Gaj i kira nun!" Golgren commanded harshly, indicating the bird. He pushed on as the handler bent to remove the carcass. As his huge mount trudged along, it trampled into the hard ground what remained of Ardnor's last missive, reducing it—and the pact between the ogres and minotaurs—to dirty bits.

Countless ships of the imperial fleet converged on Mito, certain of their ability to trap the foolhardy rebels there. They had set sail almost immediately after receiving the urgent word. The renegade, Faros, was there and could at last be cornered.

Except Faros wasn't there. Mito was far behind him. By this time, either Captain Tinza and Commander Napol had secured a viable position or they would be slaughtered on the docks. Whatever happened, they would die serving the cause to which they were dedicated. They had asked no more from him.

Faros intended that their sacrifices—and those of all who attacked Mito—supply glorious inspiration for the rebels.

"We're getting awfully close," Captain Botanos muttered. "Those storm clouds worry me, though. Even in the dark, they don't look natural."

"They aren't." Both the ring and the sword had reacted to the clouds, vibrating softly as if in warning. Now and then Faros even heard the sword whisper, *Beware her . . . beware him . . .*

"Faros?"

The rebel leader stirred. "What?"

Botanos shrugged. "Nothing. Just didn't like that odd look in your eye. Saw it in General Rahm's before he . . . uh, died."

The stormy sky shortened the day. As the last light faded, the distant mountains thrust up like claws grasping for the sky.

"Argon's Chain," Faros declared quietly.

"Is this wise? Of all directions to take, this one's the worst! It'll take a week or more to get through the southern region and even if we do, we've got to pass through the mining areas—"

"Not quite. There's a secret port on this side, one that the imperials use on special occasions. You won't find it on any map."

The captain frowned. "Then how do you—"

Faros continued to gaze at the nearing shore. "It was the last sight of Mithas we saw as the ogre galleys sailed for Kern."

Botanos wisely said nothing more on the subject. Slowly the fleet wended its way toward the obscure region. Faros expected to encounter some imperial presence but not enough to slow them drastically. From what little he had seen of the port on the day when Hotak's officers turned him over to Golgren, the facility was for military matters only. There was no civilian settlement, only a garrison manned by about a hundred at most.

The rebel leader held up his ring. It flared when he pointed the stone a little more to the southwest. "There."

Botanos had his crew correct their course. At the stern, a single oil lamp guided the ships directly behind them, who, in turn, signalled the others. An old breastplate acted as a shield, preventing anyone on shore from noticing the flickering illumination at sea. This close, the rebels could take no risks.

"Ship ahead," muttered the captain.

In the distance, several small lights marked the newcomer. Faros, studying the angle, judged it to be heading toward the same place. "Follow her."

"Aye, my lord."

Roughly half an hour later, they noticed the first lights of the port. The ship they stalked sailed serenely toward its destination, clearly unconcerned about any rebel attack this close to the heart of the realm.

Straightening, Faros commanded, "Signal everyone else to stay back. We sail in alone first."

"Are you sure?"

"We'll have a better chance if they mistake us for just one more imperial."

With the other ships dropping behind, the *Dragon's Crest* headed toward the port. The heavy darkness caused by the unnatural storm clouds now worked in the rebels's favor, obscuring them from clear sight until they were nearly at the docks.

Someone aboard the other ship, which had already tied up, called out to them. Captain Botanos pretended not to hear. Two dock workers scurried over to where the *Crest* neared, ready to help. The officer on duty, a legion dekarian, marched up as the rebel ship came to rest. His squad stood at attention behind him as he peered aboard.

"You up there! Where's the captain?"

Botanos moved to the rail. "Here I be!"

In the dark behind him, much of the fighting force had gathered stealthily. Faros stood near the front line, arm raised.

"Blasted weather!" the officer growled, holding his helmet to his head. "What ship is this? Can't see well in this dark! By whose orders are you here?"

Botanos gave him the name of the courier they had captured, then its orders—including codes—which the rebels had gleaned from its captain's cabin. The rebels did not expect to completely fool the port watch, but they would buy some time.

Scratching his head, the dekarian looked over his list. Not finding what Botanos had said, he summoned two of his warriors and sent them running into the port.

"We need to get official approval!" the officer yelled up. "You're not cited on here!"

"At least let us tie up!" Botanos insisted. "The weather's worsening and I'd like to prevent any damage to my ship!"

Seeing no reason why not, the dekarian waved the go ahead. The dock workers took lines from the *Dragon's Crest* then tied up the ship.

"We're secure . . ." Botanos murmured to Faros.

"The gangplank."

With a surreptitious nod, the captain called, "We've a crew member badly injured! Can you take 'im? We've no proper mender on board!"

The dekarian mulled this request over. "All right, but just the one and whoever's carrying 'im!"

Captain Botanos snapped his fingers. Two of the crew already standing by hurried to get the plank into position. As the board settled onto the dock, the two legionaries sent by the dekarian materialized in the distance.

"They're almost back—and they don't look happy, lad!"

Faros dropped his arm. As silent as death, the rebels poured down the gangplank. The officer on duty froze, not at all certain what he was seeing. Belatedly, he drew his axe and shouted a warning.

Faros crashed into one legionary, cutting him down before the latter could raise his weapon. The rebels swarmed the watch, killing many quickly. The dekarian held off for a few seconds, wounding one rebel and warding off another, but an arrow from the *Crest's* deck finished him.

Two remaining legionaries turned and fled. A horn sounded, ending the element of surprise. Behind Faros, rebels took on the dock workers and the crew of the smaller ship.

Leading a band deeper inland, Faros located the garrison fort. The gates had been left wide open; the commander didn't expect trouble. However, as Faros neared, soldiers began dragging them shut.

"Hurry!" he roared.

Several bolts struck down those near him. He ducked one that would have stuck him through the eye. Unlike the docks, the port was well lit, lamps hanging from iron poles. Archers among the rebels answered, firing at the gates. Two minotaurs loyal to the empire fell, slowing the efforts to seal the way.

As the rebels reached the gates, a squad of defenders rushed out. Their sacrifice went in vain, for they were quickly overwhelmed. With a wail, Faros swung his sword, severing the arm of one soldier then cutting through the throat of another. He entered the fort and was immediately confronted by another dekarian. The officer chipped at one of Faros's horns but left his side open. Faros jabbed, forcing the dekarian to fumble his weapon and reach for his dagger. Faros slashed his hand then finished his foe with a quick thrust.

More and more rebels filled the small fort. Faros spotted the commander, a broad-muzzled, gray-furred hekturion.

Already pressured by two rebels, the scarred veteran fought with admirable tenacity.

Making his way to the combat, Faros pushed aside one rebel and shouted, "Surrender and you'll be spared!"

The commander hesitated. He looked around, estimating the odds, and finally nodded. "I yield!"

When news of the garrison's fall reached the docks, the crew of the other ship also surrendered. Faros had the vessel's officers held with the remaining garrison command in order to question all.

Botanos, his axe and fur crimson with the blood of foes, joined him in what had been the hekturion's quarters. "A fine plan! Executed smartly!"

Faros was looking over messages and maps. "Have the other ships land as quickly as they can! I want every able fighter ordered off, then you and the other captains fulfill your orders—"

The other rebel shook his head. "This once I'm comin' with you—no arguments, my lord! I owe you my life twice over and, besides, someone's got to keep an eye on you for the sake of us all! I've got a fine first mate who'll take the *Dragon's Crest* where she's got to go!"

Faros let Botanos's words pass. "Get the ships unloaded then! Have that other vessel brought out to sea so that someone can take its spot!"

"Aye, my lord!"

With the *Crest* already empty, it did not take long for both ships to depart. However, only four vessels could dock at a time, and even though the crews worked as swiftly as they could, the hours raced by. Gradually, though, a considerable army began to take shape. The long voyage had forced them to abandon many of their mounts and almost all their siege weapons. The garrison supplied them with a few good horses and a pair of small catapults, but, overall, what they had was strength and courage.

The commander's quarters told Faros something about Mithas. A recent dispatch caught his eye, for it indicated the routes of the two legions nearest their location. Despite the news the rebels were on Mito, someone—Ardnor or the high priestess—was cautiously deploying legions in all directions.

"These're on their way north," he told the captain. "They look to be taking up a position south of Varga, just in case Mito was a ruse."

"Hmmm, which it is." Botanos rubbed the underside of his muzzle.

Gazing at the map, Faros pointed at a spot on the coast midway between the capital and Varga. "They probably think we'll land around there. There's some beach there, where long boats could land, that and Varga make the most sense for any concerted attack."

"That's where you did send some of the other ships . . ."

"Droka's expecting rebels to make landings where landings can be made. I can't disappoint them."

"Aye," grumbled the mariner, "and they expect us to cross where crossings can be done. You have any idea how long it'll take us to get through this mountainous region?"

"Just get everyone ready as soon as possible."

Thunder boomed, shaking the structure. Botanos swore.

"Hope this weather doesn't get worse or we'll be going nowhere fast," he grumbled.

"Oh, we'll be going fast all right," Faros promised. "The weather is the least of our problems."

For miles beyond Mithas, the storm clouds raged. Over Nethosak, the skies were at their worst and most inhabitants fled inside. Though hardened minotaurs, they had lived long enough to understand that when such weather erupted, it boded ill.

In the sanctum of the high priestess, the mood was equally tense. Lady Nephera proudly stood in the center of the
pattern where she had cast her earlier spell. Her eyes were
riveted on the massive, silver symbols on the wall, seeing beyond them to the realm of her cherished patron. Around her,
every ghost under her iron will fluttered anxiously, fearfully.
Tonight she would utilize her spirits as never before. Tonight
their pain and suffering would be tenfold.

Takyr moved among them, keeping order. A bloodlust
filled his monstrous countenance and one ruined hand
twitched as if in memory of another time, another life. His
cloak undulated eagerly.

"The time is nigh!" Nephera announced. "My son should
be here! Takyr!"

He vanished, then immediately rematerialized. *Your offspring approaches, mistress . . .*

There was a hard clang on the door. Without taking her
gaze from the wondrous sight of her god's symbols, Nephera
gestured. The doors swung open, and the emperor—black
helmet in the crook of his arm—marched in. His bravado
faltered as his eyes swept the chamber, for although Ardnor
could not quite make out the legions of dead, he sensed that
he and his mother were not alone.

Drawing himself up, Ardnor said, "It's the hour you
mentioned."

"Yes, and you have come not a moment too soon!" With
effort, the cadaverous figure turned to face him. "Join me,
my son . . ."

Something in her tone proved pleasant, for the emperor
couldn't repress a grin. He put his helmet on a bench nearby
and stalked toward his mother. Even though he paid them
no mind, specters in his path fled fearfully from the mountain of strength. Ardnor had already been touched by both
his mother's power and the dark glory of their deity, and the
shades felt the emanations.

Only Takyr stood his ground, but if he sometimes almost mocked his mistress's son, this time he nodded respectfully toward the unknowing Ardnor, though perhaps his eyes showed a hint of jealousy.

Ardnor took his place in the center then knelt submissively at the high priestess's feet. He lowered his massive horns to the floor.

"He has made you his champion, his arm on this mortal plane, dear Ardnor." Nephera put a loving—albeit burnt and fleshless—hand on her son's forehead, brushing a spot between his horns.

"I am grateful, Mother! What must I do to fulfill my rightful role?"

"Be strong of body," she answered. "Be stronger of soul."

As he knelt there, she pressed her palm into the spot she had been but a moment before caressing.

As powerful as he was, Ardnor nonetheless screamed in shock. He tried to move but struggled in vain. The high priestess's hand alone held the massive bull where he was.

Looking up, Nephera stared at her unwilling servants. One by one, then by the dozens, their faces twisted with even more pain than the suffering evinced by Ardnor. The same silver aura surrounding the Forerunner symbols enveloped the ghostly throng. As the shades convulsed, the aura swelled to include Nephera, then her son.

"My hand touches you," she told the emperor, "but it is his that blesses you. My hand guides the spell, but it is his that casts it."

Ardnor's cry lessened. Tears pouring down his face, the emperor stiffened. He gritted his teeth and in staccato bursts, replied, "Blessed—is—his—power! I—am—but—his—vessel!"

A sinister green glow formed around his mother's hand. The fur nearest Nephera's hand blackened then turned to powder. Nephera looked to Takyr, who bowed. The cloaked fiend vanished, materializing almost muzzle-to-muzzle with the high priestess.

Takyr entered the body of his mistress. She shuddered momentarily, her eyes closing. When they opened but a moment later, they were completely red, even the irises.

"Come to me," said a dark voice that was neither hers nor Takyr's. *"Come to me . . ."*

As one, the unwilling ghosts flooded into the high priestess. The body of Lady Nephera shook violently, but never did her palm leave the emperor's forehead. As each phantasm entered her, the glow around her hand pulsated and Ardnor grunted anew with fresh pain. Soon the spirits flowed in with such swiftness that his grunts became a low, constant moan.

The last shades disappeared within their host. The green glow abruptly intensified around Ardnor, who froze as if one of the statues in the halls. Nephera's crimson eyes narrowed and laughter never uttered by anything mortal echoed in the chamber.

Head rocking back, Ardnor let out a roar before collapsing. Separated from him, the high priestess also nearly fell, but her body righted itself as if some great hand had picked her up like a doll. From out of Nephera burst the ghosts. They dispersed in every conceivable direction, screaming silently with pain. They flew through the walls, the ceiling, and the floor—seeking to escape what they could not.

The last to emerge was Takyr. He was now a faded shadow, a ghost of a ghost, but unlike the others, what pain still ravaged him he held in check. Takyr waited stoically, watching his mistress.

She blinked. The terrible, crimson orbs vanished, replaced by her own unsettling ones. Nephera ran a trembling claw through her mane, now all but silver itself. Her breathing steadied and she looked around, finally seeming to register her surroundings. Her gaze alighted on her son, still prone on the floor.

Straightening, the high priestess adopted an imperious expression. "Arise, my son! Is this how his champion presents himself?"

"No, Mother . . ." rasped the emperor, sounding more like one of her ghosts than her child. "It is . . . not . . ."

Ardnor rose . . . and kept rising. He had been a giant among his kind before, but now he swelled to a height taller than an ogre. He was three times as broad as the high priestess. Like Nephera, the emperor was marked by a shocking change over parts of his fur—only in his case the touches were of a deep, ghastly green—a green that now matched his burning eyes . . . and the blazing, downturned axe branded into his forehead.

Morgion's gift.

"This . . ." the giant said, now voice growing stronger, clearer, "this is how *his* champion presents himself."

Ardnor stretched out his hand and his helmet flew to his grip. He thrust it on then extended his other hand. His mace, which he had not brought with him, formed in the air.

Turning to face the massive icons, the emperor shouted, "I am your hand, your weapon!" The walls shook from the thunderous sound of his voice. "I am your will on this mortal plane!"

The head of his mace glowed with the same dark aura as that which had surrounded him before. Ardnor fell to his knee again, striking the floor with the weapon as he did. A fissure opened up at his feet. From within, tendrils of smoke arose and mournful voices pleaded in chorus. With his free hand, Ardnor made a grasping motion, as if he sought to pull something from the depths.

Indeed, he did, for out of the chasm five black shadows appeared. They spiraled once around the emperor, then came to rest before him. Each vaguely resembled the form of a warrior, albeit of different shapes and even races.

Ardnor chuckled and glanced over his shoulder to see the beaming face of his approving mother. "Maritia has her generals. Now I have mine."

Nephera nodded proudly.

He struck the stone again and the fissure sealed, cutting off the eternal cries.

Turning the mace downward in a symbolic gesture, the First Master pronounced, "My life is yours, now and forever . . ."

The silver icons flashed.

With Takyr trailing behind her, Lady Nephera joined him. "You have been given a great gift, one even I must envy, my son! Wield it well! Prove yourself worthy in his eyes—and mine!"

"I will bring you the head, hide, and horns of Chot's nephew, Mother." He reverently touched his forehead where the helmet hid his new brand. "And for him—I'll bring Faros Es-Kalin's very soul . . ."

Chapter XXIII

The Gathering Darkness

Nethosak. It seemed like years since Maritia had been home, yet it was only months. Still, her heart lightened at the initial view of her homeland as her ships entered the harbor. She expected no fanfare and did not receive any. No one—save perhaps her mother—would have known of her coming until just a day or two ago. Nor did her arrival presage good news.

"You understand your orders, Captain Xyr?" asked Maritia as she disembarked the *Stormbringer*.

"Absolutely, my lady. I only await the word."

"It'll be given soon enough. I have to speak with my brother first."

The mariner looked past her to the docks. "It appears he urgently wants to speak with you, my lady."

"Hmm?" Maritia followed his gaze to note the arrival of a rather dour welcoming party. A dozen resolute Protectors in full black regalia rode up; at their head was an officer in Imperial Guard uniform whose shorn mane revealed his true loyalties. At his side he held the reins of one of Maritia's favored steeds.

Descending the gangplank, she met the saluting officer.

"Captain Arochus, my lady. We are here to escort you directly to the emperor."

"Where's Captain Doolb?" she asked, recalling the veteran officer who should have been the one to meet her.

"Arrested for treason and executed some weeks ago, my lady," the Protector answered without batting an eye.

"I see," the legion commander replied, hiding her shock. Doolb had been one of her father's most loyal warriors. "My guards also need mounts," she added blandly.

"Unnecessary. The emperor believes you quite safe with this hand-picked contingent. Your guards are given leave until needed."

Eyeing the Protectors, Maritia could see they were capable. Each was nearly as wide and muscular as Ardnor. If he ordered them to give their lives to defend hers, they would do so with zeal.

Still, Maritia desired her own trusted troops. Unfortunately, she couldn't countermand Ardnor's directive. Turning to her personal guard, she said, "You heard what was said. Report to me at first light."

"Aye, my lady," they responded.

Arochus was courteous if distant as he handed the reins to her. She was the sister of his master and the daughter of the high priestess of his faith, but he surely knew—as most did—that she did not follow the ways of the sect.

As Maritia mounted, she noticed other minotaurs in the area moving about peculiarly. They were going about their tasks in ordinary fashion, but with studied movements and pensive expressions that she could only attribute to the presence of the Protectors. Many looked worn and tired. Other Protectors dotted the area, guarding for trouble. Their numbers had grown, and apparently they were now acting in place of the State Guard.

"My lady?" urged Arochus.

Maritia nodded. As the party turned their mounts, Maritia saw a fishing ship unloading its catch. An official in grey robes with the look of one of the faithful watched each net and marked each catch on a parchment. Four armored figures kept a wary eye while the contents were poured into lined barrels then loaded aboard a wagon marked with the Forerunner symbols. Other wagons awaited other cargo ships. With a pang, Maritia thought of Pryas and wondered if a similar regimen had been introduced to Ambeon.

As they rode, the Protectors formed a stiff wall of defense around her. It almost felt claustrophobic. In an attempt to take her mind off their over-zealousness, the female minotaur focused on her beloved city. The buildings of Nethosak stood tall and proud. The banners fluttered over the clan houses. The streets—

The streets were edged with grime, the stones were obviously muddy. The prints of past pedestrians covered the walkways. The few citizens she saw moved furtively, looking exhausted and wary.

"It's been some time since I was here. How fare matters?"

Arochus looked surprised. "All is in perfect order, my lady. Nethosak runs with the efficiency of which your father dreamed. The emperor and high priestess have made those dreams reality. By edict of the throne, the temple oversees much of the activity needed for imperial expansion. Productivity is at its peak and work is well underway on the addition to the main building."

"The addition?"

"By necessity, the temple must grow. The same goes for temples elsewhere in the realm. I imagine that is also the case in Ambeon."

"I left before such measures started."

"The faithful work during their free time to achieve a rapid realization of the project. Even many of those not yet

converted feel compelled to offer their help." He beamed. "It
is a wonderful time in our history!"

Maritia said nothing. They went on in silence for some
blocks, then suddenly Arochus had the escort veer from the
expected path. Maritia stared as the roof of the palace, just
visible over a merchant's home, receded.

"I thought we were going straight to the emperor."

"We are, but he will be at the temple at this hour. He spends
much of his time there." The last was said with an edge that
hinted Arochus expected her to have known this.

The tromping of feet made her involuntarily reach for her
sword. Moving with a swiftness Maritia would not have
expected, the captain blocked her action with his mace.

"It would be my head if something befell you, my lady.
Please! Wait. I will ascertain things."

A regiment of Protectors burst onto the scene, a mounted
officer at their head. He took one look at Maritia's party, then
nodded curtly to Arochus before shouting something that
sent his own band twisting into the street ahead.

Maritia watched the rank upon rank of black armored figures, noticing how one seemed to blend into another. It was
as though the Protectors were all the same figure duplicated
time and time again.

Her grip tightening on the reins, Maritia asked, "What's
going on, Captain?"

Crimson abruptly tinged Arochus's eyes and his breath
quickened. "They hunt assassins, my lady! Vile assassins!"

"In Nethosak? How can this be?"

The regiment spread out through the entire block, lining
the walkways and facing the buildings. At a shout from the
officer, the Protectors began banging furiously on doors, in
some cases breaking them down. One shaggy minotaur who
answered found himself dragged outside and chained. Other
Protectors burst into his home, from which the sounds of
protest subsequently erupted.

Looking eager, Arochus said, "The assassins slew none other than five of the most prominent, most faithful! Admiral Sorsi, for one, and even two of the Supreme Circle—Councilor Lothan himself included!"

She was shaken by the news. Even her distaste for Lothan, who had for a time seen in her the prospect of a valuable political marriage, did not keep her from cursing those who had assassinated him.

"How were they slain?"

"Of that no one can say, for the bodies cannot be found, yet they have disappeared and their personal belongings were ransacked! Blood was found nearby! The logic is irrefutable."

Not so to Maritia, who frowned to hear this strange story. The officer in charge of the search dismounted. He rumbled something to the chained prisoner, who shook his head. Dissatisfied, the officer seized a whip from his saddle. He growled again at the captive, who muttered something in reply. With a furious snort, the red-eyed Protector lashed his prisoner several times.

Hotak's daughter stiffened. The quick brutality with which the armored figure struck stunned her. She turned her steed.

Arochus suddenly urged his mount in front of Maritia's. "We will be delayed and miss the emperor! Forgive me, my lady, but we must move on if we're to avoid lateness!"

He did not wait for her reply but instead encouraged her horse on with a heavy tap of his mace on its side. Maritia's steed reared, but she got him under control. Arochus, already ahead, made no apologies.

Maritia glanced back at the ongoing interrogation, but her escort blocked her view. Ears flattened, Hotak's daughter tried to push the images from her mind. She would speak with her brother about the disturbing incident. The Protectors served Ardnor's will. He surely would punish any who overstepped their authority.

The temple came into sight. Maritia saw that Arochus had understated the new addition; it almost looked as if her mother was adding a second, equally vast structure alongside the first. The massive wall surrounding the temple grounds had been torn down on the east end, and both the street and the opposing buildings had been demolished. Wracking her memory, Maritia realized some of those missing buildings had housed clans loyal to her father.

The captain must have been watching her even more closely than Maritia had imagined, for he quickly said, "Traitors, my lady. Uncovered by the combined efforts of the temple and the throne. Their properties were seized by your brother and turned over as reward for good service to the high priestess. As your father did, these clans have been ceremoniously shunned, their names never to be uttered, their histories forgotten."

"All of them?"

Arochus nodded sagely. "They were on the Lady Nephera's lists, after all."

An ominous line of Protectors stood guard at the gateway, looking akin to the malevolent statues within. Their fiery-eyed commander nodded to Arochus, barely noticed Maritia, and opened the way.

Despite the lateness of the day, the addition swarmed with hard-working minotaurs hefting stone blocks or raising beams. They did not look as enthusiastic as she had imagined. Nor had she expected so many Protectors keeping watch over the proceedings.

"Why so many guards?"

"The assassinations, of course, my lady."

Maritia looked up, where the dark outline of the addition rose high. A dome would top it. The faithful could come there and hear her mother preach.

Two guards took their steeds. Leaving their escort behind, the captain led her inside. Acolytes in the familiar white and gold robes bowed as she passed. A few others in elegant black robes caught her eye. These were her mother's elite priests and priestesses, the inner circle who aided her in private ceremonies. Even more so than the rest of the acolytes, they had a drawn, pinched look. They imitated the high priestess in their look as well as their deep devotion.

Maritia hesitated. A chill swept down her spine. It did not help that she sensed Arochus's unease, too. Just ahead lay the first of the gargantuan statues—the Forerunners themselves—and even from where she stood their unearthly figures somehow frightened her. Only statues, Hotak's daughter reminded herself. Well-crafted, almost lifelike—if such a word could be used for spirits of the dead—mere huge pieces of marble. Nothing to fear, especially for a hardened legion veteran.

Gritting her teeth, Maritia pushed on past. She sensed if not saw the partially obscured visages, the shrouded forms. The whispers in her ears were the currents of the air, not actual voices. The feeling that shadowed figures moved alongside her was an illusion, having to do with the flickering torches.

Still, it was almost with gratitude that Maritia reached her mother's personal quarters. The two female guards saluted Maritia with crispness. Nearby, a pair of hulking Protectors silently watched.

"My lady," uttered the elder female, "you are welcome. The high priestess and master await within."

"I will leave you here," Captain Arochus murmured, bowing low to her. "Your mount will be attended to and made ready for your departure."

Nodding, Maritia entered. If the outer halls had seemed dimly lit, the chambers were all but black. A faint glow from a rounded brass oil lamp sitting near a high desk contributed most of the illumination. There were also two nearly extinct candles set in niches on the wall.

From the desk, staring down with an intensity that struck Maritia as being similar to the statues, her mother said, "Welcome home, my daughter." She smiled, but Maritia felt no warmth, no pleasure. "I have awaited your arrival eagerly."

Removing her helmet, Maritia went down on one knee. Horns low to the ground, the legion commander responded, "I thank you for your greetings. I only wish I deserved them. The ogres—"

"Yes," Nephera interrupted. "I know about Golgren's duplicity. There will be time for him once the rebels are crushed."

"As to that, I feared the delay had enabled them to already slip close to Mithas. I heard nothing from you and so deemed it best to sail directly here."

The high priestess stood. Her robes hung on her as if hanging on a skeleton. She had grown gaunt and one hand remained shrouded in her long sleeve. "Much thought has been given to the events to come. You were wise to turn your fleet toward home rather than seek pursuit of the rebels. It is most appropriate that the end to this insipid insurrection should take place in the cradle of our civilization and in the shadow of the temple."

"The renegades'll come with everything they have."

Nephera waved off such a concern. "Wisps of wind attempting to topple a mighty forest."

"It might be wise to send for fleet elements stationed at Mito, Amur, and—"

"They have their own vital tasks," the high priestess said, not explaining further.

Maritia nodded.

"With the exception of those units within the capital itself, you are hereby given authority of the legions and garrisons spread throughout the imperial island. The high admirals have already been notified to follow your lead. You will be answerable only to your brother."

Maritia looked up, startled by the show of confidence. The elite units, in addition to those forces already under her command, represented a staggering array of power.

"I'm—I'm grateful."

"A proclamation has already been issued and sent by messenger to all those concerned."

"I'll begin preparations as soon as I leave. I calculate two to three days at most to set everything in motion, providing Faros isn't already at our door."

"He is not," Nephera assured her, "but I expect him soon."

"I'll organize all the ships."

"We have the full confidence in your strategies, my daughter. There's no need to explain them. Simply do what you think best."

Maritia felt as if her head was spinning. Ambeon had been an impressive enough command, but it was a frontier. Now she had been granted authority almost as great as that which Bastion had wielded shortly before he had been chosen heir to the throne.

Bastion. The thought of her other brother darkened her mood, but with this new command, she would avenge him yet.

It suddenly occurred to her that she had seen nothing of her sole surviving brother. "Where's Ardnor? I thought he was supposed to be here?"

"I'm right over here, sister."

Maritia jumped. It was not that the voice had come so unexpectedly from the darkness. No, it had as much to do with the voice itself. It was Ardnor's, of course, but with something different to it that made every strand of hair on her neck bristle.

When the emperor stepped from the shadows—seeming almost to form from the darkness—Maritia nearly jumped again. She recognized her brother, yes, but only barely. He was bigger and taller than any minotaur she had ever seen.

Every muscle in his body was taut, every vein extended. Ardnor looked as if he contained within him an impossible fury ready to explode.

He was clad in the armor of the Protectors, the gold markings identifying him as a master of the order. From his belt hung a mace almost as long as his sister's arm and with a heavy crowned head.

What caught Maritia's breath were Ardnor's eyes. Always tinged with crimson, they were now a deep, unearthly green, even the pupils. Maritia could not meet his gaze directly, which she sensed offered some amusement to her brother.

"I—I apologize," she stammered. "I didn't see you."

This seemed to amuse him more. "Caught up in the excitement . . ."

If Maritia did not look the emperor directly in the eye, she could relax more. "I meant no slight, Ardnor." Belatedly, the legion commander began to kneel. "I know that you sought my arrest earlier on the mistaken belief that I had betrayed the realm—"

"There's no need for concern on that matter, any more," Lady Nephera said. "You were swiftly deemed innocent. The Grand Lord was helpful in ascertaining the truth. That Golgren played his own little games is something he will answer for . . . eventually."

Hotak's daughter was not at all certain that she understood everything her mother said, but she knew how the temple had ways of divining the truth. Ardnor, too, appeared satisfied.

"You will redeem yourself on the battlefield, sister. You'll finally have all the soldiers you ever wanted to play with. You'll be just like Father."

"Enough prattle!" Nephera suddenly blurted, making both her children look at her. "I sense the spawn of Kalin nearing! There are battles brewing in and around the heart of the Imperium, but he is not among the rebels! Therefore he must be closing on Mithas."

"With your permission, then," Maritia interjected, once more the consummate soldier. "I shall begin work immediately. There's a lot to do—fortifying the garrisons north, shoring up the forces inland, setting the fleet into proper position, and—"

A deep rumble of laughter erupted from the emperor. "Like I said, more like Father than any of us sons ever were!"

"By all means, go with my blessing," Nephera stepped from her desk, amidst a flutter of parchments. She stood over Maritia, an imposing and at the same time, somehow eerie sight. Next to his sister, Ardnor respectfully knelt.

The high priestess touched his muzzle, then his helmed head. She then turned to her daughter. Maritia gratefully accepted the touch on her muzzle and forehead, knowing such gestures meant much to her mother. Nephera bid both offspring to rise.

"The Forerunners watch over us and guide us," Nephera intoned. "They and the power that summons them forth shall tear our enemies asunder!"

"Praise be," replied her son. Maritia merely nodded.

"Ardnor, attend me for a moment longer," the high priestess said. "You may go, daughter."

Maritia kissed her mother's hand, then turned and bowed to her brother. "Do any of the generals already have orders?"

"Order about any you wish. I've my own generals," the emperor responded with a cryptic grin.

She waited for him to elaborate, but Ardnor only stared at her with those unsettling orbs.

"As you say, then."

With another bow, Maritia marched away. Despite the unsettling sights she had witnessed, a sense of euphoria overtook her. She would have at her command a force rivaling any her father or Bastion had ever led. The last remnant of Kalin would be slaughtered on the field. Then, she told herself, Nethosak would be restored to its pristine glory. The realm itself would finally be set on its course toward the future.

Her father's dream would culminate at last.

Chapter XXIV

Through the Chain

After the failed attempt by the minotaur slaves to take over the imperial mining camp of Vyrox, Bastion's legionaries had force-marched the survivors through the mountains of Argon's Chain to the waiting ogre ships. The trek had been arduous and deadly to some. The soldiers had shown no mercy to their charges.

Faros had been even less kind to his army. All went well until they emerged from Argon's Chain. Exhausted by their journey through the mountains, they took insufficient notice of the outpost ahead. Likely even Nethosak barely recalled the insignificant, lone structure. It could only house perhaps a dozen soldiers at most, but for the precarious path through the mountains, it had little reason to exist.

Botanos, leading his horse over the rough ground, came face-to-face with the first soldier of the empire, who immediately turned to flee and warn his companions.

"Get him!" urged Faros from behind the captain, dropping the reins of his own steed.

The rebels scrambled over the rocks, but the guard knew the paths and managed to keep ahead. The small, boxlike way station loomed. As he neared it, the legionary called out. Suddenly, a shaft materialized in the back of his neck. The soldier crashed into the worn wooden door then dropped in a heap.

The door swung open a moment later and three armed figures burst out. Despite hundreds of warriors approaching, the trio stood their ground. The door behind them shut. The odds were such that the battle would be laughingly short, but it was clear that all the legionaries desired was time enough for one of their number to send a hasty message, likely by bird.

Axes ready, the three soldiers formed a line in front of the narrow entrance. Faros, in the lead, veered to his left, Botanos following. They and several others raced around the trio of desperate defenders. The next instant, a wall of fur crashed into the three as the main rebel contingent swarmed upon them.

As the clash of arms echoed behind them, Faros and Botanos scaled a fence that penned the imperial horses. Faros dashed toward the back of the outpost, and an axe slammed into the wood inches from his stomach. He lunged, driving the sword through the armor and chest of the legionary who stood there, waiting for him.

Someone inside shot a single arrow, downing a rebel just coming up behind him. Botanos, on Faros's other side, angrily pointed at a small opening near the upper part of the structure.

The scarred, oak panel slid open. Within, they could hear the rattle of a cage and the squawk of an eager bird. Faros started forward, but something snagged his foot and the sword went flying from his grip. Botanos came up and buried his axe in the dying soldier holding onto his companion's ankle.

The cage slid open. Reacting instinctively, Faros lunged for the brown form emerging from the window. His hands grappled with a fearsome explosion of feathers and talons. A sharp beak jabbed his forearm. A wing battered his face, blinding him. He squeezed, trying to crush the bird, but it squirmed and broke free. Its flight erratic, it headed up into the clouds.

From inside came a crashing sound, furious shouts, and the brief clang of steel announcing the end of those soldiers still inside.

"You damaged it," Botanos pointed out, indicating the blood and feathers on his leader's hands, most of which belonged to the bird. "It'll likely die before it reaches anyone."

Wiping his hands off as best he could, Faros picked up his sword. "If not," he said grimly, "then we've forfeited the element of surprise."

They quickly stripped the outpost of its horses and meager rations then headed for the level terrain. This region of Mithas offered scant protection from the weather. Rain tormented the rebels for a day and night, until, unable to struggle through the storm, the rebels finally halted. Even so, they had crossed quite a distance. If their pace continued, then by late tomorrow they would be close enough to see Nethosak on the horizon.

Lightning illuminated the area, punctuated by ear-splitting cracks of thunder. Fires were out of the question, and they were cold as well as soaked.

The rain came to a halt just before morning. Their fur soaked to the flesh, the bedraggled rebels rose from the muddy ground like a legion of animated corpses leaving their fresh graves. Faros gave them little time to tend themselves, aware that the need for haste had grown paramount.

Just as Faros saddled his mount, he heard a cry that sounded like an imperial messenger bird. The minotaur glanced up but saw nothing. As they moved, Faros began to spread his force out in a wide pattern. They were making good time, partly because the only weapons they had were those they carried, while the slower moving legions boasted ballistae, catapults, and lines of supply. Fortunately, Gaerth's people had provided them with sufficient food and good, strong blades.

Utilizing their few horses, Faros sent out his best scouts. The first returned with nothing to report, but those ranging farther ahead finally came back to say they had seen the outskirts of Nethosak, spotted the first of the outlying settlements.

They had also sighted two legions, the first of many more beyond. Faros called for a few of the surviving officers from those legions who had joined him. The scouts described what they could of the two forces, especially details of their flags.

One of the flags of the enemy legions bore the image of a brown, broad claw, a black, ursine silhouette behind it. "Bear Claw Legion," a former hekturion identified it. "General Gularius's likely still the commander. Sets a strong, sturdy defense while deploying a powerful, methodical attack."

Faros's ears straightened. "Methodical? Or inventive?"

"I'd not use the latter term, my lord."

The second legion, the one nearest, sported a red ruby on a field of diagonal, golden slashes. None of the former soldiers could recall such a symbol on a banner and even Botanos, who had served long time in the military, could make no sense of it.

"Maybe it's some new grouping," the captain suggested.

Faros nodded. "The symbol strikes me as more appropriate for the temple."

"We've heard talk of legions formed under Protector control, some composed entirely of the faithful. This could be such a one."

"Hmmm, their training and experience will be inferior to the older legions." To the scouts, Faros asked, "Where is this Ruby Legion?" When they had shown him, scratching out the positions on the ground, he looked to Botanos. "What do you think?"

"Aye, if there's a weak point, it'll be them . . . but that's a huge 'if,' my lord."

The rebel leader looked again to the riders. "Show me where the catapults and ballistae are."

They pointed out what they had seen and hazarded a guess as to what was concealed. "Gather those who have worked together on either type of machine. This is what I want of them . . ."

Two hours later, the rebels were on the move, guided by the scouts. Faros couldn't shake his thoughts from the fleeing messenger bird. Then they sighted the legion. The first signs were smoke then the noises of the encampment. Faros and Botanos crept up to a rise and peered at the sight, studying the enemy. The soldiers moved about with little apparent concern, further indication they were not well-trained, seasoned legionaries.

"Protectors in command, I'll bet," Captain Botanos muttered hopefully. "Overconfident."

Faros already had his sword drawn. "We don't dare hesitate." He turned back to a subordinate. "Give the signal."

A rebel waved a pair of green and white flags. The silent signal was passed on from one section of the army to the next. When the signal returned that all were ready, Faros rose and waved his sword. With a collective roar, the rebels charged.

They were already halfway to the outer perimeter before the warning horns sounded. Armored figures scurried into position. To their credit, the enemy began to swiftly form a defense.

"The left!" shouted Botanos, his veteran's eye spotting a glaring weakness. "The left flank's disorganized!"

"What about the Bear Claws?" asked a rebel keeping pace with them. The second legion was not in sight, but surely they would hasten to the rescue.

"If we overcome these quickly, we'll be ready for them!" said Faros.

"That's another huge 'if'!" the mariner scoffed, following Faros as he plunged ahead.

A menacing shadow briefly swept over them. Something came hurtling through the air. It landed with a heavy thud far to the north, missing the rebels' outer flank by a good distance. Faros grinned as he ran and shouted orders. A well-honed, well-practiced catapult crew would have never fired so haphazardly.

Ahead, lines continued to form. Officers on horseback shouted orders. Lancers moved into position and archers notched their bows.

Faros looked for the signal horn. "Fire! Have them fire!"

The rebel blew the signal horn. Many among the ragtag army paused, aimed, and fired bows. They knew how to fire on the run. A thousand arrows dropped among the legionaries. Many bounced off shields and armor. Others landed harmlessly on the flattened soil, but a good number struck their targets. Soldiers keeled over. Others clutched wounded limbs. Bodies had to be dragged with haste from the lines.

The legion fired back. Many among the first attackers fell. Those behind them leaped over their bodies and kept charging. The stricken fighters' best hope lay in victory by their comrades. The enemy's left flank now showed some cohesion. Ballistae crews had some of the machines nearly turned and ready for firing.

Faros waved his sword. The horns blew again. A second volley fell upon the legion's left flank. Many more soldiers died, then all Faros could see were the grim faces of the soldiers directly ahead. He focused on one and met that legionary's gaze.

A heartbeat later, the two armies met.

With tremendous confidence Maritia departed Nethosak to take command on the field. She recalled the chaos with which the slaves had struggled to fight in Vyrox. Numbers had been on their side then, but they had been beaten and the best of their leaders perished there. That Chot's nephew was spared was an oversight.

Unlike some of her officers, Maritia had not been quick to believe Faros's entire force was on Mito. No, he had intelligence, she grudgingly admitted, and he might try a feint. Ardnor had been surprisingly willing to let her dictate the positions of the main forces. In the short time since the news arrived of Faros's movements, she had planned for every contingency.

Vast elements of sea power patrolled the coastline, save where Argon's Chain crowded the shore. Maritia did not have her mother's supernatural gifts, but riders constantly streamed back and forth from the various legions while the trained messenger birds gave her some notion as to what was happening with the ships.

As she watched Warhorse prepare to deploy, a rider from the west brought her a missive. "My Lady Maritia! This just came!"

Reading it, her heart leapt. Several rebel ships had been sighted to the west. One had been tentatively identified as the *Dragon's Crest*, the most elusive vessel in all the rebel fleet. She hoped to capture that one intact and display the prize in the capital. Maritia had no doubt Faros had somehow managed to drop his followers somewhere in the north or northwest, perhaps near Varga.

"Send a bird to Varga. Ask for an immediate response."

"Aye, my lady!"

Hotak's daughter looked around. "Where's the liaison from Onyx Legion?" That was one of the newer legions; Maritia had trouble keeping their names straight. To her, the new names lacked the grandeur of the Wyverns or the

Flying Gryphons. "I want verification of their position!" She peered into the distance. "Why is General Domo's legion veering toward the east? They'll leave a gap the Blood Sea could pour through!"

Maritia's aides rushed to deal with these matters. One of her bodyguards stood in the saddle. "Rider from the north, my lady."

It was the courier from Onyx Legion. Never mind his shorn mane and wide-eyed stare, he proved a highly-competent messenger, exceptionally describing the position of his command. Maritia's tension lessened as the report filled in gaps in her knowledge.

"It's coming together, Father," she muttered distractedly.

"Beg pardon, my lady?" the messenger asked, puzzled.

"Nothing."

Looking past the Onyx Legion messenger, Maritia saw that General Domo's forces were heading out at last. As they marched off to their appointed position, Maritia breathed a sign of relief. Everyone and everything was nearly in place. The fleet was stalking the rebel ships. They were closing in on Faros. The rebel leader had acted just as Maritia had predicted. She almost felt some disappointment at what would be an easy victory.

Overhead, a bedraggled messenger bird flying from the east announced its arrival with a weary screech. Maritia watched impatiently as it descended to handlers. Who was sending her a message from the east? Only two legions were there; it was hardly a strategic position.

"From the outpost near Tagla, my lady," reported the soldier who brought the sealed note. "The bird's injured," he added grimly.

"Tagla." Maritia's ears flattened as she read the markings on the case. "This bird was supposed to keep on to the capital. The harsh winds around the mountains must've worn it out and it decided to alight at the first familiar-looking roost."

The seal bore the black warhorse. The note was short and simple . . . and too astonishing to credit.

Rebels swarming out of mountains! A large army! Two miles south of Vyrox, heading—

Heading in the direction of Nethosak.

Nostrils flaring, Maritia read the message again. Three days ago. The badly-injured bird had gotten very lost indeed.

Maritia looked to the east, knowing her defenses were thin there. "A map!" she shouted to a guard. "Get me a map of Argon's Chain!"

Finding Tagla on the map and verifying the obscure route through the mountains told her she had missed a vital possibility in all her planning. Now, unbelievably, Faros Es-Kalin was behind most of her lines and nearly on top of the capital.

"The hour has come, my lord," the high priestess whispered from her chair below the icons, "the end of the age of Sargonnas and the beginning of the era of the great Morgion."

Nephera looked forward to displaying the rebels' bodies, especially that of the Kalin spawn. Each rebel death would strengthen her god, make it a certainty that the Lord of the Bronze Tower would reign supreme among the gods.

She shuddered as she felt the first clash on Tagla between the insurrectionists and the legions. The deaths fueled her pleasure, for each dead one immediately became another servant of hers, adding to her power.

Thanks to her ghosts, Nephera had been aware for some time that the rebels were penetrating from the east, but she had chosen not to alert Maritia. It was good that her daughter be tested. Besides, the high priestess wished to stoke the overconfidence of Chot's nephew, lead him like the proverbial lamb to the slaughter . . . and Faros was obliging her quite nicely.

"With your permission, my lord," she asked of the glowing symbols. Shutting her eyes, the high priestess envisioned her son. She saw Ardnor impatiently waiting her orders, surrounded by a sea of dark figures.

"Ardnor, my dear son, it is time."

In her vision, Lady Nephera saw her firstborn grin. With a laugh, he adjusted his helm. She could sense the powers bestowed upon him by their lord stirring to unholy life.

Nephera dismissed the vision and returned her senses to the battle. All was happening according to her will.

Chapter XXV

Battle and Betrayal

Through the streets of Nethosak, they marched in perfect unison. A grim horde of fanatic fighters with but a single purpose—they would obey the will of their lord. From windows and doorways, the citizens of the imperial capital watched uneasily. All minotaurs appreciated the lust for war, the devotion to battle, but the Protectors inspired dread. The black wave poured toward the city gates, radiating a dark aura that made even veteran warriors edge back into the security of their homes.

At the monstrous force's head rode the great emperor. Ardnor silently stared at the path before him as if his mind was focused elsewhere. His teeth were bared in a fearsome, unvarying smile, and the hand nearest his slung mace twitched in anticipation.

Above the endless march of Protectors, a new banner flew strong. Most did not pay much attention to it, the sight of the emperor and his elite an arresting enough vision. Those who noticed, if they were old enough and had good memories, might have discovered something familiar about their ruler's chosen symbol.

A down-turned axe.

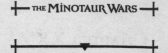

Maritia had sent word to the eastern legions as soon as she could, only to hear the horns sound from that direction just minutes later. She laughed grimly then focused on a rapid redeployment. Faros had outwitted her, but only for the moment.

She had to admire his determination. How he had dragged his followers through the mountains—and so swiftly—was a feat worthy of an imperial general, yet no trained legion officer would have attempted such a perilous journey, not with so much on the line. Still, in the end such derring-do would not save him. General Gularius and General Domo should be closing on the rebels even now, and Onyx was moving to take over her own position. In the northwest, the Gryphons had been ordered to spread their lines thin to make up for the other legion's departure. Maritia had quickly sent a message to the legions near Varga to return immediately—just in case the battle should drag on over days.

"Everyone ready?" she asked.

Seeing only nods, she mounted her own steed then gave the signal. A trumpeter sounded the call. Warhorse Legion marched to battle.

Maritia had shrewdly kept the Warhorse in reserve. Here was an opportunity for a rout of the rebels. True, using the Warhorse army would, for a short time, leave only the Imperial and State Guards as defenders of the capital, and both their ranks had been sorely depleted, but once Onyx arrived, that danger would pass.

Glancing back over her troops, Maritia saw with pride the most honored fighting force in all the imperium massing to meet the rebels. She murmured, "Guide our arms, Father . . . make our axes sharp and our swords swift . . . and I promise you that I will personally slay Chot's nephew in your name—"

Daughter . . .

Maritia's ears went taut. For a moment, she thought that her father had actually answered her prayers, then she realized that it was another familiar voice summoning her. "Mother?"

Ardnor commands you march further north, whispered Nephera in her mind. *To the edge of the hills, then turn east.*

Startled by the directive, Maritia recovered quickly. The power of her mother never ceased to amaze her, but she couldn't follow such orders blindly. "The hills? That'll take precious time!"

This is an imperial command. Would you, a loyal legionary, disobey your brother, your emperor?

Maritia had no ready reply. In her mind, veering to the south and then heading directly to battle worked better. The Warhorse would not only reach Faros faster but outflank him.

But . . . as her mother said, this was an imperial command.

Turning to an officer, Maritia shouted, "Summon riders! New orders! Alert all that we head north to the first rise, then east!"

The other minotaur eyed her curiously for a moment, no doubt also wondering at this elaborate detour.

As the word spread, Maritia felt better. She gripped the reins tight. She had no idea what her brother planned, but she had to believe that he had something special in mind for the rebels—something that would crush Faros utterly.

The left flank finally yielded. Faros's warriors poured through, forcing the soldiers to scatter and fight on several fronts at once. Hekturions and other officers shouted commands, but the novice legionaries reacted slowly and with confusion.

Faros cut through the chest of one soldier then fended off the axe of another. Ahead lay the enemy's catapults and ballistae. The former were in the process of being hurriedly moved to avoid being seized, but the latter were trained on the attackers.

One ballista fired. Screams arose as the lances flew into the mass of fighters. In their haste to fire, though, the crew not only killed rebels but also more than a few of their own comrades. The clash of metal echoed violently. Minotaurs stood muzzle to muzzle. A legionary's axe ripped out the throat of rebel. Two other rebels lanced a dekarian, their spears tossing the body up and away, so that it landed back among the imperial soldiers.

A mounted treverian materialized from out of the blue, striking at Faros with a mace. The heavy head of the weapon caught Faros's arm, ripping his skin and smashing the bone. He deflected a second blow from the officer. Fanatical eyes glared at him, as the helmed figure swung the mace again.

"Heretic!" the treverian suddenly spouted. "Criminal!"

Ducking below the mace, Faros brought his fist up. The punch shoved the legionary's muzzle straight up, causing his helmet to slip to the side, revealing his shorn mane. Shaking off the attack, the officer thrust. The long point nearly skewered Faros's throat.

Faros seized the weapon's handle and tugged. The treverian fell forward. He let out a gurgling sound as Faros's upturned blade ran him through. Shoving aside the body, Faros took a swift glance around. The way to the war machines was opening wide. Botanos, leading a pack of fighters, headed toward one catapult. Another band headed for the ballistae.

Faros and his party met the crew of another catapult. A legionary swatted at him with his axe. The rebel leader dispatched his foe with a single thrust then jumped atop the machine. Near the back, another crew member worked to set off the huge weapon's missile. Faros kicked at a soldier then dove past.

Another rebel came around to fight the legionary. The soldier parried her attack then jammed the top of his axe in her stomach. As she fell, he raised the blade for one last, hard slash at the rope that would unleash the catapult's missile. That was when Faros's sword cut through the soldier's left arm, burying itself to the bone. The soldier roared in pain, and while he attempted to keep his grip on the axe, Faros cut across his throat.

As the rebels swarmed the machine, two other members of the crew surrendered. Faros had his own experienced catapult operators take over the machine.

"Their right flank! Hit it!"

With both machines now being wheeled into a position against the empire, Faros looked to the ballistae. Two were still under legion control, but the rest within sight were instruments of the revolt. Seizing a rebel, Faros pointed and shouted orders.

Screams arose from one of the rebel crews as a legion ballista fired on one of its captured counterparts, tearing through those manning it. The new legion's ballistae were a different type than those aboard ships or used by previous imperial forces. They carried smaller shafts but three to four times as many in number. It was as if a small but incredibly swift flight of arrows had been hurled at body level, with devastating effect.

"Get those two!" Faros ordered a group of warriors. "Come around their left."

The captured ballistae now fired back, raking the rear of the legion. Many imperial soldiers fell, including mounted officers.

A catapult manned by the rebels went off. The heavy rock dropped among the defenders, the earth exploding and bodies flying. The huge boulder left a crater in the midst of the enemy. With that, the legion was all but defeated. A sweating but jubilant Captain Botanos rode up beside Faros.

"First blood is ours! They collapsed like a house of playing cards!"

"They weren't an experienced force! They were led by Protectors. The others will be more formidable."

The fighting dwindled. A female with her arm in a bloody sling reported, "Their general's dead! It's taken the fight out of what's left! Do we cut them down or try to take prisoners?"

"Give them one chance, and if they hesitate, do what you must. We've no time to waste!"

The catapults fired off a few more shots at viable targets, then Faros called for them to cease. The rebels would need every missile and bolt.

Rebel scouts returned from ahead. One of them immediately shouted, "Bear Claw Legion is sweeping north of us!"

"North?" Botanos growled. "What's gotten into their general?"

"Another legion's on its way. A stronger one yet. It's heading north, too."

"Makes no sense . . ." growled the mariner. "They're going out of their way, north. They'll not catch us until we're nearly at the capital! It has to be a trick of some sort! What do you think?"

Faros didn't hesitate. "I don't care. We push on anyway. If we let them come and fight us here, we'll never make Nethosak. They'll whittle us down."

The rebels gathered what they could and pushed their advance. One flank broke off, heading north. At the head of the army, Faros added something new—two hundred minotaurs in the tarnished breastplates of the defeated legion, their hands bound behind them. Rebels prodded their abject march with swords.

Scouts continually reported on the northern legion, which seemed to be moving not only at an odd angle but a slow pace.

Captain Botanos frowned. "They're not acting right, lad! You'd almost think that they're moving to avoid the fight!"

"Make sure the scouts keep a constant eye on them," the rebel leader muttered. "They may yet surprise us."

"And if they stay aloof?"

"Nothing matters now but Nethosak," was all Faros answered, imagining the home that he had not seen in years. "Nothing."

The black tide flowed out through Nethosak's gates like blood, filling the landscape. Great copper kettle drums punctuated their march. The zeal that drove the Protectors was terrifying. They were certain of their might, certain of the glory that the power beyond would grant them for this victory.

Spread out among the ranks, the five fearsome shades that Ardnor had summoned kept order over their elements. The specters were not wholly visible; they seemed insubstantial, but no one doubted their presence. They sat upon steeds long dead and rotted. The warriors in the ranks did not seem at all disturbed by such monstrous commanders, for these were simply another sign of the great god they served, though they did not yet know his name.

Around the emperor, other ghosts drifted. These were his attendants, ghostly eyes granted by Nephera to keep her son aware of near and far events. Through them, Ardnor saw the crushing of the first legion and noted the movements of the rebels.

What he could not see into was the mind of their leader. A fog covered the Kalin spawn, and no matter how furiously Ardnor tortured the cringing shadows with the power Morgion had granted him, they could not tell the emperor what Faros was intending to do.

In the end, his fury was such that Nephera penetrated his

thoughts in order to rein her son in. *Cease this futility, my son! You shall have Faros Es-Kalin shortly!*

"But why can't I see the bastard?" he growled, ignoring the fact he was talking aloud. None around him would dare question his strange behavior. "What keeps him from Morgion's power?"

A pathetic attempt by a waning god . . . nothing more. The Horned One's final desperate act! It was to be expected . . . and it will avail neither him nor his puppet any good in the end.

Ardnor's hand slipped to his mace again. He itched to bury it in Faros's skull. "No matter. The important thing is we'll ride them down before they're halfway to the walls."

The force with which the high priestess's presence struck Ardnor nearly caused him to rock from the saddle. *You will do nothing of the sort! You will follow my instructions implicitly!*

He opened his mouth to argue, only to be nearly overwhelmed again by her voice inside his mind.

You will not deviate from what is planned! Faros will be yours, my son, that is promised!

"But Maritia! She'll reach him first."

And she will serve her role! You will do as we discussed! This day will see the utter destruction of the rebels, and the people will know the supremacy of the temple and the Great One. They will know there can be no other emperor but you! You, Ardnor . . .

His protests faded. "Me . . ."

The outcome is assured! Follow the lead you have been given and pay no mind to your sister's task! Soon enough you will advance to center stage.

Her voice faded from his head. Ardnor's blood still raced. With a predatory grin, he whispered, "Just so the Kalin spawn is still mine."

The others closest to him pretended not to hear.

Nethosak was finally with Faro's reach. Even the most remotely-born citizen visited Nethosak at least once in their lives. The capital city embodied the empire. It had been razed to the ground time and time again and after each disaster it had arisen stronger and more impressive than before.

Faros stared at its towers, hardly daring to believe that he was home. Then he heard a horn and spotted the banner rising from the north. Minutes later, a scout breathlessly arrived.

" 'Tis the banner of the Warhorse, my lord! They're closing on us fast!"

"Find out if Bear Claw still marches away from us," the rebel leader said, ordering another scout. As the latter hurried off, Faros added, "We ride to meet the Warhorse, captain."

"Aye, lad. We couldn't escape destiny now if we tried."

Warhorse represented the empire in ways unlike any other legion. If they defeated it, news of their victory would spread to all the other legions, crippling the will of the defenders.

The rebels veered toward the oncoming legion. Even from a distance, Maritia's force was impressive. Warhorse moved without gaps in the lines, without faltering. Their breastplates shone. The mounted officers rode back and forth with precision, and halfway to the rebels, the legion simply stopped.

"She's daring us to come to them, Botanos." Faros tried to identify where her catapults and ballistae were positioned, but he could not make things out at a distance. He might be sending his force into a hellish trap. The sooner he acted, he felt instinctively, the better. "Let's not disappoint her. She and I have overdue business."

"Aye, my lord."

At the sound of horns, the rebels moved toward the enemy. The prisoners were prodded ahead of the rest. Let Maritia think him a beast without honor, Faros thought. Likely she already did.

The gap between the two sides shrank. He could now make out faces among the legionaries and finally saw the one mattered. There! The commander's standard marked Maritia's position. Her countenance was still vague, but the figure with a plumed helmet and midnight blue cloak had to be her. Only a Droka rode with such powerful bearing. He had seen it in her once before in Vyrox.

"They've not fired yet!" Botanos called. "The prisoners confuse them!"

"Let them be confused no more!" Faros made a slashing motion with his hands.

The rebels slowed. The captive legionaries were prodded forward and then they were let go. At first the prisoners reacted slowly, uncertainly, then as they moved farther away from the rebels, they began to sprint for freedom.

Those in the forefront of the Warhorse lines began roaring encouragement. When the first reached them, the soldiers quickly made openings in their ranks. Several slapped the captives on the back. Not a few used their weapons to cut the bonds of the newcomers.

"The first step is complete," Faros muttered. "Now for the second."

He suddenly urged his horse to a trot. Botanos gasped and tried to grab his arm, but Faros was already out of reach.

Midway to the foe, the rebel leader paused and waited. He was not disappointed. Seconds after his arrival, the one he had taken for Maritia removed her cloak and helm and rode out to meet him.

"Faros Es-Kalin," she nearly spat.

"My lady. A long time since Vyrox."

She snorted. "Would that I'd cut you down then."

"My sentiments exactly," he returned.

"You can still surrender, rebel. I promise your execution will be a swift one, and I'll do what I can for those with you."

"Can you restore our families? My father? My mother? All so basely slain that night? All because we shared the blood of the emperor."

"It was necessary!" Maritia snapped. "Necessary for the sake of the realm!"

"And honorable?"

She glared at him.

"Just know this, my lady; we do what we were forced to do."

With that, the rebel leader turned his horse and rode from the minotaur commander while she sat staring at him in surprise.

Meeting Faros, Captain Botanos looked furious with his leader. He rumbled, "What was that all about? All it would've taken was one eager archer or even the lady herself and you'd be deceived, or worse, lying out there dead!"

"That wouldn't have been honorable."

Faros turned his steed to face the legion just in time to see Maritia vanishing through a gap in the front of her troops.

"They've two catapults set far behind their left flank, which are aimed for just right of our center," Faros said briskly. "Behind the first three lines, there are four ballistae. The second and third lines have gaps at those points. You can tell by the small red pennants flying at each position. You see them?"

A startled Botanos nodded his head. "You were—"

Cutting him off, the rebel leader quickly added, "Another catapult to the far right, aimed just left of our center. There may be another there as well. She has a cavalry reserve near, probably to ride in once we're engaged. Also, archers are behind the main lines, already with the bows notched. They'd hit us about at the distance where she stood. Three segments of soldiers behind what we can see. The one I could make out best had a hekturion leading them, so assume three hundred fighters in reserve."

"They're larger than any legion I've ever known!" Botanos shook his head.

Faros snorted. "Did you think I rode out to admire her?"

"The thought had actually crossed my mind, aye."

At that moment, the scout he had sent earlier returned. The new minotaur said nothing, only nodded to him.

Gradic's son shifted in the saddle. "Warhorse is getting impatient and I don't want my own stalwarts losing their edge. Make certain that everyone follows my signals."

"After what you said? I'll shout the orders myself if need be."

"Then let's ride." A rumble of thunder shook the area, spooking the horses. Faros noticed his ring flare briefly. It would not surprise him if there were other things going on around him, beyond mortal comprehension. "Sound the advance!"

With the cry of a single horn, the rebels charged.

✠────▼────✠

The high priestess viewed the scene from her daughter's perspective. She tried to reach out and touch Faros's thoughts, but again a barrier rose up to block her. Sargonnas's power hid something, but Nephera could sense nothing of particular concern.

Both the Protectors and legions were in desirable positions. That her daughter was unaware of the high priestess's entire strategy was unfortunate, but sacrifices had to be made. With this last thought, the unease returned. With a snarl, Nephera glanced quickly over her shoulder; however, only Takyr stood there, awaiting her command.

No Hotak. No condemning eyes . . .

Snorting at her own foolish anxieties, she returned her focus to the struggle. The rebels were on the move. It was time to savor their destruction.

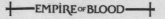

The legionaries stood motionless, their expressions guarded. Their weapons were raised, but they awaited the necessary signal. Faros measured the distance. He waved his sword at a trumpeter. Two short notes followed by a longer single one echoed in the air.

Noise erupted from the back of the legions. Huge rocks flew up in the air. Near the first ranks, soldiers gave way for hidden ballistae.

The front line of Faros's army suddenly cleaved in two.

"What're they doing?" Maritia snarled.

She looked up and saw the missiles dropping. They struck with the full force of gravity and weight, huge stones designed to wreak the greatest possible carnage, if there had been anyone to hit.

The rebels were moving rapidly, changing from an organized rectangular formation to a fluid, constantly reshaping half circle with most of the rebels flowing to the sides. The missiles burst where the center had been, creating huge craters, and scattering rubble . . . but all in vain. One or two rebels twisted as if injured by small pieces of rock, but most continued their business unhindered.

Two ballistae fired before she could call a halt. One managed to bring down a rebel who had stumbled into its path, but the rest of the lances fell short.

"Hold fire!" she commanded. "Hold fire!"

She had thought Faros a fatalistic fool who had ridden out to meet her as a last act of defiance to rally his troops. Now Maritia understood better. He had been surreptitiously measuring her forces. Small wonder she had found his conversation almost nonsensical; his mind had been on far more weighty issues.

Of course, Maritia, too, had been analyzing her enemy, but they had few war machines and scarcely any mounted units. While Faros had planned for her catapults and ballistae, he couldn't guess everything – certainly not what she had in store next.

317

"General Domo should be in position," she whispered to herself. "We'll catch you in between and eat you up, Faros Es-Kalin!" To a trumpeter, Maritia shouted, "Sound the signal!"

Horns blaring, the famed legion slowly and methodically spread out in its march toward the oncoming horde.

"Archers at the ready!"

Four hundred bows tightened.

Maritia measured. "Fire!"

The rebels' attention would be drawn by the advancing foot soldiers. They would not expect the deadly rain, but again a short series of signals blew from the opposing side. As swiftly as the arrows flew, they were betrayed by their need for a high, arcing flight. The rebel force reshaped again.

The tactic wasn't as effective as against the catapults, and scores of the enemy dropped or slowed as the shafts landed. However, the wholesale slaughter that Maritia wished did not occur.

"We'll do it with sharp blades then," she snarled.

Maritia again made a quick assessment of the rebel numbers. The advantage would definitely be hers. In addition to her own trusted army, she had added the survivors of the other legion, who had been quickly rearmed and now waited in reserve behind the cavalry.

Sword waved high, Maritia brought her right flank forward, curling it around the rebels' force. This time Hotak's daughter did not underestimate the adversary, for many, she knew, were former soldiers. A few even still wore the emblems of Dragonsbane, perhaps to stir up uncertainties among her troops.

"Get those archers over to the right!" Hotak's daughter shouted. She kept an eye out for Faros, seeking a chance to take him on.

Grunts and cries filled the air. Rebels fell, but legionaries dropped too. A massive figure with the gold rings of a mariner materialized ahead briefly, his axe cutting through the helm

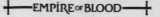

and neck of a soldier. Maritia marked him as a possible sub-commander, but before she could get close, the battle swept the figure away.

A harsh clatter arose from behind her left flank. Legionaries abruptly turned in circles, creating disorder. Some looked confused and others, strangely, lowered their weapons. Then, to her utter bewilderment, a legionary close by took a swing at her, nearly biting deep into Maritia's leg.

She managed to escape with a cut along her thigh, paying the treacherous fighter back with a thrust to his windpipe. As he tumbled forward, Maritia stared in disbelief at the minotaur . . . and belatedly realized that he was not one of her own. A ruby symbol marked his breastplate.

The prisoners?

Absolute chaos swept over the rear of the legion. Everywhere, the freed prisoners fell upon their confused brethren. Ranks disintegrated. Catapult crews had to abandon their machines to fight back. The cavalry was in disarray, many horses without riders.

The truth hit her hard. The prisoners that Faros had released to Warhorse might have worn the armor of the legions, but they were rebels.

What a fool, to have fallen for such a stunt! she thought bitterly. She should have checked. She should have had them sequestered. Never would Hotak's daughter have expected such base trickery. The false prisoners numbered only a couple of hundred, but with the main force attacking from the front, Warhorse was sorely beset.

"Where's Domo? Damn him! Where is he?"

Of the legion she had counted on in a pinch, there was no sign. Something had gone dreadfully wrong with her plans.

Chapter XXVI

The Black Tide

Warhorse seemed in complete disarray, Faros noted to his satisfaction. They still fought and fought well, but they were harried from all directions. None of the trapped legionaries could be certain that the figure behind them might not be an enemy in disguise.

The rebels were suffering, too. The ground lay littered with the bodies of those who had followed Faros through Kern twice, then across the Courrain, and finally trekked over part of Argon's Chain—all to die in pitiable fashion here.

"Drive them into one another!" Faros shouted, deflecting a legionary's axe. "Find the Lady Maritia! She's the key to victory!"

"Bet she's wondering where her reinforcements are!" Captain Botanos barked with a hollow laugh.

Bear Claw Legion would not be arriving soon. If Faros's forces had looked less than imposing to Maritia, it had not merely been because he had disguised two hundred of his best as prisoners. Rather, it was because another portion of his army had stayed behind with weapons confiscated from the defeated legion. Their rearguard fighting

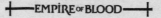

would delay the other imperials from riding to Lady Maritia's rescue.

Time was still of the essence. The rebels had a day, no more, before other legions regrouped and attacked. Faros had to break the Warhorse army and march on Nethosak swiftly.

"Incoming!" Botanos roared.

Faros and the captain jumped from their mounts, taking refuge among rocks. A flight of arrows dropped among the rebels, killing too many. Rising, Faros found the captain clutching his upper leg where an arrow had pierced the side.

"I'll be fine! Just need a few moments to bind this!" growled the veteran sailor, already working on the wound. "You just watch your head—and bring me back hers!"

Nodding, Faros returned to the fray. On foot now, Gradic's son could see less clearly what was happening. To his left, he saw a ballista crew trying to adjust for a shot at his front line.

Catching the attention of nearby followers, Faros cried, "To me! The ballista!"

They formed a spearhead. His sword led the cutting of a swathe through the soldiers trying to defend the ballista. Other rebels pushed back the remaining legionaries, widening the way. The crew saw their danger and tried to turn the machine. However, they had to grab their axes and blades to meet Faros's group.

The dekarian in charge lunged for Faros. The black silhouette of the Warhorse momentarily revived in Gradic's son the terror of the Night of Blood. Once again he saw the bodies and the laughing figures watching as fire consumed his home; again he remembered the helmed assassin who had tried to kill him.

Fueled by rage, Faros forced the dekarian to his knees. The officer's eyes bulged as he perceived the almost inhuman strength of his adversary. Foregoing his blade, the rebel leader seized the legionary's throat in one hand and slowly crushed his windpipe.

Breathing heavily, Faros looked to the abandoned ballista. "Get it turned about!"

With effort, they forced the war machine around. The weapon had already been primed. The rebels corrected the machine's aim and fired. The small bolts blasted into the legionaries. Screams filling the air, the dead and wounded twisted together in a grotesque heap.

Faros left his crew behind, slipping once more among the combatants. Suddenly a cloaked figure tried to run him down. Faros leapt to the side and grabbed the soldier's cloak, sending the figure flying head first to the hard ground. The imperial officer collided with a harsh cracking sound and lay still.

Faros seized a horse's reins and mounted. He peered around, looking for the distinctive helm and cloak worn by Maritia. There were only so many who wore it and fewer yet who were female.

He grunted in sudden pain as a blade scraped his side. Instinct saved him, his sword moving swiftly to deflect a second strike.

"Were you looking for me?" Maritia de-Droka said mockingly.

Hotak's daughter again swung her sword, forcing Faros to wheel his horse around. She attacked on his injured side, making it difficult to properly parry, even with Sargonnas's blade.

"I promised my father your head!" She slashed wildly at him, but Faros again wheeled on his horse and swung back.

Both blades came together. Sparks flew, and Maritia's sword was badly chipped. Unfazed, the legion commander stabbed at his reins, slashing them away.

The rebel's horse shifted nervously. Maritia tried to take advantage, but she had to adjust her footing.

Faros countered. His swing should have lopped off her hand, but at the last moment it seemed to veer of its own accord, striking her with its flat side. Maritia yelped and lost her grip, her weapon vanishing into the press of bodies around them.

She reached for her dagger. A swarm of fighters came between them. Faros had to seize his horse by the mane in order to keep from falling. Maritia lunged at him with her dagger. Faros blocked her blade with his forearm, scraping his hide. His mount jerked and he whirled, accidentally hitting her hard on the side of the head with the fist that gripped his sword hilt.

Maritia's head snapped back. She would have fallen off her horse, save for the timely appearance of two of her officers. One grappled with Faros while the other seized and steadied Maritia.

Faros could barely hang on. In frustration, he watched as the second officer pulled the dazed Maritia out of reach. Finally, he was able to push away from the legionary attacking him, and with great pleasure, he ran the imperial soldier through. Unfortunately, as the soldier perished, his arm thrashed and his axe caught Faros's mount deep in the side of the neck. The animal reared in agony, tossing his charge to the ground.

Landing on his wounded side, the rebel leader cried out, a moment later rolling away just as hoofs landed where he had fallen. Only the confusion of the moment saved Faros. With so many combatants and writhing bodies around, his bedraggled form went unnoticed. Coughing, he pushed himself to his feet.

A horn suddenly blared. He did not recognize the signal, which meant that it had to be an imperial alert. For a second, Faros wondered if reinforcements had arrived after all. Then he noticed that it was the legionaries who were backing away.

Warhorse was in retreat.

The empire's soldiers did not look at all pleased by the surprise command, but they obeyed. Although some rebels began to see to the wounded, the majority, enthused by the enemy's retreat, continued to harass the legion as they pulled away.

Of Hotak's daughter there was no sign. Faros located a mounted rebel. "Your horse! I need it!"

The rider turned over her animal. Leaping onto the saddle, he took another look around. Nothing. Maritia had escaped him, yet another familiar face caught his attention. Captain Botanos, his leg bound, sat atop a monster of a steed. The mariner saw him and exhaled with noticeable relief.

"By the gods, you look horrible!" he growled. After a brief inspection, Botanos added, "But still in one piece, I see, save for that bad cut in your side. Let me help you bind it."

Botanos took a piece of cloth that had once been a banner and wrapped it around Faros's waist, quickly taking care of the wound.

"Warhorse retreating," Botanos said as they worked. "Never thought I'd see that! Continues to be a time of miracles!"

"I hope we haven't exhausted our supply," Faros said tersely.

"Do we continue after them?"

The younger minotaur looked him in the eye. "No, onward to Nethosak!"

Botanos grinned, but Faros felt no pleasure. The clouds over the capital had grown as black as night. The wind had picked up too. Neither were natural. The power of the Forerunners gathered for some dire purpose, and Faros dreaded what that might mean.

Still he knew that there was no turning back.

Ardnor stiffened in the saddle as Nephera's presence filled his thoughts.

He is yours, my son! The spectacle will be spoken of in bard's songs for centuries to come! Advance!

The emperor roared his pleasure. He pulled his crowned mace free and thrust it forward. The curled goat horns called darkly. The drums beat the march.

The black plague that was the Protectors streamed forward.

The stain of dishonor could never be erased. She had lost her father's legion. Warhorse had retreated from battle for the first time since Hotak had built it into the model for all other armies.

"We must regroup before Nethosak!" she told her gathering staff, her voice rising so that it could be heard above the worsening weather. A third of her officers were either dead or missing and several were, like her, wounded. "Send word to Onyx Legion to be prepared to hold the front for us! We have to stand our ground until evening! The rebels will be met at the capital by an impenetrable wall. The northern legions will come and help us finish them off." She coughed. "Any word from Bear Claw?"

"None, my lady."

"Then they must be busy with the other rebels. We'll make do without them, if necessary." Nethosak loomed in the distance—and something like a massive, inky shadow seemed to spew from it, heading toward the retreating legionaries. "What in the name—?"

Even as she formed the question, the answer became evident. *Protectors.* More Protectors than she had ever seen in one place at any time, a legion whose numbers dwarfed even the gargantuan Warhorse. Rank upon rank of the ebony-armored figures marched in perfect unison. Each foot soldier carried two weapons—the familiar crowned mace and a twin-edged hand axe honed sharp. Around them, black-cloaked officers on devilish steeds kept order with whips and maces. Murky, surreal figures flitted among the soldiers.

A banner unfamiliar to Maritia rose over the mass, the symbol in the middle looking something like an upside-down axe. The menacing force covered the landscape as far as one could see. Even then, the ranks continued to flow out of the city.

At last, Maritia saw Ardnor at the head of this army. Her brother seemed even larger than life than the last time she had seen him. Gazing at him, Hotak's daughter experienced the same uneasy sensation she sometimes felt when facing her mother, yet Maritia also drew strength from her brother. Faros's proud fighters were about to face the perfect opponent.

"Sound the call to regroup! We'll reform and buy time here for the emperor to prepare."

You will do nothing.

The voice jarred Maritia. Blinking, she looked toward Nethosak, toward where the temple stood.

You will continue the retreat. You will leave your forces in disorder.

"But—why?"

An intense force pressed on her skull. Maritia tore at her helmet then clutched her head. Her aides, not hearing the voice or comprehending, looked uncertainly at one another.

Your task is to serve the empire, daughter! You will obey! All is planned! The pressure eased. *Ardnor thanks you for your sacrifices but now wishes you to take over the protection of the capital in his absence. He trusts no one more for this job.*

Maritia composed herself. The retreat of Warhorse might yet serve a purpose. If this was what her brother, her emperor, desired of her, who was she to question his wisdom? Her duty was to the throne and her father's legacy, which Ardnor represented.

"I will obey," she answered crisply to the air. As Nephera's presence faded, the female minotatur looked to her staff. "Belay that last command! Continue the retreat! We will fall back behind the emperor's lines and retreat into Nethosak!"

The others bowed and left to carry out her orders. Gritting her teeth, Maritia focused on the advancing line of darkness. Soon Maritia was able to pick out her brother. Ardnor—as though he could sense her attention—glanced her way.

Maritia nearly reined her horse to a halt. There was nothing mortal in those orbs.

Ardnor rumbled something to the officer next to him. The latter bowed deep then turned his mount and headed directly toward Maritia and her ragged band of retreating legionaries.

"My lady," the Protector intoned flatly upon arrival. "The emperor expresses his relief that you have survived this setback."

"Yes, thank you. I wish to speak with my brother for just a moment."

The Protector raised his hand slightly. As one, a nearby line of warriors turned their faces in her direction. Their expressions showed only fanatical loyalty.

"That will not be possible right now. The battle is imminent, you understand."

She gave up. To her officers, Maritia snapped, "You heard. Keep moving. Get everyone in through the gates as fast as possible."

"We shall, of course, guard your retreat," the black figure said.

She ignored him. Warhorse would be forever humiliated by having been ordered to abandon this fight. "Come!"

The Protector waved his hand once. The line of warriors turned their faces forward again. A path opened amidst their ranks. The Protectors moved as if puppets on strings, Maritia thought, her brother's puppets.

As they passed among the baleful figures, Maritia's gaze alighted on one of the shadowy figures she had noticed earlier. The dark shape sat astride a gaunt-looking horse. No matter how hard Maritia tried to focus on the rider, all she managed to see was the indistinct image of an armored figure. Trying to see better, the legion commander happened to glance at the steed itself.

"Gods!" she blurted. The animal's sides were sunken in, with ribs showing, ribs and thin layers of moldy flesh.

"My lady," whispered one of her companions. "Are you ill?"

"Keep moving! Go!" Maritia welcomed the sight of the gates.

They were solid. They were reality. They were the place from which Ardnor's sinister army had come.

"Patok! Take over supervision of Warhorse! If you see any of the Guard, draft them into the ranks! Bolster our numbers—just in case! Create new lines just inside the gates and have them ready either to advance to the field or hold in the streets!"

"But, my lady! Where will you be?"

Her brow furrowed. Lightning flashed, and Maritia glanced up at the sky, her frown deepening. "I go to see my mother."

Chapter XXVII

Darkness Ascendant

The sword's voice whispered in Faros's head again. *Beware...*

Protectors. They covered the land before the capital like locusts. Faros stared at the horde, looking for Ardnor de-Droka.

"He wants to put on a show for the populace," Faros murmured. "Slaughter his enemies before the gates so that tales can be spread."

Botanos glared at the oncoming horde. "He must expect to make a grand spectacle of our deaths, then."

"Look at that ominous sky, Captain. Can't you feel your fur standing on end?"

The wind howled and the skies, darker than a Protector's armor, made it almost seem as if night had fallen. A tempest threatened, but so far no rain had materialized.

"Aye. I'd kept telling myself it was nothing."

"But it is. It's everything we've feared." Faros gripped his sword tightly. "We've no choice but to face it."

From the Protectors's ranks, the drums pounded like one massive heart, slow and foreboding. The black warriors moved in perfect, relentless unison. At their head rode a fearsome giant. On foot, he would have stood at least as tall as an ogre, but even without armor he had to be twice as broad . . . all taut muscle. In one hand he clutched a long, deadly mace around whose wicked head there seemed a faint, green glow.

"Is that a minotaur or an oversized ogre wearing false horns?" Botanos gaped.

Faros continued to stare at the approaching rider. As if sensing this, somehow, the helmed figure turned to gaze directly at the rebel leader. For the briefest of moments, the two locked gazes—and Faros discovered a creature no longer merely mortal beneath that helm. The eyes radiated death and worse, an agonizing decay of not just the body, but the soul, too.

Ardnor de-Droka broke contact first but not because of any lack of willpower. With a savage laugh, the emperor looked back to his fanatic ranks and waved the mace over his head. The drumbeats stopped.

Shouting, the Protectors broke into a run.

Faros raised his sword, then slashed downward. The rebels started forward at a slow trot, picking up speed as they charged. They made no sound yet, following their leader's example.

At the front of the Protectors, Ardnor brandished his mace. The weapon flared, the unsettling green aura enveloping the head like fire.

A tingle ran through Faros. With a curse, he quickly glanced over his lines, but as yet they appeared unscathed by magic. A cry of anger, of primal vengeance, escaped him. As one, the rebels took up his cry, drowning out the thunder.

Like two massive waves, the Protectors and rebels crashed violently together. A hundred minotaurs and more perished in the first clash alone. Bodies flew up several feet into the air, so tremendous was the force of convergence. The corpses of rebels and Protectors alike dotted the earth and those still alive in the front lines stood soaked in blood. A wall of death formed on both sides as all movement in either direction utterly ceased.

The emperor, out in front of his army, laughed as he clubbed one opponent after another. No sword, no axe, held against his mace. Each time he hit, his weapon flashed the same ominous green.

Faros! Nephera's voice urged Ardnor. *Deal with him, my son! None other matters!*

The emperor, momentarily caught up in the glee of butchery, paid the priestess no mind. Ardnor knew Faros would be his eventually. There was time enough yet for sport.

As for Faros, he now realized the giant figure was Ardnor, but he could not reach him. The packed bodies and endless foes kept him from his goal. A rabid-eyed Protector pushed close and attempted to climb atop Faros's mount. The rebel leader dodged the black fighter's mace then jammed the hilt of his sword in the other's neck. Clutching his ruined throat, the Protector collapsed into the mob, vanishing underneath frenetic feet.

One of Faros's followers tried to push past the rebel leader, but the veteran fighter unaccountably faltered, slipping to one knee. Faros automatically reached a hand to help the rebel—only to pull it back in horror. The stricken warrior's muzzle and arms had developed scores of small, brown pustules. Quickly, looking around, Faros saw other rebels rapidly developing the same symptoms.

Plague . . .

Now he understood Ardnor's gesture with the mace. The implications shook Faros. The magical plague would sweep through the rebels in a matter of minutes, quickly deciding the outcome of the struggle. Angrily, he looked to the sky, seeking the shrouded constellation of Sargonnas. The god had dealt with Morgion's plague earlier. Where was he now?

No rain came when Faros summoned it, no cleansing water to wash away Ardnor's evil. Gradic's son swore at the absent deity. "Do you want followers or not? Show me how to put an end to this!"

His sword suddenly yanked away from him and pointed of its own accord straight into the dire ranks of the Protectors. Faros's gaze followed its direction—seeing Ardnor de-Droka.

"Botanos! To me!" The captain and several other mounted fighters rushed over to Faros. "The power of Morgion is among us! Our only chance is to for me to reach Ardnor and quickly!"

"Well, we'll get you there!" shouted the captain. "How can you fight 'im? He's a giant with strength beyond belief. Must be evil magic at work. Nothing's even scratched him!"

"Just get me to him."

Botanos immediately organized a spearhead with himself leading the charge. As they pushed into the sea of black armor, more and more rebels showed signs of the sinister malignancy. Rebels stumbled, clutched their stomachs, wiped their feverish brows. The Protectors conquered more ground and lives. Sickened fighters could not stand up against Ardnor's fanatics.

Ahead of Faros, Botanos swung at one of the ebony-armored villains, easily slaying him. The mariner urged on the others. "We've a gap forming! Press harder!"

Then the Protector he had killed suddenly rose up anew. There was a huge gap in the side of the neck where the captain's axe had cut deeply. Blood still poured from the wound, yet the warrior, on wobbly legs, raised his mace to rejoin the fight.

"Botanos!" Faros called. "Look out!"

"By the Horned One!" The captain barely deflected the mace. He chopped into the Protector again, striking deeper into the same wound. The Protector slipped to his knees . . . then stood up again.

Faros swore. There could be only one explanation. Now, in addition to spreading plague, Ardnor was resurrecting the dead. Indeed, in every direction, slashed and blood-soaked minotaurs were slowly rising to pursue their mission. All wore the same blank, veiled expression.

The Protector twice slain by Botanos stabbed again at the captain, but another mounted rebel bravely moved in front the living corpse. The two combatants traded blows, the rebel driving his sword into what was left of the Protector's mangled throat, but despite his head lolling to one side, the monstrous figure's mace still came crashing forward, crushing the rebel's chest. Botanos's savior slumped in the saddle, dead, but not for long. Barely a breath later, the dead rebel jerked straight. His eyes were now the same as those of the creature that had killed him. He turned on the rider closest to him.

The battle was fast becoming a nightmare. Rebels keeling over from the plague. Fighters on both sides dead and reborn as evil minions, each death swelling the ranks of Ardnor's host.

The spearhead broke up as the survivors were forced to battle for their lives. Faros managed to reach the side of Botanos, who was parrying the blow of a female rebel whose stomach had been ripped open seconds earlier by an axe.

"Find him!" desperately cried the mariner, out of breath. "Find Ardnor!"

Nodding, Faros rode past his companions and into the mayhem. His lines had almost completely disintegrated. If he did not find Ardnor soon, all would be lost. As he scanned the chaos, a dark shadow extended over him.

Faros had the impression of an armored figure, but slimmer and insubstantial. Every time he turned, the shadow shifted. There was no mistaking the sword, as much of a shadow as its wielder, which drove toward his heart. Faros's own blade came up just in time. There was no sound when the two touched, but smoke arose.

The dark warrior hissed. Its shape ebbed and flowed like the tide, making it hard to follow. When its blade came at him again, Faros reacted too late and had to stumble back. As he retreated a few steps, the rebel leader could not help but wonder at how terrible the power of the temple had grown. Death itself seemed a slave to the Forerunners.

Then, deep beneath these urgent thoughts, Faros wondered about his own family, long slain. He had seen every sign the temple controlled the spirits of the dead. If that were so, could it be then that even his father—all his loved ones— slaved for the temple? Instead of being honored spirits, were they reduced to chattel?

That thought burned into Faros. He imagined his mother, his sister, his brother Crespos, forced to follow the will of the high priestess.

With a howl, he found fresh energy and lunged at the shadow. Sargonnas's sword cut through the dark figure without any resistance—and with a monstrous wail, the demonic warrior dissipated like fading fog. Immediately, its mount lost all animation, collapsing in a disgusting heap of putrefying flesh and bone before Faros's reddened eyes, but looking around, Faros knew his small victory was a hollow one. His followers were being shoved back mercilessly, dozens collapsing and dying with each step. Then, in turn, the dead rebels almost instantly rose up and began fighting their former comrades.

From the midst of the chaos came a bellowing, sardonic laugh that could only emanate from one person. Ahead, Ardnor's huge form sat high in the saddle. The emperor swung his mace back and forth like a toy and each time he struck someone, the weapon flared green. Laughing and spouting curses, he seemed to pay little real mind to what was gong on around him, joyously caught up in the slaughter.

"Droka!" Faros roared. "Look at me, Droka!"

Ardnor paused in mid-swing. The savage grin widened in recognition. He tugged on the reins and eagerly advanced toward Faros. Thunder crackled. The sky flashed green. Faros gritted his teeth as he went to meet the giant. If he failed now, he failed everyone.

"The Kalin scum!" Ardnor roared merrily. "Ha, little ant! Smaller up close, aren't you?"

Faros looked in poorly concealed awe at the monstrous enhancement of the emperor, wondering if Ardnor was still mortal. He said nothing, instead instantly thrusting at his foe's armored chest.

Ardnor easily parried his attack. The massive warrior moved at what seemed an impossible speed. Even as he knocked the rebel leader's blade back, his mace came around to smash at Faros's other arm. The green aura flared as the crowned head struck. Faros cried out agonizingly. In addition to the horrific physical pain, he felt a weird sensation— as though some insidious poison had entered through the wound to torment his body from within.

"Still alive?" grumbled his monstrous foe, drawing back the mace. Blood, fur, and bits of flesh clung to the sharpened points. "She said you'd have some help from him . . ." He leaned forward. "Not enough, though! Let's see what another blow can do!"

Faros hurled himself off his horse. Ardnor's mace flew brushed by him, missing by inches.

The emperor laughed loudly as he turned his mount to face the smaller figure. "Scamper, scamper! Try and run, will ya? I wish it was the great General Rahm I was fighting, not some fool of a gambler who only survived because he was too lucky to die with his family!"

Ardnor pulled back the reins, making his horse rear. The horse's hooves kicked out at Faros, grazing his right horn. Shaken but determined, Gradic's son rolled under the animal and stabbed up. The blade pierced the horse's rib cage. With a shriek, the mortally-injured animal tumbled over. Ardnor let out a confused growl as he was bounced off.

As the horse collapsed, Faros quickly slithered out of its path. The former slave jumped up, looking for Ardnor. He found himself darkened by the shadow of the latter's huge, menacing form.

"Kalin trash! I trained that horse from a colt! I loved it like a son!" He barreled into Faros, the mace already raised for a strike. "That animal's life was worth a hundred of yours!"

The two collided awkwardly as a pack of fighters rolled into them. Arms and limbs tangled everywhere. Faros slipped from Ardnor's grasp as the emperor's great mace came crashing down. The head instead hit the ground, shaking the immediate vicinity and opening a yard-long fissure next to the emperor's foe.

"Stay still so that I can swat you!" commanded Ardnor, chuckling madly to himself. "Just like we swatted all you Kalins!"

He hit the ground again as Faros ducked and dodged, but the rebel leader left his side open. A Protector turned from the rebel he had just gutted and aimed an axe swing at Faros's head.

"No! He's mine!" Ardnor leaped. The emperor's mace crushed in the unsuspecting Protector's helmet and skull. Cackling over the Protector's body—which after all, was slowly collecting itself to rise from the dead—Ardnor leered at Faros. "My glory!"

Kicking out, Faros caught the giant's legs. He tripped Ardnor, who fell. Rising, Gradic's son slashed at Ardnor's open hand, but the mace came up to block the blade. Sparks flew as the two weapons met. Faros felt the pain and again the odd poison. He pushed hard, managing to force his adversary back slightly.

"A little stronger than I thought! Ha! Good! It makes the victory tastier!"

So close to his foe, Faros saw Ardnor's eyes as they truly were, utterly horrific, like those of no living creature. The power of Morgion had devoured whatever soul Ardnor had once had.

"You're admiring his gift . . ." mocked the emperor. "Yes, I am his chosen! His champion!" He shoved Faros back, laughing again uncontrollably. "You're all the Horned One could find! His day has passed, and soon so will yours!"

Ardnor shook off the gauntlet protecting his free hand. As he reached for Faros, the rebel saw the same terrible aura surrounding that limb.

"Feel his wondrous touch as I have, Kalin! Feel his strength! Come, it won't hurt much . . . at least, not for very long . . ."

Faros could retreat no further, and he found, deep within him, that he had no desire to retreat. He might die, but not retreat. Brow furrowed, the rebel leader aimed his sword toward the unprotected hand. Ardnor chuckled, as if whatever the smaller minotaur desperately hoped could not possibly work.

He stopped laughing as Faros's blade shifted direction. Even Ardnor's enhanced reflexes could not compensate for his surprise. Faros's sword cut through the mace's handle. There was a burst of green as the two pieces separated, then the aura faded away.

Ardnor instinctively grabbed for the upper piece, but Faros, counting on the magic of his own weapon, heaved his entire weight forward, driving the blade through the emperor's armor, through his ribs, and out the back of his body.

Faros exhaled, shaking.

The back side of a gauntleted fist struck the rebel hard on the jaw, tossing him backward. Somehow Faros managed to keep his grip on his sword. With a moist, slick sound, Sargonnas's gift slid free of Ardnor's chest.

Looming over his rival, Ardnor de-Droka, seemingly un-fazed, laughed darkly. "I'm His champion!" he reminded the fallen figure. "There is no power greater than that of the Lord of Decay!"

A thick, putrid ooze the color of rotting flesh slowly dripped from the wound Faros had caused. Ardnor tasted it with his ungloved fingers, admiring what Morgion had wrought of him.

"No power . . ." he repeated with a fearsome baring of his teeth. The giant squeezed the thick fluid in his fist and as it spread between his fingers, it reshaped itself. Around his hand the foul substance became a steel grip. A staff formed, rising almost three feet high, where it became transformed into a wicked ball with scores of tiny, sharp hooks all over. The unearthly new mace blazed with the power of Ardnor's patron. "Especially a useless, tired creature like Sargas! It's time he was put out of his misery . . . and time for the last of Kalin to join him in oblivion!"

In the sanctum of the high priestess, Nephera and her at-tendants were preoccupied. Nothing that went on outside went unnoticed by Ardnor's mother, and in addition to her link to her son, the multitude of ghosts surrounding her con-stantly whispered in her ears, telling her everything of the unfolding events.

The last scion of Kalin had been brought down at last, she knew. Hands crimson, Nephera watched her son pre-pare to add Faros to the ranks of her dead slaves. He would be happy among the dead, she thought, for he would be reunited with the family he so loved . . . and had failed so miserably.

"Your power is without peer," she intoned to the Forerunner

symbols. "Without compare! His champion is defeated. He is defeated."

However, for some odd reason, the high priestess did not sense the extreme pleasure she would have expected from her god. Morgion seemed distant, almost distracted.

Of course! Sargonnas was no doubt scurrying around, trying pathetically to shore up his influence over her people. Morgion was simply busy eradicating his rival, just as on the mortal plane Ardnor was busy crushing the last vestige of the insurrection.

Nephera poured herself anew into her spellcasting. The populace would finally see that no resistance stood a chance against the power of the temple. None of the rebels would be allowed to live. That had been Hotak's mistake; he had spared lives. Of course, he had not benefited from the deaths as she did. He never understood all she had tried to do for him. Now every life lost on the battlefield aided her, made her more powerful than ever.

Her gaze shifted to the slab. Still, the power she had attained was not enough. She needed more.

"Remove that refuse. Bring to me something . . . fresh."

As her acolytes obeyed, she turned her attention again to the climax of the struggle outside. Nephera delved deeper into Ardnor's mind so that she might savor the experience through him. He was caught up in the moment, she noted with an inner smile. The fool of a Kalin stared wide-eyed at his imminent death; the blade given to him by his weak god was of no use because he did not know how to properly wield it. The heart was too obvious a target.

"Too bad, Faros Es-Kalin . . . but you will never know the secrets of a god, will you?"

At that moment, there came an incessant banging on the bronze doors. Maintaining her connection to Ardnor, the high priestess angrily waved at her followers, urging them to finish dragging the sacrifice out. As the banging continued, Nephera carefully bathed her hands again. The red did not wash out completely, but tidiness had long ceased to matter.

Approaching the doors, the high priestess gestured. The doors were flung open, revealing two anxious guards . . . and the source of their frustration.

Her daughter.

Maritia stood there, her eyes darting nervously around, looking at her unkempt, wild-eyed mother and the strange scene in the interior of the temple.

Steepling her hands, Nephera calmly asked, "To what do I owe this untimely visit, Maritia? Especially when you are supposed to be actively organizing the city's defenses . . ."

"Mother! We have to take precautions! In case something should happen to Ardnor, you need to—"

"Tut, tut. Have faith, daughter. Nothing will happen to your brother. The Great One is with him!"

"But Ardnor—"

"Is about to conclude this epic chapter of our people! The last blood of Kalin will, in seconds, nourish the soil. His followers will be hunted to extinction. The insurrection shall become but a footnote in the glorious history that is yet to come." Her smile stretched tighter. "The history of our new Golden Age!"

Maritia started to speak, but Nephera had no more time for blather. She would not miss her greatest moment of triumph—the death of a rebellion and the death knell of a god.

"Please go. Leave now, my daughter. There are matters I must still attend to, and you have urgent duties, as well."

The other minotaur stood at attention. "I do, Mother, and one of those is protecting you. Just in case some of the rebels or their sympathizers make it to the temple—"

"I have told you! Such a concern is—" Nephera froze, her eyes lighting with an intensity that worried Maritia.

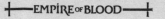

"Mother, are you all right?"

"Hush! It's about to happen!" Nephera declared, gazing up into empty space. "The death of Faros Es-Kalin!" She laughed, the sound sending cold shivers through not only her daughter but also the ghosts surrounding them. "And the death of his god!"

Chapter XXVIII

The Gates of Nethosak

Sickened with the plague, forced to fight both the living and the reborn dead, the rebels held on as best they could. Even with the outcome inevitable, they would not, could not surrender. They fought on because it was all they had left. They had been slaves and renegades, but they were still minotaurs and would die as such.

Thee Protectors were happy to oblige them. The black wave relentlessly swept forward, flowing over the desperate rebels. The ebony-armored figures had submerged themselves in the aura surrounding Ardnor, becoming extensions of the emperor's hate and depravity.

To Captain Botanos, the enemy looked unstoppable, yet like his comrades, he continued to fight. Faros had commanded him to do so. The rebels had to hold while their leader confronted Ardnor. Only if Faros could defeat the emperor would there be hope, but as the mariner looked around, he had a gnawing fear that the duel had not gone as Faros had planned.

"My father said he took no pleasure in slaying your uncle," growled Ardnor cheerfully. "Father was a fool. I can't think of anything that would please me more than your blood."

He swung.

Faros's ring flashed bright. The sudden illumination startled Ardnor just enough. The hesitation enabled Gradic's son to just barely roll away before the magical mace shattered the ground.

With a roar of outrage, Ardnor pounced again. Sword at the ready, Faros kept just enough distance between the black figure and himself. Sargonnas had given him a reprieve, nothing more, yet now his sword tugged at his hand, almost demanding he use it. It wanted to fight what seemed impossible to fight.

The rebel's eyes shifted to the giant, studying every aspect of him. His expression grim, the emperor advanced again.

Ardnor laughed. "Want to take another futile try before I gut you?" He spread his arms wide. "Why not? Choose anywhere, Kalin!"

"As you like," muttered Faros.

He leapt, swinging as hard as he could. The blade wailed as it sought its target—Ardnor's throat. The slash nearly severed the emperor's head. Ardnos's head tipped back—tossing off his helmet—and a strangle, muffled sound escaped him. His body started to weave back and forth.

As Faros gaped, the gauntleted hand pushed the head forward again. The neck sealed, leaving only a long, vicious scar.

Ardnor's monstrous eyes widened almost in admiration. "Ha! Well struck! I didn't think you had it in you—not that it did you any good, did it?"

His adversary did not answer, stunned by both his new failure and what lay beneath the abandoned helmet. The emperor's horrific orbs were terrible enough, but there, emblazoned on his forehead, stood the glowing mark of

Morgion. The downturned axe radiated malevolence. It glowed bright until Ardnor's throat was completely restored, then it dimmed slightly.

"Too bad, Kalin spawn," mocked the huge warrior. He hefted the supernatural weapon. "Well, you've had your fun—now it's my turn!"

Ardnor moved too swiftly for Faros. The mace hit the rebel's shoulder with an impact that cracked bone. Faros cried out and the sword slipped from his grasp.

"Let it end now," Ardnor urged soothingly. "This time, take what's coming to you! I promise I'll crush your skull to pieces first. Then, you won't feel the rest of it."

Tears of agony pouring down his face, Faros attempted to summon the sword to his hand. However, even though it came to him, his fingers could not quite grasp it. Again, it tumbled to the ground with a clatter.

"Interesting sword you have, ant! It'll make a fine memento!" As the emperor loomed, his eyes burned with the same intensity as the mark on his forehead. He grinned wider. Ardnor reached for the fallen sword. "Maybe I should even kill you with your own puny blade! That'd be one for the poets, eh?"

Once more, Faros attempted to summon the blade.

"Give in, Kalin! Die with a little dignity—unlike the rest of your family!"

The sword flew to Faros . . . but landed in his other hand. The weapon felt strange in that grip.

"Father," the wounded minotaur gasped. "Guide my aim . . ."

He lunged.

Ardnor met the attack. The emperor tormented Faros by blocking him so easily. "Why continue this farce? You know what'll happen! You're every bit of the wastrel and fool I remembered!"

Faros stumbled, leaving himself open to Ardnor.

"It'll be a service to our race to rid it of you!" The emperor snorted derisively, then swung with all his might.

The smaller minotaur twisted around the mace, bringing the blade up at the same time. Ardnor again saw the attack coming and barked with laughter, even presenting his throat to the blade.

At the last moment, Faros turned his blade and went beyond Ardnor's throat, beyond his muzzle—and drove toward his forehead. Summoning every reserve of strength, Faros drove the magical weapon into the mark of Morgion.

The giant's laughter became a shriek. Faros forced the blade into the skull, resisting as best he could the brutish, supernatural forces attempting to push both him and his weapon back. He held tight even as the mace in Ardnor's flailing arm nearly decapitated him.

Ardnor's scream shook the very earth. All around them, combatants stopped in mid-struggle to stare in their direction. Even the dead hesitated, their forms quavering as if whatever power that had animated them was now threatened.

Green fire enveloped Faros's sword, but it chilled rather than burned him. Frostbite swept over Faros's fingers. The minotaur shivered with the intensity but did not relent. The green fire now swept over him. His scream united with Ardnor's. The world around Faros flickered, shifting back and forth between the battlefield and a dank, decaying land where, at the edge of a cliff overlooking a bottomless precipice, a tall, tarnished tower of bronze dominated all. Shambling figures, all of them in terrible stages of rot, reached for him. Their empty eye sockets pleaded with him for a release that he could not grant.

Gritting his teeth, Faros focused only on the blade and his foe. The horrific landscape faded away, returning him to the battlefield.

Somehow, Ardnor, still screaming, had found the strength to let loose his weapon, which dissipated as it fell from his fingers. With both hands, Ardnor reached up and tugged hard on the sword stuck in his forehead, not caring at all that the edge cut his palms and fingers. Thick gore spilled from all his wounds.

Despite Faros's efforts, the giant slowly began to pull the blade out of his skull. Gradic's son pushed back, certain that once Ardnor freed himself, all would be lost, but without warning, the sword flung itself free. It flew back, dragging Faros several yards back as if he weighed nothing.

A new and harsher cry erupted from Ardnor, resounding across the landscape. From out of the skewered brand flowed more and more green flame and as it spewed forth, Ardnor de-Droka began to shrivel. His flesh dried and rotted. Even his armor grew tarnished. The savage slash Faros had delivered to his throat reopened and the huge minotaur's head lolled to one side. The wound to his chest reopened as more cold, green fire pouring from it.

His cry became a twisted, high-pitched squeal. As Faros watched in astonishment, the emperor's eyes faded then sank into his skull. Crumbling fingers attempted to hold his left in place, to no avail. Ardnor took a step forward and his left leg broke in two, the lower half dropping to the ground. The emperor tumbled forward. With one nearly fleshless hand he tried to drag himself toward his foe. Even so wounded, his hatred still evinced itself. His head somehow pivoted toward Faros, but the mouth could not utter the words the lord of the Protectors sought to speak.

Then, with an almost animalistic howl, Ardnor crumbled to the ground. The last of the flames escaped from him. His skin turned to dust, then his bones blackened as if with great age. The skull rolled away.

No sooner had that happened, than the ground shook anew. Its effect was immediate on the dead. As one, they fumbled their weapons and crumpled into piles, joining Nephera's son in oblivion.

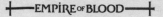

Someone shouted, pointing in the direction of the mountains. Far to the northeast, a plume of black smoke rose to meet the stormy sky. It was joined by another and another until there were five. The volcanoes of Argon's Chain had erupted.

Cries filled the sky. From the turbulent clouds descended thousands of birds, yet unlike before, they did not come this time to feast upon the dead but to fall upon the living. The huge flock attacked the Protectors, those still alive, that is, who, until that moment, had stood almost as if dead themselves.

Gasping for air, Faros looked to his followers. All trace of sickness had vanished with Ardnor's demise. More important, these two great signs of Sargonnas—in his roles as Condor Lord and Lord of Volcanoes—combined with their leader's utter defeat of an impossible foe, heartened the rebels. As the confused and distraught Protectors tried to come to grips with their loss, the rebels roared lustily and hurled themselves back into the fray.

The Protectors tried to rally, but their officers lacked morale and the shadow warriors had vanished. Nothing now would stop Faros's people. The black army broke. All semblance of order vanished. Individual combats continued, but as a thing of fear, the Protectors were no more.

Somehow, out of the swarm, Captain Botanos found Faros. The mariner dismounted then helped Faros steady himself. He eyed the grisly remains of the emperor, the veteran sailor shuddering.

"By the gods, Faros! You've done the impossible, my lord!"

"Not by the gods," the younger minotaur managed, reluctantly adding, "One god, maybe." His brow furrowed. "Now . . . I need your horse."

"For what?" Botanos asked, already helping him mount.

"There is still the temple," Faros responded, cradling his wounds and wearily urging the animal forward. "There's still the high priestess, Nephera."

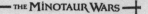

"Noooo . . ." Lady Nephera sprawled on the floor, moaning.

Maritia fought past the priestesses to kneel next to her mother. "What's happened? What's wrong?"

"He's gone . . . he's gone . . . he's gone . . ." the high priestess repeated over and over.

"Ardnor . . ." Maritia breathed. "It can't be! Nothing could defeat him!"

Nephera did not respond, save to repeat the words. Her daughter held her, trying to think. So close to her mother, she was shocked by how gaunt, how deathly, Nephera looked.

Horns sounded from without the building. One of her officers burst into the chamber, racing past startled sentries.

"Lady Maritia! Praise be that we found you! The rebels are already at the gates! Warhorse and the Guard are trying to hold them, but the Protectors are in disarray! It's as though they were nothing but walking shells!"

Signaling one of the priestesses to take over for her with her mother, Maritia rose. "The emperor is dead."

"My lady!"

"How many are there of you?"

"About two dozen mounted," he quickly replied.

"Find me a horse. I'll meet you out front." As her aide ran to obey, she looked down at her distraught, dazed mother. "We'll do what we can."

Nephera said nothing, her gaze still elsewhere.

With great reluctance but much determination, Maritia hurried out after her officer.

The handful of priestesses hovered around their mistress for a time, uncertain what to do. One brought some wine, but Nephera simply stared past the offering, her mouth opening and closing as if she spoke silent words, then the high priestess blinked. Her eyes took on a yet wilder aspect.

She rose without warning, sending her acolytes stepping back in apprehension.

"He's gone . . ." murmured Nephera to herself. "Just like before—no! Not like that! Not this time! It's not too late!"

One of the priestesses reached a hand to her. "Mistress! We grieve for your son!"

Nephera grabbed the other by the wrist, her fingers strong and tight despite her cadaverous appearance. "Never mind him! It's not too late! I can still feel the power!" She looked past her fearful servants to the slab. "There could still be time."

The rebels flowed through the gates. There they met their first resistance in the form of the remnants of Warhorse Legion. Their tide slowed, but momentum was with the attackers. Even the elements of the Guard that joined the legionaries could not hold the rebels back.

Battling his way through the melee, Faros sought some path to the temple. An opening window in a nearby building caught his attention. A graying male whose left ear had been cut off in some long ago battle squinted at the figure on horseback then at the fight below. His right hand suddenly formed a fist and he quickly shut the window.

Faros cursed. The people of Nethosak could still alter the outcome if they chose to support Ardnor's followers—and the temple.

"Break that line!" Faros shouted at several rebels. "Hurry!"

The legionaries held. They had to know their cause was lost, but they would not surrender. It was almost honorable on their part, Faros thought with a twinge.

Then, just behind the soldiers, a figure slipped out from between two buildings. Faros recognized the elder minotaur. He wore old armor and wielded a sturdy axe. Another minotaur followed the first out, this one a slightly younger female armed with a sword. Others began creeping after. Faros saw two youthful figures race to other buildings, possibly to rally neighbors. Gradic's son cursed; if the citizens joined the legion, then what?

One of the officers happened to turn and see the group. He bellowed something to the lead figure. The graying minotaur kept coming.

The legionary drew his axe, at the same time alerting another officer. The older warrior charged. The rest followed his lead. Several legionaries turned to defend from this unexpected attack. The rebels finally began to push through the distracted front line.

The graying warrior and the first officer traded blows. The former was strong but lacked swiftness. In the end he fell, but not before badly wounding his opponent. The female who had followed behind finished the legionary.

The defenders broke. The rebels crashed through, with the defenders forming two small pockets. Faros rode at full gallop. More minotaurs emerged from the surrounding area, all carrying some sort of weapon. Several cheered as he and rebels on foot poured into the capital.

A squadron of the State Guard suddenly appeared in Faros's path, but they were hardly concerned with him. An armed crowd pursued them, minotaurs young and old participating in the chase. To his right, two bands of citizens clashed, evidence that not all had chosen the rebels' side.

The deeper he penetrated into the capital, the more violent the situation grew. Everywhere anarchy reigned. He passed several dead members of the Guard, then a burning building which nobody seemed to be concerned about. Shouts came from the north, then from the east. No matter where one looked, there was fighting.

A band of cavalry bearing the mark of the Warhorse came racing around the corner, just as Faros and those with him reached the intersection leading to the temple. He dueled with one soldier, slew her, then pushed his way through the busy ranks.

Ahead lay the temple. The gates stood open and unguarded. Faros rode up the elegant path. Dismounting, he heard noise behind and saw that a cavalry unit had retreated after him onto the temple grounds. Two legionaries dismounted and tried to close the gates, but the throng readily shoved through. Three other riders fled for the vast structure, abandoning their fellows.

A momentary scrape alerted Faros. His attention distracted, he had not heard the Protector creeping down the steps. Eyes crimson, the guard took a savage swing at Faros with his mace. Forcing the weapon up, Gradic's son punched the Protector hard under the jaw. The black-armored figure stumbled back onto the steps, where Faros finished him.

Leaping up the steps, he encountered a second guard. Unlike the Protectors on the field, these seemed to have lost none of their zeal. This one attempted to strike the rebel's legs. Faros dodged then lunged. His blade easily penetrated the minotaur's armor, and unlike Ardnor, this Protector had no divine healing to save him.

As the corpse clattered down the steps, Faros dared a glance over his shoulder. Rebels and citizens were thronging to the assault on the temple. With a score of supporters behind him, Faros burst through the outer doors. He was immediately set upon by two guards. Parrying one attack, Faros killed the first. Two other rebels closed with the second, freeing Faros to forge ahead.

Out of the corner of his eye, Gradic's son caught a glimpse of armor. He looked over in time to see two legionaries heading down the corridor. The memory of the three fleeing riders flashed through his mind. They had not been trying to escape but rather had entered the temple through another passage.

There could be only one place they were heading . . . the chamber where the high priestess would be found. The legionaries no doubt hoped to spirit her away.

He sprinted after them.

The day was lost.

The empire was lost.

Maritia could not even reach the gates. The battle met her before she even made it halfway back. Rebels were swarming through the capital, and worse, the majority of the citizens she saw not only welcomed them with open arms but hurried to join their side. Fleetingly, she wondered why the citizens were so eager to rise up against her brother and mother. Against such odds, she knew, the legionaries and guards could not prevail.

Her thoughts turned back to her mother. She must help her escape to one of the smaller ports and from there they could sail to Ansalon. There, with the Wyverns and Direhounds—and even Pryas's forces—they could build a fresh base of operations. What had worked for the rebels would certainly work in turn for her. Droka would retake the empire.

With a pang, she realized what she was thinking. Leave Nethosak? Abandon the heart of the empire to the rebels? She had little choice. She hurried back to her mother. As she approached the doors, Maritia saw that, in addition to the previous guards, another pair of wary Protectors stood ready.

"Let me through! It's urgent we get the high priestess out of here!"

"She ordered that none should enter now," said the senior of the guards.

"This is our only chance to keep her from the rebels, you fool!"

The guard leader wavered then nodded. Maritia glanced at her small retinue.

"Stay here! Help guard the entrance until I summon you!"

Barging past, she slipped into the chamber. However, her concern that she might have to drag her distraught mother out by force vanished as Maritia confronted a foreboding sight.

An ominous silver glow radiated from the huge icons. Their light all but drowned out that of the torches. The silver illumination gave the chamber a pale, other-worldly look, a look not at all helped by the unearthly appearance of the high priestess.

Nephera stared emotionlessly at her daughter. "So you are back."

"Mother! The rebels are in the temple! Come with me! There's still a chance—"

"Yes!" the elder female interrupted, her expression suddenly purposeful and fanatical. "Yes, there is! He has not totally abandoned me! Even if I could not sense him, the icons prove his allegiance!"

"What are you talking about?" Maritia eyed the icons hopefully. " 'He'? Has—has Sargonnas returned to us?"

"Sargonnas?" the high priestess responded with a derisive snort, choking back laughter. "He is welcome to that cur, Faros."

The younger minotaur suddenly understood what she had heard. She looked stunned. No, she could not have heard her mother right. Such a thing could not be said! The rebel leader was welcome to the patron god of her people!

"Faros?" Maritia blurted. "You—you can't mean that the Horned One sides with . . . the rebels?"

"For all the good it will do either."

"But—I thought—but the Forerunners—!" Maritia gestured at the symbols. "Who—?"

Lady Nephera smiled in a flirtatious manner that her daughter had long ago seen reserved only for Hotak, her husband, the dead usurper whose Night of Blood had started all the bloodshed years ago. "He who is the end of all! He who allows us life by his sufferance! He who sits and views eternity from his tower of bronze on the edge of the Abyss!"

Born and raised to the legions in a time when gods were only memories, Maritia knew only Sargonnas and Kiri-Jolith well, yet her mother's words reminded her of another deity, whose despised name slowly wended its way to her stuttering tongue. "Mother . . . you can't mean . . . you can't mean . . . *Morgion?*"

The beatific aspect that suddenly spread across Nephera's visage was answer enough. Maritia stepped back, her world rocked to its foundation. "All this time?"

"She abandoned me!" the high priestess abruptly shouted, her expression shifting to one of anger and betrayal. Almost as quickly, though, Nephera calmed again. "The one true god, hah!" Her eyes glazed. "When he came to me, all was right again! The power was mine again! Order over the empire could be maintained! All that were ever needed were a few necessary sacrifices." Her face hardened and she turned from Maritia, clearly lost in a strange reverie. "Until now. Now it is understandable that he must demand more! Something of greater value . . ."

An all too-familiar sound erupted outside, stirring Maritia from her horror. Veteran reflexes took over as she recognized the commotion of fighting. The rebels had reached the doors. The legion commander surveyed the chamber, trying to puzzle out the hidden exits that she knew must be there.

Instead, though, Maritia saw the sprawled body of a priestess. She took a step toward the poor creature, only to realize that there was more than one dead body in the room.

"Mother—"

Nephera had dipped her hands in a large bowl set on a small marble stand. Instead of the water that her daughter expected, the high priestess's fingers came out covered in crimson.

"It must be a worthy sacrifice," Nephera said, still speaking to herself. "I sacrificed my husband, my son. I've used up my favored followers, but it wasn't been enough! I've displeased him and the only way to make amends is to give all that I can give . . ."

Maritia, hearing her words, stared at her in horror. There was a heavy thud against the doors.

"Mother! They're coming! We're running out of time!"

"Yes . . . you're right." The high priestess reached next to the bowl, drawing a dagger that also dripped red.

Maritia grew frustrated. "You can't fight them with that! You can't fight them at—"

The doors burst open. One of her legionaries tumbled to the floor midway inside. A brawny Protector backed into the chamber, at the same time trying to defend with his mace against two rebels. The other Protector also retreated into the chamber, his lone opponent an intense-looking, scarred and wounded figure wielding a black blade that moved like lightning.

Faros Es-Kalin.

The Protector attempted a lunge, the mace raised over his head. The rebel leader shoved aside the threat with his blade then sliced downward. The sword cut through the Protector's lower jaw then his throat. The fearsome guard let out a gasp and fell to the side.

Maritia readied her own blade, her expression a mirror of his own determination. A few steps past her, Lady Nephera stood watching both, her eyes unblinking.

"Surrender," Faros offered. "Surrender and you'll live."

"I doubt that very much," Maritia growled, positioning herself between him and her mother.

To both their surprise, the high priestess walked calmly toward the dais where a high, elaborately-decorate chair almost like a throne stood below huge renditions of the Forerunner symbols.

"Mother! Come back—"

The high priestess paused midway up the steps. Ignoring the pair, she raised her gore-encrusted hands and shouted out to the icons, "Great One! I will give you what you desire! Do not leave me! You shall still reign supreme!" Nephera eyed Faros contemptuously. "You shall still have his soul and many others . . ."

Faros moved toward the robed figure, but Maritia again blocked his path. "Keep back!"

He froze as the ring on his hand abruptly flashed. Faros turned.

What at first appeared to be tentacles emerging from a deep patch of darkness reached to snare his limbs. Within that darkness could barely be made out a burnt, decaying visage. The sickly smell of something rotting in the sea wafted past his nostrils.

Nephera laughed. The other combatants—and Nephera's servants—fled from the chamber at sight of the demonic form. Out of the blackness thrust a bony, clawed hand that reached for Faros's throat.

With a guttural cry, Faros slashed wildly. The tentacles, part of the voluminous cloak the ghost wore, went flying in every direction, the pieces dissipating before they struck the floor. He then swung at the outstretched arm. The specter let out an agonized moan as the ethereal appendage separated.

Plunging into the darkness, Faros impaled Takyr. The ghost's moan became ear-splitting. The monstrous shade twisted and turned, clutching at the air in vain. Sargonnas's blade drew in the sinister spirit, absorbing him. The phantom struggled but to no avail. His once-malevolent countenance now held an expression of utter hopelessness.

As the last of Takyr vanished into the black blade, the moaning stopped. The weapon pulsated, as Faros turned back to the Drokas.

Maritia gaped, understanding little of what her eyes had beheld. Lady Nephera, her look murderous, came down the steps closer to her daughter.

"You will pay for every bit of interference, Kalin! Do you realize all that you've undone? So many lists, so much to do, to create the perfect realm! No sacrifice was too great!"

"Mother . . ." Maritia stepped in front of the high priestess. Her resolve was rattled. "Faros, if we surrender . . . 'if' . . . would you grant us permanent exile to one of the outermost colonies? Just myself, my mother, and perhaps two attendants to assist her."

"With my guards . . . and you could never leave such an exile."

Her ears flattened. "If it must be so, to spare her life—"

"Once again, you surprise and disappoint me, my daughter," Nephera interjected in a high, eerie voice that made the fur on both Maritia's and Faros's necks stiffen. "I sacrificed all for this impending glory, and you would give it up in heartbeat!"

"It's the only way, Mother," the younger female pleaded, eyes still fixed on the rebel.

"There is always another way, if one is willing to sacrifice!" The high priestess clutched tight her dagger. Her gaze, too, focused on Faros. "Even he, who has suffered so much, knows that!" She took another step down, coming to a halt behind her remaining child. "Kolot died for the empire. Your father died for the empire. Bastion and now Ardnor, too!"

"I know . . ."

"Poor Hotak, the fool. He should have never named Bastion heir," Nephera went on. "That was when he began to lose sight of what needed to be done! We had arranged everything, created the perfect plan! He kept changing his mind, instigating more refinements! When I tried to correct matters, he only grew more furious! He didn't appreciate the temple, you see, and I was forced to understand that if a Golden Age were to be achieved, I had to remove the cause! A sacrifice had to be made and I made it!"

Maritia tore her gaze from Faros. "You . . . what?"

"Just when it appeared that I had set the empire on its proper path . . . *Bastion* brought about more chaos! Bastion, who should have been dead already! Turning on his own brother and trying to split the legions by telling his sister lies!" The high priestess shook her head. "I should have known that tusked beast would bungle things! Mixing his emotions with his duties . . ."

Nephera's daughter stared at her wide eyes.

"Yes, daughter, your father and brothers made a sacrifice for the good! Don't you understand? Oh, you can be such an insipid little thing! I take the responsibility. No one else could keep the order! Every time I finished a list, a new one was needed! The rebellion kept spreading. Your father failed, as did your brother!" She slapped the fist holding the dagger against her robes, leaving in its wake a twisted imprint of the hand and blade. "If not for me, we would all be caught up in anarchy!"

"No . . . no!" Maritia looked at Faros, met his angry eyes.

"Only I was willing to make the sacrifices—whatever sacrifices were needed! Even now, victory is still in my grasp! They weren't enough—" With a negligent wave, Nephera indicated the slaughtered priestesses. "But he's certain to grant me the power I need for the spell if I give him just what he demands! It was necessary for your father, then your brother—and now you—?"

The high priestess raised the dagger high. "Yes, it is your turn, my darling daughter."

Maritia edged back. Nephera ceased in mid-sentence, gasping. The dagger dropped from her trembling fingers. She shook her head and pointed past the two. Maritia looked in that direction but saw nothing.

"Away from me!" Nephera ordered to the empty air. "I told you! I will not brook your stupid condemnations!"

Faros blinked, also seeing nothing, then resolved to act. Weakened though Nephera was, he had no way of guessing as to what magic she might have left and dared not let her even attempt to cast. Trusting to the power of the sword and his benefactor, the son of Gradic clutched Sargonnas's weapon in both hands, and with a shout that echoed throughout the chamber, he charged the priestess.

Nephera raised a gnarled hand toward Faros as he shoved a startled Maritia to the side.

"You want your god so much," he roared. "Go to him!"

As Faros neared the priestess, he felt his body strangely slow its motion, as if the air around him was thickening to honey. He strained forward, fighting the magic. The high priestess continued to point at him, as her hand quivered and her expression grew strained.

The toll weakened Faros. In the end, he saw that he would not make it to Nephera herself, so he focused his aim on the outstretched hand. Sensing this, the high priestess shifted her posture.

The tip of his blade barely scratched the back of her hand. Faros fell to one knee on the steps, the sword propping him up. Above him, Lady Nephera eyed the scratch on her hand with growing amusement.

"So this is all your god can—"

She broke off. Her hand, already ruined, now sprouted small, red boils. Nephera gazed at her other hand, upon which was spreading identical boils.

"What—" Her brow furrowed as the high priestess gave a deep shudder. "The heat . . ." she gasped. "The heat . . ."

Maritia started toward her mother, only to draw back in horror. Across Nephera's muzzle, across her gaunt face, could be seen red, pulsating veins. Faros pushed himself away, for the warmth radiating from the Lady Droka was enough to heat the air.

"This cannot—he would not—" Nephera stumbled back to the chair. Sweat dripped from her body, quickly soaking her fur. Her hair exploded in great patches that spilled upon the dais.

She clutched at her garments, rending the top. Her breathing became a hacking cough and where the fur had vanished the high priestess's flesh turned scarlet.

Thus you have decreed, the voice of the sword said to Faros. *Thus does the Lord of Vengeance act! The servant is sent to her master in the manner of the evil she has cast upon others.*

Faros edged back.

Nephera stretched out a dripping hand to the emptiness beyond them, and something made both Faros and Maritia glance toward the shadows again.

A figure in armor with the Warhorse symbol stained in blood stood there, staring with his one good eye at the dying priestess.

"Father?" blurted Maritia in astonishment, for she and Faros both could see the strange, unhappy spirit.

Behind this shade, they could see many others forming, until the chamber was filled with transparent, silent figures all staring at the struggling Nephera. None of the ghostly visages carried any hint of emotion, yet one could not look at them and not feel their intense accusatory stares.

Hotak, his face brutally battered from the fall that had killed him, climbed wearily up the steps. The legions with him followed suit. As they neared Faros, he touched his weapon, but the ghosts passed through him. Their brief merging

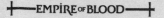

was like a light chill breeze, nothing more. He looked over his shoulder, where Maritia, too, tried to get out of the way of the specters. She stared at her father most dazedly, but although Hotak glanced ever so briefly her way, he made no sign of recognition. Like the rest of the ghosts, he seemed only intent on reaching his mate.

The ghosts swarmed around the high priestess. Although they had the substance of air, Nephera acted as if tightly crowded and pressed by them. She pushed and jabbed at the throng, even seemed to try to shove her way through them but could not budge from where she was anchored. Her actions became more manic.

As if overcome, the high priestess fell back into her chair, her form convulsing and her body now covered with blisters.

Hotak reached out a translucent hand. Almost as though hypnotized, Nephera moved to take her dead husband's hand, but before she could, the reddened flesh fell from her fingers.

"The . . . sacrifices were . . . necessary . . ." the high priestess managed to insist, scowling. "All of—"

Nephera suddenly moaned, shook violently, and sank further into her own robes. Hotak lowered his hand, watching with all the rest. A high shriek erupted from the priestess, and with one last clutch at her throat, Lady Nephera de-Droka twisted dead on her throne.

The last vestiges of the silver glow above faded. With it vanished the countless legions of spirits the high priestess had controlled. The last to disappear was Hotak.

The power of the Forerunners was no more.

Chapter XXIX

Children of Destiny

A stillness filled the temple chamber—one broken at last by the scrape of metal from the direction of Maritia de-Droka. Faros barely got his sword up in time to deflect her blade. With a ferocious grunt, she tried to shove him down the steps.

"Damn you! This all your doing!" She tried to knee him, forcing Faros to twist away awkwardly.

"She was going to sacrifice you to her god!" Faros reminded Maritia. "To Morgion!"

Tears streamed down her eyes. "I'll not let you take down my father's dream!"

"She killed your father and your brothers too!"

"I'll cut out your tongue!"

He gritted his teeth, fighting back. "Surrender and I'll still grant you exile!"

"Never! I'll see you dead!"

Hotak's daughter thrust. Recovering his balance, Faros met her blade squarely with his own.

His sword sheared the upper half of Maritia's weapon off. She blinked in consternation, then backed up the steps. Brandishing her sword stump, she snarled, "Keep back!"

"Toss that aside!" he warned her. "Or—"

He is here! came the blade's voice. *He is here!*

It was as if a veil was suddenly tossed over the chamber. Faros looked over his shoulder at the entrance but saw nothing but shadow. There was no way out. Only the portion of the room where he and Nephera's daughter stood seemed to exist—and it was clear from her startled expression that Maritia was experiencing the same phenomenon.

A voice echoing from everywhere called out, "Hail, Faros, emperor of minotaurs, champion of the imperium!"

The former slave spun to his right and growled in recognition when he beheld the tall, cloaked and armored figure with fiery fur and eyes crimson in color. "You!"

"I owe you a great debt, mortal," Sargonnas proclaimed, nodding. "You brought the Lord of Decay's servants to ruin and distracted him as I needed. The balance has shifted dramatically and the conflict is done. Morgion has learned his place . . . much to his everlasting dismay." The god gave Gradic's son a terse smile.

"And the ghosts?"

"The dead . . . all the dead . . . have gone on to their rightful places . . ."

"Just like that." Faros neither wanted nor needed clarification of the deity's words. That he knew his family was at rest was all that mattered. Eyeing Maritia, who looked in shock, he rested his sword, feeling utterly spent. "Now what?"

"My children must become one again." Sargonnas briefly eyed Nephera's remains. "The high priestess was correct about one thing—sacrifices must be made. You, Faros Es-Kalin, must assume the mantle of Ambeoutin, of Toroth, of Makel. You must become an emperor who brings the realm together, who leads it as it should be led."

"I don't want that," Faros said simply. "I never wanted that. Go away and leave me alone, Horned One."

"There are always other choices, but not necessarily the ones you wish." Sargonnas turned crimson eyes to Maritia, who was staring at Faros, trying to make sense of his surmising declaration to Sargonnas. "I have won out over the faceless one, but you may now kill each other or make a different sacrifice."

"A sacrifice?" Maritia muttered. She halfheartedly held her broken sword toward the god she had been raised to revere—the god her mother had betrayed and denounced. "What sacrifice?"

"Not her kind of sacrifice," the god replied, indicating the body of the high priestess. "A more . . . personal one." He loomed over the pair, his fiery mane tossing bits of flame as he added, "For the sake of the realm, for the sake of your race . . . the two of you must join together in an alliance. You must be wed."

"What?!" Faros blurted. "Her?"

"Never! I'll gut him first!"

The god's expression grew menacing. "You will do so for the wisdom of my decision and because I have said it is necessary."

"Where were you during the reign of Chot? Where were you to tell us what needed to be done then?" demanded Maritia. "Our patron lord! Ha! What right do you have any more to demand anything of us?"

Faros vehemently shook his head. "The blood of Kalin and Droka will never mingle . . . unless it is here on the killing floor!"

"If I marry that spawn of Kalin, it'll only be to cut his throat on the—"

"ENOUGH!"

A tremendous shock save threw both Faros and Maritia to the floor with their weapons flying, yet that paled in comparison to the deity's abrupt transformation. Sargonnas grew into a towering thing of living fire and molten earth, and his

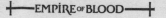

visage bore such ferocity that even the two hardened fighters could not gaze directly into it. Huge black wings spread wide from his shoulders and his outstretched hands ended in the talons of a great raptor.

Sargonnas stared fiercely at the two mortals. When neither moved or even barely breathed, he nodded his tremendous horned head and shrank once more to how he had initially appeared.

"Hear me now!" the Condor Lord declared, his voice nevertheless booming. "The imperium is in flux. There are those who would follow your lead, Faros, and those still loyal to the ways of Droka! Nethosak is yours, rebel leader, but for how long?" His terrible gaze returned to Maritia. "Is this what Hotak desired? How many more must die? Will the minotaur race fight itself into extinction? What of the ogres? Think of this, daughter of Hotak! Would you have Ambeon become a third ogre realm with the Grand Lord Golgren its so benevolent khan?"

Maritia shivered at mention of Golgren's name, but she replied defiantly, "I'll not be this one's puppet!"

"No, nor he yours! Is there nothing you recall of my ancient teachings? Kalin and Droka must come together as equals! Only that may save your people! I make no promises! Be emperor and consort, but both with an equal voice! Has not such equality been what your race have always sought?"

His words stirred something in Faros. Gradic's son tried to deny the truth of Sargonnas's words, but he could not. At last, he exhaled. "All right!" His tone was angry. He felt as though he was being poisoned by this decision. Glaring at Maritia, Faros asked, "For the good of the race, I agree. And you?"

She took longer, her face twisting with hatred. Finally, ears flat, she spat, "Done! And may my father forgive me . . ."

"A most charming display of affection," remarked Sargonnas sardonically, "but even from so salted a patch of dirt can things with time grow." When neither responded, he snorted. "I am done here then! I leave it to you to raise up or ruin the empire! Consider that, when you both seek to bring daggers to the wedding bed!" His brow furrowing, he reached toward Faros. "However, there is one thing I must take back before I go, my champion. The ring is yours and its secrets too—a mark of my favor. The sword, however, must return to me. It has other tasks to perform."

Faros glanced down at his hand, where, to his surprise, the jeweled blade had returned without his knowledge.

I could do so much for you . . . it whispered to the former slave. *I could make you more than just emperor of minotaurs.*

Something in the manner in which it made such promises disturbed Faros. Without hesitation, he released his grip on the weapon and the blade flew to the crimson figure's hand.

Sargonnas gave a smile. He clutched the hilt tight, looking the weapon over. "A fair dealing with your wielder . . . this time," the Horned One said cryptically to his creation. "A good thing for you, else I would have had to punish you again."

Even from where he stood, Faros thought he saw the deadly sword quiver. Sargonnas opened one side of his cloak and thrust the blade within, where it vanished utterly. Hands empty once more, he bowed his horns to the last scion of Kalin.

"I bid you farewell, Faros Es-Kalin, and you, Maritia de-Droka. For what it is worth, my blessing upon you both." He started to fade, but at the last moment said to Faros, "Oh, there is one more thing about the wedding, mortal."

"What's that?" Faros asked irritably, glancing at Maritia.

"It would be wise to have it as soon as possible."

It was managed inside of a month, a period of time much too long and yet far too swift for the couple. Regrettably, more minotaurs perished before the word was spread and many then had to be convinced that what they heard was truth.

From Mito came a victorious Captain Tinza and Napol, along with a wounded legion general named Voluna who had been instrumental in negotiating the surrender of the island after the governor's death by her own hand. From Ambeon came word of the abject surrender of Procurator General Pryas, whose mind, according to General Bakkor, appeared to have disintegrated at the moment of Nephera's demise.

Such news came from many parts of the inner empire. Many Protectors of the highest ranks—those most closely touched by the high priestess's power—had simultaneously lost their will and much of their sanity. Leaderless, the Protectors everywhere fell into disarray, of which their enemies took great advantage.

This was not to say that all looked forward to the clan of Kalin taking the throne again. When Maritia could not convince some of her support of the marriage, she had the recalcitrant figures arrested and brought to her personally. They soon left believers.

There were other great concerns for the empire, but as with so much else, they had to be left for the future. First, the marriage had to take place.

In that place that was the heart of the empire's heart—the Great Circus of Nethosak—Kalin and Droka came together. Sheathes of fresh horsetail grass covered the two paths taken by the betrothed. From the northern gate into the main arena stepped Faros. His mane was bound behind him, his horns polished. His fur had been treated with palm and olive oil to make it shine. Upon his glistening breastplate was emblazoned the condor symbol of eras past. A long, flowing cape of midnight blue trailed behind him and in the crook of his arm, he carried the Crown of Toroth. The Axe of Makel

Ogrebane was slung behind his back. Today would not only mark Faros's wedding but also his ascension.

Behind him marched those representative of his victorious faction, Captain Botanos at their lead and acting as Faros's patriarch. Many among them had been slaves like Faros.

From the southern gate emerged Maritia. She was clad in the dress armor of Warhorse Legion and also wore her mane loose and flowing, as was custom among minotaur females during such ceremonies. Like Faros, her fur had also been treated with oil. In her arm, Hotak's daughter carried her own helmet. The sword in her sheath had been loosely bound with a leather strap, a symbol that that she approached one from whom she had nothing to fear and who had nothing to fear from her. Faros's axe was likewise bound.

In attendance behind her was the patriarch of House Droka, portly Zephros. Behind him came a host of legion commanders, including Bakkor and other high-ranking officials, many who had once backed Hotak. A number of faces still expressed disgruntlement with the situation.

The opposing paths ended under an oak arch thirty feet high whose top ended in long, curving horns pointed upward. Upon the sides had been carved the histories of the two to be wed, symbols marking significant points in their lives. Among Faros's marks were a flame and two broken links, the death of his family and the shattering of his chains.

Two banners hung from the arch, Droka's and the condor symbol favored by the new emperor. Faros had no love for his uncle and the flag that Chot had created was one that he could live without. The condor served as more than just a reminder that Sargonnas had returned. It also indicated Faros's determination to return to the traditions his father had once prized.

When the gods had fled, the custom of using a priest or priestess to oversee the ceremony had given way to a chosen official. However, Faros and Maritia had determined that they would perform this ceremony themselves. Minotaur weddings contained no words, only gestures, for the binding of two.

Drums beat in sync with the movements of the two groups. Weapons raised, two rows of warriors flanked the arch—House Droka on the east, Faros's rebels on the west. The audience, filled to overflowing, began to stomp their feet in unison with the drums.

As the prospective bride and groom approached, the drums gave way to trumpeters at each end of the Circus. The audience stilled. Five high notes signified the beginning of the actual ceremony, at which point the constant murmuring, and every other sound in and around the vast structure ceased.

Faros and Maritia stepped under the arch then dropped down on their left knees. They put the helmet and crown on the ground beside them. Each then bent and raised their left arms, placing their forearms together and clutching one another's hands tight.

The huge drums beat slowly again. Captain Botanos, clad in the regalia of the fleet, joined the patriarch of Droka by the two. They bound the forearms and hands of the kneeling pair tightly together, using leather straps.

Their task done, the mariner and the elder retreated.

Rising together, Maritia and Faros moved in a circle. The drums guided each step, which followed a complicated pattern. Faros and Maritia never once took their eyes from one another. The two completed five circles—five for the luck of the marriage—then paused, the drums ceasing.

The crowd stomped their feet loudly, timed with the drums. Then the trumpeters blew a single note and all sound again came to a halt.

Maritia reached for her sword. Hotak's daughter brought up her blade before the rebel leader. Faros met the sword with his axe. The weapons clanged—then both figures spun so that they stood watching each other's back, the sword and axe held out against any foes in the distance.

The crowd stomped its feet and roared lustily. Zephros and Botanos came up and cut the straps holding the pair's arms together. Faros and his new mate sheathed their weapons, then clasped one another's hand again. Their free arms raised, they saluted their well-wishers.

"All is done," muttered Maritia, "in such a short period of time."

"Yes, too short," agreed Faros.

"I swore I'd do what was needed to keep the empire from collapsing, Kalin. I'll continue to do that, come what may."

"Then call me Faros . . . Maritia," he pointedly replied.

She nodded her head slightly. "Faros . . ."

At first, what sounded like thunder shook the giant coliseum. The new emperor, though, knew exactly what the sound was. Once more, the volcanoes had erupted. No one could doubt that their timing was propitious.

Then suddenly thousands of dark birds fluttered over the Circus, cawing almost as though they called out a name—Faros.

"By the gods!" roared Botanos, pointing beyond them. "Look!"

Although it was day, Sargonnas's constellation glowed bright, each star like miniature suns. The crowd accepted all these omens and the cheering and the stomping grew more intense.

"You have all the power," Maritia whispered. "He gives it to you freely."

"We have the power. He said so. We."

Hotak's daughter gave him an odd, appraising look. Pulling her forward, he signaled for silence. The acoustics of the legendary edifice enabled all within, and many more outside, to hear him as if he stood next to them.

" 'We have been enslaved, but have always thrown off our shackles'," he began, using the traditional litany. " 'We have been driven back, but always returned to the fray stronger than before! We have risen to new heights when other races have fallen into decay! We are the future of Krynn, the fated masters of the entire world!' " Faros paused. " 'We are the children of destiny!' "

The people shouted and cheered and roared.

Faros glanced at Maritia, and what he saw in her eyes surprised and pleased him.

NEW YORK TIMES BESTSELLING AUTHOR
MARGARET WEIS
RETURNS TO
DRAGONLANCE!

THE
DARK DISCIPLE
TRILOGY

AMBER AND ASHES
Volume One

Mina, the central figure of the War of Souls saga, declares her
new faith and love in Chemosh, God of Death, and leads an evil,
vampiric cult that sweeps across Krynn. The fate of the world is
left in the hands of a pair of unlikely heroes—a wayward monk
and a kender who can communicate with the dead.

AMBER AND IRON
Volume Two

The trilogy continues to follow the mysterious warrior-woman
Mina through Krynn.

AMBER AND BLOOD
Volume Three

The Dark Disciple Trilogy draws to a bloody conclusion.

**Release dates and downloads at
www.wizards.com**

THE LINSHA TRILOGY COMES TO ITS THRILLING CONCLUSION!

CITY OF THE LOST
Volume One

MARY H. HERBERT

Linsha Majere, the granddaughter of Caramon Majere, a hero of the War of the Lance, has been entrusted with a terrible secret. When the precarious order of Ansalon is shattered, she must embark on a desperate quest to save the city from an unstoppable enemy.

FLIGHT OF THE FALLEN
Volume Two

MARY H. HERBERT

As the Plains of Dust are torn asunder by invading barbarian forces, Rose Knight Linsha Majere is torn between two vows—her pledge to the Knighthood, and her pledge to guard the eggs of the dragon overlord Iyesta. To keep her honor, Linsha will have to make the ultimate sacrifice.

RETURN OF THE EXILE
Volume Three

MARY H. HERBERT

Linsha has been taken prisoner, and the only chance she has to keep her vow and save the dragon eggs is to marry the feared leader of the Tarmak invaders. On the far-away island home of the Tarmak, she finds hope in the most unexpected place of all—among her enemies.

www.wizards.com

THE ELVEN NATIONS TRILOGY GIFT SET

FIRSTBORN
Volume One
PAUL B. THOMPSON & TONYA C. COOK

In moments, the fate of two leaders is decided. Sithas, firstborn son of the elf monarch Sithel, is destined to inherit the crown and kingdom from his father. His twin brother Kith-Kanan, born just a few heartbeats later, must make his own destiny. Together—and apart—the princes will see their world torn asunder for the sake of power, freedom, and love.

THE KINSLAYER WARS
Volume Two
DOUGLAS NILES

Timeless and elegant, the elven realm seems unchanging. But when the dynamic human nation of Ergoth presses on the frontiers of the Silvanesti realm, the elves must awaken—and unite—to turn back the tide of human conquest. Prince Kith-Kanan, returned from exile, holds the key to victory.

THE QUALINESTI
Volume Three
PAUL B. TOMPSON & TONYA C. COOK

Wars done, the weary nations of Krynn turn to rebuilding their exhausted lands. In the mountains, a city devoted to peace, Pax Tharkas, is carved from living stone by elf and dwarf hands. In the new nation of Qualinesti corruption seeks to undermine this new beginning. A new generation of elves and humans must band together if the noble experiment of Kith-Kanan is to be preserved.

www.wizards.com

COLLECT THE TALES OF THE
HEROES OF THE LANCE!
NEW EDITIONS AVAILABLE!

THE MAGIC OF KRYNN
Volume One
In these ten tales of adventure and daring, the original
companions of the War of the Lance are together again. The
tales tell of sea monsters, dark elves, ice bears and loathsome
draconian troops.

KENDER, GULLY DWARVES, AND GNOMES
Volume Two
Nine short stories by superlative writers tell the tales of the
well-loved companions as they confront danger, beauty, magic,
friendship, and their destinies.

LOVE AND WAR
Volume Three
Finally, the legend of Raistlin's daughter is revealed. This story,
in addition to ten other compelling stories of chivalry, heroism,
and villainy fill the pages of this stirring addition to the
DRAGONLANCE canon.

THE TALES OF
THE HEROES OF THE LANCE CONTINUE!
NEW EDITIONS AVAILABLE!

THE REIGN OF ISTAR
Volume Four
Before the Cataclysm, in the wondrous days of the Kingpriest, marvels abounded. A kender becomes a Solamnic Knight (almost), an ogre saves the dwarven race, and gladiators compete in the bloodsport of Istar.

THE CATACLYSM
Volume Five
The Kingpriest's arrogance brings the wrath of the gods upon Krynn. The result is the Cataclysm—chaos and anarchy, despair and villainy...and inspiring heroism.

THE WAR OF THE LANCE
Volume Six
The world of Krynn is caught in a terrible war between the minions of Takhisis and the followers of Paladine. Dragons clash in the skies and a small band of friends, who would one day be known as the Heroes of the Lance, strive for freedom and honor.